That ee's hump was gone—instead there was a furious itching. At first he thought it was the shirt which tore beneath his raking nails and then he knew it was skin, thin tatters of skin!

More and more he raked at that loosened skin, felt it rip and fall away from his body. There was unde it something which moved, arose—as if for all t se years he had carried some other living e on his back.

He pulled and tore until that which he had carried for so long was released.

"Winged!" He heard Lord-One Krip's voice with strong note of awe in it. "He is winged!"

M scles moved again, stretching in a new way.

Wi ged? Was he? How could such a thing be?

Th re was a wide sweep through the air behind him. A small smart of pain as if something had scra ed on an edge of rock. Now he longed to see!

B fore him lay the globe of light. Across it he coul l see the faces of those he had followed—and ther was awe on both. Again he raised one hand—then he other—and explored by touch. There were exte ions from his body right enough. How did wing feel—if they sprouted from one's own body? Who—WHAT was he now?

BAEN BOOKS by ANDRE NORTON

MOONSINGER'S QUEST

Andre Norton

MOONSINGER'S QUEST

Flight in Yiktor copyright © 1986 by Andre Norton. Dare to Go A-Hunting copyright © 1990 by Andre Norton.

A Baen Books Original

Baen Publishing Enterprises
P.O. Box 1403
Riverdale, NY 10471
www.baen.com

ISBN: 978-1-4516-3855-4

Cover art by Alan Pollack

First Baen paperback printing, December 2012

Distributed by Simon & Schuster
1230 Avenue of the Americas
New York, NY 10020

Library of Congress Cataloging-in-Publication Data:
2011032633

Printed in the United States of America

10 9 8 7 6 5 4 3 2 1

··•) CONTENTS (•··

Flight in Yiktor

··●) 1 (●··

Cold, cold. Fold in the legs—do not move.

Cold—pain—the big one was using the prod again—pain. Stand—jump—but it is cold—so cold.

The small body edged between the two large woven baskets uttered a mewing cry. Then one claw hand flew to provide a gag against any more sound. But shivers continued to shake the too thin body.

Cold—where is cold—where is pain?

The curled body jerked as if a tormenting lash had been applied to the wrinkled greenish skin only too visible through the tatters which were not true clothing. No one had shouted those words. Yet they had come as clear and loud as if Russtif his ugly self were standing over the hider. In the head—not in the ear. Talking in the head!

The small one tried to wedge even more out of sight, and now the shudders of fear were worse.

Where is cold? Where is pain?

The demand came again, imperative—to be obeyed. Wrinkled hands covered ears, but that did not keep the

3

questions from opening like dry and curled leaves under the touch of water—an opening in the head. Once more the body jerked—

Pain—Russtif was using the prod on the other side of the tent wall, using it with the skill of a trained showman to stir up a sulky or frightened beast. And, like the words out of the air, the pain reached the lurker with a hot burst that brought a second whimper.

"Here!"

There were legs beyond the crack where the small one crouched—two pairs of them in space boots.

"No harm—there is nothing to fear."

A pallid tongue licked cracked lips. But there was something that made the fear less, lulled it a little. Beyond the wall Russtif growled and spat threats. His anger and love of tormenting that which could not fight back was like a spurt of fire.

"Nothing to fear." Again the words spun into a mind that had to listen even if the ears were stoppered against sound. Nor did either pair of boots move toward or away from the lurker. Crouch, wait for a hand to reach down and jerk out the small body, perhaps cuff hard for being there—for existing at all.

But this was not Russtif and the boots did not move. Slowly the head, covered with dry tangles of thick hair, came up, drawn against all will by the new note—the very strange note—in that mind voice. Large eyes looked up and out.

Very far from Russtif these two. There were always strangers about, some of them as odd in their way as Russtif's imprisoned performers. So it was not their difference, rather the way they stood shoulder to shoulder looking down. Not with disgust nor cruel curiosity but in another way the lurker could not understand.

"Do not be afraid." It was the male who spoke now, uttering words in the trade lingo that was common speech all through this quarter which catered to the entertainment of ship people. He was very fair of skin and his hair was white—though he was not an old man. Those eyebrows so pale even against his skin ran up at the temples to join the hairline, and his eyes were green, luminous as if there were tiny fires behind each.

"There is nothing to fear." That was the other one, the female, who spoke now. Beside the fairness of her companion she was a fire glowing—hair as red as one of Russtif's oil lamps was braided and looped about her head to look like a heavy crown. She was—

The small body uncoiled. Claw hands went out to the big basket and drew the hunched body up as far as nature would let it. For it was a very crooked body, hunched forward by a misshapen burden at shoulder level, so that the head had to be raised to an uncomfortable angle to see the other two at all.

Arms and legs were thin, their greenish skin encrusted with dirt. The mass of uncombed hair was black, gray with dust at places, but black underneath.

"A child." It was the spaceman who said that aloud. "What—"

The woman made a gesture with one hand. There was a listening look about her. Could she hear Toggor, too?

"This one, yes," she said. "But also another. Is that not so, little one?"

The answer was pulled out by the intent gaze of her eyes—coming before thought muffled it with caution.

"He—Russtif—he would make Toggor play. It is cold—too cold. Toggor hurts from the cold—from the pain whip."

"So?"

She stooped to set a hand beneath the chin of the small, bent and maimed figure. From her touch, from the tips of her fingers, something warm and good flooded right into the shaking body.

"Toggor is what?"

"My—my friend." That was not quite the way of it either, but they were the closest words that could be found.

There was a hiss of breath from the man; the woman's lips fitted tightly together. She was angry—not like Russtif, all noise and quick to aim a blow—but neither was her anger turned toward the one before her.

"We may have found what we seek." She spoke above the bowed head to her companion. "And who are you?" Again warmth flowed from her.

"The Dung one." Long ago had that name of the lowest been accepted. There was no other. "I run errands. I do what I can." A pride which was seldom felt made shoulders hunch a little higher.

"For Russtif?" The man indicated the tent behind.

Dung shook his head. "Russtif has Jusas and Sem."

"Yet you are here. It is Toggor. I—I bring him—" The claw hand fumbled in the front of the single ragged garment. Once more truth was pulled forth by that warmth of the other. "I bring this." He held an unwhole-some-looking lump of stuff. "Russtif does not feed Toggor enough. He wants him to fight for food. Toggor will die"—the sharply pointed chin quivered—"there!"

They could all hear the crackle of the prod and a rising mutter of obscenities from beyond the tent wall.

"Toggor fights and they bet on him. Russtif never had so good a clawed one before."

"So," the man said, "let us see this fighter, Maelen. Also Russtif. He interests me."

The woman nodded. She dropped her hand from beneath the pointed chin to lace a hold in the tatters which crossed the bowed shoulder hump. What did she want with Dung?

"Come." Her hold unchanging, she urged him forward just behind the man who walked with the swing of one who has spent most of his years in space, and who was now heading toward the entrance to Russtif's domain at the other end of the tent. Whether or not the lurker wished to accompany them was not asked. There was no breaking that hold which was drawing Dung along. Somehow the thought of fighting for freedom had vanished.

There was the thick and nasty smell which was Russtif's—one of uncleaned cages with weak and sickening captives—to fill the nose as soon as they had pushed past the open flap. Things rustled and squeaked until Russtif roared and the silence of fear snapped down. He was a big man who had once been proud of his strength but now was entombed in rolls of greasy fat. His bare skull shone with oil in the light of the lantern he had set on the table where there was also a cage—Toggor's place of prison. Now he looked up with a sullen scowl. Then that changed, by a visible effort, into a showman's ingratiating grin.

"Gentle Fem, Gentle Homo, how can I serve you?" His back was to the table now, and he had dropped the prod on it. It was then he caught sight of Dung.

"Has the trash made some trouble?" He took a ponderous step forward, his hand lifted as if to aim a blow at the hunchback.

"What trouble is this one noted for making?" asked the woman.

"A thief, a piece of walking dung, a monster like that? Why, whatever comes to hand to upset honest people—"

"Such as Beastmerchant Russtif perhaps?" asked the man.

Russtif's smile slipped and slid but still he caught it. "Such as me and everyone else. I caught this sewer scum tampering with a cage just two eves ago. Luck was with him then, or else he would have smarted for a good *lessoning*. Trash should be thrown away and not come to annoy others."

"Opening a cage? Is perhaps the cage that one?" The man pointed to the one on the table.

Russtif's smile did vanish then. With the hand in sight he made a fist which might have fallen like a hammer blow on the hunchback.

"Why do you wonder that, Gentle Homo? Has the trash been spewing out some vomit that you would believe?"

"You have a fighting smux is what I believe," the woman cut in and Russtif hastened to draw on his showman's smirk again.

"The best, Gentle Fem, the best! There have been stellars wagered on this one—not just market coppers—and stellars won!" He moved along the edge of the table now so they could better view his possession.

The woman stooped a little so she could see most of what looked like a ball of hairy rags squatting in the center of the cage. Under her hold Dung gave a quick start and then stood very still. She was mind speaking to Toggor. The smux did not answer. It was as if he did not or would not listen.

"These be—good." Unknowingly at first, Dung's mind reached out to become a part of that other steady stream of reassurance.

Toggor's answer never came in words such as those that had struck Dung. Rather it was feeling: pain, fear, and sometimes but very seldom, a rough kind of contentment. Thus Dung thought "good," even "help," which Toggor somehow seized upon avidly, as if Dung had indeed flung open his place of hopeless captivity.

The handful of legs folded tightly to the haired body was visible. Those vicious-looking claws at the end of the first four were clamped together as the creature answered Dung's reassurance rather than the more concise broadcast of the woman.

The smux was no thing of beauty. Had he grown larger he might have been such a monster as to set human kind to flight. His body, covered with spiky hairs thick enough to look like quills, was a grayish red like a fire coal smoldering in ashes. Each quill was tipped also with a darker red as if blood-dipped. There were eight of the long hairy legs, the fore pairs equipped with claws which were sawtoothed on the inner sides. His body was two ovals attached, the smaller fore one to larger hind one with a waist no thicker than two of his legs held side by side. His eyes—all six of them—were now retracted into his ball of head, concealing the stalks on which they were mounted. All in all he was ugly, and, with that ugliness, he gave off the promise of quick and vicious attack.

Now his abdomen dragged on the floor of the cage, and Dung knew Toggor was both filthy and hungry. To be dropped into a rounded half sphere with another of his kind and a piece of raw meat flung in for a victory prize should arouse every fighting instinct of the smux. At Dung's thrust of thought he raised one foreleg and clicked the claw there in entreaty—a friend had food.

Russtif kept his hand well away from the prod. Would he dare to move when these two strangers were here? Dung did not know, but breaking the long-held rule of his own survival, he wadded together the bit of offal he had sneaked from behind the butcher's and, measuring the distance carefully, while Russtif was watching the woman, his small eyes leering, Dung threw the bit of food into the cage. Toggor was on it in an instant, grasping the unwholesome-looking piece and bringing it to his mandibles.

Russtif roared and swung one of those hammer fists at Dung, but it did not crash against the side of the hunch-back's head as he expected. It was the woman who swung her lightly held captive out of the way, and it was the man whose hand came down in a sharp chop across the beast seller's wrist, bringing an angry cry out of him.

"What you do?" Russtif seemed to swell as if his bulk had suddenly increased.

"Nothing."

"Nothing? You let this trash throw poison to my smux

and it is nothing? Ho, let the wardens decide whether this is nothing."

That Dung had not expected. That Russtif would allow the law such interference was unheard of. Yet the beastmerchant was slipping farther along the edge of the table, his eyes turning from the spaceman standing at quiet ease, to Toggor, to the woman, almost as if he expected they were about to unite against him. Dung made a second attempt to wring free of the grasp which had brought his misshapen body into the tent, fruitlessly. Though that hand twisted in the rags across the hump did not tighten, yet moving away was impossible.

"The smux—quote a price on it." That was not the man but the woman who said that quietly. Russtif grinned a little, showing broken, black, rotted teeth.

"There is no price for good fortune, Gentle Fem." He had stopped his crabwise retreat from the two, standing now at the end of the table with Toggor's cage between them. The smux had finished the bit of near-carrion Dung had scraped out of a discarded *E* tube and had closed himself once more into ball form which was his only protection, since Russtif had soaked the poison from his claws only an hour ago.

"There is always an end to good fortune," said the woman, standing tall so that only the tips of her fingers touched Dung, yet light as that touch was now, captivity remained. "Also for everything there is a price. You have fought that smux ten—double ten—triple ten times, starving it between so that it will come to battle as you wish. There is a flicking of life force in it now. Would you kill it rather than profit?"

Dung's dark tongue swept across pale lips. "Toggor." He was not aware that he had spoken aloud until he heard his own word.

The spaceman moved his wrist out into the open, closer to the lantern. That light showed a cal dial, its light steady. As Russtif saw that, his small eyes held a new glitter. Everything this off-worlder said was true. The smux was—or had been—a strong contender, the best he had ever been able to find. He had marked the day he had had it out of the hands of the drunken crewman who had wanted to raise a stellar to see him back to his ship, as a fortunate one for him. But who knew how long the thing would continue to live? Russtif was greedy, but there was an undercurrent of sly profit sense in him, too.

"Off-worlders cannot run gaming," he pointed out. He was absentmindedly rubbing the wrist the spacer had struck with the fingers of his other hand.

"We have a license to buy," the woman cut in. "We do not choose fighters as such, but only strange beings or creatures."

Now Russtif made a wide gesture that took in the other cages and prisoners. "Take then your choice, Gentle Fem; we have such in abundance here. There is a hopper from Grogon, a dry tongue sucker from Basil, a—"

"Smux from—from where, Beastmerchant? From which world comes your lucky fighter?"

Russtif's thick shoulders arose in a shrug. "Who knows? By the time such come—and they come seldom—they have been traded perhaps a dozen times. And surely the thing itself is not prepared to snicker out its home world. It fights—fights to eat. It sleeps. It lives after a fashion, but no one can bring charges that Russtif deals in a thinking species. These are all below the official recording, and the records will tell you so."

Dung could have protested. Alone among Russtif's captives had the hunchback made contact with Toggor. The creature's mind pattern was different, very hard to follow. It wove in and out when he tried to communicate more than the most primitive messages or emotions. Yet he was sure that smux had more powers of thought than Russtif believed.

The spaceman tapped the edge of his cal dial with a forefinger, the small click-click underlining the restlessness of the caged creatures about. Russtif's own cal dial showed.

"The thing brings in a stellar—"

Now the woman laughed, and there was a note of scorn in that sound. "A stellar a battle? And for how much longer? It is weakening, is it not? At the last fight did it not nearly lose a claw?"

Russtif's eyes narrowed. He stared at her insolently, though he was careful to keep his voice at a respectful pitch as he answered.

"I did not see you there among the wagerers, Gentle Fem."

"Nor would you," she replied. "But I speak the truth."

Again Russtif shrugged. "A stellar this bit of ugliness did win. And he will win again."

"Two stellars." That was from the spaceman and it came crisply.

Dung gasped and then raised his stick-thin fingers to cover his betraying mouth. Two stellars—it was a fortune beyond imagining in the haunts of the outcasts where the hunchback sheltered.

"Two stellars, um?" Russtif rolled the words around in his mouth as if he could taste the sweetness of such an offer. "Three." A brainsick fool who would make such an offer could perhaps be edged upward yet again.

"Do not bargain." The woman's voice was not raised. It was neither harsh nor threatening. Yet Dung shivered and sunk his head lower, not wishing to see her face. Though the hunchback had scurried away from threats in all the years of harsh memory he had never heard such a tone before. What was this woman? Certainly some great lady, such as one would never think might venture into such a hole. She should come carried on the shoulders of stout chair veeks with outrunners and speakers-for-the-great in attendance. Who or what was she?

The effect her order had on Russtif was made plain in the way his fists fell upon the table and his eyes took on a reddish glare. Dung expected to hear foul words ordering these two out of the trader's sight. Yet no words came. Instead, a purplish flush covered the beastmerchant's oily jowls and he looked as one who might be choking on his own spittle.

"Two stellars," the man said again, and his speech was as quiet as the woman's, although with none of that compulsion in it. Yet it was also not to be denied.

Russtif made a noise like the honk of an enraged grop, the purpling color still in his cheeks waxing deeper. He gave a sharp shove to the smux's cage, sending it skidding along the greasy tabletop.

"Two stellars." He choked out the words with the same

enthusiasm he might have given had the offer been only copper.

The man began tapping out on his cal the transfer from his own holdings to Russtif's.

The skidding cage was about to dive over the edge of the table. Dung's skeleton hand caught it, and for the first time the hunchback dared to try to reach Toggor again.

"These are good." Anyone would be better than Russtif, to be sure, but there was the additional promise in the mind touch of the woman. One could not lie with thoughts as one could with words.

The woman did not try to take the cage, but neither did she loosen her hold on Dung's rags. Instead, she gave a slight pull which brought him around and started him for the open tent flap. Then they were out in the twilight where other tents' smoky torches and impulse lamps gave a measure of sight. A moment later the man joined them.

"Trouble?" The woman did not use speech, but had mind touch that Dung found easy to catch.

The man could not laugh in that mind-to-mind communication, but there was something in his answer which was light as laughter.

"Trouble? No, he will be slightly puzzled perhaps for a space, and then congratulate himself on a bargain that *he* made. I wish we could clear out that whole den of his."

"Think freedom?"

Dung caught not only words but a picture—a picture that showed paws, and insectile legs, and tentacles looping through wire, mastering the catches on the cages in the tent behind. "Bend so—push. Go, little ones, go!"

Dung felt a touch on his own grime-blackened hand.

The smux had thrust a foreleg through the wire netting, was grasping with a claw the catch of the cage. Like those in the tent, Toggor had caught that message and was following the promise that was like an order.

Gasping, Dung held the cage against his body. But that gesture came too late. Toggor had already freed himself and caught with all four claws at the rags across the pinched chest of the hunchback. Dung dropped the cage, then nearly stumbled over it, except a strong hand caught at his bony shoulder, pulling the small figure back on balance.

Dung cupped both hands about Toggor, having no fear of any cutting slash from those claws, for the smux fitted itself into the hollows of his palms as if those were a safe home nest. Now those hands swung out to the man who stood so straight and tall that Dung had to stretch his neck painfully to see his face, offering Toggor to him who had paid that unbelievable sum to free the smux.

"Hold him well, little one. Bring him that we may tend him—he still hungers and thirsts. And"—the mind speech was softer than any Dung had ever heard in a short hard life—"so do you."

Thus one who had always slunk through shadows now walked as straight as an ungainly and broken body would allow, a friend sheltered in hand and a stranger on either side acting as if one was as tall and well-formed as themselves. It was beyond belief yet it was the truth!

••◉) **2** (◉••

Twice when they passed some patrolling guard, sent to keep the peace among the dealers in the strange and rare who gathered like an untidy fringe about any space port, Dung hung back, and would even have dived for the shadows, but for that grip on the rags across his hump, steering him straight ahead until they passed the invisible boundary which kept those in the Limits from the respectable portions of town.

The lingering twilight was enough for Dung to see the stares which greeted their party. Passersby, used to strange sights issuing from the Limits, seemed to judge their small group even stranger. Yet neither of the spacers appeared aware of the comment they caused, and Dung was brought along as one who had every right to walk there.

They came to one of the large shelters for travelers, light beaming richly from its wide doorway, house guards on duty. Dung, straining his neck upward, ready to twist away from a blow or kick, saw that the guard on the right did move forward a step as if to question their passage, but retreated again when the spacers paid him no attention.

Together the three crossed the wide lobby with its ring of luxury shops, its throngs of people, making for one of the transport plates Dung had heard of but had never seen. They had it to themselves, other people drawing back as they approached. Their carrier whirled upward and then sped into one of the open hallways three stories above the lobby. It was stomach-turning for Dung, who gulped and gulped again. The invisible plastaglass sides did not give any suggestion of protection.

Dung swallowed hard for the third time as they stopped before a door and the spaceman put out a hand to press against the lockplate, letting the door withdraw into the wall to give them entrance. Toggor stirred and pushed against the sudden involuntary tightening of Dung's hold. This was such luxury as trash from the Limits had never seen. His misshapen feet sunk into a thick carpet that was a lush green and gave forth a tangy, spicy smell.

There was no smoking torch or lantern here. The walls themselves glowed, and that glow grew more brilliant as the door rolled shut behind them. A wide couch heaped with cushions ran along the left-hand wall, and other cushions were piled one upon the other at various points here and there—each flanked by a low table or double sets of shelves on which were a number of things Dung did not have time to study, for that grasp on his rags drew him to one table which the spaceman swept free of tapes and a queerly shaped bowl.

"Put the smux here." The woman did not use the mind

touch but the trade tongue, and loosed Dung to gesture to the now clear surface. "Or will it run?"

Dung licked lips dry with that never-ending fear. They had bought the smux. Perhaps Dung had only been necessary in its transportation here. Now there might be no longer any need for this one misshapen and twisted body.

Obediently his thin fingers uncupped and set the spike-covered body in the place the woman had indicated.

"Stay," Dung thought. "These are good." Though how he could be sure of that!

Toggor crouched, drawn into a ball with legs hugging his pulpy body. The eyestalks on his bristly head extended a fraction with all the eyes facing outward and around, ready for attack from any direction.

The man went to the wall and tapped on a row of buttons there. There moved out a section on which sat a tray with a number of small covered boxes and dishes. He brought the tray to the table on which Toggor crouched.

"What does it eat?" Trade speech again.

Dung's own mouth watered and his belly pinched with longing as the spaceman snapped off the lids of the dishes and showed a variety of food. "Meat," Dung said and stood, hands behind his own body lest they move of themselves and snatch some of that bounty.

"Well enough." The spaceman moved two of the dishes a fraction closer to the smux, but Toggor made no attempt to try their contents. That in-and-out pattern which could reach Dung spelled out the smux's wariness.

"Toggor wishes to know where he must fight," Dung interpreted.

"There is no fighting, only eating. Tell him so!" The woman no longer had any hold on Dung, but her hand moved to the upbent head, touched lightly between and above the reddened eyes.

"No fight—eat." Dung strove to fit his thoughts to the pattern Toggor could catch.

For a long moment it seemed the smux did not understand, or, understanding, did not believe. Then a claw flew, with a speed which made it hardly visible, to the nearest dish to seize upon a cube within and transfer it to clashing mandibles.

When the smux had fed a second time and was now using both foreclaws to empty the dish, the woman spoke again, this time no trade talk but words that were clear in Dung's head.

"Eat you also. If there is other which you want, just say it so."

Dung felt as Toggor must have moments earlier: that there might be a threat to come. Why had he been brought here and offered—But also, as it had with Toggor, hunger got the better of wariness and he grabbed for a flat round of bread-cake already spread with lumpy gorberry jell. It was crammed swiftly into mouth. His eyes were not on stalks, able to watch all sides of the room, but Dung used them as best he could while he ate, ate so fast that the taste of the food was lost in the swift chewing and swallowing.

There seemed to be no trick. He ate more slowly when no hand came forth to snatch away food, no foot raised to boot his bag-of-bones body. In all the seasons Dung could remember never had he been offered freely such a wealth of food.

None but well-cleaned dishes were on that tray when smux and Dung were done. The smux balled up, his legs wrapped about his body. He might doze now for several hours. Dung eyed the piles of cushions and wished he could do likewise. But those who had brought him here were not yet through.

This time the spaceman caught Dung's shoulder and drew his captive to a wall, over which he passed his hand. A second door opened. There was a tight little room therein—no cushions, nothing but bare walls and floor.

Ah, rightly had Dung feared them. He was to be shut up in there. Twisting his body did no good; there was too strong a hold on him. His rags tore as the spaceman stripped the rotten cloth away from the hump, away from Dung's body. Bare so that all the bruises mottling the greenish flesh could be seen, the hunchback was placed well inside, and the door closed before he could throw himself at it in one last despairing attempt to escape imprisonment.

Out of the wall shot streams of water, warm against the skin. Two metal arms unfolded from the shining surface of the cell and caught him. To hold him under that flood to drown? No, they were brushing down the small body, rubbing to dislodge the grime which had always been a part of Dung. No more struggle. Standing still, a faint pleasure grew within him—clean as never any such as Dung could be. Even the wild matted hair was washed and combed back, its wet and curling ends brushing the hump.

The skin of the hump was different from the rest of the grimed hide which covered his body. He had never seen himself in any mirror, but his fingers had long ago told him it was thick and hard, almost like the covering on his nails, with a ridge down the middle of the back which only by painful contortion Dung could touch. Through it he had little or no feeling.

The water shower died away, and the door which had sealed came open again. But the spaceman did not drag Dung forth. Rather, he stretched an arm above Dung's head and pushed a thumb tight to the wall.

Water had come before, now it was wind, warm and drying. Dung swung slowly around as he realized its purpose. Even the hair which had lain so lankly back arose and answered, to fly up and out.

Then the wind was cut off, and when Dung looked up in disappointment the hand of the spaceman reached inside the place of water and air, holding toward him a folded piece of cloth. Dung took it and shook out a small robe, clean and white and of a soft wooly texture unknown to any beggar in the outer Limits.

To be fed, and clean, and wearing a whole garment— Dung's wildest dreams had never taken him so far before. Regretfully the claw fingers caressed the soft folds about the top-heavy body. One walk into the night known to Dung, and that covering would be snatched by the more powerful.

He came out of the washing place blinking. It had been a long time since tears had come to Dung. There was a far memory of a time when sobs had choked his throat and shook his body, when there had been pain and more pain. Then there came the day when there was a door left unguarded because Dung was a useless unknown thing, unneeded. Strength had come, enough to creep away and begin life in the shadows. But there had been a time before—so far away and dim now. Being clean and clad again triggered that memory. However, fast on it followed fear so deep that Dung dropped to the floor, folding in upon himself, waiting again for what had ended that other good time, blows and hurting in the head with the threatening thoughts.

"Why do you so fear, little one?"

Dung would not look up. The words in his mind did not hurt, but who cared what became of Limits trash or would want to know the past of such a one?

"*We* wish to know, little one. And there is no need to fear."

Dung struggled to raise his head the higher slantwise.

"I am Dung." He said it and thought it—thought the vileness which had given him his name.

"Never so. You are what you believe, little one. Do *you* call yourself by that name for filth?"

She was too clever, she guessed, she knew.

Now he allowed his hands to cover his face. His face, yes, but who could hide thoughts? And both of these could pick his thoughts out as Toggor picked scraps of meat from within an orker shell.

"Farree?" She spoke that name aloud. Now they would laugh and push him out the sooner into the coming night, the outer Limits which would be the worse because he had left for a space.

"Dung!" He corrected aloud, his voice rising squeakingly high. "Dung!" If he did not claim that other name, perhaps he would be allowed to escape all but the jeers.

The woman dropped to her knees, bringing them near face-to-face so he need not hold his head at such an angle to view her. Her hands reached to gently touch the grotesque shoulders.

"Farree. Hold by what birth gave you, little one. Do not accept what unseeing ones force upon you."

Dung's head shook uncomfortably from side to side. What did this one who lived in luxury know of what one faced in the Limits?

"You are not of Grant's World?" It was the man who spoke.

Dung shivered. In truth he did not know from where he had come; the early days were so overlaid now by the terrors and torments that had followed.

"I am Dung." He must hold to that, to do otherwise was to stand bare of body and defenseless in a ring of Limits bullies. He had seen the weak kicked and pummeled to death for daring to show any spirit.

There was a pulling at the clean robe about him, and he looked down to see Toggor catching hold with his foreclaws, drawing himself up the cloth. Dung had never handled the smux before this twilight, but there was nothing to frighten or disgust him.

"Good." Not a word, a feeling projected by the smux and filling him with warmth—it was like a burst of shouting. The smux might be living for the moment, but he was triumphant in the joys of that moment. Dung wished that he could share the creature's relief and joy.

"You can, if you wish."

Dung stared at the woman fronting him still at his own level.

"If with this stranger-brother you can communicate, then—" She looked around and up at the man and straightaway he opened another inner door of the room.

What came dancing into their presence then was a creature the like of which Dung had never seen, although those who dealt with strange life forms had given him his only shelter. Among the bizarre his own affliction had seemed less conspicuous.

"Yazz. I am Yazz." The words seeped into his mind as the newcomer pranced around him, uttering sharp mouth sounds into the bargain.

Its body was as tall as Dung, its head topping him. Four slender, golden brown legs supported smoothly rounded flanks and a sleek-haired barrel. The head was triangular. A mane with a froth of frizzly hair near-covered its large eyes and then rose to curve down its long, slender neck and shoulders. Those eyes peering carefully at him were a bright red like the gems a Lord-One might wear, and its muzzle was open far enough to disclose gleamingly clean teeth of a golden yellow several shades lighter than its coat.

It had a wisp of tail, which fluttered from side to side as it stood, still now, viewing Dung. "What are you, brother one?" Its head tilted a little to one side as it surveyed him. "No, there are two of you." It had apparently sighted Toggor. "Large, small. Different. What?"

The words came into Dung's mind smoothly but less forcibly than those of the man and the woman.

"I am . . ." Dung began to reply and then suddenly hesitated. Never before had he had to explain what he was: a wretched mistake in a world which named him trash. "I am—me," he answered dully. "This"—he had taken the smux into his two hands again—"is Toggor. He is a smux."

That he was answering the questions of what was manifestly an animal seemed now no stranger than anything else which had happened since the two off-worlders had found him.

"What do you do?" Yazz returned. The creature was bubbling with what Dung realized very dimly was content—happiness—though to define happiness was beyond him.

What did he do? Fight to live and yet every day come closer to the knowledge that for him there was little reason to go on struggling at all. "I—live." He said that aloud, not in thought.

"You live." It was not as if the woman was agreeing with him, rather that she was confirming some necessary belief. "Now comes a time when you may do more. Since you can talk with the Little Ones—there is a place for you, Farree—"

"I am Dung," he corrected her again, but inside him there was a small spark of wonder aflame. Did these two—could they—He did not even want to think of the brightness which might just be true.

But it would seem that this wonder of wonders might be after all, for the man said then: "You have no kin, you are apprenticed nowhere?"

Dung laughed, a broken cackle which had seldom left his lips. "Who wants Dung? I am of the trash of the Limits."

The woman's hand suddenly laid fingers across his lips. He could smell more strongly the spicy scent which seemed as much a part of her as her skin or the glory of her hair.

"You are Farree. Say not that other name. And now you are apprenticed if you wish. We welcome one who can talk with our small ones."

So it was that Dung became Farree, though to him it remained like a dream from which he might awaken into the despair of the real day. He ate voraciously what they provided, never knowing when they might tire of their careless generosity. He learned to keep his body clean and to answer to that other name, but he shrank from going out, from leaving this refuge from all he had ever known.

Though these rooms in the towering rest place for travelers were not the home of the two he had learned to call Lady Maelen and Lord-One Krip (even though they objected to his names of state), to him they were greater palaces than any of the nobles of Grant's World, whom he had only seen at a distance. No, this was only a temporary resting place; these two were truly out of space. They had a ship of their own finned down in the repair field where various changes on it were being made. Strangest of all was the fact that these changes were being made to accommodate bodies which were not human nor even of human shape. They were to hold in comfort animals!

Once or twice he wondered if they looked upon him also as an animal, one with superior talents for communication. But better to be an animal, with such a life as they were giving him, than Dung. Always they talked to him as if he were straight and tall and of as fair a body as they. At length (though he never asked any questions, lest by doing so he would offend) he learned that it was in their minds

to gather together animals, even such as Toggor, and to
transport them from world to world showing that indeed
all life was kin and that creatures were to be welcomed as
brothers and sisters rather than be kept in such slavery as
Russtif had held the smux.

So far they only had three such—for the venture
depended, Farree came swiftly to understand, on the
ability to communicate by the mind touch. There was
Yazz, who also had been bought from a showman and
remembered a past in the high mountain country before
she was entrapped by hunters; there was the smux; and,
kept in a hut near the ship, there was a bartle the spacers
named Bojor.

Had Farree not seen the bartle loosed from a chain and
coming to pay homage to Maelen by licking her feet, he
would have raced from the hut as fast as his bent legs
would carry him. For a bartle was one of the menaces in
stories of the early days on Grant's World. He had seen
bartle claws strung on ident disc chains and worn with
pride by any fortunate to have them.

When the bartle arose on his hind paws, he topped
Lord-One Krip. His body was massive enough to make
three of the man's. This being the shedding season, great
patches of coarse hair lay on the floor of the hut, and the
sleek underhide shone through in green-gray spots.

The off-worlders visited the bartle for many hours each
day, the man grooming out the dead fur, both of them
communicating with the beast. Farree, who knew that
only one of those huge paws needed to descend on him to
leave a smear of broken bones and blood, kept his distance
at first. But, caught up in the mind exchange that held the

other, he began to think of the shaggy beast as another person—odd and queer to be sure, but no different in that respect from many of the aliens which he had viewed from hiding around the port.

The alterations in the ship were slow, and soon Lord-One Krip spent more time there, urging on the fitters, for it would seem that for some reason he and the Lady Maelen wished to be in space as soon as possible.

In space! Farree's thought shied away from that, and he refused to think again into the future. Then he would be back in the Limits again. This time—this time when there was no more—

Sitting in the doorway of the bartle's place he had begun that train of thought that he could no longer shove away. They would go with the bartle, Toggor, and Yazz, and he—he would—

"Come with us!"

Farree gave a start. His hands clenched and his head swung at a painful angle so he could see the Lady Maelen's face. He had thought her busy with clipping the bartle's claws. The big beast had been biting at them, being no longer able to wear them out upon the stones of the distant canyons. No, she was not looking to Farree but he was sure that he had caught that thought.

"You did. You come with us."

"Off-world?" He swallowed, and it hurt as if his inner throat was raw.

"If you wish it, it is so." She did not look at him even now, but there was such certainty in her thought that he had to accept that she meant it.

"If I *wish*—" He could not quite believe. This was

more of the dream from which he hoped there would be no more waking. "If I wish—Lady—" His hands twisted the robe across his misshapen breast. "There is no other wish in me—"

"Then it is so." Now she did look at him, and she smiled. He felt as if he were Yazz, and wished to creep close and nuzzle at her hands and signal with a tail he did not have. The dream was continuing!

"There is trouble again with Kem-fu." Lord-One Krip had come up without Farree noting. "The fittings must be re-laid." The man was frowning and tapping his fingertips on his cal as he did, Farree knew, whenever he was disturbed.

"Yet he set those himself." Lady Maelen got to her feet. "Why now this difficulty?"

"Ask me not. It was almost as if—" Farree saw the frown on the man's face deepen. "As if," he continued after a moment, "he was deliberately delaying us. And the moon—"

"Why would he deliberately delay us? There would be no reason for it."

"No reason except Sehkmet and what was wrought there. That was a raider snatch first, and, when we spoiled that game and uncovered the great treasure, the Guild did not take it kindly. It depends upon how far the true story has been spread. And who was really behind that operation to loot the tombs of the sleepers."

"But what would they get from us? Our share of the finding fee is safe now, and they would have no chance at it. What we do here has nothing to do with any Guild or raider plotting. That is finished, and on Yiktor there is nothing which would draw them. They seek large returns, not the looting of a small planet where lordling has fought lordling until nothing flourishes to tempt even a Free Trader."

"Revenge, perhaps, or for us to furnish a lesson. I will have the inspectors out before we up ship, and that is the truth if I ever spoke it!"

The Lady Maelen smiled. "It is probably just that this contractor deals with such a ship as he has never seen before. Thus he goes slow and makes mistakes."

"The moon," returned Lord-One Krip shortly.

Now it was Lady Maelen's turn to frown. "We have allowed time; surely we have allowed enough time."

"True enough, but time runs fast. We must lift ship in the next seven days if we are to make it."

"Kem-fu—" Farree did not understand all this about moons and treasure, but he did know much of what went on in the Limits. "He loses much at the tables in the Go-far. It is known that he is in debt to Gerog L'Kumb."

Lord-One Krip looked down, startled. "What else do you know, Farree? This is of importance. Great importance."

••●)3(●••

Though Farree had half, or maybe more, of the lore of the Limits collected mindwise, he had to do some sorting before he answered.

"It is said . . ." He stopped. He wanted to be very careful to separate rumor and what he knew from observation and actual overhearing of news. Such a one as he was so much a part of the general trash of the Limits that few watched their tongues when he crouched or shuffled nearby.

"It is said," he began slowly once again, "that Gerog L'Kumb has as much power in the Limits as the Lawspeakers of the Great City. Yet he is seldom seen or heard to use it. For one to speak his name is enough to make a desire an act. He has his own eyes and ears everywhere. And, Lord-One—"

"Krip," the other corrected him mechanically.

"K-Krip." Farree stumbled over the saying of that name without any honorifics. "If it be his wish to delay the work upon your ship, then it will be delayed. It is said that oftentimes he does such until he is paid more, and then out of the ground come the needed men and straightaway all is done as was first ordered."

"Extortion." The Lord-One's mouth became a thin line.

The Lady Maelen nodded. "And we are fit victims for such a game. Perhaps that he also knows."

Farree drew as deep a breath as his constricted lungs would allow. "Let this one," he said then, "put on rags and go back to the Limits. To no one he matters, and that he has been gone for days—that would not have been noted. While he was sheltered by you, few here knew it, either. Is that not so?"

"And if it has been noted and reported to the Lord of the Limits, and you appeared again, what excuse—"

Farree lifted his head as far as he could. "There are Lords in the upper town who keep twisted ones such as I for as long as we afford them a certain amusement. When we are no longer of interest we return to the Limits—if we are lucky."

"And if you are not lucky?" asked Lady Maelen. Farree shivered and doubled his fists. "There are other ways of amusement, Lady. To them such mistakes of birth are to be used and discarded at will."

"I do not think that I like the customs here," she declared. "So, little one, you could return to the Limits as one who has served your purpose with us?"

"As long as I stay well away from Russtif, yes, that I could do. And men talk before beasts—though you have shown me that perhaps the beasts might also undo plans if they met such great ones as you thereafter. In the

Limits I am such a one as is not worth as much as Toggor would win in a battle match."

"I do not like it," she returned promptly. "To put you into such danger as that—"

"Lady, I have had ten seasons in the Limits and still I live." Farree held himself as erect as possible. "I am not lacking in a game of peering and prying. If time is what you fear, then it is best for you to use any tool to hand— such as Dung." For the first time in days he used his old name, the one he had hoped to forget.

Lord-One Krip looked to the woman over Farree's upward-straining head. "If this is meant to hold us planet down as he thinks, the Guild may be behind it. They would not have taken kindly to our interference with their looting on Sehkmet. And if we are bucking the Guild— the sooner we know it the better. What do you know of the Thieves Guild, Farree? And are you still as willing to venture in, if it is a matter of theirs this L'Kumb busies himself with now?"

The Thieves Guild! Farree's pointed tongue caressed his lower lip. To go up against the all-powerful Guild— yes, that was a different matter. Yet he believed that he could sink once more into the Limits and pass from sight of anyone save perhaps some grotesque scavenger such as he had been.

"You will take me, Lord-One, to the gate. Perhaps you should drive me forth with kicks and curses, having discovered that I stole from you. That would be as they expect." He put a hand out to the door of the bartle's hut. "It is moon dark for three nights, and the shadows are my old home. I can listen very well."

A small body thudded against his own, and, as limited as that force was, he near lost his balance. Toggor had crawled out of Lady Maelen's belt pouch to spring at Farree. He scuttled up to that unsightly hump and squatted in the narrow hollow between head and shoulder. When the Lady reached for him, he hissed sharply, warning her off.

Farree strove also to dislodge the smux, but the mental contact came sharper and clearer than he had ever received it before, as if the days spent with the off-worlders had honed a weapon to an edge fit to shave a hair.

"Go with. Hide, but go with!"

The Lady drew back and nodded as if the smux was suddenly one of her own kind with whom she was in full communication. Perhaps contact with the creature for some days had given her that power. But Farree was afraid.

"Russtif—" He made a mental picture of the beast seller.

"No see—hide." With that the smux burrowed under the edge of Farree's robe, his claw tips tickling as he made his way from hump to breast and there settled himself, the stiff bristles of his hair rasping Farree's skin as he clung to the inside of the garment.

"So be it," the Lord-One said. "Two days we shall wait, while I also shall try to discover why our work goes so slowly. Then you will return, whether you have learned anything or not." He slipped one of his long-fingered hands under Farree's pointed chin and stared down into the hunchback's wide eyes with such command that Farree was forced to agree, knowing well that he could not deny that order. These two were not like any others he had known, and he could not guess what form their control might take—even an unrecognized molding of his own mind to obey.

He stood as soon as the Lord-One released him and scooped up some of the dust and straw by the door, smearing it with a careful hand down the fore of his robe.

"You shall shout evil after me, kick me form—" he told the Lord-One. "Do this with no lightness. Any who watch—as you may be watched—must be deceived."

"Well enough!" The Lord-One reached down to grab his knotted shoulder and hurled him out of the hut. As Farree sprawled forward on the ground, one hand curved over the hidden smux to protect it from harm, he felt the pain of a well-placed kick. Loud in his ears were curses noted in the trade lingo and others which must be in the Lord-One's own tongue.

A booted toe scraped along the side of his tousled head, and he uttered a cry of fear as he scuttled, first on hands and knees, and then on his feet, away from the hut across the field toward the gate. Behind him came the Lord-One, yelling curses and accusations that this was a thief no honest man would want around, and when Farree slowed by the gate the boot caught him again, this time in his side and with enough force to leave a bruised hurt. The two guards on duty only laughed, and one of them swung the stock of his gas rod, thudding it home with such vigor above the hump that Farree nearly lost his balance again.

He ran as he had run many times in the past, heading for the nearest straggle of buildings marking the Limits. Out of somewhere a clod of hard earth struck his ear and brought another cry out of him. He scuttled between buildings, twice slipping in the noisome scum that marked all but the main ways of the Limits, and kept on running until a sharp pain under his ribs brought him up to hold a tent rope, gasping.

Though his robe was not tattered, it was bespattered with dirt and foulness, and he believed that his appearance was little better than when the lordly ones had led him forth from this place of ever-abiding terror and despair.

However, his wits had not been dimmed along with the cleanliness of his robe. Now, even as he breathed in gasps, he looked about him, trying to fathom where to lurk to learn what he had come to pick up. To keep well away from Russtif's section of the Limits was also necessary.

This was a section of drinking booths ready to catch the lower ranks from any ship which finned down on the landing field. Though it was not alive with custom as it would be later on, there were enough men in the shacks to make a din that Farree found loud after his days in the upper town. He dodged a staggering, singing couple who wavered out of the nearest den and slunk along behind the crude buildings.

Toggor was riding right under his chin now, eyestalks were extending over the collar of the robe. The smux seemed to be watching their surroundings with a purpose, Farree thought, equal to his own.

He approached L'Kumb's gambling establishment and squatted down near its door. There was an old superstition which he loathed—that to rub the hump of such as he would increase a man's luck. He had never willingly allowed it before, but now he had a purpose in which he could accept debasement. Thus, he squatted with his thin knees poked up, both hands resting in the dust of the ground, his head turned up as far as he could. His back was to the wall of the shack. He tried to tune in the voices inside, but he found them too muffled to follow—save for the cries brought about by success or failure.

A man wearing the worn leather of a space officer— lighter spots on the breast from which insignia had been ripped away—trod purposefully forward. Farree recognized the type: a planeted junior officer who had been fired from or missed his ship and was on the downward road into the floating trash of the Limits. He was darkly browned as became an off-worlder—even his scalp, for it had either been shaved or he was naturally hairless.

In spite of the evidence of his worn clothing, he did not look like one of the lost. There were no dribbles of Graz from the corners of his wide mouth and he walked with the alert stride of one who had purpose in life. As he came, Farree saw that he shot sharp glances about him, even over his shoulders, as if he thought he might be under surveillance. From one of the Limits guards who wanted a larger bribe than could be gotten out of that shabby belt pouch? The pouch was not flat, Farree saw, and he noted that the spacer's hand was never far from it. Therefore he must be in funds—and so would be welcome in L'Kumb's establishment.

Then those keen eyes, which seemed to belie the role the other was playing, caught and held on Farree, and the spacer swung a little out of his way, his hand dropping to thump the hunchback sharply between his bowed shoulders.

"Wish me luck, Dung." He fumbled inside the vest he wore and from an inner pocket produced a bit, a section split from a well-worn stellar, snapping it to the ground before Farree's bare toes.

"Luck." Farree mouthed the word obediently but absently for he was surprised. To his memory this off-worlder was a stranger. How could he use the noisome name known to the Limits? How many strangers might then have heard of Dung and would mark his coming and going?

The man had already turned away and was passing through the doorless entrance of the shack. Farree's hand closed over the fragment of metal he had been thrown. Though he wanted to hurl it from him, that gesture would be foolish. He needed to eat if he stayed for any time in the Limits, and this would provide him with a bowl of stew at Hangstna's tent, as long as he was content to enter the kitchen half and bestow it on Mug the waiter-bartender.

Toggor moved and wriggled out of the neck of Farree's tunic, swinging down onto the hunchback's knee where he squatted, retracting three of his eyestalks and whirling the others about in a way which could make a viewer a little dizzy to watch.

"What? What see?"

Perhaps his association with the two spacers and their communication from mind to mind had strengthened Farree's own powers. The swing of touch in and out that had always been a part of his contact with Toggor was less, and he had caught what was surely a question much more easily than he ever had before. A thought of his own struck Farree, and he touched the smux on his bristled back just below the head. Could he use the small creature

to go where he could not venture without risking an end
to his mission?

"Toggor see?" He shaped the message so that it was a
question, and promptly enough came the answer.

"Toggor see—what?"

"In." Farree jerked a claw thumb at the shed. "Hide—
see?"

But it was not going to be easy. The smux drew together into a ball as always when threatened by something
greater than himself. The sense of refusal struck without
words to center it.

It had been only a passing thought. Farree resigned
himself regretfully. All kinds of parasites and vermin
roamed the Limits—some of them deadly. He had fought
twice for his own life against the slashing-toothed vir that
hunted in packs and, when forced by hunger, were known
to have set upon sleeping drunks and left nothing but
well-stripped bones behind.

For the first time Farree was startled himself. The smux
apparently had followed his chain of thought, though it had
not been deliberately aimed at him. For Toggor curled up
three eyestalks, turning one lidless appendage to watch the
door of the shack and the other two on Farree. The message
followed the direction of the pair of eyes.

"See—in—what?"

Yes, what? He was sure that he could not implant in the
smux's very alien mind the purpose of spying. But he
could try something as a test—a watch on the spacer who
had just entered, perhaps.

"See—him." He pictured as best he could the man who
had just thumped him for luck. "What he—do."

"Toggor be caught."

"Toggor small. Hide, watch." Farree scooped up a handful of the evil-smelling dust of this path between shacks and poured it on the lifted edge of his already much-befouled robe, mounding it there with busy fingers. "Toggor covered with this." All of the eyestalks had arisen again, and more than half of them watched that dust sifting through the hunchback's fingers.

Farree did not add anything more. He was no Russtif to command obedience from the smux. He had asked; now it was up to Toggor whether the other would agree or not. The smux reached out a foreclaw and dabbled it in the dust that Farree had mounded on the edge of his robe. The claw scooped up a fraction and let it slide again through its hold. Then brought up a second lot to toss it over the bristles on the back.

Farree needed no other reply. Delicately, so as not to drop any motes to irritate the outstanding eyes, he took up pinches and spread them on the smux. The creature hopped from his knee hold, landing out in the dust, and proceeded to draw in his eyes and then roll across the ground. Moments later the smux looked like a clod of earth. Farree picked up the small creature carefully and set him by the open doorway. Putting out foreclaws, Toggor pulled himself in and out of sight.

Farree was suddenly rocked back by a wave of mixed fear and rage. He would not have believed that so small a creature could have projected that to him. There was a frazzled mind picture a part of it, something dark and ugly and—

There was only one thing, he believed, that could have brought that response out of the smux: Russtif!

Instant agreement sped thought-swift. The beast seller was there—with a wavery figure that Farree thought might have been the man he saw enter moments before. There was a third bulk, but Farree could pick up no more than the fact someone else was present. Farree drew himself tight against the rotting timbers of the shaky wall. When he put out a hand and scraped his nails along it splinters loosened. If he could just—

"Near you?" he asked Toggor. He was sure that the smux had not gone far into the room inside. And if those three were in good sight then they must be not too far from the partition against which he now huddled.

"Here," Toggor beamed in reply—though where "here" could be Farree could not be sure.

He put an ear to the boards where he had scratched. But he must also keep an eye for any passing by who might sight him. There were voices right enough and words—but not the words of gamblers. He treasured what he might catch.

"—no pilot."

"See that remains so."

"Stellars, stellars like bits." That was Russtif; Farree could never forget that growl.

"Tell—"

"Why share?" Russtif again.

"L'Kumb knows. Never get away with—"

"His plan—why always his?" That voice was raised a little. There followed a thought which broke through Farree's concentration.

"This one comes. Trouble moves—"

And come the smux did, slipping through the hole in the board and leaping for the folds of Farree's robe. Then he scrambled within at the neck.

"Bad one. Look. See."

Fear froze Farree in turn. He jerked back from the wall and scrambled on hands and knees around to the back of the shack. There he forced himself to halt and watch around the corner he had put between himself and the alley. If the beast seller had indeed sighted the smux, he might be issuing forth to get him.

Russtif did come out, but he did not glance down the alley. Tramping heavily across its mouth, he was gone. Farree's heart ceased its leaping beat and settled down to steady rhythm again. The animal dealer was followed by another man—not the spacer Farree had wished luck but a tall fellow wearing the uniform of a guard, one who stood for a heart-stopping moment at the mouth of the alley. But he, too, failed to glance down it. Rather, he looked after Russtif and then shrugged at some thought and turned in the opposite direction.

Farree settled down to wait for the spaceman. Somehow he believed that this off-worlder had importance to his own mission. He had to wait for quite a while—perhaps the man was trying his luck after all.

When he came out he strode across the alley mouth in two steps, but Farree had already planned ahead how he could follow. There was a back way he had spied out and, though his pace was not a run, he had learned to be fast in his own way. Stones and blows had taught him much about the need for speed.

He was always the length of a tent or a shack behind the spacer, keeping to the shadow which had risen fast as the sun had gone down. There was more activity on the "street," and that would grow with the night. As long as it was not more than now, Farree could follow.

The man turned, heading along one of the crooked ways that led through the Limits to, at length, give upon the respectable streets of the upper town. If he crossed into that Farree dared not follow. There he would be as visible to the first passerby as a scarlet lurpa among dudan lilies. He was growing breathless and tired also, for he was not used to long stretches at his highest speed. And he had to pick always a shadowed way which often led him off the right path.

To his relief the spacer did not cross over into the upper town, rather turned in at the door of one of the more respectable buildings of the Limits—one which offered lodging to such travelers as could still pay half a stellar each morn. Rubbing his ribs where a sharp pain bit at him, Farree hunched down in the nearest pool of shadow, unsure of his next move. Why he had chosen to follow this stranger he was still unsure, but the man was an off-worlder, a spacer plainly down on his luck, for no spacer would stay planetside for long if he could help it. Farree had heard the Lord-One Krip say that their own ship needed a minimum of crew or it could not raise. He had hired one crewman, a spacer who had been planeted when the captain of a prospecting ship could not afford a needed rebuild. The crewman had been willing to sign on for his own need to get to a more traffic-filled field on another and richer world. Was this man Farree had followed such a one?

4

Would he play the role of a beggar at the back of the rest place? It was well known that the trash did this from time to time. However, should the spacer sight him, the man might think it was too much of a coincidence that he had seen Farree by the gambling tent and saw him also here, more than halfway across the Limits. What had he learned? Little enough—that there was a reason why someone would have difficulty in finding an off-world crew. There was only one trying to hire such now—the Lord-One Krip.

Farree hesitated, trying to plan his next foray for knowledge when he saw another come down the street, walking boldly and swinging a silencing club. The guards had tanglers and stunners, but most of them relied on their clubs to keep order, preferring to leave a half-dead, beaten victim in the street rather than take the time and trouble to bind and deliver a prisoner to their general headquarters.

Farree squeezed backwards as far as he could go, careful

not to catch the eye of one trained to sight just such a disturber of the uncertain peace as the hunchback was deemed to be. He breathed slowly and shallowly, with as long a pause between each breath as he could manage. There was the wreckage of a crate of more than usual substance pulled into this space between two structures, and Farree made the best use of that that he could.

The guard did not hesitate, turning directly into the rest house as the spacer had earlier. Farree tried to think clearly. Perhaps this one carried some message—one that would mean much if he could report it to those who waited for him near the port. But how might he worm his way into the building, see those he must spy upon? Though it was now heavy twilight and only the few and far between street lanterns gave any glow, he knew better than to try and win past that doorway yonder.

Bristles scraped against his chest. The smux—could Toggor give him partial sight, a fraction of hearing, as he had at the drinking hole? Farree put his hand gently into the front of his befouled robe and felt the claws grip so that he could draw the smux out.

Farree's night sight had been trained to the peak of what his species could achieve during the years in the Limits. There was coming and going in the crooked street now. And at least four of the passersby turned into the rest house. He watched for his chance and crossed to shelter once more against a slimed wall, bringing out Toggor as soon as he settled himself in the best shadow concealment he could find. The smux's eyes were all up and out, fanning about his head at their farthest extent.

"What—do?"

Toggor seemed free of any fear. Farree studied the wall against which he crouched. The lowest story of the building was stone, very old and fitted block upon block with crumbling mortar in between. It might once have been an important building like those of the upper town. The second story was squared timbers, also rough. Farree thought that his own thin fingers could find openings there to draw himself up.

But the weight on his back was not meant for a climber, and would hinder any such attempt.

Instead, the hunchback held the smux closer to his own head as if the proximity would better broadcast the thought he labored to send.

"Man." Laboriously he pictured as best he could the spacer, not sure that the alien mind of the small creature could pick up the identification. "Find in—" He patted the stone of the wall with his other hand.

A little to his surprise the smux seemed almost eager to go, climbing over his fingers to latch foreclaws into one of the mortarless divisions between the blocks. Farree leaned as far as he could backward to watch the creature climb easily aloft. He reached the narrow sill of one of the slitlike windows. But apparently there was no entrance there for him. Instead he scrambled around to the wood and pulled up claw over claw. Then he was gone!

Farree looked around wildly. Had Toggor lost grip and fallen? No—there was a beam, not of thought, but emotion. Hunger, hunt—the smux had come into the runway of a vynate. Farree felt the bitterness of defeat. Once on the trail of one of those pests he could not hope to turn Toggor aside.

But neither would he loose the thin thread of mind touch that tied them together. The smux's hunger became strong enough to make Farree's own belly rumble, and he thought of a meat cake, rich, dripping with gravy, such as he had eaten only that morning. Hunger—then the attack—

He shivered, still making himself share the frenzy of Toggor as the smux tore into flesh, was spattered by blood, and then feasted to the full. Never before had Farree shared minds with a hunter, and he found his body trembling, his own hands clawing out as if he were faced with good food. Now the smux was satisfied. He must either summon it back somehow or—

Would Toggor now wish to sleep after his kill? If so, how could Farree retain any control over him? He clasped and unclasped his fingers, drew a deep breath, and probed. Perhaps his very uneasiness added strength to that call, for he reached the twittering mind of the small creature on the first try.

"Eat. Good. Eat!"

Farree began to despair of getting below that satisfaction of the successful hunt. He held on and kept trying though he felt that the smux was finding him an irritation but apparently not one Toggor could throw off. Deliberately Farree made his demand.

"Find. Find the man." Into that order he tried to pour the full extent of his mind hold.

"Eat!" The ecstasy of the hunt still held, and Farree could have beaten the wall beside him in his frustration.

"Find!" There were beads of sweat on his narrow forehead, matting the heavy thatch of his hair. "Find."

His mind touch wavered in and out more and more. The smux was caught up in his own world, triumphant, free to be himself perhaps for the first time since he was captured. What power could Farree raise which would bring Toggor again under his control, light as that control was?

"Find!" Though he realized that it was dangerous, Farree loosed his awareness of the world about him, built up the picture of the spacer, and beamed it savagely to the creature in the walls above. "Find!"

There were only the thinnest of threads uniting them now—and those Farree could not be sure of. The smux might continue where he was in the wall runways of the vermin, hunting and slaying to eat. Why should Toggor answer or want to come out again?

"Find!" Farree's full attention was on building that thread, on attempting to rouse the smux out of his lethargy. Then, suddenly, the thread was broken. There was only emptiness. Farree's head touched the wall up which Toggor had gone, failure making him weak. The smux had chosen his own way. He was gone!

Somehow Farree got to his feet. That the loss of the creature was his fault he understood only too well. He had been so intent on gaining his own ends that he had forgotten he was dealing with an assistant who had really no common interest with him. The smux could live for days, he was sure, scouting the runways, a killer such as no vyn could escape.

"Find!" He sent a last desperate and despairing silent cry into the nothingness where Toggor had been. Dared he wait and hope? He could not make up his mind. The spacer and the guard—there was manifestly a tie between them, one into which Russtif was also drawn. Then, out of the nothingness, there came a weak signal.

"Man!" That fuzzy picture was so bad it could have been either the spacer or the guard. But Toggor had been set to locate the spacer, so—

Wild with relief, Farree had to keep a tight grip on himself to allow his thoughts to simmer down to calmness, then to sharpen into the meet prod.

"What do—?" That he had been wrong about Toggor made him feel a little dizzy. "Man. Man."

Twice? Maybe that signified another meeting—the guard and the spacer. If he only had a hearing hole such as he had found back at the shack. A few words might make all the difference!

Two fuzzy shapes were beamed to him now. They were close together, facing one another. Then they grew sharper as if the smux were making a supreme effort.

Anger. Anger and threat. The smux could not report words, but the emotions he picked up were warning enough. Whatever those two planned meant trouble. Trouble for the off-worlders? Farree could not be sure, but he believed that it pointed to such.

There was an alteration in the scene the smux projected. One of the fuzzy figures stood up, disappeared out of range. The other remained where he was—that was the spacer, Farree was sure, since it was he Toggor had been sent to track.

"Come." There was nothing further to be learned, Farree was sure, as long as the smux could not provide him with ears.

"Another comes," the creature on spy aloft returned.

"Show me. Show me this other as well as you can!" Would that plea bring him anything? Toggor's sight was not his, and what was clear to the smux was badly blurred for him. Yet another figure did join the spacer now. To Farree's joy there was a distinguishing mark to this one. He wore the uniform of a spaceman, yes, but across the breast was a splash of vivid color. Smux's sense of color was also not human. He registered in shades of red and yellow seemingly, having no other shade or hue to project. This splash was yellow.

"Come!" He wanted to get Toggor away from the tempting runways hidden in the inn's walls. Now he wondered if he *could* draw the smux away from so rich a hunting ground.

There was someone coming out of the front door of the inn, humming as if he were free of a burden. Farree cowered as the guide went by. It was sheer luck that the man turned north instead of south, heading toward the narrow way where the Limits touched the upper town.

Toggor had broken off touch again. Farree could only hope that that meant the smux was returning to him, not starting another hunt. Twice more he beamed, "Come," without any answer. It was dark enough now so that the wall above him was shadowed. Those lanterns which lit the street did not send any beam this far back. And there was a hum of noise carrying up from the other side where lay the bulk of the Limits—that district was coming into its nightly life.

Then Farree saw movement within the shadow which lapped against the wall. Before he had more time than to draw three breaths the smux leaped from the sill of the narrow window above to land on his hunched back, running lightly around to burrow again into the neck opening of his robe.

Farree raised both hands and clasped them gently around Toggor, so relieved that the smux had returned to him that he could have gone forth humming as had the guard. Into his mind shot an impression of two wavering figures moving out from a room above. He crouched low in the dusk, his eyes upon the doorway of the inn. Then they came: the spaceman he had followed here, together with the other who wore the badge, which was not as brilliant as Toggor had pictured it for him but certainly was vivid.

Anyone in the Limits knew the meaning of that. Unlike the one who accompanied him, this second off-worlder still belonged to some ship's company. Yet Farree was not knowledgeable enough to know which.

Unlike the guard, the two headed downslope toward the distant landing field, and Farree again slipped through the pools of dusk between the lanterns, tracking them. He caught words now and then, but they were not in trader lingo, and he did not understand. Save that the spacers were talking earnestly as they went.

They did not pause at the gaming places nor the drinking dens but threaded a way straight for the port where the brilliant lights about the ships provided a beacon against the murky ways of the surrounding territory.

There were three ships on the landing apron, spaced well apart. That which belonged to the off-worlders, Farree knew, was the closest to the gates, and there was scaffolding about its outer skin though no workmen were visible at this hour. Beyond was a small Patrol skimmer, a messenger vessel which had landed only two days earlier with information for the local League council. Beyond that stood a merchant-class vessel, larger than that which the off-worlders had claimed, with a battered, space-scoured insignia on one fin.

The two he followed passed the gate, and the guard there asked no questions as they went on toward the ship under reconstruction. Farree must follow them. But to get past the light, which was full at the gates, and the guard there—could he?

Hunkering down in a noisome pocket between two of the nearer Limits tents, Farree bent his head forward until his forehead rested on his crossed arms. He strove with frantic need for an answer.

It was as if he whirled out into a space that was filled with almost invisible ribbons floating and spinning, seeking the right one to guide him to his needed goal. There were flashes of thought, which he tried earnestly to shut out that he might seek single-mindedly. Then—

"Little brother!" Not the muddled response he got from Toggor, but as clear as if the words had been spoken in one of his prick-pointed ears.

"In." Certainly he had little to report—only the two meetings. Yet he also had a strong feeling that the news he carried was needed, and there was little time. "Bring me in."

For a heart-shaking moment he thought that he had lost contact—that it was as it was between him and Toggor—his talent was too limited, too diffuse to hold.

Then there came strong and steady the answer: "Be ready—near the gate."

He went forward on all fours, feeling the prick of Toggor's claws and bristle hair as the smux rode in the fore of his robe. So he reached the edge of the shadows— beyond which lay only the merciless light of the gate. There was someone approaching from the opposite side, and he saw the hood of a cloak slip back from the head of that brilliant hair as deep as any Milisand ruby in shade. The Lady was coming for him herself.

She halted before the guard and spoke, the murmur of her voice carrying but not her words. Her right hand was up, and she twirled something between her fingers with a rhythmic movement. "Now!"

Farree had to trust. He ran forward on his spindly legs, both hands pressed over the smux lest he lose Toggor. When he stumbled over a stone and it moved with a click, the guard did not look around. Then Farree dared the gate itself, putting all his strength into a dash which carried him by the Lady Maelen and the guard with a speed that near sent him sprawling forward. But he kept to his feet and hurried toward the hut where the bartle was housed.

Outside of that was the Lord-One Krip, and with him the two men Farree had followed from the Limits. The hunchback pushed himself behind the hut, hoping that he had not been sighted. Why the guard had not seen him when he was in plain sight at the gate he could not guess.

He lay nearly flat now as Toggor climbed up and back to squat upon his hump. The Lady was still at the gate, with the guard listening to her as if his position depended upon her words. But she had dropped her hand and the shining thing had disappeared. Finally the man saluted and she turned away, coming back toward the hut. Farree drew a deep breath and huddled where he was. He heard a little chirping call. The smux scrambled down and scuttled to the fore of the hut, leaving Farree for a moment or two a little angry that the creature would so readily obey that summons from another.

"Well enough. If you bring a quittance from your captain then we shall deal." That was the Lord-One Krip talking. "We sign only until first planetfall, you understand."

"That is to my advantage also, Captain." It was a new voice—that of the spaceman who wore the insignia? "Also the *Dragon* already carries a senior astrogator. When do you lift?"

"Soon enough. See me tomorrow with your papers. And yours, Quanhi—have you full clearance for hire?"

"I will bring a statement from the councilor. I am fit again and want nothing more than to be free of Grant's World. Few enough ships touch here to give me much chance."

"We will consider."

"Right enough!" Together, the two Farree had followed turned and went back toward the field gate.

Farree crept around the side of the hut, putting it between him and the gate. He made a last dash and took himself inside before Lord-One and the Lady Maelen entered. The bartle moved uneasily, and Farree heard a low growl out of the dark. But another shape stood over him, licking at his face—Yazz giving her usual exuberant welcome.

"What have you learned?" The Lady Maelen came first, and at a twist of her fingers there was a dim light in the hut.

What had he learned? Bits and pieces. Perhaps none really were of importance. Yet Russtif had a place and a part, and the dealer in beasts was for Farree the symbol of evil, an evil that could reach out and touch these two. He could not have found words to explain what the Lady and the Lord-One meant to him, he could only offer all he could summon to their service.

"Those who were there," he began in haste so his words were almost a gabble. Then he caught hold of himself. "One, he who wears no badge, met with Russtif and a guard. They said—" He summoned the few words he had caught: "No pilot—stay that way—stellars like bits—and L'Kumb—he plans something. The badgeless one meets with a guard again and then with he who wears a badge."

"Stellars like bits—" Lord-One Krip repeated. "Where would such a speech *be* the truth?"

"On Sehkmet," the Lady Maelen returned promptly. "That tale is one of the legends of the star lanes now."

"But that world is fully guarded. No raider, or even a Guild-owned vessel, could set down anywhere there."

"Yet those who found it first could carry away information of perhaps other finds—a danger we considered from the first. And the clutching fingers of this Guild extend far. Perhaps they think to plant one—two of their own among us."

"We would read them."

"Would we?" the Lady Maelen asked then. "It is well known that the Guild has access to many discoveries that even the Patrol does not know. Remember, on Sehkmet there were mind shields which we could not break."

"But those were—"

"Of the dead old ones, you would say? We cannot be sure they do not otherwise exist. What mankind has once discovered can be found again." She turned to Farree. "You heard no more?"

He shook his head. "It is said that Russtif would link with L'Kumb if he could. It was in a gambling hut that he met with the badgeless one—"

"Pitor Dune of Chamblee, suffering with spotted fever, was left here when his ship lifted four months ago. And this other, Quanhi, who wishes a full berth for himself as astrogator," the Lord-One Krip said slowly. "We have a half crew at least. And now the rigger has his men on the jump to get finished, saying frankly he must have the money."

"It links," the Lady Maelen said slowly. "We have had trouble in finding men. Yiktor is no major base, even now when the League plays more a role in her current history."

Lord-One Krip laughed. "Ah, but they do not know what powers the Thassa have—the Thassa and She Who Slept."

The Lady shook her head almost violently. "Not so, Krip. Nothing did I learn from her. She was—the real part of her—long dead or gone elsewhere. I but banished the will which kept her waiting. But we bewilder you, small one."

She smiled down at Farree. "Know that we are Thassa, a people so old we have forgotten our beginnings. It was given to us to find a mighty treasure of the Forerunners on the planet Sehkmet and there was trouble there, for the Guild would also plunder it. The Guild lost and the winning was ours. We seek a ship of our own and so here we found the *Far Seeker* for sale, one which will serve us well. But the time is short. The three rings will shine on Yiktor our home world, and to that world we must go. It is a tangled tale in our past—you will have the hearing of it some time."

"I?" Farree strove to lift his head higher. As if she knew what frustration moved him, the Lady knelt and laid her hands one on each shoulder.

"If you wish to come, little one, then it shall be so," she repeated the earlier promise.

Farree drew a deep breath. To stride the stars as if he were straight and strong and stood as tall as the Lord-One himself—that was something he had not dared trust. "Yes—oh, yes!" His own hands flew to his shoulders to cover hers where they rested warm and welcoming. "Oh—yes!" He could have shouted that aloud.

"So be it." She nodded. "Now let us think concerning this man Quanhi who seems so willing to come—"

"He thinks we lift for Greater Marth," said Lord-One Krip.

"Let him continue to think so. The voyage tape I hold myself," she answered. "And we need no astrogator in truth once the tape is locked in—only the port authorities require we have one aboard. As for those trying some tricks with us—" Now it was her turn to laugh, raising her hand to gesture to the rest of them, Farree, Yazz, and Bojor the bartle as well as the smux clinging now to her own shoulder. "I think we may have some surprises for them."

••●)5(●••

He whom Farree had spied upon came again to the bailie's hut. The hunchback shrank to the rear of the hut, trusting the big animal. Toggor sat on his shoulder, eyestalks aloft, and beamed what Farree already guessed—that this was the one he had watched.

The man was young, though it was always difficult to tell the true age of any spacer since ship time and planet time were different and those who spent most of their days within the hulls of the sky ships did not age so swiftly. His badgeless uniform was shabby, but he seemed clear-eyed and quick to answer, not as if he were someone rightfully grounded.

"For the voyage only, Dune," Lord-One Krip repeated. "And are there any more willing to take service?"

"I can get you twenty," returned Pitor Dune. "That you would want them is another question. They may have been grounded for more than illness or ill luck. Quanhi is, however, a good man."

"I have said we would take him, as you heard, but to change ships in mid voyage—" Lord-One Krip began.

"May be the sign of an unsteady crewman, yes. What excuse does he offer to *you*?" Lady Maelen asked of Dune. She might be checking stories.

"None, except he can expect no further promotion within the *Dragon*, and that is an outland trader which does not set down on many worlds with larger ports and more traffic."

"We shall take him when he brings quittance," Lord-One Krip returned. "In the meantime, you also bring your papers as you promised."

The crewman started out across the field. On Farree's shoulder the smux moved, and the hunchback caught a fraction of emotion once more—uncertainty, shadowed by fear. Behind him Bojor gave a deep grunt. Instantly Lady Maelen turned her head to observe the tall beast. Farree caught her questioning concern.

It came as with the smux—no words, only the feeling of wrongness, of the need for being aware.

"We are warned," the Lady commented. "It seems that there is something about our new shipmate which the small ones do not like." She was beaming soothingly, promising that there would be no trouble with the strangers.

Once more Lord-One Krip questioned Farree.

"Russtif, yes. His interest I can understand. He was overpaid for one of his slave things," the Lady mused. "Yet had we bargained, that would have given him time to wonder, to think . . ."

For the first time Farree dared question the off-worlder.

"Lady, he will think, does think. From him perhaps others have learned."

She made a face and shrugged her shoulders. "I lose

my caution when I answer a help cry. Perhaps we were wrong. But the man was ugly enough to have killed this little one." She held out her hand, and the smux extended a long curl of tongue to touch the tip of her finger.

"You have fitted the tape?" Lord-One Krip changed the subject.

"Last night when the workmen left," she answered. "I have learned much, and perhaps even this new body of mine retained some level of knowledge. When we lift we do so for Yiktor."

New body? wondered Farree. What story lay behind that? But he dared not question now.

"There has certainly been a change in the fitters," her companion returned. "They have kept on the job steadily this afternoon. Tomorrow we can move Bojor aboard. By the next sunrise we shall lift ship."

"Providing we get this astrogator Quanhi. But, Krip, of this I am sure, we shall get him, and for no reason which means us well. Our only protection is our sealed tape that cannot be withdrawn by any except my own hand."

"And that tape was bought on Ballard. The *Dragon* last raised from that world," the other answered her. "That is an open port—"

She nodded. "If we go threatened from the left, we can only hope for aid from the right. On no other world are such tapes for sale, and we had to deal with those outside the law of the League in order to get it. News travels near as fast as thought. Ah, here comes our new shipmate and with him Quanhi—you are sure that this is the one who met him in the Limits, small one?"

The Lady moved aside a fraction from the doorway and

Farree could see out into the lighted field. He would be certain of that emblazoned badge anywhere, but as for the man—he could not be sure. So he reported.

"Quanhi," Lady Maelen repeated the name. "And of no world—perhaps a Free Trader then."

"Not so," Lord-One Krip snapped. He was frowning now, his attention all for the man coming toward them. "We shall see how much this one desires to become one of the crew," Lord-One Krip observed. "Stay in the shadows," he spoke now to the hunchback. "It is better that they do not see you and perhaps speak of you."

Farree speedily hunkered back, Toggor riding on his shoulder. Bojor moved aside as if ordered, giving only a snuffing sniff in the hunchback's direction. Yazz was lying full length, lost in the shadows at the back of the hut.

The man from the other ship looked even younger in this stronger light than the other—with an open expression which Farree found hard to think of as belonging to a plotter. He answered Lord-One Krip's questions freely and openly but—

In spite of the order given Farree and his own uneasiness, he sent a single tendril, thread fine, toward the other's mind. And he met—

Nothingness!

Not a barrier, not the swirl of alienness which marked the smux, the bartle, and Yazz. Simply an emptiness, as if no one stood there at all. That was so frightening that, for a full moment, he shivered and strove to the edge even farther away. Yet when he opened the eyes he had squinted shut, there was a man like any other walking the Limits or the upper town.

He had heard tales—always told with gusto but never believed—of how, on some distant world, there were beings with the look of men but who were in truth machines. Those would even think when properly supplied with the right tapes, just as a ship could be guided, once in space, to a chosen world. Was he now fronting one of those fearsome things neither living nor dead?

Like their bargain with Dune, this other one was quickly struck, but, as the astrogator left, Maelen spoke softly, using a language Farree did not know. He heard harshness in the Lord-One Krip's quick answer.

The Lady looked over her shoulder to where Farree crouched.

"Mind touch?"

He knew what she meant and first shook his head and then, fearing she could not see, answered in words.

"There was nothing. Nothing at all!"

"A shield," Lord-One Krip said then, "and that is surely Guild. But if they knew us they also know that we would detect such at once and be warned off."

"A machine one?" Farree ventured.

"What do you know of such?" Lady Maelen asked.

"Only stories," he answered. "No one believes them true."

"Yet once such things were," she answered slowly. "Once the Thassas knew such. But also I do not understand why they would send us a well-shielded one."

"They may think that it is only with each other and with the animal ones we can communicate," Lord-One Krip said slowly. "Yet the Guild have the reputation of taking nothing and no one on trust. There are many races and species in space. The Zacanthans in their rolls of history have only a partial listing of such and their attributes both physical and mental. They did not even know of the Thassa until we met on Yiktor. There may be many others—even a race born with a natural mind shield. Still, it argues planning on their part. This is a warning, for it goes with all we know of the Guild."

The Thieves Guild had spread and entwined world after world—where star overs went, sooner or later the Guild followed. They were reputed to be masters of strange knowledge and devices which they stole or bought before the Patrol realized that such existed.

Farree ran his tongue across his lips and then asked in a small voice: "Could it be known that time is of importance to your plans, Lord-One, and that you would chance taking whoever offered because of that?"

"Yes," Lord-One Krip replied, "that makes sense. However, these two may have defenses or weapons of which we know nothing. And to blast off with such aboard—"

Toggor moved. His eyestalks were all extended to the farthest limit and swung so that they pointed after the man who had just left.

A fuzzy picture in Farree's mind. One which the Lady Maelen must have picked up as quickly as the hunchback.

"He is not a machine—that one," she said. "The smux finds true life there and danger."

"Yazz, Bojor." The Lord-One looked to the two other animals.

"Live. Like Yazz. Live," answered that one at once. The bartle growled, sitting up on his broad and weighty haunches, making gestures of holding something in his front paws.

"I think," Lady Maelen said slowly, "that we may have our own warning alerts from directions which our new shipmates will not guess. They can accept animals performing because of threats or promises, but not little ones who share with us that true life of all that is equal in Molester's scales of being. We shall mount our safeguards. You have made your own lock installments on the cages?" She turned to Lord-One Krip.

"Yes; we shall test them this night. It will serve that our little ones are firmly housed and yet—" he smiled a little grimly—"that will be only a cover."

Farree had been in the ship before, but that had been a hurried visit and only to that section meant to house those the Lady Maelen called her "little ones." Though she used the same term for Farree himself, there was a difference which was subtle but which he had caught. He was perhaps as ignorant of worlds beyond this planet as the animals, or even more so, for those had roved the wilds far beyond the Limits. Yet to these two off-worlders he was common kin.

Now he lay in the bunk which had been assigned to him. For the off-worlders and their live companions had chosen to go within the ship though it was still fin down. However, what he was thinking had nothing to do with the events of the past two days. Rather he was caught up in what he had never experienced before: a waking dream of wonder. That was centered upon something he had seen in the Lady Maelen's quarters.

A cube which seemed transparent and clear of any

content—one which was only slightly larger than what he could hold comfortably in his two hands. When the Lady touched it, there had come a swirl of color within as he watched in astonishment. He might have been poised in the air above another land—one so far different from the Limits that dream was all he could find to call it.

There were wide plains—small within the limits of the cube's space, yet the longer one looked at the scene the wider those spread, as if one became smaller than a sand jumper and had been pulled into the picture. There was green—great stretches of green growing things, starred here and there with brilliant splashes of color, some widely separated, some massed together. Growing things also, but the like of which Farree had never seen before.

Far down in his cramped memory something stirred even as it had when they had asked his true name. Color, growing things—There were none such in the Limits, yet he recognized them for what they were instantly: a mantling of rich, tall-growing grass and—flowers. Faltering memory produced a name for him.

His nostrils expanded. Yet there was nothing save the air of the ship to fill them. He had expected something else: clean, strong, unlike the sour stench of the Limits. Why did he think of that?

"Yiktor." The Lady Maelen's word had cut through his searching of memory. "The Thassa wander wide over these plains, though their own private place is near desert." She was, he saw by an upward glance, concentrating on the cube with an intent stare. "We shall be in Yiktor! In the circling of the rings."

The scene within the cube swirled again from clarity into

a fog of mingled color. Farree gave a small exclamation of protest. But the cube did not clear entirely. Now there hung a ball of light within it, and around that three distinct rings of radiance grew and held.

He felt a greater wonder than even the flower-studded land had given him. This was a thing out of the sky—a miracle of light unlike any he could have imagined. The sight brought no faint recognition with it; it was totally alien to anything he even had heard described.

The Lady reached out long fingers and caressed the cube as she had done at times the bartle and Yazz, as if she needed the reassurance that they did exist. Farree felt a strong wave which was both of sadness and of joy— though, before this moment, he could not have believed two such diverse emotions could be interwoven.

Then she lifted the cube and instantly the picture was gone. She took a soft piece of spider silk and wrapped what was now only a clear and colorless artifact, then placed it in one of the wall compartments.

Farree longed to see again that flowery land, to feel that he had been drawn into the dream and become a part of the whole, accepted and at—at home—

"You saw," the Lady spoke slowly as she turned from the compartment she had locked with her thumb seal. "Yiktor, which I . . ." Now her voice failed for an instant before she added, "which I long for and to which we go."

She clasped her hands together, rubbing one over the other as if some substance had escaped the cube to moisten her fingers. "Yiktor," she breathed for the third time. Then her glance wavered from the compartment door, and she looked directly at Farree.

"You saw. But there was something else—you remembered."

Oddly enough he felt suddenly threatened by her words. It was as if her probe could pierce easily into an inner part of him—a far inner part which cowered away from light and knowledge. There was a growing pain within him, which he found hard to handle.

"I did not remember," he countered quickly. "There was always the Limits—just the Limits."

"Your kin—your father—your mother?" She was not going to let him escape. But she need only keep mind touch with him to know the answer to that. The Limits, always the Limits—but then the man—

For the first time in years Farree was remembering the man. He was only a shape, faceless, to be feared, yet all-powerful. He had died drunken and Farree had fled. He himself had been even smaller then, a misshapen lump of flesh which no one could look upon except with distaste or fear. Like Toggor, he had been alone. His kin? Who would claim kin with such as he? He had never seen his like even among the beggars, some self-mutilated to arouse pity. From them he had kept apart, moved by the queer feeling that were he to seek a place in their stinking, shambling guild he would be, in a strange way, lost.

He was stronger than he looked, and there was a core of determination within him to keep him going on his own. How long had it been? The refuse of the Limits did not reckon years, only seasons—hot and cold. And he did not add those up.

Before he realized what she was about to do, Farree

felt the Lady's hands at the neck fastening of his robe. She pulled at the cloth, bringing it down to bare his hump.

He flared with a thrust of sick anger. Then her mind speech touched him quickly. At least she had not put hand to that monstrous roll of flesh which he bore always with him.

"This is no hurt, yet it looks as if it were old scarring." She shook her head. "A healer I once was—a Moon Singer who could bring good out of ill. And much have I seen of bad wounds and injuries. The Thassa have their own dangers, which do not equal those of other species. This looks more like a shell—"

Farree jerked the cloth of his robe, fastened it tightly once again. "No Singer can make me straight," he answered sullenly.

But she did not let him go. Though she did not touch him again, yet he realized that he must answer her. For the first time he resented with more and more bitterness this mind tie between them. What had once seemed to him to be an opening gate to understanding now took on the bars of a cage.

"No, I think not. But for everything there is a reason. Do you suffer pain?"

He had to answer with the truth. "No—except the pain of its weight. It grows heavier with the passing of time." Against his will truth came out of his mind. He had suffered the pain of kicks and cuffs aplenty, but the weight on his shoulders which curved him forward had never hurt. There was an itching which came at times, more often recently. He had been driven once or twice by the force of that to rub his back against the stone walls of the inn within the Limits.

"If you suffer pain, Farree," she addressed him now as she might the Lord-One Krip, "come to me. Though I am an exile from the Thassa, yet I still hold some power in these." She held up her hands and flexed her fingers.

Now, as Farree lay circled on his side in his own place (for he had been given a small cabin of his own, to his unvoiced wonder), every bit of that came back to him. She had meant it, and he knew also that it was an offer he could not take. Or at least he thought at this moment that he could not. The burden was his own, and none but death might lift it from him.

Yet he kept remembering the pictures in the cube and his inner excitement grew. It was necessary for these two he held in unbreakable awe and reverence to go to that world of flowered plains and three-ringed moon, and they were taking him with them.

That they took off a day later with two on board who must be watched did not alarm Farree. He knew too well how to keep wary eyes and those thoughts which tied the rest of that company into a force none without mind touch might even deduce existed.

He who had the mind shield could be seen, and the other, though they were careful not to probe below his surface thoughts, could well be open to search if it became necessary. There had been a flare of protests from the astrogator when he discovered that they were traveling by a sealed tape. But on a privately owned ship that was not too uncommon, and his arguments had been few enough.

It was Toggor who provided their first sentry. Though they were in free-fall for a goodly space of time and Farree was miserably sick and fought to conceal that fact, the smux loosed its legs and swam in the air, catching at fittings for anchorage from time to time.

The Lady Maelen stayed with Bojor, who suffered the most for lack of proper weight and had to be constantly reassured that this was not something that would last forever.

Once in hyperspace the weak gravity of the ship gave them at least a chance for footing. Farree, out of some inner uneasiness, made it a point to learn how to get about without help—wishing that he had the smux's confidence.

There was no time except that rigidly marked by the ship's instruments. They kept to a series of watches wherein either Lord-One Krip or the Lady Maelen was on duty with one of their hastily assembled crew. For Farree there were no stated duties, but he would lie on his bunk for unknown periods of time, linked with Toggor, learning more and more how to channel the smux's foggy sight so that he so went exploring through the ship by that remote means.

Separated by division into watches which the off-worlders had devised, there seemed to be no reason for the two crewmen to get together. Nor did they.

It was during the tenth sleeping time that Farree awoke out of a troubled doze. He did not know what had haunted him so that he had not rested as deeply as he usually did. Then he looked out into the middle of the small cabin and saw, scuttling across the floor, Toggor, who had just pulled himself through the crack of the door.

The smux's claws reached up and Farree put his hand down for the creature to climb.

Just as Toggor had once registered pain and cold, so now he registered again fear. Whipping up the hunchback's body, he sought a hiding place at the neck of his robe.

Farree sat up and dangled his thin, stunted legs over the side of the bunk, both hands over the smux's lump on his breast.

"What—?" He began and then realized again that the direct mind touch was not clear. Instead then he strove to disentangle emotions. He got what startled him first and then led to a flare of anger.

Toggor's picture was very fuzzy and it had been at floor level. There was something which was clearly part of a pilot's seat and then—then a boot, metal plated as were all in space, swung out and over the questing eyestalks, aimed to crush the smux. There was a quick flurry of movement, which Farree could not untangle, but it was plain that one of the crew had attempted, or had chanced, to nearly crush the smux, who had fled in a burst of fear. Which of the crewmen—and why?

Patiently Farree struggled to subdue that fear, to get through the icy curtain of it for an answer.

Crewman—he could get no clearer answer than that. To Toggor perhaps both men looked alike. The fuzzy figure bent over, trying to claw at the wall of the command cabin. At least Toggor saw it so.

Farree had no idea of the duties aboard ship. The man might have been busied at some regulation task. But he was shaken enough by Toggor's report to try to raise Lord-One Krip whose watch should be ending about now.

What he found with the mind touch—nothing!

That nothingness was as strong as it had been for Quanhi. It was as if the off-worlder had ceased to exist.

The answer brought a fear as deep as Toggor's had been. Farree swung off the bunk, reached in to one of the compartments below. He brought out something which he had discovered in his earlier exploration of the ship: a stunner. The weapon was not made for hands as small and weak as his. But he could carry it. Though his inability to take hold with both hands would slow him on his travel through the weak gravity, weapon held butt to his chest near the lump that was Toggor, he left the cabin. Mentally he sought Bojor and Yazz as he went. Both of them reported no trouble.

Lady Maelen—dare he try to reach her or would that betray him in turn to the one with the mind lock?

..•●) 6 (●•..

Farree scented it first in the central core, which held the ladder rising from one level of the ship to the next. It came as only a trace of a cloying sweetish odor which reminded him instantly of the noisome stews of the Limits and had no place in the sterile air of a space vessel. It wafted through the air from ducts on the next level, and Farree felt dizzy as if he floated out in some vast space with no ship to enclose or support him.

The Lady Maelen! Her cabin was here. He reached the door port and was stopped short. Across the surface, wedged well into the frame, was a bar making a prison for one inside. He put down the stunner. Then he swung his full weight on that bar. It was immobile as if it had been welded into place.

Panting, he huddled there, daring to use mind touch. Though he was sure that she whom he sought was inside, he touched—nothing! Just as the same answer came to his search for Lord-One Krip. Yet he could not believe that either of the off-worlders was dead.

Not up to the pilot's central cabin—not yet. Taking up the stunner, he pulled his distorted body down instead, seeking the special quarters which had been installed for Bojor and Yazz on the lower level. His eyes smarted and he felt a burdening need for rest that he was sure was a part of the drugged vapor which had been fed through the air duct. However, as he went lower, trying to breathe as shallowly as possible, the traces of that sickly sweetness vanished. By the time he had reached the lower level all he could smell was the odor of the bartle, the acrid scent of its shaggy fur.

"What happens?" Yazz's quick demand caught Farree as he swung from the final hold on the ladder and approached the cage of the larger animal. Pressed tightly to the wall between them was Yazz, bright eyes ashine in the gloom of this level, lips drawn back to show fangs near as formidable as those of Bojor.

Farree came quickly forward.

"Trouble." He could only advance his own fears but that was enough to alert both animals instantly. There came a single yap of reply from Yazz, a deep-chested growl from Bojor. Both of them now planted themselves, ready to issue forth were their doors opened. Outside the ship, planetside, both would have been formidable opponents. Within the confines here, it was another matter. Farree crouched down before the two animals and mind cast as well as he could what he had discovered, intensifying his fear of the pollutant in the air supply. Both of these were quicker to touch than the smux, and the channel between them and the hunchback was clearer.

"No food," came from Bojor. "Since last sleep no food."

Farree could guess the reason for that. To the crewmen there would be no reason to feed either the bartle or Yazz, the two animals having no value. The hunchback dragged himself across to the far wall. There were the levers he had seen tested and retested by the Lord-One Krip before they had lifted from Grant's World. He swung his weight on the nearest and it gave, allowing to fall into both cage-cabins the flat cakes of nutrient which were the voyage supplies.

Both animals wolfed down the food while Farree examined the fastenings of the cages. Those had also been carefully installed, and, though the builders had not realized it, pressure on one side would allow those within to use a paw for escape. Though Bojor had been cautioned against far roaming in the ship.

Farree applied that pressure. Now the cages might look intact but their occupants were free as they wished or needed to be. There was a skittering sound and the hunchback swung around, groping for the heavy weight of the stunner.

It was Toggor who came sliding down, one set of claws hooked loosely about the woven metal rope which formed the bannister for the ladder. All the smux's eyes were up and open. From the small creature flooded excitement and fear, but excitement was the stronger of those two emotions.

"What happens—" Farree beamed the question which Yazz had earlier used to greet him.

Once more he was greeted with a fuzzy picture of the crewman in the control cabin. Now that hazy figure was pounding on one section of the wall, and from him, through the smux, there flooded a raging anger and frustration.

Whatever he had tried to do in that place, he had not been able to accomplish it, and he was in a murderous mood.

"The Lord-One?" Farree asked then, picturing for himself the best replica of the off-worlder he could hold in mind.

What returned to him was a door with a bar as firmly across it as the one he had found sealing in the Lady Maelen. Perhaps overcome by the narcotic in the airstream, Krip had been downed and then imprisoned.

There had been only one of the crewmen in the smux's sight. Where then was the other?

The rumble of the bartle's growl and a click-clack of fangs from Yazz suggested they, too, had picked up Toggor's report. But if both the other-worlders had been sealed within their cabins after being overcome, why and how had Farree escaped?

Unless, Farree guessed, he seemed so negligible an opponent to the crewmen that they saw no reason to fear him and he had been classed with the other of Maelen's little ones. Well. He breathed deeply, inching forward to the ladder. No, there was no taint of the gas here. He was free, as were Toggor and the other two when they needed to make a move.

He had gone through the ship with Toggor and he knew it. Each cabin, storage place, walkway, was impressed firmly on his mind. Now, the stunner lying across his knees, he turned once more to the smux who was surely the one of them best suited to moving about unseen.

"Other man—" He spoke that aloud in a low voice as well as mind beamed. "Other one—"

A bit of the frustration of that one in the control cabin remained with Farree now, even though his contact with the smux was so limited. It would seem that the creature gained something from his demand, for he returned to the ladder rope down which he had come and began to climb.

There was another point which Farree must keep in mind: undoubtedly both of the crewmen were armed, and probably with far more potent weapons than the one he handled so awkwardly. A force blade or a laser could end any confrontation before he began.

He—

With all the directness of a blow, touch came to his mind then—the Lord-One Krip!

"Maelen?" A questing call sounded through his head as if it had come to his ears as a great, rousing shout.

There was no answer. But Farree cut in: "Her cabin— it is barred. Is yours also? Toggor reports it so."

"Farree!"

"Yes. I am free and with Yazz and Bojor. Toggor goes aloft. One of the men has been trying to do something in the control cabin but has failed. I do not know where the other is—"

"Sleep gas. And you?"

"Must be too far beneath their notice," the hunchback answered wryly.

"A force bar," came back quickly. "It must be detached. Can you—"

Farree interrupted with what he saw as the truth. "I cannot move while I do not know where they are—"

"Wait!"

He felt that also—the searching thought—though it was not beamed at him. Once more Bojor growled and this time raked his claws down the inner side of the door. Farree held up a hand in a signal which apparently the large animal understood.

"They are both shielded now," the Lord-One Krip aimed at Farree again. "I cannot find them—"

"There is Toggor. He has gone to search above—"

Instantly the prisoner seized upon that. "Seek him. I will feed you—seek him!"

Farree's whole twisted body quivered at what happened. There flowed into his mind such power as he would not have believed he could hold—nor did he try to contain it. Instead he thought of the smux, picturing him tightly and allowing that additional force to scrape along the path of his own thought.

For the first time the picture he received in return was far less fuzzed. At an odd angle, for the smux must be at floor level and the others towered far over him, Toggor was again surveying the control cabin. One of the men knelt on the floor, and there were tools laid out. He was working on a panel, which seemed to resist any attempt to loosen it.

"That is persona locked!" There was relief in Lord-One Krip's thought. "They can never open it without wrecking the tape there so that it cannot be used."

"What do they want?" Farree dared to ask. His head hurt so that he was rubbing his forehead with one hand. To provide a mind path for the Lord-One was like trying to contain a burning river.

Abruptly, as if the other sensed his pain, that flood

ceased and he lost contact with the smux as quickly as if someone had snapped a barrier between them.

"The voyage tape," came the answer. "They wish to switch tapes. It can't be done. The lock answers only to— to Maelen!"

There was anxiety to be felt, as if the Lord-One Krip had seized upon a perilous answer. The Lady was a prisoner: they might be able to force her to do what they had not been able to accomplish. Farree wondered briefly why they had not already tried that method.

"Perhaps they fear—" Lord-One Krip beamed. "There are many tales of the powers of the Thassa, and she is a Moon Singer. Since her duel with evil on Sehkmet there are even more tales. Yet we cannot hope that rumor alone will keep them from her."

"Yazz has fangs, elder brother." For the first time one of the others interrupted.

Echoing that was another hot, half-formed thought— the hazy rendering of an attack by the bartle on a barely realized human figure.

"Not yet," Lord-One Krip answered with a direct order through mind probe.

Farree resumed touch with the smux, and now that creature was turning about in the control cabin. What the hunchback caught was not the man still laboring futilely with the paneled wall but another dimly projected picture of the second settled in what Farree had been earlier told was the astrogator's seat.

It was, he decided, as if that second one was only waiting the result of the first's labors to go into action on his own.

So they were both in the control cabin! He kept only a thin tendril of connection with Toggor and began to edge up the ladder, the stunner against his chest, one hand on the guide lines to draw him on.

He passed the level which held his own cabin, panting with the effort he must use to reach the next level, needing to depend on his sole handhold to aid in negotiating the steps. Unused to the weaker gravity and with no magnetic boots it was a harder climb for him.

Once more he fronted the Lady's cabin with that pressure bar in place. He laid his weapon down within hand's reach and strove to move the barrier. It was beyond his strength, as if it had been riveted in place. He tried mind touch, and this time he did not meet the blank nothingness—rather a hazy, fluctuating return which might have been that of someone coming out of a deep sleep.

"Wake!" He pressed his own thought to the utmost strength. "Wake!"

The return was stronger, the alert and forceful pattern which he had come to associate with the Lady Maelen. She had fully roused. Now her demand for information was nearly as sharp as that of the Lord-One. It was he who gave her first answers. Then she turned her mind send back full on Farree.

"The bar—how is it fixed?"

He squatted, stunner in hand, to study the locking barrier and project the picture of it. So—and so—and so.

"Locked by persona!" flashed back an answer when he had done. "Now—"

But what she might have added was interrupted by a flash from the smux.

Toggor had dropped away from the cabin, was coming back down the handhold. The two in the control cabin were on the move, apparently descending to the next level. Farree himself skittered down the ladder and took refuge temporarily by the door of his own cabin. If they came that far, he might duck inside.

The odor of the sleep gas was gone from the level of Lady Maelen's prison. Perhaps they had some way of filtering it out of the air.

"We come." The united mind touch of Bojor and Yazz reached the hunchback. Swiftly he countered their suggestion. Neither animal could make a swift and easy ascent of the ladder, and they both would be too easy for the crewmen to pick off with either stunners or the fatal laser beamers.

Farree listened with his ears as well as his mind. Toggor had not withdrawn to this level. Instead, those eyes on stalks were watching the ladder near a closed door, which might mark the cabin of the Lord-One. Would the crew members believe that Krip was the one who held the information they must have?

"Care—" A single word from the imprisoned man. Farree had a fleeting impression that the Lord-One suspected these two had in their power some way of judging or listening to mind speech. Farree swiftly closed that channel but he kept his thread of contact with Toggor. It might well be true that the enemy could sense a human thought exchange but would not suspect it between their prisoners and the animals.

He heard above the vibration in the ship's walls, which remained a steady hum, a metallic clatter, and then voices came down the well of the ladder.

"Don't try anything, Thassa. We have a mind lock. We also have these. Those hands of yours—how would you like a roasted finger? Or a charred ear—that should be enough to scramble your thoughts, wouldn't it. Come out and get up to the control cabin. We want that tape pocket opened—and right now!"

"Persona set." That was Quanhi. "Clever, aren't you? But what has been set can be unset just as quickly. Get moving!"

They had the Lord-One with them—there followed the clip of magnetic boots on the ladder. But it was the Lady Maelen who had set that lock! How soon would they learn that and return for her—perhaps leaving the Lord-One maimed as the spacer had suggested?

Farree's anger burnt as it had before during his short life. Before he had had to stifle it—had been helpless against those who aroused it. Now—now there surely was something he could do! He had the weapon to hand and Toggor to run scout for him.

"And us. And us—"

That quick assurance came from below, surprising him again with the eager anger which moved Bojor and Yazz. The bartle—could the beast force the lock across the Lady's door, releasing her?

"I come." Bojor's only half-sensed message, which Farree had to strain his mind below the usual channel to intercept, was almost as angry as a vocal growl.

"Not yet." The bulk of the animal and its difficulty with

the ladder might cause too much of a delay. Farree tapped his stunner against the step above where he crouched and tried to think.

Once more he made his way back to the level where the Lady Maelen's door was barred. Holding the stunner and continually glancing from ladder to door, Farree ran his hand across it at his chin level. It was easy to feel the thumb indentation of the persona lock was made to answer to one of the crew and him only.

He had closed his mind, nor would he try to open to the Lady lest they be checked upon by those others. Farree stationed himself near the upper ladderway, his attention for all that was above. Then he dared to give the signal to the impatient two below.

The passage of the thick-bodied bartle was a tight one and preceded by a number of grunts and half-voiced growls. Then the heavy shoulders and the tufted head appeared, and a moment later Farree retreated up a step, leaving full possession of that level to Bojor.

Long talons were unsheathed and wound about the bar. Farree watched the shoulders tense until their thick covering of bristly hair stood erect, and knew the animal was exerting its full strength.

At that same moment from overhead came an alert from the smux: "One comes!"

Perhaps the enemy had already learned that only the Lady had the true answer to their riddle and would bring her up to taste their method of coaxing. Farree clung to the ladder, wedging himself as best he could to the centermost part of it where the steps were the widest. He lifted the stunner with both his hands on the firing pin and waited.

Legs in dull gray spacer uniform appeared—then the rest of Pitor Dune. There was nothing of the disreputable Limits crawler about him now. Rather he swung down as if he were the master of the ship.

Farree fired. He had not aimed at the head, but for the center of the body, and a moment later the man folded in upon himself and tumbled forward before the hunchback could get out of the way. He heard the shout the half-paralyzed man gave even as the body knocked him flat, both of them landing against the shaggy flank of the bartle, who growled and showed fangs.

The hunchback wriggled out from under the bruising weight of the crewman and pushed him aside, farther along the floor, toward Bojor. The bartle used teeth now as well as talons to fight the stubborn hold of the bar.

A sudden thought caught Farree as he struggled away from the man screaming oaths at him. He fought to enter the bartle's mind with the plea to stand clear for a moment. Then he pushed and shoved the inert but cursing man to the position before the door and hooked up one of his hands to press the thumb in the hollow. There was a fifty-fifty chance of this one being the warden.

But the bar did not yield, and Bojor, irritated at being disturbed during his own efforts, swept both Farree and the crewman aside with a powerful blow. The helpless man slipped through the opening at the center of the ladder well and was gone before the hunchback could move to stop him.

There came a shout from aloft: "What's to do? Is the witch bitch out? Answer me, Dune." When there was no answer, the ray of a laser clipped into molten droplets part of the hand rope, seaming a line across the steps.

At the same time Farree tried to urge Bojor back out of the line of fire. The creature gave a last deep grunt and the stubborn bar loosened a fraction. Prying at that end, the bartle was able to pull it fully free and allow the door to open.

The Lady Maelen stood just within. She had a second stunner in one hand, and there was a look of grim purpose on her face. But she did not speak nor mind send an order—rather signed with one hand. The bartle rumbled deep in his throat once again and then moved cautiously back and onto the ladder, pushing his bulk through the level opening to descend. Farree, also obedient to that signal, set his crooked back to the wall and waited for orders, his own stunner ready.

"One of them is gone?" Her question came not mind to mind but in a whisper so faint that it barely reached him. He nodded and pointed down the ladder well.

"Listen, witch bitch," came a shout from above. "Do you want your fancy man here to fry?"

"Do you wish," she called back, "to planet where we have friends and then strive to explain where we are? Our voyage is already past the turn point. Whether you would or no, you are now bound by the ship's tape, and nothing save a destruction of the whole guide system will prevent it carrying out its instructions. Do you wish to die in a drifting derelict?"

"Friends waiting?" The unseen captor above appeared to catch upon only one of her arguments. "You have no friends, witch bitch. You were exiled by your own people and cannot return without breaking their laws again. Yes, see, I know you, wearer of other bodies! Now, do you yield or do I cook this fake Thassa of yours?"

"I swear to you by Molester, there is no way you can change the tape. We have gone too long and too far." She was standing very close to the upper ladderway, but out of sight of the one who must be above, perhaps just above, as the last call had sounded much closer.

"So it is Yiktor whether or no, that is what you would tell me? Well enough, there are those on Yiktor who can take charge of you as easily as I can cook this friend of yours. Wait and see—"

But the gloating voice stopped almost in mid word. Instead there followed a cry of disgust which became one of pain. Down the ladder thudded a squat-barreled, ugly-looking weapon which Farree knew was a laser. It hit against the edge of the lower well and flew into the air, falling straight out of sight.

There was a second scream of pain fast becoming agony. Then Farree saw Toggor swinging down the rope, his claws gleaming bright scarlet and dripping greenish droplets. It had been many days since the smux had been out of the hands of Russtif. His venom had not been forcibly drawn. It might not be enough to actually kill a man, but the pain from any smux wound was, as Farree knew, intolerable.

"All clear!" There had been sounds of a brief struggle, and now the Lady Maelen leapt for the ladder and started up them, Farree following.

They found what they sought on the level below the pilot cabin. On the floor, one hand a brilliant scarlet as if it had been scalded, lay Quanhi. His eyes were shut and the rest of him limp. As first Maelen and then Farree came through, it was to see Lord-One Krip backed against the wall, rubbing one fist with the fingers of his other hand, and the knuckles of that hand were skinned. Maelen turned, and, without a word, played the stunner she carried straight upon the head of the already unconscious man.

"Let him sleep in peace," she said. "But first—" She knelt down and ran her fingers through the short dark hair of their prisoner. "No webbing shield. There must be"— she shook her own head as if she wanted to deny just what she said—"an implant of some kind."

"Maybe they were mind washed," Lord-One Krip suggested.

"This one was protected from the beginning. Pitor Dune was not—at least on the surface. On ship he was. I wonder where they wanted us to planet."

..●)7(●..

"Not, I think, on Yiktor," the Lord-One returned. "But they would expect us to land at the port and—"

She smiled a little then. "We shall surprise them. Into the Dry Waste we shall go, if the tape proves true and he who set it had no reason to lie. Also I scanned him as he took payment. What he might have done is relay our navigation points to another. That the arm—and ear—of the Guild are long is well known."

"Manus Hnold gave his word," her companion returned. "He is Free Trader—and they are used to keeping secret landfalls which might have future use."

"We are close now to turnover, little kin," she said to Farree. "Seek you now your own place, for with turnover comes ship shift. And these others—" She looked down at the man Lord-One Krip had silenced and beyond him to the ladder well. From below still arose the dulled sound of curses. "They must be put into stass also."

It was not easy, handling the limp bodies of the two crewmen, though the bartle had strength enough—had there been room—to toss them both easily about. But at length each was bound down with safety straps on his own bunk and Bojor and Yazz were back in their cages, taking their own precautions against the spill of turnover.

Toggor crept once more into the fore of Farree's robe and lay flat as the Lady and the Lord-One went into the control cabin and strapped down. The hunchback was in his own cabin, the stunner made fast to the straps which were his protection. He forced himself to relax and waited for the queasiness and giddiness of the reentry into normal space. As he lay there his mind was as busy as his body was inert.

The Guild. Its tentacles of power ran from star to star, perhaps magnified by rumor, or perhaps not even rumor could suggest the full tale of its controls. Where there was law, there was also the Guild—that was a matter of balance, and it had always been so as far as Farree knew. Each planet was supposed to police itself, the Patrol only in command where there was off-world interference or against independent worlds where the Guild had carved out niches of "safe ports" for itself. There were worlds where rumor said ships planeted and exchanged cargoes that were not of the usual kind and paid for in unknown ways. Wherever there was an unusual find also—there the Guild appeared sooner or later.

His present companions had spoken of Sehkmet—of a Free Trader forced by power failure to land on a supposedly dead planet only to chance upon a vast treasure of Forerunner artifacts and knowledge that was already being harvested by the Guild. That the Guild would not take kindly to having that operation broken up he could well-believe. And Lord-One Krip and the Lady Maelen had had a hand in that breaking. He gave the small nod which was the only movement his present bonds allowed him. Yes, the Guild could well be after them.

He waited for the rise of fear within him. There was that and a shiver of excitement, for he knew well that, had he been given the same chance again, he would make the same choice. To Lord-One Krip and the Lady he was not the scum of the Limits, but one, Farree, to be trusted.

Turnover! He was pushed against the bunk, the padding within it seeming suddenly leaden, far from the soft surface on which he had rested a breath or two earlier. There was a sharp pain in his head, and then the giddiness and nausea hit together.

Later, the spasm past, he dared to loose the protecting belts and ties and climb up to the pilot cabin, wedging his small body into the seat of the com officer they lacked. Both the Lord-One Krip and the Lady Maelen were absorbed in watching a screen, where pinpoints of light were growing larger and larger as their ship bored on through normal space.

The Lady Maelen broke silence first. "We shall earth at night, I think. The code—" She reached forward and the fingers of her right hand sped across a board of buttons. "That will see us past any orbital guard. We must hope that that has not been changed."

Time passed, and then they were centering in on one of those balls of light. Farree wriggled forward in his seat to watch their goal come rushing toward them. They would orbit twice, he had understood from the plans earlier made, and then set down under mech-pilot on the spot to which their tape had pointed them across the star lanes.

It all seemed like a dream to him. The outer star-spangled space was cold and lonely, he thought. And how could a twist of ribbonlike metal bring them in without any action on their part? To trust in such was a little more than he could accept as the time grew short before they must set down.

At last he deliberately closed his eyes and turned his head into the bargain. He did not want to see a world come rushing up toward him. It seemed that he would spatter against it as a fos-beetle spatted against a screen, unable to waver in its flight to avoid the barrier.

A giant hand perhaps as large as the bartle's whole body pressed him down. There was a pain which shot through his hump as if he had been slashed by a knife, and he tasted the salt-sweet of blood in his mouth. Then darkness and nothingness fell like the space between the star worlds.

"Farree," a voice called. Reluctantly he crawled back up out of the darkness in answer. He looked up into the face of the Lady Maelen. She passed a damp cloth over his nose and mouth, and it showed the dark red of blood. He felt an ache through his whole body, but he caught at the webbing of the seat, which had been loosened, and drew himself up.

"I am all right," he made quick answer, refusing to let them believe that he was merely a charge upon them, as if he were indeed one of the "little ones"—those to whom cages came as prisons. He felt her probe and met it quickly. No, he wanted no care, only to be treated as she would treat one of her own straight-backed kind.

She drew back. "You *are* of our kind, Farree." She did not speak that mind to mind but with her lips, as if she acknowledged relationship by word instead of thought.

He did not try to answer her. One needed only to look at him to know that she spoke in pity only, and the notion of her pity brought a fierce surge of anger which he could not voice.

Lord-One Krip was still seated in the captain's swinging chair, and now his fingers played across the board which the Lady Maelen had earlier used. Farree became aware of something else: the vibration that had been a part of him while they were en route was gone. The ship was motionless and silent. On the looking screen there were tall rises of bare rock. They had indeed landed and, from the look of it, not at any port.

There was a greenish light upon those rocks. Lady Maelen took a step forward and touched the man's shoulder lightly. Though no word or mind speech Farree could catch passed between them, the scene outside the ship changed.

Gone were the light-touched rocks with their deep indentations of shadow. Instead they saw a moon in a sky which was not dark. For around the globe of that gold-bright coin were two rings of light, stark and clear. Beyond them, a hazy surround of a third was yet but a palid shadow of the others.

The Lady Maelen flung her arms up as if she stood in the open reaching to touch that wonder.

"Three rings—not yet but soon!" Her voice held a triumphant sound as if she had won through some hard battle to reach this time and place.

"And where"—Lord-One Krip leaned back in his seat, his still hands resting upon the edge of that board of many buttons—"are we?"

"Sotrath will lend us light. If I only had long sight I would—"

But the three in the cabin of the ship were not to hear her words, for ringing into the mind of each of them came a challenge, so clear and sharp that Farree reeled and saw that even the Lord-One Krip had caught at the edge of the board, holding so tensely that his grazed knuckles stood out as white knobs.

"Who comes thus into the Quiet Places?"

For a long moment Farree thought that there would be no answer. Then the reply came from the Lady Maelen.

"I am she who was judged, she whose rod of power was taken from her. She who wore fur and fangs and—"

"And comes again in a new body! Whence got you that, Singer who was and now is not?"

"Thus." There was a tingle in Farree's mind; that was the only way he could describe it. No passage of thought, rather a high sweet sound as if someone sang without words. How long it continued he could not have afterwards said. It trailed up and up into notes he could not hear but which still fed that tingle in his mind.

Once more that other voice spoke. It came from nowhere but arrived with all the authority of a guard: "This is a thing which must be thought upon. Not lightly are the People answered by a flouting of their Law."

Lady Maelen bowed her head as if she stood before a speaker and surrendered her will to that other.

"Let it lie upon the Scale of Molester. For such a judgment I am ready. Those with me are guilty of naught save striving to help—"

"All those with you?" resounded the voice. "What of the two who lie prisoner in body within that ship?"

"They shall be delivered to the judgment of their own kind."

"They are trespassers by your aid into a place which is forbidden to all save the People and those they summon."

"Sotrath has summoned us. Three rings will shine and then that which is crooked can be made straight—"

That which is crooked—straight!

Farree took a single step forward. Surely she did not mean that! She and the Lord-One had picked him out of the Limits, cast off his casing of Dung, but there was no magic in the world—this or any other—that could straighten him, three rings around an unknown moon or not!

There was a bitter taste in his mouth as he swallowed, not born of his blood this time but from his thoughts. Yet he was given no time to sift those, for again the voice rang clear.

"Unto Molester shall it be, even as you have said, you who are not—"

There was a kind of echo in his mind, but the words were sharply cut off and Farree knew that the speaker had withdrawn. Once more the picture screen in the control cabin showed, not the sky, but towering cliffs about them. The bright light of the moon brought those sharply into focus, and the picture began slowly to move from right to left as if the ship itself was turning on some giant spindle.

The cliffs ended. Before them now stretched a wide plain unbroken by any growth higher than a few thick patches of dead-seeming grass.

This was an empty land appearing only as a wasteland. Then once more cliffs arose to wall them in. Lord-One Krip leaned a little closer to the screen.

"This I have seen."

"He did well, that Hnold. We are within short distance to the meeting place," Lady Maelen returned. There was warm satisfaction in her voice. "Let me but go and all shall be readied."

"Wait!" His hand went up as if to back his command. "Look to the—"

He pressed thumb hard upon a button and the screen ceased its turn. Before them were still tall cliffs under the clear moonlight, but in the sky above the ragged edge of those cliffs something moved, striking fire now and then from the same moonlight.

"A flitter!"

The Lady Maelen's lips flattened against her teeth in a grimace. She, too, leaned closer to the screen. "But this is the Land of Beyond where only the Thassa move. And the lordlings of the inner lands have no sky flight!"

"Others do," he returned grimly. "Such as those we have on board."

"Wait and watch!" Her hand on his shoulder pushed him fully down into his seat again.

The airborne transport came on, fully into the moonlight, where the rocks seemed to reflect back the glory of the rings to show the clearer what passed either on earth or through the air. The craft had no riding lights, and yet it appeared to hold a course that would bring it to their own landing place.

Guild? But how could the two prisoners have summoned such support?

"They were waiting," said Lord-One Krip in a low voice.

"That they could not have been!" she protested. "The tape was unchanged and brought us—"

"Perhaps they expected their men might fail," he returned. "They had ready then a secondary plan."

"Which will not serve them either." Her fingers dug into his shoulder as she watched the oncoming flitter closely but with no expression of alarm. "See!"

The small craft boring through the moonlight had nearly reached the lip of the cliffs. Then it seemed to waver—almost as if the same wind which rippled the grass patches was strong enough to seize the flitter from the control of those on board. The craft sideslipped to the right, drew level with what Farree could believe was an effort, slipped again. It near-skimmed the top of the cliff, and then it made an abrupt turn and half circled to put itself back on the same course it had followed toward them.

Only no longer was its flight swift and sure; it slipped from one side to the other in jerky motion. The craft could have been a bird netted by a sure fling of a hunter, struggling for its freedom to no purpose.

So jerking and fighting the craft passed out of sight behind a taller pinnacle of the cliff rise and was gone.

"The Thassa have their own defenses," the Lady Maelen said. "None approach here unless they are of the blood or are summoned. This is the Old Place and here lies the heart—" She stopped suddenly and looked curiously abashed, as one who talks of hidden things and then realizes her words can be heard by those who have no right to listen.

"Will they crash?" Lord-One Krip asked in a level voice.

Now she frowned. "Not so. Our defenses are not to destroy—not even any evil which may come. They will be but diverted and also they will forget—"

"Not if they, too, are mind shielded."

She frowned. "I do not know. A shield is made to keep out thought thrusts. It is not intended to stand up to the force of the Elders acting together. We shall see how well any man-made thing may last against the full force of the Thassa."

"Let us hope," he said in the same level tone, "that the force is fully effective then. Do we go?"

"Not yet. With the dawn perhaps. Maybe then the summons will come. We cannot enter without that."

Farree lay once more curled on his own bunk with Toggor squatting beside him. This was a long way from the Limits yet. He rubbed his forehead. There was something—a pale shadow of a shadow of a memory that once he had lain within a ship before. Still, how could that be? His only clear memory came from the noisome sink of the Limits and that was all he thought he had ever known. He wondered—pushing away that shadow which made him uneasy and aching—what the dawn would bring. That Lord-One Krip was also uneasy this night, he sensed.

However, if there was any crack in the confidence of the Lady Maelen he could not detect it. She was restless, yes, but not as one who awaited trouble, rather as one who would be out and doing—one who stood before a door, impatient that it be opened to her.

He wondered about the Thassa and that voice out of nowhere. Had it perhaps rung out also in the minds of those in the flitter, warning them off in a way they could not protest? Or had it taken charge of their bodies as he had heard tales of among the spacers, forcing them against their wills?

He thought and later he slept while, in his broken and fleeting dreams, he looked upon a three-ringed moon and felt power drawing him to—to—but to what he could not remember when he awakened.

It was Toggor tugging with a claw at one of the locks of his unruly hair that brought him out of that drowse. The smux radiated hunger, and Farree felt an answering emptiness in his own bent body. He slipped into the narrow slit of the fresher and allowed the mist there to wash him, coming out to a fresh robe and sandals. Then he went to the galley, smelling, even before he opened the door, the fine odors of food.

Lord-One Krip was at the table, an opened ration tin at hand, but he was not eating. When Toggor gave a squeal and leaped onto the table, he shoved the tin at the smux, who clacked claws over it and immediately began to eat.

Farree was a little daunted that the other had made no sign of seeing him nor given any greeting. But he got his own tin and crawled up on the empty seat opposite the man, waiting for him to break the silence between them.

"She is waiting still." Lord-One Krip might have been talking to himself, for he did not look in Farree's direction at all. "But what if . . ." He did not finish the question, and Farree dared now to do it for him. After all, he was a part of this company, too, and if trouble lay before them it was his right to know.

"What if the—the voice—says we must leave?"

For the first time the man looked at him. There was the crease of a frown between those upward-slanting brows.

"Then we go."

Greatly daring, Farree asked, "Where are we?"

"At the meeting place of the Thassa. You do not understand, little brother." He clasped his hands before him on the table. "I am not Thassa"—with the fingers on one hand he pinched the skin on the back of the other—"though I now wear a Thassa body."

"One does not wear bodies," Farree cut in sharply. "One *is* a body." For a wild moment the thought of another body—a straight, tall, humpless one—filled his mind. What if what he had just denied was the truth and he could change? There were many wonders on other worlds, but never had he heard such as that!

"The Thassa *wear* bodies." He could see that Lord-One Krip meant in truth what he said. "To become a Moon Singer, a one of power among them—they change bodies with animals, running wild on the land and learning from them other scents and desires. I was a crewman on a free trader, and here on Yiktor I was taken by a lordling who would have of me the secrets from off-world—or else use me to wring such from my captain. He gave my body to pain."

Farree hunched under the burden on his shoulders as if rolling himself into a ball. He knew what Lord-One Krip meant. Such had been his own portion.

"I was—damaged. Maelen was a Moon Singer and also the leader of a troop of little ones—animals who gave shows she devised. She saved me by singing me into a barsk."

Farree swallowed. "An animal?"

"An animal"—nodded the other—"one which was notably fierce and supposedly untameable. It was not one of hers but one which had been captured and badly treated, and which she was curing and trying to mind free. So did I live on Yiktor for a space. But then there was a Thassa body—a Kinsman to Maelen—a Thassa who had taken on animal form but been killed in that form. His body was empty of mind, for the animal transformed with him had gone mad. So—I became Thassa—for my own body was judged dead by my shipmates and spaced after they had taken off. For this act Maelen was condemned by the Thassa and her wand of power taken from her. When she left this world she, too, was an animal—and as such she traveled with me. Until Sehkmet. There—well, there were bodies, very ancient bodies, who could change at will. And one of them was a woman. She would have ruled, but Maelen invaded her, freed her captives and the inner core of evil which dominated her, so her body became Maelen as you see her now. We have returned to Yiktor with this ship—for it has long been Maelen's dream, as you know in a little—to become once more a Moon Singer and then to go out among the stars with her furred folk, proving to all that life is sacred and those considered the lesser may, in their own way, surprise those who see them as that. When Sotrath bears its three rings is a time of great power, and we have waited for that to return. But now, just as that flitter was guided from the inner land, so may we also be sent on our way."

"She does not believe that." Farree did not know how he knew that truth, but he was certain he did.

"She is—Maelen. Once a Singer under the moon, one cannot be stripped of such powers easily. And on Sehkmet she found a battle such as few even of her people must ever have faced. Thus she believes what she wishes to believe—"

"Belief is a comfort and a weapon, a wand of power, and a pointed laser." Maelen stood in the doorway of the cabin, her eyes alight. The long cascade of hair, which she usually kept tightly braided, flowed free around her shoulders, though locks of it wavered a little, as if stirred to rise by some magnet. Her drab ship's uniform was gone. Instead, she wore breeches and boots of a russet color close to that of her hair. Her shirt had a wide stiffened collar forming a tali fan behind her head, and she had a sleeveless jacket of some yellow wooly stuff which was not unlike fur.

Farree heard Lord-One Krip's breath come forth in a low sound of wonder. The Lady Maelen turned slowly around as if to allow them to view her. In the drabness of the ship she was almost like a flame glowing with warmth, for that eagerness Farree had earlier sensed in her was now a consuming fire.

"Come!" She beckoned to both of them. "The Thassa gather. Soon we shall be summoned also."

She swung up to the control cabin, Lord-One Krip on her heels, Farree moving more slowly behind. The screen was on and they looked out into or onto a sun-drenched world. There was life—no flitter in the skies, but rather there came at a steady pace wagons with covered tops and huge earth-crushing wheels pulled by teams of shaggy-coated four-legged animals that plodded steadily onward at a ground-eating pace. Nor could Farree see that any held the reins, any walk beside them with a goad in hand. Rather the animals had the air of being about a necessary business of their own.

The wagons were brightly painted, colors vivid, against the dull gray countryside over which they plowed. Now he could see figures on the front seats of some of the wagons, though they were still too far away to be well viewed.

They were all headed for a break in the wall of the cliff, one so regular in size Farree could almost believe it had been squared off by some ancient intelligence. For as he looked upon that roadway he had a feeling of age—of age and forgotten story.

Then, once more, came that clear voice in his head: "The Thassa gather. Come you who would speak."

Maelen threw back her head. She did not reply in that wordless, voiceless sound but in a thought touch as firm and clear: "We hear and we come!"

··●)8(●··

They stood out under the open sky, a wind rippling around them, pushing at their bodies, making a flaming banner of the Lady Maelen's hair. Behind them Yazz and Bojor snuffled and snorted, their pleasure at being free of the ship projecting a warmth reaching from mind to mind. The wagons went their way still, and it seemed that not one among them was interested enough in the ship even to look in their direction. Perhaps strict order drew them forward. But there were fewer of them now, a straggling end to the push of that company.

The Lady Maelen led her companions toward that same break in the cliff wall. And, as the sun slanted across the rock, Farree, holding his head at the best angle his deformity would allow, saw strange markings on the stone. As if once there had been carvings there, now so worn away by time that their ghosts alone still haunted the rock.

Beyond a narrow passage through the cliff lay another open space, and there the wagons had been staked out, the animals that had drawn them loosed to graze at will.

Here were squared openings set in patterns as if the rock itself had been mined for a city of dwellings. Again the ghostly markings ran across the yellowed stone. There were the people of this company also, and after each wagon had taken its place they headed toward one of the openings—larger, more wreathed with the patterns.

Farree heard Lord-One Krip draw a deep breath.

"The gathering," he said as if he spoke his thought aloud.

"The gathering!" echoed the Lady Maelen but there was a note of excitement in her voice, whereas Lord-One Krip appeared to be less eager to take the way toward that open doorway in the far wall of the cliff.

They were approached by some latecomers passing the same way, but to Farree's bewilderment and growing unease these Thassa ignored the party from the ship as if they did not exist. But neither did either of his companions try to exchange greetings or even glances with those whose pace now matched theirs.

So, of that company and yet apart, they came into a vast assembly place within the rock. The floor underfoot inclined gently to a center where was a dais, and on that stood four of the Thassa. Farree studied them eagerly, hoping to read something in their attitude which might token that the ship's party was not trespassing but was to be welcomed.

But, though the four stood watching, their eyes appeared to go above, beyond, or to either side, not toward the three from the ship. The last of the Thassa split into two small groups and took their stations on either side of the broad open aisle which led down to the dais itself.

Now the Lady Maelen stopped short and stood, with Lord-One Krip a little behind her and Farree still farther back, aloof in that crowd of strangers where he felt more than ever his crookedness.

It was not dark within this hall cave for there were globes of light suspended overhead to provide the same light as the moon had flung the night before across the outer world. Now around them there raised song without words, entering into one's very skin and bones, becoming a part of one.

It seemed to Farree that that song could put wings on the listener, lift him up and away from the body, freeing the innermost part of him to float and fly above all which tied him to the earth. He forgot time, and space, and himself, and was only what the song bore with it.

At last that died away in a slow sobbing as if the fading of a people or a life was now a part of it. Farree smeared his hand across his face and so wiped away tears—he who long ago had learned that weeping availed nothing. It was the dying of something great and wonderful, that last of the singing, beyond his small power to describe, and it wrung him, bringing with it all the feeling of alienness he had ever known.

There was a tearing in his chest, and a fierce aching awoke in his hump. He put his hands over his ears, trying to shut out that dying song. Then he saw that one of those on the dais had shifted the silver wand she bore in her hands. The end of that pointed now in his direction just as he was aware that she saw and knew him. Straightaway the sound ended—for him—though he still half crouched, too aware of the burden on his shoulders and the pain which held through that. But he was released from the sorrow borne in the song.

The wand swung, pointed now to Maelen. "What now is your tale—in this time and place—exile?"

It was the same voice which had questioned their landing, ringing again in their heads.

Maelen moved forward. Lord-One Krip stepped up beside her. If she faced a foe, then he, too, would front that hostility. Not to be left behind, Farree followed, his head at a straining angle to watch that company of four.

"Standing words cannot be altered. As was said here once before to you who sang and then forfeited that right."

Farree thought that that came from one of the two men flanking the woman with the wand.

"The third ring waxes, the power rises." Maelen faced them proudly with such a bearing as might a warrior waiting for the first order to advance.

"It waxes—" That was the other woman. "Well, well— the Old Ways are not to be denied. Speech is yours, you who were once a Singer."

"I am Maelen."

"That is the truth. Yet you come wearing a new guise. Do you again meddle as you once did with changing?"

Maelen threw open her arms as if she was so loosing all shields she might hold against any of these.

"Read, Older Sister."

There was silence, so deep that it might have been that this hall was now deserted. Yet Farree felt a stirring in his mind at too high a level to follow. Thassa bespeaking Thassa, he guessed—not for such as he to hear.

They stood motionless, all in that company, as if caught in some twist of time unending, unchanging. Then the woman who had challenged Maelen broke her statuelike stance and turned her head, first right and then left. She might have been speaking soundlessly to those with her, sitting in judgment. But it was the other woman among the four who touched minds now.

"You have been along a strange path, Singer-that-was. There abides in you now that which we cannot assess—save that you have used it as you could for the good of those who trusted you. Singer, no. We cannot judge for you. You must name yourself. Are you asking such a naming?"

"The third ring waxes," Maelen returned slowly. "No, I ask not any power which does not come to me openly and is earned. But I am still Thassa, and this thing which started on another world and with another race is not yet ended. It will again be my debt on the Scales, and Molester shall judge in the end as all of us are judged."

"On the Scales then let it lie. You do not judge—"

"Am I still exile?"

"You are what you are, by your choice. Thassa is not closed to you nor"—she now leveled the wand and pointed at Lord-One Krip—"to you, once stranger, who have worn our seeming well. Nor—"

Once more the wand centered on Farree. And he saw a look of vast surprise cross her face, the rod quivering in her hand.

"Go with Molester's Hand above you, small one," she said slowly. "His Scales shall weigh you and in the end it shall be the truth for you also."

He wondered at the way she said those words, as if she pronounced some judgment. Yet one that was not a heavy one for him. Perhaps, he thought, with a stab of the bitterness that was always with him, her surprise was that such a one as he had ventured into this company. Dung of the Limits might have no place here. He dropped his head and looked downward to his clawlike hands with the greenish skin, his feet which were no better, looking too small and weak to support that burden on his back. Thus he saw Toggor's eyestalks looming out of the neck opening of his robe, turning this way and that as if the smux must acquaint himself with all this company and the moon-glow hall in which they were gathered.

"You have not yet come into your inheritance." That loud, clear voice rang in his head. "We are what Molester shapes, and for each shape there is a reason and a duty—"

It was the bitterness which made him brave enough to answer with the mind touch, "And if the shape is spoiled in the making, Lady?"

"There is nothing save that which is ordained. You will come into that which is yours at the proper time."

He supposed she meant when he was dead, which was hardly an encouraging message. Then he remembered Lord-One Krip's own tale of how he had been, at a time of great need, transferred by Thassa power into the body of an animal and then into a man's form again. Could such work for him? For the first time Farree thought seriously of that part of the off-worlder's story. Would it be better to run like Yazz on four feet, or claw a way in Toggor's form, than to shamble as Dung? That was a thought to consider.

However, though the words of the Thassa Elder might promise change—what change and how? He breathed a little faster and then became aware that around him the people were starting to leave the hall within the cliff. Only Maelen and Lord-One Krip did not move, and, seeing that, he also stayed where he was.

The Elders did not leave the dais, but she of the wand made a small beckoning gesture, and Maelen and Krip moved toward her. Only Farree remained where he was, still bemused by that thought of another body, unburdened, four-footed perhaps. Though where was even a beast that would change places with such as he?

Those on the dais had come forward to face the two from the ship, and again there was a flow of thought too high and fast for Farree to catch. He dropped cross-legged on the stone where he was, and Toggor climbed out to hold the folds of his robe and project the feeling of hunger and impatience to be fed.

Then the smux suddenly loosed hold on Farree and with a leap reached the stone of the floor and caught a big-bodied insect that had swung from circling about one of the moon globes above, transferring the morsel to his mouth with a message that such prey hardly made up for the hunger in him.

"Come, Farree." Lord-One Krip looked back to him. "It is back to the ship for us now."

Yet the Lady Maelen remained still with those leaders of the Thassa as he rose to shamble after the off-worlder. No, not an off-worlder here where he wore a Thassa body, whatever might lie within that.

"What do we—you"—he caught himself quickly not to

claim too such familiarity with the Lord-One—"do now?"

The man shrugged. "That remains with Maelen and the temper of the Thassa. This she had longed to do—to return here and be again a Singer, a companion to little ones with fur and feathers."

"But—" The question Farree might have asked was swallowed up by sound from the sky above them: the beat of a flitter coming low above the valley which led to the hall, swinging on toward the ship. Lord-One Krip began to run and Farree could not keep up, only trotted along as best he might. He noticed as he passed that none of those gathered by the wagons looked skyward.

There was something here to which he could not put name, but it made him feel that he was forcing his misshapen body through a turgid flood which sought to cover and stifle him.

The flitter swept on, and he fought to follow Lord-One Krip into the open where the ship stood. Was that strange wave of strength broadcast from the airborne craft, or was it some side issue of a protection summoned by the Thassa?

Farree stumbled around boulders, having twice to stop and draw enough panting breaths to send him on. He could see Lord-One Krip ahead but he, too, moved as if caught in some flood that would wash him back instead of forward, a current of power raised to keep him from his goal.

They reached the end of the valley, and there Krip halted, the whole tense posture of his body showing that it was not by his will. He was struggling still.

Farree felt a sudden push of new force against him, and

he could not breast it for himself. Rather he clung to another boulder and stood as straight as he could, watching—almost certain now that this force came from the flitter and was not a protection raised by the Thassa.

The flitter set down not far from their ship. Men issued forth from the flitter. Two of them went toward the inclined way leading from the smoking land about the fins into the center of their ship, and two others took their places between that and the open mouth of the canyon, standing with feet slightly apart and weapons ready in their hands—That pressure kept Krip and Farree away from them, helpless against what they would do.

Once more his own shoulders' burden began to ache, weighing him down, as if the pressure against him had sought out his weakest portion of being and there centered upon him. Lord-One Krip no longer struggled but stood where he had been stopped, his arms folded across his chest. Farree could feel the thrust of thought he hurled toward those at the ship, though it was pure pressure in the mind, not coherent words and phrases.

They were not gone long, those two who had invaded the ship, and when they came back they had the former prisoners with them, walking easily, not hampered any longer by their bonds. Then, together, those from the flitter and the two others lined up before the ship's fins. One of those who had gone aboard had in his hand what looked like a square box which the downing sun caught and awoke into an eye-hurting burst of light. He placed this carefully on the ground and knelt beside it—

The current of power that had entrapped them within the canyon was in a single moment reversed. Farree gave a shout of sheer astonishment and fear as he was swiftly drawn forward in spite of his attempts to anchor himself to one or another of the boulders his small body scraped by.

If that force reft him from anchorage, it was not as successful with Lord-One Krip. Just as he had earlier striven to pass some unseen barrier into the open, now he fought fiercely, as attested by all the movements of his body, to remain now where he was.

Farree had not the personal strength of the other. He scraped stone painfully, looked vainly into the face of Krip as he was drawn past the man. The Lord-One's features were stark with effort. He looked to Farree and a single thought passed from him to the other.

"Hold—where and how you can."

Only, if Krip was able to hold, there was no hope in any such battle on Farree's part. He was aware only of a movement at his breast. Toggor had leaped from his clawhold there to seize upon the Lord-One's arm.

This desertion brought a new stab of fear. Farree never knew how much the smux could guess or knew of the ways of men. He had operated under Farree's urging in the ship and back at the Limits. Now he might be acting on his own, and his action brought home to Farree his own complete helplessness.

In one last attempt to withstand that force, the hunchback flung himself forward on his knees and caught with both hands at a stunted scrub, striving to keep his hold, only to have his fingers loose of themselves and make him scuttle along on hands and feet like some unwieldy shell-encased monster.

"One!" He heard that voice dimly and then a second.

"One, but the least of them!"

"Put it on alpha then—"

He had crawled until he could see their boots clearly. Having once lost his feet, that treacherous wave of force kept him low, so he came as a spirit-broken animal might slink to Russtif at the crack of a whip.

"It is on alpha. I tell you we deal with the unknown. And—"

There was a startled cry from one of Farree's captors. The hunchback now sat within touching distance of that shining box. He was soaked with sweat from his fight against the power, tasting blood in his mouth where he had bitten down on his lip in that agony of struggle. But Farree looked up to see he who knelt by the box, swaying back and forth, a look of torment on his face. One hand was going forward to the strange weapon, advancing plainly against his will.

One of the other men from the flitter gave a harsh exclamation and joined his fellow by the box, slicing a hand down with vicious suddenness so that it struck against the wrist of that groping one. There was a cry of pain and the first man nursed his wrist against his body.

"Take off! While we can!" It was Quanhi who yelled that. "They have strengths we don't know—"

"Nobody can withstand this." The one who attacked his fellow said that grimly.

"No? I see Krip Vorlund over there still. Did you think to bring him crawling to us like this?" The toe of a boot flashed out to catch Farree in the ribs, and the pain drowned out the pain he felt in his hump.

"There are Thassa here, and it is the cycle of the third ring. No one on Yiktor goes up against them—"

"So we just go?" demanded the other.

"So we go, but not empty-handed. We have this one, and perhaps he is less idiotic than he looks. Gompar knows what questions to ask and how. He'll spill out his insides easily enough."

It would seem that this speaker had command of the force, because they did turn toward the flitter. Farree was picked up and slung aboard, then a tangler was turned on him and before he could hope to move the sticky cords had netted him in.

He had already striven to reach the minds of those who had taken him—and came up against the blankness of shields. Now he was a small ball of misery and fear pushed to the back of the flitter where he lay, his hump rubbing painfully against the wall, as the small craft arose with an upward leap.

None of those aboard paid him any more attention. He made himself push aside panic and take stock of that company. Their former captives sat well to the back, crowded in not too far from him, and the four who had come to their rescue occupied the fore seats.

They were dressed uniformly, in space suits, and had their hair bristle short as did most crewmen. The leader seemed to be the man now at the controls of this small ship. It was never easy to guess ages, but Farree thought that he was younger than Quanhi. He had a seam of scar from one corner of his mouth to his jawline. Otherwise there was nothing about him to suggest that he was any different from any crewman Farree had seen off duty in the Limits.

The man by him was, in spite of his spacer clothing, a different type. Had Farree not seen him here, he would have thought him a wealthy tourist, the kind who sometimes ventured into the Limits for a thrill and then often complained of thievery or ill-usage. He was stout—almost enough so to appear bloated—and his features were of an unusual smallness, squeezed together at the forefront of his head, with a high, bulbous forehead and a neck which in the nape was marked by two rolls of fat. It was on his knees that the box of power rested, now fitted into a case. He kept running his pudgy hand about its surface as if he felt chilled and this kept warmth for him. His lips were pushed out in a petulant pout, and it was plain that he was far from satisfied with their just-past action, yet he made no protest in words.

There was no way that Farree could either see out of the flitter or even mark the time they spent in the air. His bonds allowed him no movement, and he could guess that what lay ahead was nothing to try to anticipate.

They came in at last for a landing, which jarred Farree again against the wall and would have brought a whimper of pain from him had he not once more bitten down upon his lip. To let any of these see that he was frightened would be the last thing he would do. He clung fiercely to that, and for a moment thought of how Lord-One Krip had told him of running in the body of something called a barsk—so fierce an animal that all feared it. What would happen if he could claim now the claws, the strength, the bulk of Bojor?

However, there was no chance of that. He would remain what he had always been: too weak and helpless a creature to stand against anything thrust upon him. Even now, one picked him up and slung him easily to another man waiting at the hatch. And as that one carried him he got his first look at what lay about him.

He was upon an open plain with no sign of the cliff which had broken the other one. Instead a mound arose, plainly not a natural one. On that was a broken, ragged heap of tumbled-down stone walls while a tower in its middle pointed a finger to sunset clouds. As much of a ruin as the place looked, there were dwellers within. He saw movement along the near-broken walls as he was carried up the incline to where the tower stood.

A courtyard with walls and half-destroyed buildings verging on all four sides surrounded the tower, but it was to the latter that he was carried. Then, being carelessly knocked against the wall, he was transported upward to be tossed like a bit of unwanted refuse into a narrow room with a wider arc of wall narrowing to nearly a point where the door now slammed into place, leaving him alone.

A window broke the arc of the far wall, but there was no furnishing here, only the bare stone that already had given him bruises. He had landed on his back and the pain in his hump awoke from an ache to a burning stab, until he managed to roll over on one side, facing that high window where all he could see was a narrow slit of sky.

For the first time since he had been taken, Farree had time to think. It was plain that the Thassa part of Lord-One Krip had managed to keep him from being swallowed up in the same trap. But what could these who held him, Dung from the Limits, hope to learn from him alone? He knew so little: only that some time ago the Lord-One and the Lady

Maelen had helped to break up an operation of the Guild and could still be in danger because the Guild could not allow its might to be flouted easily, or because they had certain knowledge which went beyond that particular action and which might lead to another discovery.

Good enough reason for their capture and the attempts to take over the ship. But Farree had not been with them during that earlier exploit and certainly had no knowledge that could be sifted out for the Guild's profit. Maybe they intended to use him for a bargaining piece . . .

Farree's mouth twisted wryly. What was he to the two of the Thassa that they should risk anything in his behalf? True, they had taken him out of the morass of the Limits. However, they had a feeling for helpless animals as he had learned from their talk. But one did not risk all for an animal and certainly he, Farree, could not rate any higher than that. It would seem that he was now as much on his own as he had always been in the Limits and with far less to help him here.

··●)9(●··

It would seem that none were in a hurry to make what use they could of him, for he continued to lie alone, wrapped by the near-strangling cords of the tangler, in the tower room. Hunger awoke in him and thirst, both of which he had known too many times before to yield to now. He lay and watched the scrap of sky, which was edged by the high window, and he slept for a while or at least had no memory of the passing time. It was dusk beyond the window when the door was at last opened. Quanhi came in to stir him with one boot toe.

The spaceman pointed a laser on lowest beam at one stretch of the tangler cords, and those straightaway began to shrivel up until the ashy remnants fell away and Farree was free of bonds. His whole body ached dully as the boot reached out once more to prod at him.

"On your feet, Dung. You are needed."

His arms and legs were so numb from his bonds that he found it almost more than he could do to get to his feet. But a stubbornness in him would not let him crawl, and he made it, though he wavered toward the wall of the room and had to steady himself there.

"Move—or do you want a touch of this?" The spacer twirled his laser, and Farree lurched forward. Though there was the pain of returning full circulation and the ever-present aching in his hump, he managed to keep his feet and go on.

Though the curve of a stair which hugged the wall, cracked and worn as to steps, nearly defeated him, Farree at last reached the ground level of the tower and was herded on into another section of the ruin. His glimpse of the open before entering the other building gave him a chance only to see that there was indeed a force here—men coming and going, all of them wearing space clothing.

However, the room he was now herded into might have been lifted out of some Lord's holding back on Grant's World. Hangings of a blue-copper cross-spinning covered the ancient walls, and there was actually a matching carpet under his feet. He was brought to a halt before a table of silvery wood. Behind it were two folding chairs of tapestry and precious gonder wood. The table itself had been recently used for what Farree would have thought a feast, but the soiled plates and cups had been pushed to the far end, and now there were several boxes set out before the two men seated there.

One was the overfleshed man from the flitter, and his hands still caressed that box he had brought from the scene of Farree's undoing, stroking it as if he so pleasured a pet animal. His companion at the table was of a different pattern. There was in his look, his every movement, an air of command that led Farree to believe he was fronting the leader of this outlaw company. Though the face before him bore no disfiguring scar nor was he high-nosed in manner like one of the upper city Lords, Farree, after one meeting with those eyes, shivered and longed to draw himself into a ball as Toggor did when threatened.

It was the fat man who spoke first: "This is the one which was drawn . . ."

Had there or had there not been a thread of uneasiness in that? Farree thought he distinguished a suggestion that the fat one was not as pleased with his capture as he might have been.

"And the others?" the leader asked quietly, even mildly, as if he lacked much interest in the proceedings.

For a moment the fat man was silent, and even his pudgy hands ceased their gentling of the box. He pursed his lips as if he searched for a proper word or would get one out of his captive if he dared.

"The others?" the leader repeated in the same quiet tone.

"They withstood . . ." The admission was dragged from his companion, and Farree saw those hands tense on the box.

"Yes. The Thassa . . ." The leader could have been merely beginning an observation, but Farree was aware, by his own feelings of tension and fear, that the fat man changed position a fraction, nearly as if he winced.

"They are reputed to have more than one skill," the leader continued after a pause. "How do you think they have continued to exist for centuries of planet time with the Lords of Yiktor both jealous and afraid?"

"We had none to test," the fat man said with a note of defense in his voice. "Our material—"

"Was such as this?" the leader gestured toward Farree.

"He was with them the whole time." It was Quanhi who volunteered that.

"They gather strange life forms for the showing, do they not? What could they find more strange than this lump of offal? You"—his hard eyes caught Farree's and held them captive—"what were you to these Thassa?"

Farree had to moisten his lips with tongue tip twice before he could find answer. "I helped with the animals, Lord-One," he said in a hoarse whisper.

"Helped with? Or were one? Do you not know by now that these Thassa consider themselves above the rest of us?"

"Commander." Again it was Quanhi who dared to interrupt. "This one helped in taking back the ship—"

The leader gave a single bark of laughter that was more like a burst of oath. "A mighty opponent indeed. I wonder that you acknowledge his part in that."

"Commander." The man refused to be silenced. "He speaks with thoughts like those others."

"Yes, as you have said before several times. Well, Dung, can you read my thoughts now in your twisted head?"

"You are protected, Lord-One," Farree answered with the truth.

"Just so—protected. But so were the two aboard that ship and yet they fell into a Thassa trap. However, as you are not Thassa, we need not take the precaution of silencing you. In fact it is better not. Seek your friends—your masters—whatever those witch people are to you, and beg for their help. I will wager that such a call will bring nothing, but one can always hope, and these Thassa are ridiculously mindful of their own—even their animals. Now"—he leaned a little farther across the table—"let us get to the matter of what Dung knows about his betters. Why did Vorlund and the woman come here?"

"I do not know." Farree barely got the words out of his mouth when a heavy-handed blow from Quanhi sent him forward to come up against the table edge with bruising force.

"Let me fry a finger from him, Commander. Such a reminder—"

The man at the table held up a hand which instantly silenced the other. Farree might not now be able to read minds but he could feel the emotions heating in this room and that from Quanhi was a tinge of fear.

"Dung, do you know what these Thassa do with those they take?" inquired the same low and level voice. "They change people—men—into animals and animals into men. Do you wish to find all that is you behind the hide and fleas of, say, a zirider?"

He spoke of a mound of foul oozelike flesh which fed and crawled and was an abomination in the eyes of all unfortunate enough to meet it. Farree shivered. Not that he believed that he—that anyone—would be so treated by those he had met wearing the name of Thassa, but the picture of the creature in his mind made him ill.

Apparently his shiver informed them that such a fear did lie deep in him. But how wrong they were. To be an animal—a swift, beautiful runner such as Yazz, a mound of strength and courage like Bojor—to him who was Dung—what could be a more welcome change?

"I see you understand me. Did you not know that they would not keep such an abomination as you with them? You would find yourself furred or feathered or caged soon enough. Now, let us ask again: Why did Vorlund and the woman come here? The Thassa have no ships, and that one which brought you is too small to carry many. But only a few recruits and they could cause us a problem—a small problem. Did they ever mention the planet Sehkmet to you, humpback?"

Farree considered quickly. He could well pretend that the fear of the animal transformation governed any answer. And what did he have, in truth, to say? He was not sure why they had come to Yiktor—save that the Lady Maelen was moved by a pressing desire to set down here when the three-ringed moon swung in the sky and that that had something to do with her powers. He was having to think faster than he had ever been pressed to do before, weighing one fact against a supposition and a guess against a fact.

"They said only that there had been a great find there and that they had something to do with it. It was a matter in the past which they spoke little of."

"A matter of the past reaching well into the future—which is now. Yes, something was found on Sehkmet, and they had a hand in it—those two." Though there was no change in the Commander's set expression of half boredom and flagging interest, still there was a note in his voice which suggested that he might not be broadcasting fear now but rather anger.

"You read minds, I am told." He leaned forward a fraction to look down into Farree's face only inches above the top of the table. "Therefore you could know what they did not say as well as what they said. Now what of that?"

The hunchback shook his head. "Lord-One, those can cut off their thought by will even as you are shielded. I could read only what they willed me to—the small things that they thought it needful for me to know."

For a very long moment the other simply observed him. The dark eyes were expressionless and there seemed to be no surface life in them. It was as if the Guild leader could shutter them at will.

"That could almost be the truth, Dung. Only I cannot be sure, can I? We shall do some probing when Isfahan gets here with the reader. There is nothing human which can hide a thought from that. So you will share our hospitality for a time. If you wish to bespeak your friends—"

Farree had already made a decision, the best he could summon in the here and now.

"Lord-One, when that summoned"—he pointed at the box the fat man still so jealously guarded—"did I not come? They did not, but saved themselves by their own ways. Therefore why should I believe that they care now what happens to such as me?"

"The truth again. The Thassa do not fight, nor war even when they are attacked, but always withdraw. They will be in no haste to rescue one who is as you—a misshapen thing out from the slime, which they might have taken merely for an experiment."

Perhaps that was the truth. Now that he was not near the Lady Maelen or the Lord-One Krip, how could he be sure that it was not? He need only look down at what he could see of himself and think a bitter truth or two. On Grant's World he had had some value. What was he here but some refuse swept up during their escape—of less worth than Yazz or Bojor?

"I see that I have given you something to think about. Consider it carefully. Return him into keeping."

Return him to the tower room they did, though they shoved into his hands a roll of nearly stone-hard ration crisp and a canteen of water. He ate slowly, chewing at the hard stuff with caution lest he break a tooth. It would have been easier to put some drug in that scant ration of water than in the roll of hardened nutrient. There could be no sleep gas here, but neither had they re-bound him. It might be well that they thought him so safely caged that they need take no such precautions anymore.

He could not put his back against the wall; his hump was still tender. Now he sat cross-legged in a corner of the room farthest from the door and tried to think.

What he had gained when Lord-One Krip had told him of the past and other hints garnered along the way—even what his present captors had said—all linked together. There had been a find—doubtless a big Forerunner one (such could make the finder wealthy beyond dreams) on a world named Sehkmet. The Guild had been busied with looting it when in some way Krip Vorlund and the Lady Maelen had spoiled their action. Now the Guild (and he did not doubt that the Commander here was truly a Guild Veep of some standing) had a double reason for wanting to lay hands on the two Thassa again: once for retribution and once to learn if there were more such finds to be uncovered.

Nor did he doubt that the Guild controlled that which would win their desires—first from him and then from the Thassa. It was a well-known fact that the Guild was ever on the search for new weapons—or old ones of lost and forgotten races—which could be used with effect. This one which had brought him into their hands was surely such. Yet Lord-One Krip had been able to withstand its demanding call.

Thankfully there was little they could get out of him. He was very glad that he had not been deep in any plans the Thassa might have made. Certainly he could fight and he would, testing his will to the uttermost. But in the end they would wring him dry as one wrings a washing rag. That they could and would use him as trap bait—that he also supposed to be the truth. But he had no idea that any Thassa would venture into the heart of enemy territory to have him out. They had treated him well, near as if he were standing tall and fully human. But . . .

He slowly turned his large head from side to side. Put that shadow of hope out of mind. He had no chance of being plucked out of the hands of the Guild. It was all he could do to fight down the waves of dark fear that rolled over him until he was breathing in small throat-hurting gasps and the sweat rolled down his cheeks like tears.

There was no weapon. He had no Toggor this time to even give him a hazy picture of what lay outside. His hands, thin and long as they were, were only collections of brittle bones that could be easily snapped by a single kick or blow. And they had mentioned laser burns . . .

Farree's head fell forward until it rested on his drawn-up knees. He wound his arms about his legs until he was near a ball of distorted flesh and bone open to any attack which might come. But his mind . . . ? Feeling very open to evil he sent forth a questioning tendril of thought.

Time and time again that came against the blankness which he knew marked a shielded man. There was no chance at all of contacting any of them. Then he found a spark of thought—not coherent but rather all emotion, and that emotion was mainly hunger underlaid with wary fear.

An animal of some sort, perhaps the same type of vermin as might be drawn to an inhabited building in the Limits. It was a very limited mind, but it was not shielded. He saw so little by its aid—only a dark run which he guessed was within the walls. But he rode with it, beginning by very slow sendings to build up the sensation of hunger which should bring the creature he had netted out into the open.

Hunger—the kind of hunger he himself had known only too often in the past. It was easy to think hunger— impress it on the hurrying creature in the wall. There was thin light in the haze of the run; the hunter must be approaching some exit to the outside. Hunger! With the same pressure he had used with Toggor he fed that need—hunger!

The creature was out of the wall into full light. But the picture was so hazy he could not be sure just where it was—within one of the buildings or clear in the open. Hunger—food—feed! He bore down upon that order which the minute brain of the hunter could hold.

There was a sudden leap which caught Farree by surprise. And now—food—he could pick up every nuance of that feeding, the tearing, the gulping—then—

There was a sudden sense of spinning, of falling, and at

the end—Farree withdrew touch in a hurry. That creature he had "ridden" was nearly dead. He filled his lungs deeply, clasped his hands upon his arms with a nail-cutting grip. Almost he had gone into death! He could only believe that the forager had been caught and killed. Yet—insofar as he was successful—there was or had been one mind within these walls which had not been shielded. He had not only found it but made use of it after a fashion. Where there was one there might be more.

Also—and this was something new he had gained—he had not had to focus on a clear mental picture in order to make contact, as he always had or thought he had had to do with Toggor. Now, his eyes closed, his body still in that tense ball, he began another search. From the single window in the wall so far above his head there was framed the sky. What life, other than Guild men in flitters, rode that sky? Awkwardly at first and with little success he thought of sky, and vaguely of a winged creature which rode the winds there. He knew little or nothing of birds. Their like did not abound in the Limits, save a few lice-covered eaters of carrion haunting some of the darker ways.

There was something about the—

A trace of thought! Farree poured all his strength into touching that, wrapping about it, finding its source. This was an air dweller, a flyer—and again it was hunger and the lust for a hunt that moved the unknown. He strove to see, but the difference in their sight organs was too much or—

It was as if someone had pressed a button. He could see: the earth spread below him like a great floor. The buildings on the knoll were a gray-black stain with flickers of light here and there. He could—

"Who?"

The hunger and the desire to hunt had been cut off as sharply as the change in vision had come to him. There was—another!

"Thassa?" He thought that.

"Thassa." There was no mistaking the sharp assent which came to his single-word question. "Who?"

Farree strove to mind picture himself in all his misshapenness. He could not be sure if the other were to follow him as he had followed the trace of the flying thing.

"Here!" That was no bird thought; rather it spoke in his own mind even as he strove to contact it a second time.

"No!" He had respect for the Guild. Mind shielded they might be, but in dealing with the Thassa they might also have alarms that could betray such an entrance as much as if an enemy of his captors rode into the gate.

"Not so." The answer came so firm and loud that Farree uncoiled and looked sharply at the door, almost sure that had been uttered aloud rather than by mind speech. "You are—"

There came no other word for a long breath or two. Then with the same clear sharpness that mind voice said: "We are on a level not well known—not known." There seemed to be almost an aura of surprise in that. "They have their safeguards, but those are for minds such as theirs. They will not know. What has happened?"

"Thassa you are," Farree thought back slowly. There was no mistaking the kinship of this voice to the one which had come to them earlier in the ship. "Why?"

"Why? Because you are open to us and all else is closed save vermin of the walls and that which flies. Who are these and what is their purpose?"

He was sure now that this was one of the four who had stood in judgment over Maelen at the gathering. Perhaps the one who had sealed his ears to that intolerable dirge that the people had sung back in the audience chamber.

Though he would have wished the Lady Maelen that was his own wish—though the Thassa meant hardly more to him than a name, yet what was threatened touched those he knew. He ordered his thoughts quickly and strove to relive in his mind that meeting with the Commander.

"So." The mind voice had but that comment. "And they think to perhaps use you as bait in some trap?"

"Which will not work," he answered quickly. "What am I that any should venture for me here? But they bring other machines—"

"Machines!" The other voice made that sound like an oath. "Already they have profaned the Old Place with their flyers, and now they would seek to use other things. But have hope yourself, little one. I say this and it is never a thing lightly promised, though you do not know us well enough to understand that. The Song has been sung in your hearing. Now you are under the wands of the Singers and what comes to you also touches us. You are not forgotten. Think you on that and be steady as you have been!"

Abruptly, as with the flying thing, the voice was gone, and he had a strange sensation as if in some manner it had drawn that which was the inner part of him a short way after it. But no, that was no escape. He was still crouched here—Dung of the Limits. He could not see that there was any hope of escape. Were he on his home world, a number of things would come to mind; here was nothing.

He wondered over that promise, if promise it had been. From Maelen, he might have believed in it and taken heart again. But from one he did not know—the many sorrows of the past made him doubt. They might wish to help him, he allowed that. But that they could do anything he did not believe.

Thus it was his own fight. He thought of that creature that had run in the walls—if there were many of them and if they could all be aroused to attack some food supply. What might he gain from such a skirmish? He had no idea but he filed that possibility away. There was at least one flying thing he had touched—though it might be wholly under the control of the Thassa and might not be within reach again. If only he had Bojor!

Though even if he could summon that giant to him he doubted that he would. A laser would bring the bartle quick and painful death and avail him nothing. Once more he rolled himself into a ball and tried to shut out the thoughts from his mind to sleep.

At first he thought that sleep was impossible. His mind kept repeating that interview with the Commander and his helplessness as a prisoner. But many times before he had carried fears and torments into sleep, and this time it was also so.

However, he dreamed—not one of those broken and distorted series of pictures that had been his uneasy nightmares in the past. This was as clear as a mind picture and very vivid, so that he saw it all sharply and knew also that this was no dream but a fragment of sleep-unlocked memory of a time which seemed to him utterly far in the past.

He was crouched upon a bundle of dirty carpets watching two men. One of them, wearing a crumpled and much stained spacer's coverall, was—

"Lanti." The other man spoke the name even as it had come to the dreaming Farree's mind and reached across the stained table to catch a fistful of Lanti's shirt at the neck to jerk up the head which rolled loosely on the man's shoulders.

Lanti's mouth was slack with a drool of spittle from one corner, and his eyes turned up in his head. He breathed noisily. The one who held him struck a sharp slap on each side of the face.

"You blasted fool—answer me! Where did you planet then?"

But the man who was Lanti only puffed his lips and then snored. With a grunt of obscenities, the other let go of him and allowed Lanti's head to fall forward onto the table. He pounded a fist on that dirty board before him and then reached within his own jerkin and pulled out a piece of cloth. From its wrapping he shook out a scrap of something which glittered and welcomed the light in the place.

Seeing that, the dream Farree made a small movement forward and the man was instantly alert, turning to look at him. Such was the expression of demand upon his hairy face that the very small Farree gave a tiny whimpering cry and waited helplessly for a blow to follow.

••●) 10 (●••

The man in one lumbering movement came to stand over him, scowling down at the small figure. He still held that glittering scrap between two fingers but Farree did not look at it.

"Dung." The big man slapped his face, even as he had done to Lanti, rocking him over so he lay nearly facedown on the filthy carpets. "What do you know about this? He has dragged you about with him so you must have some value. Is it that you know?"

He could sense the cruelty rising in the other. In one of those huge hands his brittle bones would snap easily; he could be turned into dead rubbish to be flung into the street.

"Far—" Almost he said the name which he must not. Lanti would beat him again if he did. If this bravo did not slay him first. "I—I know nothing, Lord-One." His voice was a harsh croak hardly above a whisper.

The second blow fell, only this bully mistook his strength and sent Farree speedily into unconsciousness. When he awoke once more he was sore, so stiff and sore that the slightest movement was a torment. There was the gray light of morning around, but Lanti still sprawled across the table, his face turned away. Of the other man there was no sign. For several long moments, while feeling came back to his legs and arms, Farree waited.

Outside this hut he could hear the normal sounds of morning: the groans and oaths of men on their way back to ships, and the rattle of pots and pans in those eating places which sold first meals. But the hut inside was utterly silent. At last Farree moved, humping himself off the carpets, daring to approach the table. That his first known enemy was unaware was a gift of fortune he would not throw away. He stood as tall as he might to survey Lanti. The bloated face was a grayish color, the pouting lips blue. Greatly daring, ready to dodge if the man awoke, Farree put forth one hand to touch the other's dangling hand.

Slept? His flesh was cold. With even greater daring Farree tried to sense the other. There was nothing there—none of the faint traces of identity which one carried even into the deepest of sleeps. Lanti was—dead!

If he were now found here! Farree scuttled to his noisome carpet nest and brought out a square of cloth he had earlier garnered. He moved around the table, his small hunched form not unlike that of one of the sus-spiders, gathering up a half-gnawed slab of bread, the tail end of a flat eel, not pausing to eat, though his empty stomach yearned to be filled, but ready to take the food with him. A weapon? No—the two sheaths at Lanti's belt were empty. He had already been plundered of both his force knife and his stunner. Farree's only chance would lie in flight and hiding. He did not know why the other man had abandoned him—but perhaps he had discovered Lanti's death and had prudently put a distance between them. All this end of the Limits knew that Farree was Lanti's captive and the hunt might be up for him now.

Clutching to him with one hand the bundle he had made of the food, he slipped in the dawn light out of the hut and sought the shadows, speeding at his best hobbling pace away from the only place he had known on this world.

Before this world, before Lanti, what had there been? He turned to that over and over again. Always to meet with dark as if a part of his mind slept endlessly—or was reft from him by some form of small death. Almost, once, he had remembered—when he had seen that scrap of glittering stuff in the bully's hand. But even then there had been a barrier.

He had always guessed that he must have come from off-world, and he could not understand why Lanti had thought to bring such a miserable creature with him. Farree must have had some value beyond his own misshapen body. Some value beyond—

Farree awoke. For a moment or two he was disoriented. These chill stone walls about him—they were not of the Limits—then, even as he blinked his eyes, all which had happened came flooding back. The promise which had been made that the Thassa would help. How much dared he count on that?

He tried to school himself to forget it. Those to whom he was now captive could bring to their aid things he was sure the Thassa, with all their might of minds, had never thought of. No, he dared not depend on promises.

By the window so far above him, he thought the sky

was that of morning. And he was very hungry and athirst. To ask—to beat on that door hoping someone would hear him—No, better to go without than perhaps make them remember that they had him to hand.

He had just made this woeful decision when the door did open and a man in a spacer's clothing, but one he had not seen before, came in. In his left hand he carried one of those cans of rations made for emergencies and in his right was a stunner. He said nothing but gestured with the weapon. Farree withdrew to the far wall and watched the other set down his burden and go out again. There was an audible thud which he believed signaled a bar on the other side of the door.

The ration was meant to be both food and drink. It was a tasteless semiliquid, but he knew that it would strengthen and revive him, and he devoured it to the last drop. That done, he turned the container over and over in his hands. Now, were this only some wild tale such as men told in their cups he could put the can to good use as a weapon of sorts and break out of his prison. Only this was no tale, it was the truth, and he thought the only time he would see beyond that door was when the Commander had some use for him. At least they intended to keep him alive; the food proved that.

Bait for a trap?

Slowly, as carefully as if life itself depended upon it (which might indeed be so), Farree sent out a mind touch, not aiming it at anything human but keeping to the lowest level he could reach. Within moments he found another of the wall-living vermin. The creature was sleeping, and it was easy enough to take over.

He slipped in and the thing awoke, felt the hunger

Farree carefully suggested, and whipped into one of the runs in the thick wall. What he received was hazy, very limited impressions of, first, those tunnels familiar to his guide, and then a sudden open space in which he could distinguish little, just enough for him to identify furniture, some part of a room.

The craving for food was tempered by the animal's native caution. As it made short rushes from one cover to the next, Farree fought the other's alien field of vision for something he could identify. There came a sensation of heat and he believed that his scout was close to a fire, undoubtedly one intended for cooking. Then the hazy glimpses which he could not identify fully steadied and remained the same and he believed that the creature crouched in some sheltered hiding place.

Fear—a vigorous stab of it, filling all that small alien mind—a smaller mind than Toggor's and of a different pattern. Toggor! If he had only been able to bring the smux with him into this captivity! All the mind touch which they had used in the past would have given him a better chance to work with this other-world creature whose very form was unknown to him so that he could not build up a mind picture that might clarify his probing. He wondered where the smux was now. And somehow that loosed his hold on the vermin from the walls and before he knew it he had sent out a thought tendril which he knew would not be taken. Only—it was!

Farree was not able to smother the sudden ejaculation of astonishment as the familiar pattern of the smux was there. It was very tenuous, to be sure, yet once touched it could not be mistaken.

The Thassa—or the Lady Maelen or the Lord-One Krip—must be very close for him to have picked up Toggor's send, closer than was safe. As he had done with the bird, he reached forth and strove to use Toggor for a connecting link.

If the Thassa or his late companions were there he could not make the connection—there was only the smux. Still, Toggor was growing clearer all the time as if he were approaching the ruins where the enemy had set up headquarters.

That the smux had made such a journey on his own Farree could not believe. However long that trip in the flitter had been, surely the Thassa had no comparable form of transportation which would bring Toggor. Still, there was no mistaking the smux's mind and—

It was backed—strengthened—carried—not by any one mental thrust but by a uniting. Farree had not the training nor perhaps even the gift to sort out the will and the power that projected the smux's own small range of thought. Nor could he reach behind Toggor as he had with the skydweller. Yet there was a new warmth rising in him. It was plain that Toggor was approaching, and that he would have a better ally here than the native things which he could not picture and so could not actually possess.

Farree closed down his mental link. He could not help but believe it might just be possible that those who held him could somehow sense such communication. Let Toggor get within the right distance, and he could trace Farree by his own gift without revealing his presence to those who held this ruin as their own.

Now it was a matter of waiting. Farree found that impatience was a hard goad to elude. He wanted so much to use Toggor for eyes, to see what the smux would see, to feel—

He sat as upright as he could, his back awakening into the same ache as had kept him company for the past few days, as he strove to get to his feet under that window which was too high for him to see from. Toggor—Toggor was suddenly afraid.

He was—he was above ground, with no strong hold on anything—being whirled through the air in a manner over which he had no control—and he was crying out to Farree for help and comfort—to be released.

Had he been picked up by someone of the Guild guard? No, this severe fear came not from being handled but rather from being not handled, swung along in an open space where there were no good clawholds for safety's sake.

In the air? Had he been tossed? No, Farree could not feel that he was so helpless as he would have been had he been flung, say, over one of the ruinous walls. In the air, yet not thrown.

There was a whirling of hazy sight and then—Above in that single window there was a shadowing. A bird—or at least a flying thing with feathers—had lighted on the stone sill. It carried a squirming object fastened to a cord about its neck and now it dipped its head and that cord slipped off. Farree was beneath the window, his hands upraised, and with a desperate snatch he caught the smux as it fell toward him.

There was a net about Toggor which Farree swiftly

peeled away. Once free, the smux caught his shirt front and swiftly made his way to his favorite perch, inside the collar, his stalk eyes extended to their farthest level for sight.

Farree tried to reach the smux with thought send but all he received was a breathless, sickening sensation of being swung through the air. Toggor had not yet recovered from his journey. But there must have been some overwhelming reason for the smux to have been sent to this prison, and Farree knew that it might hinge upon a space of time, something to be done as soon as possible.

There was no way out of here except the window, and the flying creature, having delivered its burden, was gone.

The hunchback squatted down again in the corner of the room from which he had best seen the door, and carefully detached Toggor's hold, lifting the smux on his two palms so that the eyes swung and arose on level with his own. Once more he attempted to establish mind contact.

And this time he achieved a hazy impression of the Lady Maelen. Also something else—that Toggor was rebelling against some task which had been laid upon him. Exploration of this place? Perhaps the rough stone outside the window would provide clawholds either up or down. Farree thought carefully and then pictured the vermin of the walls which he had contacted earlier.

Immediately Toggor's attention was caught and riveted upon that suggestion. As he had routed out his prey back at the inn in the Limits, so was he ready to try the same here. But Farree was loath to let the smux go. Though he had touched minds—or rather scratched minds—with that runner in the wall ways, he had no idea of its size or natural armament. It might prove too much for the smux. It was plain at once that the smux did not agree with him. A hunter's lust for the game welled up to possess most of Toggor's mind.

Once more Farree crawled over to stand beneath the window, but the smux did not loose his hold on the shirt. It was plain that he had no thought of taking that way again. Then how? There were no cracks in the walls of this tower wide enough to take the smux, and the door fitted tightly to the floor so that every time it was opened it rasped harshly in protest.

Just as Farree thought of that, the portal to his cell did open and once more the guard appeared, but did not venture any farther than the threshold. Toggor moved with the flashing speed he could show upon occasion and was into the shirt, well hidden, before the door was wide open.

Though the man held a stunner he had brought no food, only beckoned to Farree to come to him, and the hunchback obeyed. He foresaw another interview with the Commander and perhaps worse to come. Somewhere along their path to that questioning he must loose the smux. Thus he shambled slowly, his head bent forward as one who had been broken in spirit and planned nothing.

The guard waved him on to descend the crumbling stair, and down this he went. He was only too aware of the scrambling Toggor was doing in the shirt and hoped with all his might that his guard would not see the movement.

Luckily the inside of this place was dusky enough to be full of shadows, which just now were comforting and promising. He felt the smux thrusting its way into his sleeve and allowed his arm to dangle, refusing to wince as the clawed feet dug into his flesh for the other's descent.

They had reached the ground floor, and the guard said in trader tongue, "Wait, you!"

As if he were weak and tired, Farree leaned back against the wall, holding the smux-supporting arm straight down. The claws moved from one hold to another. Farree could only hope that there was no trace of venom leakage from any of those sharp tips. Then he felt Toggor loose all contact and felt a soft plop against his leg in the shadows— the smux was on the move.

Farree dare not watch that quick scuttle into the greater dark. His guard was raising his free wrist to his lips and reporting in code into a disc banded there. A moment later he waved the hunchback on again and Farree had to go, leaving Toggor to follow his own desires, not even having any chance to impress on the smux what was necessary. But perhaps those who had sent him had already done that.

Out of the door they went. The sunlight was so great a burst of glare in this parched land that Farree had to shade his eyes after the murk of the tower room.

"On with you, Dung." The barrel of the stunner struck the hump hard and Farree had to bite his lips to keep from screaming. The tenderness of the lump which burdened him had been growing more with each day. He wondered if that meant some ill he did not understand. Now he staggered a step or two before he could control the wave of pain and walk as best he might in the direction the guard pointed him.

The tower stood alone, not connected with the other

ruins about it. Most of the buildings were roofless, had even lost half a story to time and wind and storm. Only the one he had visited before was intact. There were some men lounging by its door. Five he counted. But there was no way for him to assess the full number of the enemy sheltering here.

"Here comes the luck piece, Jat!" Two of the lounging men were playing pitch and toss with black and white counters. He who spoke leaned forward as Farree approached, holding out a stiff finger.

The hunchback longed to dodge that touch now but knew deep within him that it would be best to keep hidden the fact that his back burden was so tender. They might well make a torturous use of such knowledge. So he suffered the slap of those fingers stoically and tried not to show any pain.

"Luck for all of us if we need it," one of the onlookers commented. "And need it we might."

"Your lips are too loose, Deit," commented Farree's guard. "Better not let the Veep hear you."

"I signed on for service, not sitting around in rock piles—we all did."

"We all did," agreed the guard, "and you don't go back on a sign-up. Not with him in there—" He gestured with an outstretched thumb at the door just behind him.

"Get on with you!" Once more that punishing jab, but this time high on his arm, and that was as nothing. Farree went inside the building. Again he was surprised at the carpeting, the hangings on the wall, the various bits of a less austere life which the Veep of this company had carried for his own comfort.

For the second time there were the two at the table: the man in uniform and he who was so fat he bulged in sections out of his chair. He was intent upon a small picture com; the Commander was more at ease, smoking a spice stick, the scented air of which fought with the mustiness of the ancient room.

Neither of the men paid any attention to the entrance of Farree. He and his guard stood together back by the wall until the fat man gave an impatient push to the viewer before him.

"There is no silencer according to the reading, but this will not reach into that valley."

"Nor will it ever," commented his companion. "These Thassa have their own protections—"

The fat man pouted petulantly. "What kind of learning can defeat a far viewer?" He put thumb and forefinger together and clicked them against the silent screen.

"An efficient one it would seem." The Commander drew deeply on the spice stick and then expelled a puff of bluish smoke. "Is that not so, DUNG!" His voice lost all its calm laziness and snapped as a leader might snap an order and expect to be instantly obeyed.

Farree fought to remain steady. He had feared and hated Russtif but that was nothing to the emotion this man raised in him. He could feel the threat behind those words as if a whip had been snapped in his direction and flaked a scrap of skin from his cheek.

"I do not know what the Thassa can do." He offered the truth but was afraid that it would not be accepted.

"Yet you have traveled with them, you have gone into their forbidden valley. And they do not allow that to any they do not believe is one with them. Or are you so weak and poor a specimen of living thing that they treat you as they would one of their 'little ones'—those beasts they gather about them, changing places with them? Which are you, Dung, man or beast? Perhaps they have already worked their will upon you and in truth you might have claws and fangs. Yet I do not believe that—not yet."

The fat man pushed aside the viewer with one hand and looked also at Farree.

"Get to the truth," he said sulkily. "Verify him!"

Farree knew what he meant, and he had the greatest need of holding on to himself, not to shiver and cry out. They meant to use upon him one of the enforcing machines which spacers told so many tales about. Within the influence of that he could hold back nothing that these two wanted. They need only ask their questions, and the machine would at once betray and subvert any desire of his to keep information hidden.

"Very well. It will be illuminating at least. Why do the Thassa want you, Dung? You are a sorry specimen. But perhaps for those who deal intimately with animals your ugliness does not matter. We shall see."

The Veep made a gesture with one hand, and before Farree could move the guard beside him grabbed a hand-hold on his shirt where it hunched across his tender hump, bringing, in spite of all effort, a murmur at the pain. He was so swung to the right and pushed down on the seat of a chair which another of the spacer guards had jerked forward.

One of them held his head cruelly at a backward angle while another one forced a silvery band well down on his forehead and into his tangle of black hair. Wires ran from this up into the space overhead. He could not tilt his head far enough back to see where they ended. But now he was a prisoner to a power he feared more and more as his helplessness became so clear.

"What is your name?" The fat man was the questioner.

"Farree."

"Farree?" There was a slight frown on the Commander's face as if he were trying to capture a small thread of memory. "What are you?"

"A hunchback." He made a true answer, trying to see if he could so limit their knowledge gained from him.

"And what else?" The Commander leaned a little forward on the table. He pointed his smoke stick straight at Farree as if he could use it at his wish as a laser to send the other into smoking refuse.

"Farree." That was also true. He held to the thought that if he limited any answer to the exact question he might not be so great a traitor after all.

"You were born in the Limits?"

"I do not know." Again the truth, and they could not reach behind that for something he did not know himself.

"A man knows where he is born, unless he is an idiot," puffed the fat man. "We do not believe you are an idiot."

"Why do you say you do not know?" The Commander showed none of the irritation of the other, but he was the more dangerous of the two and Farree had known that from the beginning.

"I cannot remember."

"You were wiped?" The Commander no longer stared

at him so intently, but was looking over his head at whatever there betrayed his speech as true or false.

Wiped—a memory erased for some reason. Was that the truth which he had not faced during all the seasons in the Limits?

"I do not know."

"What do you first remember?" The Commander had back his gentle, ruthless voice.

Because he dared not try any tricks with the truth this time, Farree spoke of that which had been in his dream— the death of Land and his own escape into the jungle of the Limits.

••●)11(●••

"Lanti." Again the questioner repeated the name. He looked to the fat man who was still running his fingers around the edge of the visa-screen. That other shrugged.

"Who knows of the actions of one man among millions?"

"He had a purpose—"

"Do not we all unless we are being wiped into nothings? A kidnapping?"

"How could this"—the Commander indicated Farree—"be supposed to be anything worth the worry or a copper nick in any market, Sulve? Unless he knows something. This bit of something which was taken from Lanti—or which at least he knew about—what was it?"

"I do not know."

"You do not know!" parroted Sulve in his high voice. "There seems to be very little that you *do* know, doesn't there? Why did Vorlund and the woman take you with them?"

Why had they? Because he had touched minds with

the smux? But he must keep Toggor out of this if it were possible.

"Russtif dealt in wild creatures, they were hunting such, and they discovered I could mind touch with some of them."

"Thassa reason right enough—perhaps." The Commander scratched a thumbnail across his chin. "It is known that the woman once showed trained beasts—and doubtless changed bodies with them from time to time as she did on Sehkmet."

Sulve's fat hands were suddenly still. "This one?" he jerked his fat-rolled chin toward Farree.

"No, the inquirer would have recorded that. Did they promise you a new body, a furred one, Dung?"

"No."

"But you dealt with the animals, that is so? And still you are human to the eighth—" The Commander's eyes had traveled from Farree's face to a point hanging above him—perhaps the indicator of this truth machine.

Human to the eighth point, Farree heard that clearly enough. Not human to the tenth and full! He looked down at his claw-thin hands and the greenish skin which covered them. Was he then no freak of human kind, but something else—something which was perhaps to all of these as Yazz and Toggor were to him? He considered that and shivered. Perhaps he was not so different from Yazz and Bojor as far as the Thassa were concerned after all.

He tried to straighten a little and the burden on his shoulders flashed a thrill of pain through him. Now the very question they had asked him became all important: Who *WAS* he?

"Why did they return to Yiktor? Was not the woman in exile?" Sulve took up the questioning.

"I do not know." The truth, always the truth. The Lord-One Krip had told him, but he had not yet heard it from the Lady herself.

Both of the men were staring at the point above his head now and a slight frown had returned to the Commander's face.

"What said they of Sehkmet then?" he asked abruptly.

"That they had helped to find a place of the Forerunners—a great treasure—and there were Guild men there who were defeated."

"Nothing more?"

"Nothing." Farree made quick reply.

"Ah." The Commander picked up a tube lying on the table before him, setting aside the smoke stick. He pointed it at Farree and the hunchback gave a cry he could not smother as a pain like a flow of skin-burning acid struck him full on.

"What said they of Sehkmet and this time the truth—"

"Only that the Lady Maelen is now wearing a body found there—that she defeated something strange and not of flesh and blood to claim it." Farree could not see that that was of any importance, but it was the rest of the truth about the past—something which these two might well know and so be able to check his word.

"You see, you can remember when you are prodded," the Commander commented. "Play no more games with me. Did this Maelen and Vorlund return here to gather a force to search elsewhere, hoping or knowing that such luck would continue?"

"I do not know. There were three rings and power—"

"We all know of the blathering about the three rings, Dung. And the Thassa have their own power. But this Maelen possesses something else, does she not?"

He was turning that rod of torment around in his fingers, playing with it as he divided his glances between Farree and what was overhead.

"I do not know." Farree tried to brace himself for another blast of that body-shaking pain. The frown was plainer on the Commander's face.

"What you know, it seems, is very little if at all what is needed. Let us take up the matter of Lanti."

For a moment it looked as if Sulve was going to protest, but if he was not in accord with his partner he did not voice any objection.

"Who was Lanti?"

Once more Farree told the story of his first memory— of the spacer who had died over a spilled drink and given him freedom of a sort.

The Commander stubbed out his smoke stick. "In other words, Dung, you know little or nothing which is of service to us. Why should we keep you alive?"

Farree made no attempt to answer that. He had in him still that core of belief which had not let him whine in the Limits and which, even in spite of the pain, kept him from crying out here. Human to the eight point only was he? Then he would prove that his stock, whatever it might be, had some rags of courage.

Sulve tapped those rolls of fat which were his fingers on the edge of the viewer. "He is not worth two copper units—not even one of inguaw wood."

"Perhaps not in himself. But as bait—yes, as bait. They have been sending over those flying eyes of theirs. There may be some merit in keeping him a while longer."

He clicked his fingers, and the same guard who had forced the head circlet on Farree came to yank it off, his hair pulled painfully in the process.

"The tower again," the Commander ordered. "And the viewer for you, Sulve. If they come ahunting this misshapen blotch, we can at least know it once when they are beyond that impenetrable wall of theirs. They will not remain there forever."

"Time—" began the fat man.

"Time governs itself. We cannot thrust it forward nor draw it back. They depend upon the third ring of that moon of theirs. It may be only superstition, but I am inclined to believe that it is more than that as far as the Thassa are concerned. Remember, they were an old stock before the first lordling arose here to take land for himself."

"Worn out—"

"No!" The Commander shook his head firmly. "Do not make the mistake of the untraveled, Sulve; you should know better. Because a people does not huddle in cities, is not tempted by trade goods, it need not be primitive. I have heard much of the Thassa—and I do not believe that they are in decline, but rather have passed into a new way of life by their own virile choice."

A hard grip on Farree's arm dragged him near off his feet so he had to scurry to keep up as he was led from the room and across the broken pavement in the courtyard. They had learned nothing from him about the Thassa, and what good his memory of Lanti might serve he did not know. He dared not try a cast for Toggor—Sulve might be able to pick that up. Farree had heard many tales of the superior equipment the Guild was supposed to use. And what good would the smux do free in this place when the hunchback could not communicate with him?

He was soon back in that room at the top of the tower, flung into a corner and the door slammed against him, trying still to keep his mind clear of any thought of Toggor. That the small creature could unbar the door was impossible and there was no willing bartle to be summoned this time.

Once more he hunkered down, his arms around his knees, and allowed himself to think—not of the Thassa or the Lord-One Krip or the Lady Maelen—but rather of his vivid dream the night before and of Lanti and of who or what he himself might be.

Points on the human-man-alien scale had been decided long ago. There were creatures near the alien end of that scale who possessed attributes that even a higher "man" could not understand. Thus—

Eight points—and what did those points consist of? Somewhat for his body form: he had two legs, two arms, a head, and a humanoid body. He could be a crippled "man" as well as an alien. His skin was greenish in tint, but that was nothing, for the Thassa were white of skin and hair, and these two who had just questioned him were space-browned and had dark hair. He had seen "men" with two pairs of arms, with the scaled skin of the Zacanthans and their lizardlike neck frills, with the soft fur pelts of the Salarki and their feline features. All came and went through space and no one remarked at their differences.

But in all his seasons in the Limits he had never seen one so bowed of body as himself. Why had Lanti had him? He was sure he had come from off-world with that one and that he had had some importance in Lanti's plans before the spacer became so soaked in var juice that his mind was not far from a mush. Therefore, if Farree had had importance once—

And he had revealed that to the Guild!

Farree sat up, murmured at the pain of his back. But that was not harsh enough to drive out of him the thought that he had indeed revealed much to his interrogators. Not perhaps the information which they had sought, but concerning himself. The Guild was noted for the thoroughness of any hunt which might claim a profit. What had Lanti stumbled on which had produced that incandescent rag of stuff which his questioner had also shown to Farree?

That a report of all he had said would be referenced to the Veep in charge of this sector he was sure. Then maybe they would come for him again. They might have a way of breaking a mind seal—though that could also mean his death. What had he done, save make the truth perhaps more dangerous than he imagined?

Never had he felt, even in the worst times in the Limits, so helpless. Then he had had some chance at mobility, been able to run, to hide. Now he was trapped, and even though Toggor had come to him through the aid of the Thassa, that meant little or nothing. Dared he try to touch minds now with the smux, or did the Commander and Sulve have a blanket over this place which would pick up any telepathic activity? Since they were all shielded against that themselves, it would seem that they were prepared to face such.

They could be reading him now as one would read some message in a viewer, using a machine which he himself could not detect. If so, they would expect—what?

Thassa first surely. Since they had reft him away from those mind controllers, they would believe that he would try to reach his late companions for aid. So—not Toggor! Rather the Thassa in particular—build up a series of thoughts about some imaginary feat being planned by *those* under their three-ringed moon!

He had never tried such a thing before—that of false thinking, of imagining that which was not so in such a way that it could be taken for the truth. If it were possible about the Thassa, why, so it could be with Lanti.

First, the Thassa. Yes. Some order to his thinking. Slowly and tentatively he began to build up a mind picture of Lady Maelen—of her commanding a body of beasts—and into that he pushed all he knew of beasts, not only of Bojor who had served them so well on board the ship but also others—some such as he had seen in Russtif's cages and some which were entirely imaginary but as monstrous as he could make them. He thought of the Lady taking council with both Thassa and the beasts.

So—Maelen was taking council with her furred and feathered—and scaled—troops. They would come with the night—surely with the night. He had been squatting with eyes closed and putting all his effort into that mental picture of what he was supposed to expect. But a sound cut through his absorption, and he looked up to see a waving claw reach within the window above and hook onto the inner stone.

Fiercely he strove to keep all thought of Toggor away—of the Toggor that was—but suppose that Toggor was twenty, a hundred times his present size; such with huge envisioned claws would make an opponent worth reckoning with. Thus Toggor might be used to menace this whole Guild operation—as long as the subterfuge remained unbroken.

Now he opened his mind to Toggor and the usual hazy in-and-out messages passed between them. The smux had explored the lower reaches of the tower as well as what lay above: a flat roof surrounded by a parapet, which had seemed gigantic to Toggor but which Farree thought might be perhaps only as high as a man's waist. If he had some way of reaching the window, of climbing aloft, he might find himself a hiding place which would defeat them all—if he could sink his thoughts into nothingness. But there was the distance between him and that window. Could he only defeat that, he was certain he could squeeze his body, in spite of the hump, though.

Thinking carefully of a smux as large as Bojor on the march to rescue him, Farree arose to run his thin fingers across the surface of the wall. There were no holds between the old stones. In this part of the ruins there was nothing that he might climb to raise him to that door on the outer world.

He flexed his hands vainly and stared upward, defeated. The door, barred and probably guarded, was the only way out of here. He wheeled to face that and projected a picture of the giant smux without, ready to break him free even as the bartle had dealt with such a problem on the ship.

Toggor leaped from the wall to Farree's shoulder, bringing an answering pain from his tender hump. The eyestalks of the smux were all extended and he was staring at the door as if expecting something from that direction.

There was! Farree heard the grate of the bar being drawn. Then he moved. Gathering Toggor in both hands, he tossed the smux through the air, and he landed, even as Farree had planned, on the niched stone which formed the top of the door opening.

The smux reversed himself quickly and hung by two claws at the very edge of that shallow shelf, eyestalks retracted, ready to drop. Farree hunkered down again like one without hope, but he twisted his head around so he could see the smux in action. There was already a greenish bead forming on the foremost claw; the venom was coming.

A man slammed into the room, weapon in hand, and swung that toward Farree just as Toggor loosed his hold on the stone above and leaped for the back of the guard. There was a flash of claws at the man's throat, almost too fast for Farree to catch.

With a sharp cry only half uttered, the man staggered, dropped his stunner to reach for his neck with both hands as he wove back and forth on his feet, his face a grimace of pain and fear. It was Farree's turn to jump, and he caught up the stunner as the guard staggered on past, to bring up against the far wall and fall to his knees, his hand still clutching at the back of his neck. Toggor was already off that struggling body. Farree swung the stunner around and pressed the button. The writhing man straightened with another muffled cry and lay still, while Farree stumbled out of the door, the smux clinging to him, and slammed that shut, thick and heavy though it was.

He thrust the stunner through his belt and reached down for the bar which was almost too much for him to manage. However, at this time he could have accomplished miracles he was sure, as he thrust it home in the slots awaiting it. Now—

He crouched at the head of the stair looking down. Without knowing how many Guild men were here and where they were stationed, to descend that stair, even armed, was more than he dare try. Down? If there only was a way up!

A dim picture cut into his mind: a section of vaguely outlined wall and on it—

Farree swung around. The smux had left him, was at the foot of that stretch of wall, reaching with its claws for something. Spikes—there were spikes in the wall itself. Not stairs but surely a way to mount the wall. As shadowed as that was Farree thought he could sight the outline of an opening, closed by a trapdoor, perhaps, but if barred it could only be from this side.

The smux was already halfway up the wall, swinging from one clawhold to the next. Farree set about following. He tested each of the rust-covered holds before he put his weight upon it, and, though the rust flaked off on his hands, there was enough solid metal within to support his weight.

Then he was clinging with one hand and both feet as he set his palm against the closed trapdoor in a push. The old wood resisted. Farree, gritting his teeth, tried a second time and felt a fraction of give. That was enough to encourage him. Now he held on with his hands, arching his body so that it pressed against the door. His hump was instantly aflame with pain, but he refused to slack his attack, and at last the barrier lifted enough for him to get one arm and shoulder through the slit. It took but a moment or two then for him to crawl forward and lie in the open air, the smux pulling gently at the long locks of his hair and uttering cheeping noises. His back was bound by a band of agony so that he had to use every fraction of determination to move again and allow the door to fall into place behind him. The top of the tower was covered by a mass of brush and dried grass, and he saw huge bird droppings. It was a nest which might have been well used for more than one season. There were bones too, cracked and splintered, some quite large, which made him wonder about the size of the nest builders if they used such animals as their prey.

A skull rolled under his hand as he got unsteadily to his feet and hoisted himself a little against the parapet to peer down at the main body of the ruins. Below the outer wall were two flitters, doubtless the air transport for those in residence here. He saw two men making their way toward the still-roofed building where he had been taken for interviews. But, for the rest, there was nothing to show that the ruins were at all occupied.

It was a dull day with no direct sunlight, yet he could sight a shadow to the east which suggested that there lay the hills and cliffs the Thassa claimed as their ancient territory. Dry clumps of grass, with here and there a wind-twisted bush, were gray instead of green, and there were a number of outcrops of rock, some large and standing as if to suggest the ruin he was in had had much older neighbors of which only a few wind-chiseled remnants remained.

Temporarily he was safe, but lacking food and water he could not remain where he was indefinitely. Nor could he expect any help—in spite of all his brave imagining of an hour earlier. Toggor scuttled back and forth through the noisome remains of the big nest, the long-dead fronds and branches cracking under his weight, small as that was. Farree caught a flash among the fronds which gleamed even under the dead gray of the sky and pulled out a knife with a stone-set hilt. His find was still in a scabbard— rusted there, perhaps, through long exposure to the weather. He worked at it determinedly until he could draw it, and to his great surprise found the blade dull but still only speckled here and there by corrosion.

This lucky find sent him kicking aside the rest of the mess and searching through what had sunk to the bottom of the nest. There were more bones: three skulls which suggested they had once served animals perhaps the size of Yazz. But there were other things, too: a time-tattered strip of skin on which were set medallions centered with blacked metal and dust-layered stones—perhaps once a belt. There was a goblet of tarnished metal which he thought might be silver. A part of a sword, only the hilt intact, the blade a lace of erosion. He had heard of birds who sought bright things and laid them in their nests, and this seemed to be such a hoard. Among the objects also was a box wedged shut past his opening until he hammered at it with the sword hilt and pried with the point of the knife.

It came open at last, but what Farree found himself looking at was a heaping of thick black powder. If that was the remains of some treasure he could give no name to what it had once been, and threw the box aside in disgust. Some of the powder curled up in a puff to sprinkle over the matted stuff of the nest which he had clawed away in his hunt.

There was an odd scent in the air, and then a tendril of smoke arose from one of the besprinkled branches. A touch of flame followed. Farree jumped back, realizing that the fire would include all of the nest stuff unless he moved quickly. He pushed the branches away as fast as he could from the door which led downwards, knowing that if the worst followed he could retreat. Probably right into the hands of his captors, since surely this mounting fire on the roof of the tower would be sighted by someone!

The stuff was tinder dry and crackled from branch to branch with the running of flame. Where the powder had fallen from the box there were larger bursts of glare—not red or yellow, but violently green—and from this thick coils of greenish smoke began to arise.

Farree squatted by the trapdoor. If he could stand the reflected heat from the burning nest he would be safer there than down in the tower itself. He had pulled aside a number of dried bones while rooting in the mass and these he piled now beside him, breaking them into brittle slivers and short, pointed pieces. If he did not have to withdraw he had ammunition of sorts to pin the hands of those reaching for him, just as he had still the stunner he had taken from the guard.

Thinking of that brief encounter he summoned Toggor to him and induced the smux to run envenomed claws along the points of his longer weapons, poisoning them as an added weapon against any storming his place of refuge.

The heat of the fire was hard to face. Toggor crawled within the breast of Farree's shirt and clung as if this youth's body, hunched together as it now was, plus the distance of the fire, would keep him from the shriveling scorch of the flames.

That green smoke still shot skyward, though a breeze at a higher level caught it and fashioned it into what looked like a giant finger pointing toward the distant cliff land. If the Thassa did have any sentries or scouts, they must be wondering at what activity now topped the ruins.

There was shouting from below. Farree fingered the stunner and pulled closer to hand his collection of poisoned darts. He now heard the pounding of feet on the stair within. The magnetic-soled shoes of a spacer were not easy to mistake. He could not count how many were in that storming party. Could they even know that he was responsible? He had felt no mind touch since he had been here aloft and now, in another vain attempt to make a stand, he pictured Thassa—Thassa and giant beasts on the march—even winged monsters here aloft.

··●) 12 (●··

The green smoke did not dissipate as a breeze swept over his tower perch. Instead it appeared to grow thicker, though it still slanted toward the distant cliffs. There were louder sounds from below. Those who garrisoned this outpost were gathering. He could see men running across the courtyard toward the tower. Even Sulve appeared in the doorway of the headquarters, his head turned up from his beefy shoulders to watch the phenomenon above.

Farree waited beside the trapdoor. He even dared for a moment to loose mind control, but all he encountered was a low emission from Toggor and those holes in space which marked the brain-shielded Guild men.

Now there was a puff like a small explosion, and Farree saw that the fire had reached the box and was feeding greedily on what was therein. Surely if any of the Thassa were on sentry duty they could sight this pillar of rolling puffs. Though what good that would do him, Farree had no notion.

Beside him the trapdoor heaved. He caught up one of

the envenomed splinters of bone and readied himself. The door swung up and back from a mighty shove, and the barrel of a laser appeared in a hand. The one who held it remained as far out of sight as he could, only, in order to keep his perch on that ladder of spikes, he had to balance himself with one outstretched hand against the frame of the door.

Farree struck and his blow went straight. There was a yell of surprise and pain from below and both laser and hand disappeared, the latter with the splinter still standing up in flesh aquiver from the strength the hunchback had summoned to plant it home.

The brilliant white of a laser beam lanced up into the air but Farree had already taken refuge behind the upthrust door, his only shelter. He thrust once more from behind that, aiming blindly downward. Once more a longer bone spear he had chosen went home.

Fire from the laser ignited more of the debris of the nest. But though it glowed it seemed to be quickly extinguished by the flames of green which were already consuming what was left of the dried stuff.

Farree put his shoulder to the door and slammed it down. They could easily burn their way through that, he knew. He had no way of latching it from this side. So he squatted on its surface, making himself the only possible lock. The poisoned bone splinters had hit twice and the one or ones who had been struck by them would have something to think about.

The fire in the nest was near burnt out, so strong had been the gust from its first lighting. How long would he have before they could force the door that even now trembled under him? He knew that someone was pushing at it. Only the awkward stance that must be held by anyone climbing up those spikes of the ladder was in his favor.

Toggor crept out of his shirt and crouched on his shoulder. "Farree?"

His name, not called aloud, but as clearly uttered in his mind as if it had been shouted. Thassa—not only Thassa but Lady Maelen herself! He took a deep breath. It sounded as loud as if she stood before him, but he was sure that she could not be out on the open land between this perch and the cliffs—the Guild would keep too close a guard for that.

"Here." He made answer, suddenly reckless enough to do that clearly, not caring at this moment whether any equipment of the Guild was able to pick up his call. Then he added, since his place of refuge was already known: "On the tower."

"Who holds?"

She was keeping her questions to a minimum of revelation and he would do the same: "Guild."

Though the fire was fast dying, the smoke showed no sign of abating. Its green finger reached farther out and out over the level land beyond the outer wall of the ruin. It was curiously thick, not diffusing in the air even though he felt a breeze against his cheek, an upspringing of wind which should have torn it asunder.

"Where?" That demand was ever clearer.

"On the tower," he answered, once again.

"Stand ready."

Ready for what? he wondered. Surely the Thassa, weaponless as he had seen them, could not hope to overrun the ruin and pluck him forth. But it was the behavior of the smoke which astounded him.

The reaching finger suddenly curled back upon itself. As it did, so it thickened, took on an almost solid quality. He felt as if he could reach out and grasp a tangible handful of it.

Back it came toward the tower. He swallowed. There was something ominous as well as unnatural about that return. He had no desire to be caught by the rolling folds of the stuff. But he could not retreat down the ladder. He still heard a muffled clamor from below, and he might well meet a laser head-on if he were to try even opening the door a crack. The grayish sky overhead had darkened, but the smoke was very plain against it. When it reached back as far as the outer walls of the ruin, the questing tip of that finger—or tongue—began to settle, seeking the lower stories of the battered buildings. At least it was not headed toward his own perch; none of it had sprayed out in his direction.

He dared to get to his knees, still holding in both hands his bone weapons, not crawling off the door, yet allowing himself a wider view of the smoke as it dipped down near to ground level. The nest had been consumed, and the end of the smoke before him had become only ragged tails which arose to follow the body of it, as if they had been summoned by order.

From below came shouts, and the pressure on the door beneath him was gone. He got to his feet, ready to drop his full weight upon it if the need again arose, and looked down.

The smoke did not touch the ground, but hung above

it at about the height of a man's knees. And it was not dissipating. Rather it was like some shapeless animal hunting, ready to engulf anything that moved. He saw Sulve draw back and slam the door in the faces of two of the guards who cursed and then ran for the dubious shelter of one of the roofless buildings. No one ventured forth from the tower.

Now there was a heaving mass covering all the open space of what had once been the courtyard. A sound brought Farree's head up—made him look beyond the ruins to the reaches of the land outside.

There was movement about the flitters which had been parked there; he thought he saw a body being tossed to one side, and strained to watch more carefully, though he was held by the need for staying where he was, making a barrier of the trapdoor.

Suddenly there was a sound which no one from the Limits could ever mistake. The flitter was preparing to take to the air. Farree squatted down once more. He had no idea what that off-world ship might carry which could scoop him up prisoner. Transferring his bone splinters to one hand he took out the knife he had found in the debris, determined to do what he could to defend himself.

The small craft spiraled upward into the evening sky. Already the outer of the three moon rings was partly visible. Farree wished that he had faith in it enough to believe that he was going to come out of this unscathed. He waited, cold with more than the rising winds of dusk, winds which made no impression as yet on the smoke below but which grew more and more chill and lashing here above.

From the sky the flitter was descending, and then from it came the unmistakable mind send of the Lord-One Krip. "Stand ready!"

Farree was sure that this was no trick of the Guild. A man's voice might easily be imitated but he had never heard that a thought pattern could be concealed. That was Krip Vorlund overhead and he—he was to stand ready!

It was not too dark to see now that a rope ladder had fallen from the belly of the flitter. Farree thrust his bone splinters and the knife into his belt, settled Toggor with almost rough haste within his shirt, and waited.

To climb a swinging ladder in the air—his mind flinched from even imagining such a feat. But this was the way out he had longed to find that until now there had been no hope of discovering. The flitter hovered overhead, and he was able to grasp the ropes in his hands. There was a third, he suddenly discovered, one equipped with a hook, and he clasped that into his belt before he started the dizzy ascent into the evening sky.

"Hold tight!" As he clung desperately to the ladder the flitter lifted and swung him on, through the air, toward the outer wall and away from the trapdoor and whoever might try to reach him now. The ropes cut his hands, so tight was his grasp, and he dared not look down. Then he heard another order: "Climb!"

At first Farree thought that he could never loosen his grip, never reach for the next hold bobbing above him. Somehow his body obeyed, while his mind remained frozen by such fear as he had never known before. Only climb he did.

There was a surge of power from the flitter, and now

the wind tore at him. A brilliant white beam cut through the air where he had dangled only moments earlier. Someone was alert, free of the ruins, and aiming a laser.

A hand reached down to him from the opening in the belly of the flitter, promising safety. He was not even aware he had climbed far enough for the hand to reach him. But fingers gripped tightly at the cloth across his hump. The flesh beneath answered with white-hot flashes of pain, but he was dragged on up and into the flitter. He looked up into the face of the Lady Maelen. She reached over his prone body and pressed a lever which closed the opening as he remained where he was, too weak with relief to move.

The small craft was shaking, and Farree guessed that it was being driven to the full extent of its power away from the ruined keep. Whether they were bound back into the Thassa country of the high cliffs he could not tell.

For the moment he was content to lie where he was, breathing heavily. Toggor crawled out of his shirt and squatted on the deck beside his head, all eyestalks erect and turned toward him as if the smux knew concern.

"We are descending now," the Lady Maelen said in trade tongue. "We cannot enter the inner places in this off-world craft."

The inner places? Had it taken so short a time to reach the heart of the Thassa country? Apparently the swift flight of the flitter had been even more speedy than he had imagined. For they were setting down. As they bumped to a halt, which jarred Farree's body and brought an answering thrill of pain from his hump, the Lady Maelen moved to open the cockpit door. But the Lord-One Krip did not rise from the pilot's seat. Instead he was leaning over the panel before him, drawing his stunner. Reversing the weapon and making of it a club, Lord-One Krip calmly hammered at the dials on the panel of controls, splintering their protective covering, and then the dials themselves, until he had bared a network of wiring which he proceeded to tear loose and twist out of shape.

"It will be a long day—several of them—before this ever flies again," he commented when he was done. "It is better that we be on our way."

Once outside, they looked up. Evening was fast becoming night but the sky was alive with the glory of the third ring, and Farree saw the Lady Maelen gazing up at it, her hand raising to gesture in the air as if she truly gathered that light and brought inward a portion of it clasped between her palm and fingers.

Before them was the entrance to the place of the hall. There were heavy ruts in the soil, from the regiment of carts that had passed that way before them. Lord-One Krip's touch on his shoulder headed Farree in that direction.

Once more he came into that place where the cliffs themselves were honeycombed with the very ancient doorways and the hand of time lay heavy on the half-arid land. But they did not go to the hall again, rather made their way to a lesser opening that was hardly higher than the heads of the two who escorted Farree. Within the entrance to which there was no bar or door shone a pale light which might be a portion of the third ring blazoned proudly across the evening sky.

They were waiting there, the four who had stood on

the dais of the hall, though they were not standing in judgment now. There was a subtle difference that Farree could sense without being able to set name to it, but he thought that whatever difference the Lady Maelen had had with these, the leaders of her people, had either been resolved or postponed to handle a more immediate problem.

"Welcome, little one." The voice he knew. It had cut into his thoughts too many times since this venture on Yiktor had begun for him to mistake it, or the speaker: the woman who stood a step before the other three.

"What have you learned that you could awake the Eor-fog?"

"The Eor-fog?" he repeated aloud in the trade tongue. All at once fatigue hit him hard. He wanted nothing so much as to curl up in sleep, a sleep without dreams, and remain unwaking for a long, long time.

The mental picture which flashed into his mind in answer to that question was of the thick green smoke which had issued from the powder in the box. He replied speedily with the truth, that he had found the box and that its contents had had no meaning for him.

"A nesting place of the grok. But those have been gone from here for many seasons. Fortune stands at your shoulder, little one, that such a thing could have happened."

He thought that he could well echo her statement. Looking back now, he could see that luck which had abided with him in the time he had been captive to the Guild. Perhaps the old superstition was the truth and his hump was a mark of luck—though one he would do without if he could.

"They thought to use me for bait." He brought out his only explanation for his remaining alive and in good condition.

"Yet the trap sprang on *them*," the Thassa leader said.

"They have lasers." He would not have her believe that perhaps they had seen the last of that company in the ruins. Whatever else the Thassa could mount in the way of offensive weapons, he could not tell.

"They could well have great weapons," Lord-One Krip spoke across his head in warning. "If they believe that we control some major find—"

"They may have what they please," the woman returned shortly. "Thassa control is now sealed to them."

Farree dared then to raise his voice in his own warning. "They may have patience, too. And can your land"—he thought of the arid country about—"give sustenance to all your people indefinitely?"

"Perhaps not. But there are other places to hunt for olden weapons besides a grok nest, little one."

He thought she was entirely too confident. As if she were the Commander and her forces set to harry a people who seemed, as far as he could determine, ready to depend upon intangibles for defense. Though he remembered how the flitter had been forced into another flight pattern the first time it had flown a scouting mission near the Thassa valley.

"You are tired, little one. Rest safe and know that you sleep within such a setting of sentries as those without have never met before."

It was a dismissal, and he went willingly enough but certainly not with a quiet mind. After his venture with the smoke he could believe that there were unusual weapons possible but that they might in the end triumph. He had lived too many years in the Limits under the ever-abiding shadow of the Guild where the indwellers spoke with awe and dread of what that organization could do and had done in the past. He still believed that the Thassa leaders were too confident.

But he went willingly with the Lord-One Krip to another of the cave rooms and there ate of dried fruit and strips of something which might be meat but which he believed was not, drank his fill of a sparkling fluid which was more than water but not a wine. Then he curled on a pile of mats with Toggor still beside him and waited for the sleep he craved. It was late in coming.

The Guild had wanted him for bait, yes. Almost the trap might have sprung. He realized suddenly that he had never really believed that the Lady Maelen and the Lord-One Krip would come searching for him. Perhaps it was a matter of duty for them, the same feeling of responsibility as he had for Toggor—that they could not leave him in enemy hands. That was the only reason he could accept.

Had he been anything else to the Guild? Though he had closed his eyes for sleep, what he saw again was out of his vivid dream: Lanti sprawled across the table and that other shaking him by the shoulder, drawing back in frustration and disgust when he realized the former spacer was dead. That scrap of stuff which the other had held—Farree tried to fasten his memory on that, sift it for its value.

Only what he saw now in the wink of an eye, the draught of a breath, was not the filthy hut of the Limits but somewhere else—

It was as if he were aloft again, swinging on the ladder, only there was no fear in this essay into open space, flight was something right and brought no fear. He looked down as if he rode on the back of a bird, not in any flitter, for the free air was all about him and he knew that he was here by *his* will and not because he had no choice.

He was looking down upon a rippling land of brilliant green: groves of trees whose leaves were clasped lightly about gems of eye-pleasing color which he knew were flowers or fruit. For the first time Farree could remember, he was truly alive, feeling no telling weight upon his shoulders, able to move his head freely. He was straight of body; without touching his shoulders he knew this. This again must be a dream, but one he clung to fiercely. If he never awakened from it, then he was repaid for all the ills of the past.

He descended through the air, lightly, easily, depending now he knew upon nothing but his own will and body. Grass rose shoulder high about him and there was the sweet smell of—

It was the scent which broke the dream, pulled him back into the grim reality of his own world. Yet it was a pleasant scent, one which he knew. He opened his eyes and the Lady Maelen was kneeling beside him.

There was a small furred creature on her shoulder, bobbing its small head against her throat. Behind her Yazz stood, tasseled tail aswing. "Farree . . . who is Lanti?"

Before he had time to truly align his thoughts, he answered. "I was with him. I think he brought me from another world to the Limits—me and something else that was worth more."

"Tell me," she urged.

He felt himself scowling. To have been awakened out of that dream in order to recall bitter memories was—hurtful.

"How did you know of Lanti?" he demanded.

"I saw him."

Farree hunched his body together as he felt a flow of anger beginning far inside him. "You were in my dream!" he accused her. He had met them mind to mind, yes, but he had never given them the right to monitor him without his knowledge. What more had she read from him that he knew nothing of? He felt as defenseless as he had in the hands of the Commander. At least then they had used a machine and had given him reason to know that he was about to be invaded.

"You cried out," the Lady Maelen said slowly. "It was a cry of hurt. I would have given you peace—that is all."

Perhaps she was right and had meant him only good, that he would again feel at ease.

"No!" There was deep concern in her voice, and she put out her hand as if she would gentle him as she might an animal that had been ruthlessly abused.

Only he was no animal! He was as much a man as a Thassa, even if he only held relationship by human standards to the eighth point! Perhaps the Thassa themselves, for all their humanoid appearance, were farther apart from the off-worlders who used that scale than he knew.

"Please." He was not aware that he had shrunk from her touch but maybe he had, for her hand fell to her knee.

"Please." She spoke the trade speech aloud; perhaps

she knew that to mind touch now was more than he would allow. "Bad memories can lighten if they are shared."

"I have nothing to share." He pulled up and faced her almost as if she had been sent by the Commander to win out of him some last scrap of truth. "You know it all. I was with Lanti in the Limits—beyond that there is no memory."

"You were erased?" She was studying him so intently that he longed to be able to enter the wall of the stone chamber to hide. There was a new alertness in her eyes.

"I do not know. I do not care." He said that with all the fierce firmness he could summon. He saw that she would accept it.

"It can be reversed, you know. If you should want—"

"I do not!"

She raised both hands so her fingertips touched her forehead in the way of an oddly formal salute.

"Your pardon, Farree. Know that all will respect your barriers until you give them permission to do otherwise."

"It—is—well . . ." He stumbled a little over that. And remained sitting until she was gone out of the chamber. There was a small chittering noise and he saw that Toggor was climbing upon his knee. He drew one finger down the back of the bristly shell which was the outer plating of the smux. Did Toggor also know resentment at times when Farree strove to catch his thoughts? What did the animals which the Lady Maelen loved and companioned with— what did they think of that companionship? He knew that Yazz and Bojor welcomed her effusively after they had been separated for a space—that they perhaps companioned with her by choice. Perhaps they welcomed the fact that another life form could communicate with them and that they were not frustrated by a lack of touch. He was no trainer nor owner of animals. Only Toggor.

Now he put out his cupped hands and the smux climbed into the hollow. He raised them so that he could meet him stalked eye to skull-enclosed one on a level.

"How is it, Toggor?" Tentatively Farree tried the mind touch. "How is this for you? Do you feel that I am forcing that on you which you would find freedom from? I am not Russtif to hold you captive, either body or mind."

He received no thought no matter how hazy, only a feeling of peace and contentment as the smux rocked a little from one set of claws to another in his hands.

••●) 13 (●••

Farree ate, he drank, he slept deeply and dreamlessly. If those of the Guild made any foray into the country of the Thassa, he knew nothing of it. When he at last awoke it was to see a band of clear and clean moonlight across his short legs, feel about him an ingathering of spirit. Had it been the latter which had drawn him out of that deep sleep?

No thoughts touched him directly. Perhaps the Lady Maelen had set a barrier to stop those, as she had promised that he would not be asked more than he wished to give. But, even though none had been sent to arouse him, he was as one hearing distant and summoning music. For just a moment there was a troubling deep in his mind as if something stirred there which might flower if he let it. But instantly that same barrier which he had striven to raise against the Thassa fell into place and he was free.

There was a basin of water in a small side crevice of the cave room and handsful of moss for towels. He shed his sweat-dank clothing and washed the whole of his crooked body. His hump was still unduly tender to the touch, it also itched, as if his pain had abraded the thick, corrugated skin, and he was careful in his drying as far as he could reach.

His shirt was so grimed he hated to re-cover his now clean body with it. But he did not have to. Near the crevice he found a small pair of breeches in the same pattern as those the Thassa wore and a shirt, wide across the shoulders, which gave room for his deformity. A chirping sound broke the silence of the cave and he saw the smux, throwing a grotesque shadow across the beam of moon-light as he came toward him, eyestalks erect.

Once more Farree sensed the aura of well-being and contentment which Toggor broadcast as he came. It would seem that the smux was well pleased with these lodgings, bare as they were. Farree reached for his belt to draw in the generous folds of that shirt when sound rang about him.

It was like the deep note of a huge gong, and his body vibrated with it. The boom did not seem to come from any one place, rather as if it were truly born of the very air about him. Three times it sounded, and he found himself moving out of the cave room as one who had been summoned and had no will except to obey.

He crossed the end of the valley, avoiding the sleeping beasts. Above him stretched a sky, which he twisted his small neck to see the more. There was the full circle of the third ring, and when one looked at it from here it was no true moonlight cast apart by some natural process of Sotrath itself, but rather a rainbow-touched encasement of the lowering moon. His flesh tingled, he felt alive to the last hair on his overlarge head, to the smallest tip of nail on his claw hands. It was as if the body he wore drank the radiance of that light as he would drink, after a long thirst, water from a clear fresh-flowing well.

The light appeared to draw the remainder of the ache from his hump, though the itching of his skin under the shirt grew worse until he longed to draw off the garment and use his nails on his own skin. In spite of that discomfort, his sense of well-being was acute.

There were none of the Thassa in sight. But he could hear again their song, issuing from the hall ahead. Only this time it was not a tale of loss and of long ages, but rather a cry of welcome to something which gave life anew.

Almost he expected to be turned back as he drew into the shadow of the long-eroded doorway. But there were no gatekeepers nor sentries here. The way was open and he passed on, drawn by the cadence of that song for which there were no words he could understand, only the rising melody.

Then he saw that through some ingenious means the light of the third ring was here also, banding across both the four Thassa who stood on the dais and the others who had come to gather below. In the glow their white hair held rainbow sheen; they were each enshrined in an envelope of light which made their bodies look almost tenuous, as if they were now only shadows. No, shadows were of the dark—rather wisps of iridescence.

He saw a Lady Maelen who was different. Her bright hair stirred about her as if each lock had a vibrant spirit of its own. The glow wrapped her round as it did all the others.

Farree halted inside the door and stood watching. Perhaps, in spite of the drawing he had felt within him, he was not one of these—perhaps it was better to keep his distance as a stranger.

The itching on his back grew stronger. He found himself rising on his toes, which were bare against the ancient stone, almost as if he were reaching again for some skyborne aid which would swing him out across that company, lift him even farther into the banded light. He flung his arms wide and lifted his head as far as he could from his crooked shoulders so that the moonglow touched his face. It was more than light now—it was welcoming warmth, like the soft pressure of a friend's hand sweeping aside the tangled hair on his forehead.

His feet moved—rocking back and forth. He began to feel the imprisonment in his misshapen body as a punishment, something that kept him chained to crookedness and sorrow when just ahead of him, inches beyond his reach, was all he had longed for and never thought to have.

The song was dying away—the desire in him died with it. He stood quiet now, and he could have wept that what had been promised or offered he had not been able to take. He was only Dung after all. There was bitterness in that which came welling up inside him as part of that sensation of irreparable loss.

There was silence now, and he stepped back under the very arch of the doorway. What if he had blundered on a secret thing and they were to find him here? He wanted to give no offense.

"Welcome."

Clear in his head, as clear as that voice had ever been, came the single word that Farree knew was to make him free of that company. He did not know why, but again he was drawn forward and now he walked slowly down toward the dais. That which had emitted the glow of the ring was fading; also, shadows gathered and lengthened. The Thassa no longer stood each and every one robed in glory.

However, it had not been his presence which had broken the spell. He knew that as he came hobbling forward. She who stood behind and above the Lady Maelen was holding out her wand. As if that had been one of the laser weapons of the Guild there was a glow at its tip, and he truly thought that he could trace a dim line of light straight from it centering upon him.

Welcome he was. There was no chance to misunderstand the wave of good wishing which arose from all that company. Then it broke as individuals and couples passed him heading for the door. Yet he was still held and summoned.

The Lady Maelen and the Lord-One Krip had made no move to leave. As Farree came level with them they fell in, one to right, one to left of him, all three facing the four Elders on the dais. She who had drawn him lifted her wand, and he felt that drawing vanish. Yet he also knew that he was not so excused from her presence.

"There is much in you, little one." Her thought speech was pure and somehow musical as if some lost tone of the night song still held in it. "Sotrath draws you even as it draws those who are sons and daughters of this earth. Yet you are of different stock and have yet to come into your heritage."

Out of all his bewilderment and unhappiness he dared to ask her then: "Who am I—what am I, Great Lady?"

She shook her head a fraction and there was a twinkling of the small crystalline gems which headed the pins holding her mass of hair.

"Who are you? Ask that of yourself, little one—for your like we have not seen before. What are you? That you must also learn for yourself."

"I am—Dung!" Again something had seemed just within his grasp and had eluded him.

"You are what you wish to be. Are you truly what you have named yourself?" Her mind touch was quiet, like a soothing hand laid across a child unhappy from a nightmare.

"I am—Farree!" He defied that other part of him which was sourly bitter. He saw the jewels glitter again as she gave the smallest of nods.

"You are even more, as you shall know when the time comes, little one. We have some of the farseeing, but we are pledged not to use it for ourselves. We must not be led into making choices, only face those clearly and alone of mind.

"But this I tell you, Farree—the time will come when you shall truly know what you are and who. And it will not be an ill time—but a good!"

Some of the warmth which had been among the song's notes and had flowed from the great third ring caressed him softly again. He tried to bow, though with his twisted body it was an awkward salute.

"For such farseeing as you give me—thanks, Lady."

"One does not give thanks for the truth. But there is another matter for us now. Come!"

The other three who shared the dais turned as one and

started away, and he fell in behind while Maelen and
Lord-One Krip followed, Farree still between them. So
they came into a side passage of the hall and at last into a
room which was not all austere and comfortless stone but
had around two sides a bench padded with woven lengths.
More such hung across the bare stone of the walls. Again
by some trick of the long-ago builders there was an
opening in the roof through which fed the light of the third
ring to give radiance to the room, for there were crystals or
gems set in patterns on the flooring now flashing rays from
one to another. Farree watched them in wonder, hardly
daring to step out upon such a carpeting, as they winked in
subtle patterns almost like the lights upon the control board
of a ship. Yet these were rocks and gems, and they were far
from any off-worlder thing.

The four Elders settled themselves on one bench and
motioned the other three to take that nearer the door. He
settled down there between the Lady Maelen and Lord-
One Krip. Then one of the male Elders pointed with his
rod to a portion of the wall and it opened, coming forth
from it, on a tray transported as if by wings, a tall goblet
which glistened with life in the moonlight.

That was borne to Maelen. She accepted it and drank a
single mouthful; then she passed the cup to Farree and
nodded encouragingly. He drank and passed it on to
Lord-One Krip. Once he, too, had accepted and drank,
the goblet turned and was away again.

"It seems that these off-worlders who follow the lower
path are here well housed and intend to stay until they
have accomplished their purpose." He who looked to be
the eldest of the Elders broke the silence first.

"Perhaps it is we who have drawn this trouble upon our people—" The Lady Maelen spoke in answer. "That we did on another world in fear for our lives, and more than just our lives, has sent ripples to Yiktor."

"They were here before," the woman who had spoken to Farree said. "I know not what they seek, but we have our own barriers and guards and they have not penetrated those—"

"Save when they sought to draw us forth." Lord-One Krip spoke sharply. "Those machines were tuned to one persona pattern, thus only Farree was forced to answer. Somewhere they had prepared to so cage us." All four of the Elders inclined their heads in agreement.

"Therefore the quicker we go, the less the threat—" he continued. But the woman held up a hand in a gesture that silenced him.

"We are the Thassa and the years lie many and heavy behind us. Nor are we the less now because we have discarded much which the off-world holds in high regard. We cannot be hunted by their hounds—"

"Perhaps not, but you can be destroyed. And do not think that such a thing is beyond the minds of those who try to hold the gateway of your land. What they cannot take, they remove."

The faces of all four of the Elders were set sternly, and she who seemed their first speaker slowly shook her head from side to side.

"Let them try." There was such confidence in her words that Farree did not know whether to accept them and be content or whether to wonder at the disbelief of those who had never been off-world and did not understand the spreading and iron-handed power of the Guild.

"Their presence here can be reported." It was Lord-One Krip who offered that. "The Patrol—"

Again her head moved right and then left. "They move against the Thassa in their own lands. These come brazenly to do what they will. We are not so far from our sources even in these days that we cannot defend our own. Do you think that these would retreat even if the three of you were taken and laid at their feet?"

Lord-One Krip's mouth set and his shoulders squared as if he were about to reach for a weapon.

"The tales concerning the Guild are many and black. I cannot believe that any bargain they made would be honored. But there is this—time may be against them. This is not yet a world they control. Their nest in that ruin is the largest consolidation now of their power here—else we would have heard. Therefore a pact with them would buy—"

"Nothing!" Her word had the force of an aroused one's oath. "We do not treat with such as these. However, they may force us back into a path we forswore long ago—that we would meet open force with open force. When we chose what lies here"—she touched her forehead with the tip of her finger and then spread out her hand level and empty between them—"against what we might carry thus, the balance shifted and the Scales of Molester were set anew. It is our thought that these invaders will not be easily turned aside, bemused by illusion. You say they are mind guarded—thus our first defense is negated. Very well, if illusion cannot grip them, then we shall summon the power. These are the hours of the third ring when the power ascends, and during the height of it we must make our move. No—"

She looked straight at Farree and under that regard he felt like a small crouched animal without any burrow in which to hide, as if all he was spread out before the four for their reading. "Picture," she ordered, "what you know of these men."

He began with that force which had drawn him forth from shelter, compelling him to deliver himself to the enemy. He continued with his trip in the flitter, his coming to the ruins, and his imprisonment in the tower—then his meeting with the Commander and Sulve. Then, for the first time he was interrupted by a raised hand of one of the men.

"This Sulve has been heard of. He is outwardly a merchant whose ship is in port for repairs."

"I believe him Guild," Farree answered. "They are supposed to have their men in many places—mostly unknown."

"True enough," Lord-One Krip agreed.

"It matters not what he seems to be." The woman sounded impatient now. "Let us know the rest."

So he told the story of his two interrogations, one under a machine which would prove the truth or falsity of his answers. There was a shade of another expression on the face of the Elder, one Farree could not read.

"So they depend always on machines. They have no trained Deliverer with them," she commented. "This machine"—she spoke now to the Lord-One Krip—"such are in use off-world?"

"The Patrol are said to have them, and they are used by the law on several worlds. But what is known to the law sooner or later comes into Guild hands."

"I do not think," the Lady Maelen said, "that they could read Thassa."

"They will not get a chance!" Again the male Elder flashed with some heat.

"Can you," Farree began slowly, one part of him struggling against the other which was all sober reason, "equip one who is not Thassa with false information and plant him to be re-taken?" For a long moment that seemed to stretch and stretch there was quiet in the room. He wanted to cry out he did not mean what he had said, that there was no way he was going to be trapped into returning into the hands of the Commander. For there would be no games played then—his very mind might be peeled and segmented so that the false would be made plain enough to those whose powers he had feared and held in awe all his life.

"I think . . . not!" That was Maelen. "There is Yiktor itself to work for us."

"Perhaps." The woman made a dismissing gesture with her hand. "But the full story is not yet told. What happened then, little one?" He told of the coming of the bird with Toggor, of how by the smux's help he had set up the trap for the guard. Toggor, as if he knew well he was being discussed, came out of Farree's shirt to sit upon one of those knobby knees, his eyestalks well up and all turned in the direction of the Elders.

For the rest Farree hurried over his climb to the tower top and the nest there. When he spoke of finding the small box, the man among the Elders who had not yet spoken leaned forward and demanded: "There were symbols on this box—you could read them?"

Farree shook his head. "It was very old—"

"That it was!" the man agreed. "We knew not that such still existed. But if it was there, what else may still be ready to hand?"

"How did you know how to use it?" again he asked Farree.

"I did not. It was very old and worn. I forced it open, and the powder in it touched the dried nest stuff and aflamed."

"So. The Scales dipped in your favor then. This is something to be thought on. Only yet your story has no end—give us that, little one."

Farree spoke of his improvised weapons of bone and the assault on his perch, of the strange cloud of smoke, which, instead of being wafted away by the wind, had sunk into the courtyard. Then he ended with the message of hope and the coming of the flitter to bear him away.

"Well enough," the Elder who had questioned him about the box said when he finished. "You gave them the truth and it did not serve them; you have escaped them, therefore their wraths or that of their leader, will be great. I know that we may look forward to some new attack on their part. And since you are not Thassa and so vulnerable to what they may launch in the form of controls . . ." He hesitated.

Farree moved a little on his seat. Uneasiness and wariness arose within him. He had half offered, in spite of all good reason, to be bait, even as the Guild had thought to use him. But they had not accepted that from him. Now—now he must make them understand.

"What if they set some control on me and I prove a key to open your fortress?"

"Forewarned is forearmed," Lord-One Krip made answer. His hand closed about Farree's upper arm and he kept a grip there as if he feared that the hunchback was about to take off forthwith to tempt the Commander and his men into the open.

"There are none that can touch you here now." The Thassa Elder spoke with such conviction that Farree was compelled to believe her. "We have a defense which has not grown any the lesser through the years but stronger, as we have learned more and more concerning our own powers of self."

"They will not give up," Lord-One Krip said slowly. "Even if we see them evacuate the ruins and seemingly depart, we may be sure they have not given up."

"Nor shall we. There will be eyes aloft and eyes afield. Those who go on two wings and those who trot on all fours will keep them ever under eye."

Farree drew a deep breath. The bird which had brought Toggor, Yazz, other animals either linked by mind to—or even exchanged with—a Thassa. What if all the Thassa became one with the birds and the animals of this world? How could those still in human guise know or prepare to defend themselves against such an overthrow of all which was natural by their own thinking? Hand clutched on hand before him. What would it be like to have a fine, well-shaped body like Yazz—to be free of the miserable itching burden always on his back? Could this be done for him? His life as a humanoid had not been such that he would not willingly relinquish it for this other and freer guise.

"Not so!" She had read him, this Thassa Elder. "It is not given for all to make great change. Even the Thassa cannot do that as they please. Would you condemn Yazz to your body then?"

Farree set teeth on his lip and bit hard. All his thoughts had been for himself, that was the truth. No, he could not ask that any—animal or man—take on the burden that he wore.

"You must be a Singer." The Lady Maelen must also have caught those thoughts. "And there must also be to hand one furred or feathered who needs the strength of man—one hurt in mind or greatly beloved to the Singer. It is not an easy thing like putting off one kind of clothing and assuming another." She was kind, but he did not need her kindness, he thought sourly for that moment.

"I have been thinking upon this matter of the Eor-fog," the other Thassa man spoke. "That such a weapon was left in a grok nest is a mystery beyond all mysteries. It has been so many tens of tens of tens of seasons since the last of the weapons was destroyed. Certainly these ruins were built even later as an outpost for the Lord Janger's land. Where did the grok find that? There was nothing else?" He looked to Farree.

"This"—the hunchback drew the knife from his belt— "and a sword—I think it was a sword—which was rusted past use. Some scraps of leather which might once have been a belt. And bones—many bones."

"If Janger had come across any such arms," the woman

Elder commented, "he would not have been overrun during the march of the clans. But there remains no record of usage. Who knows where the grok came upon it? They are easily attracted to all bright and shiny things. The cock brings them to the nest to attract a hen to what he has built for her."

"The grok do not range too widely," answered her companion. "This was a better hunting land then. And the nest was old. It might well have been built in the first year Lord Janger set his own masons to work. These lordlings look for omens and fortune favors. The Lord Janger's war sign was a screaming grok—he would have never had such driven from his own inner keep. No, the box came from somewhere near."

"You are saying?"

"Saying that perhaps there are other supplies here in the heart of Thassa holdings—only waiting to be found!"

"There was the surrender of all!" the woman Elder protested.

"Something might have been overlooked. I would advise that, instead of setting all the seers upon actions of the enemy, we put some to hunt those places where we have not walked hereabouts—to see what time itself may have hidden for future finding."

··•) 14 (•··

Moonglow was gone with the deepening of the dawn. Farree stood in the valley of the Thassa watching a mustering of the clans and then an outspreading of men, women, and even children—each small group heading toward one of the carven doorways in the cliffs. But he remained with Lord-One Krip and the Lady Maelen and their place was apart: up the throat of that canyon which led to the valley and to the edge of the plain on which still stood the ship that had brought them. By them danced Yazz on impatient feet, ready to be gone; while Bojor hunched from side to side, swinging his heavy head aloft as far as nature would allow it to reach, the nostrils wide above the tooth-fringed muzzle as the creature tested the air.

That the Guild would have reason to explore their ship was something they all agreed upon. Though there was nothing within it that could possibly give any service to the Commander's force—not now. Star maps, yes, but Yiktor had been their true goal and on Yiktor they had landed.

Whatever other voyage tapes were in stock within would lead only to false trails, and so perhaps would serve better now than weapons to confuse the enemy.

They did not enter the ship itself as that could prove a trap, but took places behind the fallen rocks which lapped about the foundations of the cliffs and so set themselves to wait and watch. This waiting and watching left the mind open to thought, and thought now plagued Farree. He kept returning to that dream-released memory—the one of Lanti. Who was *he*, and how had he come into the hands of that discredited and disgraced spacer? For, thinking back, it was plain that Lanti had had some reason to keep apart from the others of his kind who came to enjoy the tawdry pleasures of the Limits. The hunchback fought hard to fix on some point further back in time than the spacer's confrontation with the big man, striving to picture better that glittering scrap of something which had brought that one to hunt out Lanti and his captive. For he was certain that he, Farree, had not been with the spacer of his own will.

Only, when he struggled so to remember, he came always to a dark wall. What was sealed thereby he had no way of telling. Perhaps it was best that he did not know. Yet, no matter how many times he told himself that, the same number of reasons for remembering followed. Until he became aware of something else.

From behind the rock which he had chosen for his vantage point he could see the Lady Maelen and crouched behind her, his jaws moving rhythmically as if he chewed upon cud, was Bojor. There was a stir—not from them, rather in the warmth of the desert air itself.

Down from the sky wheeled a flying thing which was wide-pinioned and descended in a spiral, with only a few flaps of wings to keep it on course. It was black, yet the light struck rainbow points of color from the sleek fur on its body and along its wings, which appeared clad in skin and hair instead of feather wreathed.

It landed on the very rock behind which the Lady had taken refuge, and he could see that its head had no bill, rather a sharp muzzle with a show of teeth to suggest that it was a hunter and a formidable one. It was very large, perhaps its head would near top Farree's were they to stand side by side. Its second pair of limbs, which had been folded tightly across the upper section of its body, unfolded and reached out, naked claws showing, as if to menace the woman it now faced.

There was a shrill chittering sound and the wings flapped noisily as if the creature wished to take off and was compelled against its will to remain. Maelen's hands moved as had the claws. Not reaching for the winged one but in a kind of pounce and retreat pattern as if she played with some prey in a cruel fashion.

There was mind send—but of such a pattern as Farree could not follow. The thing took tiny steps that with the beat of the wings raised it a fraction from the rock only to let it drop again to its perch. Large eyes gleamed a brilliant gem-flash green and the overlarge ears twitched back and forth.

At length one of those uneasy jumps did take it into the air, and it beat its way up, to hang overhead, a wild flutter of wings keeping it steady above the rock on which it had perched. The Lady Maelen's right hand moved in a half circle and the thing wheeled out, circling about the silent tower of the star ship, once, twice, thrice before it was gone, soaring up until it was only a speck in the sky, a speck which headed toward the distant ruins if Farree could judge aright. He believed that so another pair of eyes had been added to their own scouting mission.

It was hot and grew hotter as the sun arose. This was a barren land, where even the patches of bleached grass looked dead on the root and fought a retreat against sand, gravel, and rock. Toggor had early made plain his opinion of their station by retreating into Farree's shirt, drawing in his eyestalks and apparently going to sleep. The hunchback also discovered that watching monotonously while nothing happened was a base for drowsiness. Since the departure of the winged one there had been no movement beyond the cliffs of the Thassa.

Thus it was almost with relief that he did see a dot in the sky—the creature the Lady Maelen had dispatched? No—there was no mistaking the sound. There was a flitter on the wing.

Surely the spaceship and flitter would draw any attention, whether it was the Guild who came now or some other cruiser—perhaps even a local planet guard. He knew very little of Yiktor save what he had learned from the Thassa, but they were only a small handful now and kept to their own barren land.

The flitter did not approach the downed ship straight, but circled. Though, Farree noted, it kept its circle from invading the air over the cliffs.

"C-2 double 3: Reply. Are you in trouble?"

It was not the clear mental call of the Thassa, but

rather an actual voice out of the air overhead. Surely a Guild detachment would not use that approach! This flitter must serve some local form of the law.

Farree looked questioningly to the Lady Maelen. She had not moved. When he turned his head cautiously, he could see no trace of motion in the Lord-One Krip. Whoever these newcomers were, the Thassa wanted no contact with them.

"C-2 double 3: This is port command. Are you in trouble?"

The newcomers, lower now, could certainly see that the downed ship's landing ramps were out.

"This is a type four planet. C-2 double 3—landing is allowed at the control port only. What is your difficulty?"

That encircling approach the flitter had made was very much closer to the ship now. The smaller craft was preparing to set down. Farree saw movement ahead, a small body flitting from one tangled growth of grass or standing stone to the next, working its way purposefully toward the silent ship and the newcomer. Too small for Yazz—and besides, that prancing champion could not have made such a stealthy advance. It must be some other one of the animals the Lady Maelen could and did command. It squatted finally not far from the ramp of the spaceship, and when it was still it melted so into the background that Farree could not distinguish it at all.

The flitter set down and a figure got out, a stunner, plain by the length of its barrel, in hand. "We are coming in. This is control from Central Port." The voice rang loudly. Farree thought that it came from the flitter rather than the man who had landed, and was magnified to a shout by some instrument on board.

There were two aground now. They did not advance toward the ramp together but separated, weapons in full sight. One remained at the foot of the entrance ramp while the other climbed inside. There was a wait—the intruder must be investigating the ship with caution. In time he returned and gestured with an outflung arm so that his companion started back to the flitter.

He did not make a straight track but swung in and out across his first path, apparently in search of some track that might have been left on the ground. Though it would take an expert tracker, Farree was sure, to find any such.

The searcher halted and beckoned. His fellow ran down the ramp to join him. Farree felt that as long as the control men were present there was to be no attempt to attack the Thassa. The Guild would lie low. Oddly enough, he felt no confidence from this belief. Part of him wanted to front the Guild again, to have done with the suspense.

The strangers inspected the ground thoroughly, one of them even getting down on hands and knees as if he possessed Yazz's sense of smell and would hunt along their last trail—day old as it was. Finally the two gave up and returned to the flitter, which took off—but not soon enough to miss the return of the flying creature Maelen had sent out earlier. The thing saw them and shied to the north, sailing to a greater height, apparently making for cover.

It need not have feared. The flitter arose easily and turned to go back the way it had come. Farree realized the gravity of the craft's visit. Any ship that did not planet at the port probably was, in their eyes, outside the law. They might continue to fly patrols in this direction, waiting for the crew of the deserted spaceship to return. Thus the Guild would not move, nor could the Thassa show outside their valley for fear of questioning. And all knew that the Thassa had nothing to do with off-world ships. Not all the Thassa—

Farree wondered. Who knew about Lord-One Krip, who had been a Free Trader? And what of the Lady Maelen? Surely their story had caused talk on this portion of Yiktor. But just as surely they had nothing to fear from the laws of this or any other world. It was the Guild who must go underground.

"Perhaps—" Lord-One Krip's mind touch came almost as clearly as had the voice from the flitter. "Yes, my story is known—probably too far too many here. Also what happened on Sehkmet. The Guild have their own ties with the law. We are better without allies."

As the flitter disappeared in the distance the Lady Maelen straightened in her hiding place and Bojor moved back to give her room. She leaned against the rock that sheltered her, both palms against its rough surface, her head turned to the north where the creature of the skies had disappeared.

Scrambling over the smaller rock came the furred one Farree had only glimpsed when it had gone forward to scout the landed flitter. It leaped for the Lady Maelen and she caught it in her arms, cradling it against her breast as if it were the child whose size it matched. Again Farree caught only broken words of whatever message it delivered, as its sending range was far above his own thread of mind exchange.

"It is true—" Now came her own send verifying. "Ista 'read' them. Those were not Guild, nor do they even know that this is the heart of Thassa territory."

"What *do* they know?" Lord-One Krip broke out sharply.

"What they shall learn by their path of return flight." She was smoothing the dark fur gently. "Ista put it in their minds to swing northwest a little."

"The ruins—the Guild." Farree voiced what Lord-One Krip must also be thinking. "They will see—"

"All which is open," Lady Maelen agreed.

"Which may be nothing," he returned. "The Guild will have their own precautions and hidey-holes."

"Perhaps. I would like to know how swiftly they can take to cover and whether they now have their flitters in hiding. There is little place there to conceal those. This may well bring another player into the game."

It would seem, however, that the visit and retreat of the guard flitter was not to end their own attending to the empty ship, for neither the Lady nor Lord-One Krip moved to withdraw. And waiting without any prospect of someone coming was a tedious thing, Farree discovered.

Toggor crawled out of his shirt and made raids where he could crook a claw under a stone and turn it over, scooping up grubs and insects so exposed. Farree ate his own rations and drank sparingly from his water flask.

It was the coming of the winged one for the second time that broke the dullness of the afternoon. Circling down, it perched on a rock which brought it eye-to-eye in height with the woman. This time Farree was not even able to catch the faintest wave of whatever message passed between them. The creature bobbed its head twice and a moment later took to the air again.

Then came the Lady Maelen's send: "There has not been grok here for as long as the memories of the jam exist—which means during at least one of our generations. But there is a height in the north where they had a second nesting place. Near that are caves. Also"—now she spoke slowly, almost as if she were thinking her way through a problem—"those in the ruins have been seen twice scouting in that direction, and what they must so seek is—"

"A storage place!" Lord-One Krip was quick to answer.

"There are none—or so I would have sworn. The Thassa destroyed all that existed when they turned their backs on the old knowledge and took to the roads and open places."

"A man would have said that Sehkmet was an empty world also—until raiders and the Guild proved that untrue," Lord-One Krip replied. "They have access to machines which can give them readings. They may even have a sensitive among them."

"A sensitive?" Farree broke in.

"One who can release energy in such a way as to spot, either on a map or on the ground itself, objects which are foreign to the land—things that have been handled and used by some intelligent creature."

"Would not such a one have found the box?" Farree ventured.

"Of a certainty he or she would—had they been searching. But the ruins were of the plains people, and they depended only on steel in their own two hands. Thus one of their old holds would not have been explored. These—to them the Thassa are a puzzle, a puzzle and a threat because they have never been able to understand us. Thus they would go nosing as closely as they could about the edges of our home place, breaking the peace as they will discover."

The furred one the Lady Maelen had been nursing in her arms suddenly came to life again, and she sat it down on the rock where recently the jam had perched. It leaped once more into the nearest clump of spike-armed bush and began working its way back to the ship. Bojor sniffed and moved a fraction from where he had been crouched upon his haunches.

Once more there was a distant dot in the sky, and the far-off troubling of the air. A flitter—was it the same one?—was returning. Farree caught Toggor and stuffed him again inside his shirt so he would not lose track of the smux during any quick move.

That craft made a wide circle about the sky-pointing ship, but this time there came no shouted message from the sky. It circled twice, and Farree could see that it bore no insignia. This flitter must be from the Guild, though the boldness of such an enterprise in the open light of day bothered him. It argued confidence on the part of those inside, and confidence on the part of the Guild meant arms and men ready to withstand any attack.

The third circling was much closer in, and finally the flitter set down at almost the same place that the guard ship had earlier chosen. Three men descended from the cabin. All were armed and moved cautiously, retreating toward the ramp of the ship backwards, facing the cliffs as intently as if they already knew that there were three sentries on duty there. Three? No, more if one counted Yazz, who still crouched in shelter with Lord-One Krip, and Bojor—as well as the furred one in hiding now.

Once reaching the ramp one of the men darted up it, his two fellows keeping guard. Then the second, and finally the third. Were they there to search the ship as the guards had done, or were they ready to raise?

Neither of the Thassa had moved. Farree, feeling more and more like a child or one of the animals who could be roused by command but did not have a voice in any plan, twisted from one side to the other trying to keep those two in sight.

Farree could not tell the time as it passed. He expected every moment to see the ramp rise, the ship take off. Surely that was what had brought this party here. But there was no change. At last movement showed at the side lock and down ran the three men, sprinting for the flitter as if pursued by the bartle or some even more threatening beast.

"They have discovered the persona." Lord-One Krip's message came with a faint suggestion of laughter. "It would require a full production yard to breach that control lock."

"It would seem that they have also seen more than they like," Lady Maelen answered. "Sadi projected well even when there were mind locks against her. She showed them one five times her own size and all teeth and talons at ready! She makes an excellent guard. And if they used those weapons of theirs, it was to no account."

Illusion? Farree wondered and was instantly answered. "Illusion and not from one of us. Sadi projected what would frighten *her*, and she did it on a mental length which apparently their shields are not set to handle. See!"

The last of the men had barely reached the ground with a flying leap from the ramp when there appeared behind them, filling the full of the hatch door, a beast such as Farree had never seen before. It was larger, leaner in bulk than the bartle. Its head was split halfway along with a mouth which sprouted two rows of fangs, spittle dripping from them as if in anticipation of sinking home in frail flesh. The forefeet which projected now onto the ramp were taloned with great claws that looked as if they might rend apart the very envelope of the ship's hull.

All three of the men were firing lasers, but the shaggy coat of the apparition absorbed the worst of that attack easily and took no hurt from one of the most formidable weapons known to the space ways. One of the men broke and ran *faster*, quickly followed by he who had stood beside him. Only the third retreated in good order, still firing uselessly as he went.

The huge menacing form at the head of the ramp pulled back so that only the head with that murderous threat of fangs still protruded. There was a wait which Farree ticked off to himself—twenty-five in whispered counting. Then the flitter arose and began circling the pillar of the ship once again as if seeking another way in. Farree almost believed that they might, should there be some opening, drop a man even as he had been hoisted up from the top of the tower in the ruins.

But it would seem that there was no other way of

penetrating the ship, and the flitter was not armed with anything other than the weapons that had already been used to no purpose.

Finally it winged away eastward. The massive head winked out of being. Then the small furred creature Maelen had earlier held and caressed came racing down the ramp and across the land toward the Lady's rock.

"Well done!" Lord-One Krip called that aloud as if the small beast could hear and understand. The Lady Maelen stooped and caught the guard up in her arms for a second holding and caressing.

She set the animal down on the rock before her, stroking its upraised head.

"Sadi will watch with Yazz," she said, "and with the old one here." She reached over to scratch behind Bojor's ears. The big animal stretched his neck to the farthest so that she could reach behind his jaw also. "I think that we had better take thought to what lies northward—to that which has drawn the interest of those others so much that they have already made three trips in search of it." Her hand swung to point in the direction where the jam had first appeared. "Nor do we know what brought the Guild here in the first place. That we ourselves have returned to Yiktor could not have been foreseen when they settled in. For that was done at a much earlier time than our coming. Thassa memory is long—but is it long enough when there was also a will to do away with something that was future danger? The Elders of another day may have even memory-wiped our stock lest some be tempted to return and use something which was not right for us."

That they considered the animals guard enough for the

ship seemed strange to Farree, but nothing or very little which the Thassa did could he compare with the actions of those he knew from the Limits days. He trudged back through the canyon to where the temporary settlement of the rest of these aliens was—Aliens? He was the alien here, even more divided from the rest than he had been from most of the Limits dwellers.

Yet he discovered, though he could not see that he contributed anything to their aid or defense, both the Lord-One Krip and the Lady Maelen took it as a matter of course that he was to be one of the party pointed north. They began the journey at moonrise, with the glow of the third ring making the plain almost day bright.

With them went a third Thassa, one Maskay, who, Farree gathered, had roamed much in that direction and had contact with the wildlife thereabouts. It was difficult to tell age with these people, but Farree thought him perhaps a generation older than his other two companions. And the Lady Maelen appeared to look to him to set the direction and the pace.

They halted before the rings were quite faded by the coming of the grayish predawn light to encamp on the top of a small rise where a trio of wind-twisted trees gave shelter. There was a seep of water at the bottom of that knoll, though it quickly funneled away in this arid land. This seemed to be one of the landmarks Maskay knew well.

He stood under the downswing of one of the wide branches and pointed on northward.

"It is another night's journey if we take to plains pace, and then come the hills. That is a dry land and the spring at Two Prong is of bitter water. Only the jam can live in those heights."

"Yet you have been there, Kinsman," the Lady Maelen said.

"When I was young and foolish, I went many places that were strange. And little or nothing did I learn from such wayfaring," he returned with a smile.

"Yet the jam live there and like all living things they must have food and water—and—"

"Hush! And under cover. Down with you!" Lord-One Krip swung out his arm and caught Maelen's waist, pulling her down, while Maskay jerked back under the tree.

It was very plain to hear now—the thrum of the flitter. Through the last haze of the third ring it bore across the sky. Farree waited for it to hover above them, to sense by some off-worlder equipment that they were here. But it passed overhead well up in the sky and kept on to the north, exactly as if the pilot had a definite goal in view.

"Guild!"

"Are you sure?" demanded Lady Maelen of Lord-One Krip.

"There is a difference in the beat. That craft is not made for short patrols but is a long-range flitter—for exploration."

"It flies"—Maskay put into words Farree's thought—"as if those aboard it know where they would land and also as if they must be there in a hurry."

"True. I wonder if they have found what they seek. If so it is best we make the same discovery and as soon as possible."

Farree tried to stretch his head a little and then

stopped, warned by the pain in his back. His whole body ached from the pace they had kept and he was not sure he could go on—not without more rest. Yet he was also sure he was not going to be left behind.

••) 15 (••

Once more Farree lay in hiding above a machine that was not of Yiktor. A flitter at rest on a ledge thrust forward from a mountainside like a great shelf. He could see the shadow of a head within the bubble of the top cover, but the door was also open, and he knew others had gone forth.

Through the ring-lighted air above dived and soared at least two of the jam, providing eyes for the Lady Maelen, who lay full length on the lip of a second ledge across the narrow valley. So aptly balanced were those two outcroppings that one could well believe them the work of some intelligence, taming the mountain ways by a bridge that had long since vanished.

There was a noticeable trail upward on the opposite side, beginning not far away from the flitter, angling along the side of the cliff toward its high summit. They had sighted nothing moving up that path, but the jams had reported that earlier those from the flitter had taken that way.

There was a similar trail on this side of the gulf also,
and they had explored it via the jams—to pace it themselves would have been to offer the flitter a clear sight of
them. It did not reach clear to the full heights on this side
but ended abruptly in a straight cliff wall that had no sign
of any opening. And Maskay had set out a half day ago to
hunt farther to the westward, setting the length of a night
for his explorations.

Farree found himself drowsing in spite of the need for
sentry go. They had hurried after the sky craft when it had
been sighted yesterday, but he had found it hard going
with his shorter legs and the weight of his hump. Though
he would not have voiced any complaint even if they tried
to wring it out of him, now his body was one ache, and he
felt as if he could not force himself to any further effort at
all.

The barren lands which surrounded the heart of the
Thassa country had given way to coarse grass and woods
scattered here and there. Here in the mountains was
growth also, wind-gnarled trees for the most part, growing
in pockets. Far above there was the bluish-white shadow
of snow early fallen or late thawed—it could be either.

One of the jams drifted across the gap between them
and the flitter to hunker down on the rocks that concealed
the Lady Maelen. That the creature was reporting, perhaps
from Maskay, Farree was sure, and a moment later the
mind touch aroused him.

"There is nothing above save a road which is now
encased in ice. It seems that those look in the wrong
direction for their treasure. It may well lie on this side."
She passed along the report and her own interpretation.

"But the way here leads nowhere—only to barren rock," he dared to protest wearily.

"What seems barren rock," she corrected.

Illusions again? He would not deny that the ancients of her race might have set such to cover their trail. But how to make sure of that?

"I go, before those others and Maskay return." It was Lord-One Krip who answered.

"You could be seen—"

"If I walk, yes. But if I creep . . ."

Farree had hunched around to face that trail. Perhaps it had originally been cut into the stone on purpose to give fair footing, perhaps it had been so worn below the surface about it by countless feet over a period of uncountable years, but it was plain that it was now a trough. The hunchback looked to Lord-One Krip. His body was slender, but even if he moved on hands and knees he certainly would show up to any watching this side of the cliff. Though he shrank from what he was impulsively agreeing to do, Farree cut in: "To creep is what I have done most of my life. Dust me well with the soil." He was already scraping up his own handfuls and smearing it across the backs of his legs and across his hips, leaving the tenderness of his hump to the last. "I can make it best."

The Lady Maelen turned her head and looked at him as one who is weighing one thought against the other. Then slowly she nodded.

"There is something in what you say, Farree."

He had so wanted her to refuse instead of accept that once more that old cord of bitterness awoke in him. They were willing to use him even as they used the jam, the bartle, any and all of the life on this world. The rainbow of the rising third ring swept over him and it seemed to bring with it a soothing. Even his painful hump felt a touch of coolness—which could not be the truth, as since when had a radiance of light had substance?

Farree shucked off his belt bag and tossed some more of the gravelly soil on his back, biting his lip against the tenderness of the hump, the small flashes of pain he felt when anything touched it now. He crawled on his belly until the upward slope of that path faced him. Then he asked the question that he should have voiced earlier. "If there is illusion, how may it be broken?"

"Try to pierce it," she answered him. "Illusion can distort sight but not touch—unless the one who tries to break it is totally under control." Fair enough, he thought. His deluded eyes would at least serve him until he reached the solid wall at the top—or the wall that only appeared solid. He began to crawl, the rock harsh against his hands, panting a little with the effort of keeping as flat as he could in the depression of the way. He went slowly, with many pauses, hoping that if the one with the flitter had any long-seeing glass trained on this side it would show only a portion of his hump—a rock bedded against rocks.

Sotrath climbed above the horizon and the three rings were clearly defined, the elusive third spreading glory over all the land. Flecks of glitter answered from the stone under him, the wall ahead. On and on he went and then froze and flattened himself to the stone as a warning reached him from below. "The others are returning."

He was tempted to look for himself, but there remained the matter of time. The Guild men could well try this side of the cliff now, having been baffled on the other. So he strove to speed up his crawl and yet not reveal that anything moved there. He lay during one of his periods of stillness, his pointed chin resting on his crooked arm as he looked ahead. To his relief it seemed that the wall was not too far above. Now he felt the pinch of claw on his shoulder and remembered that Toggor had not been left behind. Could the smux be sent ahead to prospect for an opening? Did an illusion fashioned to deceive the eyes of his species also confuse animals? He did not know, but the knowledge that the smux was still with him was a warming one.

The path up which he hunched his way was leveling out. Yes, he could see the wall before him. The path, if path it really was, ended abruptly at its foot. He was out on a level space. Putting up a hand he chirped to Toggor, and the smux obediently climbed into his palm and turned toward the stone. He lowered it.

On Farree inched until he was within touching distance of the wall. For a moment he hesitated. To his eyes it was so firm a barrier that he could not believe it was illusion only. He put out his hand and his palm met solid substance. But it would be necessary for him to test it fully from one border of the sunken roadway to the other. Edging along, he began at the outer side, Toggor clawing along beside his hand. Not here—nor here—nor—He stopped with a gasp of astonishment and fear. Before he touched the fourth time, Toggor was gone. One moment he had been there brushing the side of Farree's hand and the next he had disappeared!

Frantically the hunchback struck the wall at the same

point where he was sure the smux had vanished. There was a solid surface right enough, but there was also a crack through which he could feel a slight stir of cold air. Quickly he traced that crack. It ran only for a short distance, but where it ended there was a second crack, this ascending vertically. He returned and felt his way back, found another vertical crack. There was certainly a sealed opening, perhaps a door. He thumped it, hoping for some give in it. There was none. Perhaps he was too near the ground to move it, or perhaps it *was* sealed past any of their forcing!

He lay with his head close to the crack and tried to search out Toggor with the mind touch. The return was very faint, as if the smux answered from some great distance, but at least he was alive and within, though Farree would not have believed that crack wide enough to admit him.

Still lying with his head against the wall, he mind sent his discovery to the Lady Maelen. The rainbow of the third ring washed over him, brightening those flecks of glitter in the rock. In fact, as he glanced up the wall against which he now lay, he could see that the speckles were drawing together to form a dim pattern, or perhaps awaking one which had been deliberately set there generations ago.

"I come." That was the Lady Maelen.

Farree turned his head a little and saw her, lying belly fast to the stone, as he had, and pulling herself forward a few inches at a time. Even so, it was not long until she took his place by the unseen door as he edged back to give her room. Her hands went out in a wider sweep than his could equal and then she nodded.

"It is true. There is a door here and—" She lay now on her back and looked up at the surface of the wall where those particles appeared to move together and outline to form shapes of their own. "There is here an illusion set. But, by the Third Ring, O Sotrath, to Thee thanks of heart and mind! By this Third Ring of Thine we can see!" She began to hum, so faint a sound that it was hardly as loud as the clatter of Toggor's claws on the rock. Farree once more felt the power of that singing.

The glittering bits waxed brighter—taking on the rainbow hues of the ring itself, now red, now blue, now green, now yellow—or a swirling mixture of them all together. But as they gathered to make lines and curves on the surface of the wall, Lord-One Krip sent a thrusting thought.

"They are aboard the flitter—and it is rising in this direction!"

That warning from below was as sharply clear as if it had been shouted aloud. Yet the Lady Maelen did not move, nor was there a falter in the low sound which issued from her lips. More and more did the pattern clear on the door in the rainbow sparks of light. And that light now outlined the portal itself. It promised an opening of a size to let the three of them enter abreast.

Now the noise of the flitter was loud enough to drown out the sound of her song even though he lay beside her as flat as he could push his body. He did not turn his head to watch the enemy—not yet—for the wonder of that design of lights held him entranced.

"They come."

The second quick warning was not needed, for the

drone of the flitter rolled above the cliff and echoed and
reechoed from the rocks thereabout. Now Farree did
lever himself up and face about in time to see the forward,
upward sweep of the craft. It might well be that the two
of them had already been sighted and were easy game for
those on board. He waited, shrinking inside, for the flash
of a laser beam to cut out at them.

The light of the third ring was a mist growing ever
stronger. Perhaps in that they were not as good targets as
Farree feared. He was aware of movement beside him, of
the Lady Maelen getting to her knees and then her feet,
still facing the closed door in the cliff as if she had all the
time in the world to deduce its secret and need fear no
interruption in that task.

He scrambled up in turn, his back now to her and the
door, facing outward. Small as he was, he could not protect
her whole body with his, but he would do the best he could.

The flitter was heading straight for them, as if it meant
to crash against the cliff and crush the both of them.
But at the last possible moment it swerved in an almost
perpendicular climb that carried it up to the mountaintop
beyond.

Surely they had been sighted! Farree could not understand why they had not been cut down, at least with a
stunner. Perhaps those thought to let Maelen open the
way for them and then take them.

He glanced back at the woman. Her arms spread wide,
she was touching with the tips of her fingers this and then
that of the circling patterns of color her singing had
brought forth. But there was no answer. At last her mind
send, as strong as Lord-One Krip's warning, rang out.

"Come! This is Thassa sealed and in this body it will not answer to me. Come!"

He sprinted up the road which had been such a laborious climb for the other two and faced the doorway between Maelen and the stones. She set her own hands upon the backs of his and moved them from place to place in a swinging pattern. At that moment Farree had little hope that Maelen's suggestion would bring any success. He turned his head upward as far as he might to see where the flitter had vanished in that last upward swoop.

The sound of the craft still echoed loudly in his ears, and he could only hear at intervals the hum of song that Maelen still wrought to open the door.

Back and forth Lord-One Krip's hands moved under her control. Then—at last—there was a grating. The sound of stone scraping stone—of something long held moving again. A crack appeared, not as the thin line the ring outlined but as a darker space. Forward moved that layer of wall and Maelen pulled Lord-One Krip to the right side, Farree taking three steps to their one to join them. Outward it moved but not far, as if the disuse of centuries had so frozen it that there could be no real release. But there was an area of dark. The Lady Maelen, dropping her hold on her companion, squeezed through it, Krip following closely on her heels, and after them Farree.

His hump scraped the stone in spite of his turning side-wise and the pain of it made him gasp and stumble. Then he was in the dark where only a pale radiance of the ring reached in from the outer world. Maelen had swung about, and Lord-One Krip reached out a long arm and jerked Farree to stand beside him as the hum broke into words—a chant which sealed the entrance to this place of darkness, leaving them in a lightless place of age-old stone.

Then there was the gleam of light again. Far softer, and more limited as to reach, then the radiance without. However, they could soon see after a fashion by the small globe balanced on the Lady Maelen's palm. Farree felt a clutch on his breeches and reached down to scoop up Toggor.

The Lady Maelen tossed the globe of light and Lord-One Krip caught it deftly. She was breathing in small, fast gasps as if she had been running, and there were beads of sweat trickling down her face like tears.

Lord-One Krip held out the globe and swept it from side to side, but all they could see were rock walls shading off into clouding shadow and a dark opening before them where perhaps the road they followed continued on into the heart of the mountain.

"They may have a distort with them," Lord-One Krip said. "If so, it will not take them long to—"

"Ah, but we shall not wait!" There was purpose and power in her answer, even though she stumbled when she took a step forward. Farree caught one of her dangling hands, set it upon his shoulder in spite of the ache of his hump, and stood ready to be her support. To his satisfaction she accepted his aid, and he felt her lean against him as they moved on, Lord-One Krip with the globe of light going ahead.

Perhaps it was because the third ring's beam did not reach here, or because that which had been awakened by its gleam had been only on the outer door, but here there were no glittering bits on the walls to add to that limited light. The stone, though it showed the marks of tools here and there, was otherwise bare.

Their road ran straight for a space and then began an upward slope. At first the incline was not enough to cause them any difficulty as to footing. Even as he climbed, taking what he could of Maelen's weight, Farree was listening.

If those hunting them did have a distort, they could open this way as easily as an innkeeper could slash open a melon.

Then a sweep ahead with stunner or laser would bring the three all into Guild hands. He was glad of that upward slope for that very reason.

As they went that became more pronounced. Until Lord-One Krip, crowding against the right-hand wall, lit pockets chiseled there, meant surely for fingergrips. Farree steered the Lady Maelen until she laced fingers in the nearest. He could no longer support her and climb, as he had to stretch nearly tiptoe to set his hand in any of the holds, for these were hacked nearly shoulder-height for Thassa.

Their retreat slowed nearly to the same crawl which had sent him up the outer road. The Lady Maelen, nearly drained of strength by her singing, shifted from one hold to the next with obvious difficulty, though she made no complaint. Finally Lord-One Krip stopped short and said: "Take this and the lead, Farree. I will see to Maelen."

He obediently crowded past the other two, obliged to hold to them before he could accept the globe and use his other hand for the wall. Steeper still grew the road. So far they moved in a silence broken only by the sound of heavy breathing or the faint swish of some article of clothing against the wall. Toggor climbed to Farree's shoulder and extended all eyestalks, staring ahead as if he could either pierce the dark so or was trying to. It was a chitter from him that brought Farree to a stop. The smux saw or scented something ahead.

"Stay!" For the first time he took it upon himself to order those two who had commanded his life since they had met in the Limits. "There is something ahead." It was Lord-One Krip's strength the Lady Maelen needed now, and not his lesser aid. Farree pulled himself forward at the same slow speed with which he had climbed the road without, expecting any moment to see the way before him once more walled, and he wondered if the Lady Maelen could sing again an open door.

What the limited light of the globe showed him moments later was a stair leading up. Only down the side of this trickled moisture which had stained the stone with encrustations and given life to some strange and ominous-looking growths pallidly yellow and dankly gray in the globe light. There was movement in one such growth as the light fell across it. A thing of thin spotted wings flew up nearly in Farree's face.

"There is a stair," he called behind. "But it is wet here, and the footing may be even worse—there is water . . ."

"We come," was the only answer Lord-One Krip made. Farree realized that, in truth, they had no choice but to go forward. He waited by the foot of that stair and only when the other two reached him did he take the first step, grimacing with disgust as his fingers found the next handgrip half full of a growth which gave forth a putrid smell as he could not help but crush it.

So they went, slow step by step. Luckily the treads were wide and gave them room to stop now and again for a breather. There seemed to be no end to that upward climb. However, after a space the seepage ceased and they were free of the fetid growths and those slimy things which lived among them, eyeless hunters of the dark.

Again it was Toggor who gave warning of a change in their road, chittering in Farree's ear. He passed a warning to the other two. It had seemed to him that the Lady Maelen, instead of gaining strength as she was aided along, was slowly failing even more. Now here was a major test for them all. A crevice rent the road before them, leaving only a small space where the three huddled together as they looked ahead. There provision had been made for travelers but it was not one which Farree wanted to try.

Reaching out into the dark, in the center of the way, was a span just wide enough for one person at a time to walk. That stretched into a dark where the globe, no matter how far Farree tried to reach with it, did not show them a far side. He had taken command of their going since the climb began, but dare he lead them over that narrow strip of rock above a chasm? He was not sure. Yet neither could he give the Lady Maelen any help—it must be he to go first.

Already he felt top-heavy and weak of leg. Could he better crawl than try to shamble at his usual pace across? He fumbled with the globe and then plucked Toggor from his position on the hunched shoulder. Tucking the globe into the front of his shirt, Farree placed the smux beside it, giving one clear order. He felt the movement of the foreclaws against his skin and knew that the smux had grasped the ball of light, would hold it with all the safety Farree was able to devise.

Dropping to all fours, the hunchback ventured out on that bridge. He arose again to a sitting position, his feet stuck far out on either side, his fingers gripping the stone with a grasp which scraped his skin painfully. So he pulled himself along with nothing but the very muffled light to show mere inches before him.

As it had in his trip up the sunken road, time seemed to reach forever. There was no end to his scraping advance. His hands were cut and sore, his body ached from the stretching he must do. Yet there was something stirring far back in his mind. Not a feeling that he had done such a journey before—not a distinct memory—but rather that there was a far better way of accomplishing such a journey if he could only remember how. That blocked recall was something which weighed him down now when it was most necessary that he keep a clear mind.

There was an end to the bridge at last. He edged forward, wiping his bleeding hands against his shirt, to make a scrambling half-fall onto a wide space which was indeed the lip of the rift and seemed solid before him. He ripped the globe out of his shirt with a speed that brought Toggor with it. The smux dropped to the stone while Farree used the globe, getting to his feet and walking a bit forward, hardly daring to believe there was this solid flooring beneath his feet.

He did not go far, but swung around and did which it took all his strength of will to accomplish, squatted once more to make a return journey, with the light again at the fore of his shirt—Toggor ordered to keep it so as he himself lurched, handhold by handhold, out into the open on the narrow span. He met them near halfway across. Lady Maelen seated and hitching herself along in the same position he had chosen, Lord-One Krip behind to steady her. Now Farree was forced to go backwards, so offering them what light he could and holding fast only to his contact with Toggor, urging the smux to give all possible assistance with the light.

••●) 16 (●••

Even the third ring's spectacular radiance did not reach this far down into the gloom. They had gone through the mountain upward, across that dangerous open of bridge, to come out upon another ledge perch. The bulk of a second peak overtopped them so they were deep in the shadows here. They made the full round of the ledge and found only one place where there seemed to be a promise for descent, though that way was by a narrowed thread of footpath nearly as daunting as the bridge they had mastered in the caverns behind.

What lay in the dark depths of the rift into which they might descend they had no idea. Had they indeed come to the end of any road of escape? Lord-One Krip took up the fading globe of light and made for that dubious path to explore the possibility of their getting into the depths.

Lady Maelen sat with her back against the wall, her eyes closed as if she had not yet recovered the strength she had expended in the opening of the door. Farree prowled up and down the perch they shared in a vain attempt to forget his back. Something, perhaps it was his journey across the bridge, had started in his hump, not only the fierce ache which he felt all through his body, but also an intolerable itching, so that he wished to shuck off his shirt and score his own flesh with his broken nails. He could not sit still and endure this.

Toggor clacked claws across the stone and bent all eyestalks to survey the path ahead. When Farree passed near him he gave one of his flying leaps and caught hold of the hunchback's arm, climbing quickly to his shoulder.

Farree could no longer see even the faint gleam of the globe on the path. Either that roadway had taken a turn—or perhaps the light had at last failed and Lord-One Krip was feeling his way step by step down the slope. To remain where they were if the pursuit was up behind them was folly. To be caught on that perilous way was perhaps even more, yet the uneasiness which filled Farree made him consider that the less of dangers.

"Lady"—he approached Maelen—"can you walk or descend?"

She turned her head slowly and eyed him as if he had recalled her from some long journey. "They come?"

He attempted to send a probe back through the roadway of the mountain but picked up nothing—not even the deadening defense which marked those wearing their protection against mind send. "I read nothing. But the longer we stay here—"

"Yes." Even her voice sounded as if it came out of the dregs of fatigue. "I will try."

He lingered beside her as she crept to the head of that narrow downward path. She did not attempt to get to her feet. Farree leaned forward to catch, as tightly as he could, a hold upon her belt. So linked, they made their way after the vanished Krip at a slow pace, with frequent halts. Farree kept one hand locked upon her belt and the other feeling for handholds along the walls. To his great thankfulness he discovered that there were such, perhaps chiseled by the same makers who had left the similar aids within the inner passages.

The strain on his shoulders brought the fiery pain back again but it was better than just to sit or stand waiting— for what he had no idea.

They came to a place where the trail they crept along doubled back upon itself in a risky curve around which they crept or scraped a painful way. It was there that disaster struck.

The Lady Maelen must have trusted a loose stone for anchorage. She cried out and slid toward the edge. Farree braced himself, not knowing whether he could hold or not. She was kicking her legs, striving to find some purchase as he anchored himself desperately. His left fingers were deep in one of the handholds—those of his right hand laced to her belt. However, he had to stand and take the strain of the increasing weight of her body, made worse by her frenzied attempts to find a hold for herself.

The pain across his twisted shoulders was so intense he might have been caught in the full beam of a flamer, unable to help himself, unable to hold her long. There was a sensation of being torn in two—of agony. He felt as if the skin over his hump had parted. Still he held. And, through what seemed to be his blood drumming in his ears, he heard a cry.

"All right—I have her."

He was clamped into the linkage he had set himself. To free his fingers from the hold on her belt was more than he could do at that moment. There was liquid running down his back, spattering into a pool between his legs. He could not let go even if he would.

Then the weight which was the Lady Maelen no longer pulled him sidewise. Other fingers plucked at his fingers on her belt, prying them loose one by one. He had fallen to all fours when that strain had gone. Now he toppled forward, to lie face down, his shirt wet through, though there was no longer pain in his back.

He was hardly aware when there was a grip on his hand which now dangled over the edge of the path. The night air bit with a chill tooth at his back through what seemed to be rents in his shirt. But before he lapsed into semiconsciousness he felt a hold on first his wrist and then the upper part of his arm, drawing him away from the rim of the depths. For a moment he fought that, but the strength had gone out of him and he had to loose his hold to that grip and the sideward pull.

Then he was down from the path, on a surface which might be another ledge or at least was much wider than the way he had taken with the Lady Maelen. That pain which had centered so in his hump was gone—instead there was a furious itching. He twisted out of the hold upon him and got to his knees, stretching backward with both arms to claw at the burden on his shoulder. At first he thought it was the shirt which tore beneath his raking nails and then he knew it was skin, thin tatters of skin!

There was pain, but it was nothing compared to what

he had felt earlier. More and more he raked at that loosened skin, felt it rip and fall away from his body. There was under it something which moved, arose—as if for all these years he had carried some other living entity on his back.

The thin light of the globe was before him. He did not look up, only pulled and tore until that which he had carried for so long was released. It moved seemingly of its own accord. He raised his head now, could raise it higher than he ever remembered doing. Muscles he had no knowledge of moved, seemingly by instinct. That on his back was unfolding—stretching—no longer in more than a few quirks of cramped pain—reaching outward.

"Winged!" He heard Lord-One Krip's voice with a strong note of awe in it. "He is winged!"

Muscles moved again, stretching in a new way. He felt a sweep of air about his small body and he dared to reach back again with one hand. What he touched was like the softest of down laid over taut skin.

Winged? Was he? How could such a thing be? Somehow he stumbled up to his feet. That which had weighed upon him all his remembered life was gone. He cautiously thought of wings and tried to move such if it were true that he had them.

There was a wide sweep through the air behind him. A small smart of pain as if something had scraped on an edge of rock. Now he longed to see!

Before him lay the globe of light. Across it he could see the faces of those he had followed—and there was awe on both. Again he raised one hand—then the other—and explored by touch. There were extensions from his body right enough. They felt slightly damp, and he had the sensation that they must be fanned in the air to take moisture from them. How did wings feel—if they sprouted from one's own body? Who—*WHAT* was he now? Oh, *what* was he? He edged halfway around so that those others might see the better.

"Is it true?" he demanded, wondering rather if he were unconscious from some fall back on the trail and this was all the result of feverish imagination.

"It is true!" the Lady Maelen assured him. "Your hump held wings—they are growing larger—"

"But—I am not a bird!" There were also flying reptiles and perhaps even weirder things on the many worlds from star to star. But his was a man's body—or at least humanoid. And in all his years of listening to travelers' tales in the Limits (and very strange some of those had been) he had never heard of a winged man.

Once more he fanned those straightening wings (they must, he decided, have been closely cramped within that hump) and felt his whole body lift a little. Frightened, he clapped them together. He had no idea of flight, and he thought that that must be learned. Yet in him now moved the wish to take to the air—to spiral out into the dusk, up into the circle of the third ring which was a glory now far overhead.

Even his neck felt odd, and he had to rub at it. He was able to lift it high, to hold it straight as he never had before. No more peering out on the world from a painful angle.

Then, as if a hand had reached forth and touched him on the shoulder in warning, he remembered what they fled and where they were.

"Down"—he looked to Lord-One Krip—"we must get down."

"We are down," the other answered. "This is the bottom of the gulf. And—but come and see for yourself."

A few steps on and Farree discovered he must keep the wings furled if he would walk, and he dared not try to fly, not yet. They were once more on a road or else a smooth stretch which was flanked here and there by stones fallen from the heights around. There were in walls about them the same kind of doorways chiseled into the stuff of the cliffs on either side as he had seen in the Valley of the Thassa, though this did not widen but was a narrow way between two chiseled walls.

Their small light could show them no more than those openings were too regular to be natural and they seemed to go on and on. In the darkness ahead, where the light from the globe could not penetrate, anything might be waiting, and Farree forced his mind to turn from what now was on his shoulders to search out any hint of a living thing before them.

He picked up small anonymous stirrings that were certainly animal or bird and were too far from the general thought pattern for him to follow. But of anything stronger, more threatening, there was not a hint now. Lord-One Krip, the globe half-muffled in his hand, led again, but Lady Maelen clung to his belt rather than accept Farree's assistance and the winged man was alone. Cautiously as he went he fanned the wings slightly, not daring to trust them but sure that they needed that stretching and drying. He had peeled the rest of the rags of the shirt from his body and used those to sop up the runnels of moisture which dripped down his shoulders across his chest, which was no longer squeezed forward but was slowly coming into line with his shoulder points.

Winged! What was he then: some species so far removed from those with whom he now traveled that they would find him utterly unnatural? He watched the two moving through the dark, outlined only by the feeble glow of the light, and wondered what would happen to him now. In some ways he longed once more for the familiar weight on his back, the old knowledge that he was handicapped by something that could be understood.

Now he needed to keep those new appendages clipped close lest they scrape against the stones between which many times they had to squeeze a narrow passage. Yet they went so slowly, perhaps because of the Lady Maelen's deep fatigue, that his awkwardness had time to disappear. With each step he took there was a new confidence rising in him.

The fact that this rift among the heights must once have had meaning grew more and more evident the farther they went. The dark openings on either side were so cleanly cut that he knew them to be of the same fashioning as those in the valley where the Thassa had their meeting place. What lay within those portals the two he followed apparently had no desire to see, for their path was ever on.

They came at last to a place where the narrow slit widened out into something which was a sky-roofed valley. Yet not one like unto that of the Thassa meeting ground, for here the desert aridity was lacking.

Above the radiance of Sotrath and the third ring was

once more open, and the land before them was brightly illuminated. There was the glisten of moon rings on water, for the whole center of this basin appeared to be a lake. That body of liquid was buttressed about by a thick cloak of vegetation such as Farree had seen nowhere else on this world.

Large growths of trees which supported looping and tight vines made a wall about the lake. Farree, without ever thinking of what he did, eager only to see ahead, used his wings for the first time—fanning the air and leaving the ground.

He immediately discovered that flying was an art that must be practiced, as any other exercise. His initial soaring was too abrupt and carried him up too far, the rhythmic beat of his newborn wings was something he had not mastered, and he made leaps in the air rather than sustained flight. Still, those leaps had been enough to show him that the lake encircled an island that was so centrally placed that it might have been the pupil in a great unblinking eye. On that island there were walls and a tower not too unlike that from which the flitter had lifted him days earlier.

His two companions made no attempt to force a path into the thickly cloaking growth but had collapsed rather than seated themselves on the last space of open ground before that dense stem and branch began. The Lady Maelen sat with her head turned up to the sky, her eyes fixed upon the glory of the third ring, her mouth a little open as if she now drank sip by sip from the brilliance. As Farree watched, perching a little above the two on a last outcropping of fallen rock, she stretched wide her arms as one waiting to embrace something or someone before her.

Lord-One Krip sat with upturned face also, but his eyes were not on the glory in the sky but on Farree, as the winged one realized. And there was wonder in his face which was slowly overcome by an expression of purpose. "What lies beyond?" he spoke rather than thought. Perhaps he feared that thought send might interrupt what the Lady Maelen was doing.

"A lake and on an isle, in a ruin, a tower." Farree answered promptly.

"Can you reach it over that?" Lord-One Krip motioned toward the thick intertwining of the growth. It was only too plain that without some form of cutting tool they could not hope to blast a path farther on.

"I can try." But still Farree was distrustful of those wings. They were too new, too far removed from all he had ever knowledge of, for him to truly believe that they could be successfully used to climb into the sky more than on the short soarings he had already attempted with more than a little bemusement and uneasiness.

Purposefully now he fanned them slowly, turned his head as far as he could to sight their sweep. They were not feathered—he had already determined that with his hands reaching behind him—rather they seemed to be covered with a skin which had a soft, velvety texture almost like close-shorn fine hair. Now he stood and dared to take a small leap into the sky using the wings to support and sustain him. He had discovered a bit of the beat which would lift him and applied that rhythm.

Up he went into the splendor of the ring-bright night.

When he was sure, having rounded in a circle over the other two, he ventured out above the growth, fearing to have his wings fail and let him fall down into the matted vegetation. But awkward as he was, he was learning with every movement he tried, more and more of what it took to steady himself in the air, to do what humanoids had always wanted: reach the clouds.

Only there were no clouds here—just the darkness of that tangled wood which ringed the lake, the sparkle of the water which reflected the third ring, and the island beyond.

Out over the lake he beat his way, not trying any high soaring as yet. Then he was above the island. There was growth here, too, but not a matted wall of it such as grew on the shore. Here were tall plants scattered in clumps, heavy with flowers wide open as if the moon instead of the sun brought them their nourishment. From them came a heavy perfume so that Farree, as he flew over them, felt as though he bathed in the scent. And his mental search brought no hint of life here.

He came in, to settle on the wall which ringed the tower. Now that he was close he could see that time had not struck so heavily here as it had on that castle where the Guild had taken up their den. Rather this surface was smoother than any stone he knew of and it was near white in color, veined darkly with straggling rivers of lines and splotches. There was glitter, too, from points along those paths of darker shades, and when he touched a near one he felt a roughness as if there were some other thing, perhaps a gem, inset in the veining.

Along that wall he walked, using the wings to steady

and balance himself, looking down into the interior of the place which was wide open to the glory of Sotrath. There were no other buildings within. Only that tower, and it was thickly agleam with the sparks of fire such as passed beneath his feet.

He had kicked off his boots before he had taken off, and under the long-hardened soles of his feet he felt small sparks of heat, as if every one of those small stones was a flare of a tiny fire. Having made a complete round of the outer wall, he dared to glide down to the pavement below. As he had noted from aloft, here the small bright stones were set in patterns, not following any twist of veining. And each was different. As he landed in one such design, which was a concentric series of circles, there came that which almost sent him soaring again. A flap of wings did carry him upward so that his feet no longer touched the stone, for out of somewhere—the tower, the very sky above him—there had sounded a sharp note of sound as if he had struck two knife blades together.

He waited, his head turned from side to side, watching, mind seeking. The sound echoed and died. There was no answer that he could detect. But he was suspicious of those patterns now—some kind of alarm? Or was it a greeting meant to assure some people long dead? There had been Thassa like caves along the road to the valley, but the tower seemed unlike their form of building.

The side of the tower which faced him had the dark opening of a door, though there was no sign of any windows on any level. To enter so might mean that he was an unwary smux venturing into a trap.

Smux! He had all but forgotten Toggor during the

wonder of his transformation. But the smux was still with him now, claws tightly clipping his belt. Having received no intimations of life from the tower he applied touch to Toggor to see if the smux could pick up something too subtle, too far from his own species' mental processes to record. But the result was that Toggor knew nothing.

A wing-assisted leap took Farree from the circle which had brought forth that answer to the very edge about the foot of the tower where he noted the patterns did not reach. There he settled once again. There was a faint reflection of the moon and ring light. Enough to show him that there was no door here to bar passage. But the dusk which lay within was daunting. He had been foolish not to bring with him the globe. Even if he could see only a few steps ahead, he would not shrink so from investigating it.

Smux—send Toggor in again? But the creature's night sight was little better than his own. When he hunted within the walls for prey he used scent organs. And here the constant small breezes brought the overpowering odor of the flowers to kill any such clue.

There was no use lingering here—Farree would either completely explore this structure or he would have to return with the admission that he had been routed by fear. But he did not even have the slight advantage his wings gave him in the open!

Clapping those together and furling them as far as he could, Farree took a deep breath and started into the tower. He half expected a second warning of sound, perhaps even the snap of a trap. But what he did meet was a firm barrier of—nothingness. He could not see—he could only feel as he passed his hands up and down that barrier as stout as any double-locked door. Yet he saw through and beyond it as far as the light penetrated and there was nothing—though his hands told him there was. At last he loosed Toggor but the smux was also baffled by a barrier he could not penetrate. So—the builders here had their guards after all. Perhaps this one had been alerted by his own touching of the pattern in the pavement without.

However, as he had learned in the Guild fort, there was always the roof. Urging Toggor to fasten himself once more to his belt, Farree stepped back far enough to get wingspread and then leaped upwards, with the beat of the wings indeed carrying him to where he could grasp the parapet of the tower.

Here, too, there were patterns on the surface. Farree could see no hint among them of any trapdoor such as had been his salvation before. He did not propose to get down and go exploring, not without knowing more of what he faced. Thus he set himself to studying the patterns, setting them firmly in mind.

That done, he sought out with mind reach, and the Lady Maelen, strong and clear as she had ever been, caught his cast and answered. He told her of the courtyard below, of the invisible door bar, and now of these patterns aloft.

"Show me," came her calm answer.

Trying to picture each in turn, he began with the one immediately below his perch on the parapet. It went so and so and so. While the one beyond that was thus, and this, and that. Thus he strove to set up the clearest mental pictures he could.

He felt her growing astonishment, her excitement.

"Thus and thus?" came her demand with a newly mentalized design. Farree looked, but that design was lacking. He returned that message and could sense her disappointment. "Then this or this?"

Part of that surely—yes! But not as entire as she pictured it for him.

"Below. Look to the court below!" came her order then.

As he had crouched on the wall and surveyed the patterns from a lower point, now did he again, moving with care along the parapet so that he might view all below for her. Some were so intricate in their convolutions that it was difficult for him to sort out their beginnings and endings.

"It is a maze," she returned. "But I must see for myself. I have to see."

"I cannot carry you," Farree pointed out. That his strength had not been great enough to hold her from slipping on the trail was a fact. Also, he did not believe that she and Lord-One Krip could fight their way through that wood and across the water.

"You can carry that which I may use." Back came her answer in a rush. "Come for it, Farree, come for that!"

..●) 17 (●..

Farree winged back across the band of tangled vegetation and set foot on the ground not far from the two who waited. Lord-One Krip was busy with that bag which had been clipped to his belt through all their journeying. What he brought out now was not food as Farree had expected but rather a shining square of what seemed to be bright metal, well polished and no bigger than Farree's own hand. He rubbed his fingers across the upper surface as if to remove some unseen covering and passed it to the Lady Maelen, who held it firmly and looked to Farree.

"Those patterns," she said, "are protective devices of a sort, yet they do not follow those which I have learned. I must see them."

Farree shifted on his perch. The more he looked at the entangled maze of dark greenery before them, the less he could conceive of cutting any path through that without any tools. Perhaps a laser might clear the way but otherwise—

"Look." She was holding up that square of metal.

"Have you seen one of these before? The tourists use them for recording sights they wish to remember clearly. It works thus—or better have Krip show you, since this is not a thing of Thassa world."

He had taken the square back from her and now flipped it over to show two impressions on the back into which a man's forefingers might fit. "Let the reflection of what you would preserve so show in the mirror and then press here. Wait for the count of five and press again at this other spot and then it will clear and you can move to the next. It is simple and there is room for twenty shots before the power is exhausted and it must be recharged."

Lord-One Krip held it out and Farree accepted it gingerly. Yes, it sounded simple enough but he was unused to such off-world wonders and he only hoped that he could follow those directions without failure. Also there was something else to mind. He stood up, the picture square in his hands. He did not look to the tower in the lake, the very top of which was visible from where he stood, but rather back along the way they had come. Those who followed—surely they must be nearing now the end of that road through the mountain and might arrive at any moment. What then? Did they have time for such a task as they had set him now? What if those others could crouch in the rubble of the way and take both of the Thassa with their long-range weapons?

"Not so," Lord-One Krip answered his unasked question. "We keep guard and they, as always, will betray themselves by the nothingness their mind shields project."

"Still they will come—" Farree was as certain of that as he was now aware that he wore wings. Nor did he believe that even those could carry their prey away from those who followed.

"And we shall go," Lord-One Krip returned, "into that—" he gestured to the thick growth ahead.

"There is no way!"

The Lady Maelen smiled. "As long as the third ring holds, I have power, though my people would not have it so. However, since I have returned I have discovered it is not only the wand which controls, but rather the will and energy of the one who uses such. Yes, we can go but not from here. We shall move on to the north so that we give them no hint of what we have done. But you, winged brother, have that which will serve us best." She nodded toward the thing he now held.

Since he had no argument which would stand against her determination and self-confidence, Farree took off once more, rising above the screen of the thick brush and trees, heading for the island in the lake.

Only, as he winged so he felt naked and open to attack by the Guild hounds sniffing on their trail who could easily pluck him down with one laser blast. And he was glad when he settled again on the tower, a point from which he was sure he could record the best.

Slowly and with all the care he could summon he held the square of metal out over the first selection of the patterns below and pressed the depressions, counting aloud. He moved around the parapet of the tower, making sure that his record—if he was truly recording something—took in all those whirls, spirals, triangles, and arcs below. Having made the full circuit which would set those in order, he turned to the ones on the roofs and added them to his store.

They did not have much longer before Sotrath was gone and the third ring with it. Already that was fading into the grayish murk which preceded the sunrise. Clutching the picture taker to him, he arose aloft far enough above the lake as to hope to catch sight of the other two. But there was nothing in the place where he had left them nor anything to be seen along the northern edge of the forest ring. He dropped, to skim just a little above the tallest of the trees in that jungle, looking and then daring to send a mind call.

"The lake," came his answer. "Wait by the lake."

There was a ring of light gravel or sand between the edge of that jungle and the water. To that he dropped, folding his wings, still being surprised at how completely those crimped into place. There was yet some aching through his shoulders, but he judged that was from the use of muscles which had not been called into duty before and that it would vanish the longer he made use of his new appendages. The silent, undisturbed surface of the lake drew him now and he looked down into its surface as he might into a mirror.

He was—Farree could hardly believe what he saw there. For all his days he had gone misshapen and maimed among other life. Now he was complete. The tips of the wings arose a good five hands above that head which he was able to hold completely aloft. And the wings themselves were not dull but were covered with a satin-shining surface on which were dots and designs of a light green, the color of his skin. They were more magnificent, he thought, with the first swelling pride in himself that he had ever known, than any Lord's cloak of war or office.

He swung out farther over the water to see the better, and knew with every minute, every movement he was more and more what nature had always intended him to be. But what *was* he? Surely he had never been born on Grant's World, or someone in the Limits would have recognized him for what he was. Lanti—had he taken him there? For what reasons? Unless he had been meant to be sold to such as Russtif as a curiosity for showing after brutal training. There was something about his wings which brought a flash of memory. That brilliant scrap which the other Limits rogue had brought to Lanti too late to get an explanation. A piece of—wing! Surely that had been a piece of wing!

He felt cold. Perhaps it was from the predawn wind which had come to ruffle the mirror surface of the lake. But it might have been inside his small, spare body. Winged people hunted for their wings! It would not be the first time according to the legends often repeated in the Limits that a sentient race—and plenty of animals, too—had been wiped out for some special gain on the part of an off-worlder band. Maybe even Lanti had taken him to raise his own pair of wings so when the time came they could be harvested. Perhaps the spacer had wished to impress the Guild with treasure which was a part of Farree. Now that cold filled him, and he dropped back upon the apron of gravel between water and wood. To be hunted for his wings!

"Farree." The sharp mind call alerted him out of that momentary nightmare but he did not take to the sky. Stay on the ground, caution warned him, not let himself be seen by any hunter who had broken out of the mountain ways and now cast about for a fresh trail.

He saw, to his amazement, a quiver in that green wall, a lifting of branch, an uncoiling of vine, and then the Lord-One Krip came out into the open, leading Lady Maelen by one hand. She walked with her eyes open and staring ahead as one might walk mindlessly after some great shock. But she was also singing—a murmur of sound which had in its tempo something of the rustle of leaves, the scrape of branch against branch under a light wind. It would seem that even as her singing had wrought miracles in other places, even among the rocks, here it had tamed the ring jungle enough to let them through.

She pulled free of her companion's grasp and turned to face the woods from which they had just emerged. Now she held both hands out, palm up and empty, and her singing arose through a flight of notes such as might be caroled by a bird, then came to an end.

Lord-One Krip had already reached Farree and was holding out his hand for the mirror picture maker which the other surrendered to him with the hope that his use had been good enough to answer their questions.

The Lady Maelen, once more looking aware of what lay about her, came quickly over the pebbly beach to them.

Lord-One Krip had touched a place on the rim of the mirror, and now there appeared from the side of that square a strip of colored designs which certainly resembled those Farree had aimed to take with his mirror device. As this unrolled, the Lady Maelen laid it out on the gravel, pulling it straight before crouching down to inspect it closely. Sometimes she lifted a fingertip to trace one of those patterns as if to impress it the stronger on her memory.

"It is truly a locking," she observed. "As strong in its

way, Krip, as those persona locks off-worlders use for their most precious possessions. Here and here"—she made quick stabs with her finger—"are markings I have knowledge of—these are close to what is so used today. But others." She shook her head. "I can only guess that if one passes over them without proper preparation the result may be perilous indeed."

"What does all this protect?" Lord-One Krip put into words the first question in Farree's own mind.

"Something of the Thassa—but not of our time," she replied. "Here may be what those others have been seeking."

And these traps"—Lord-One Krip swept a hand above the roll of pictures now lying flat upon the ground—"will keep them from entering and finding what they seek?"

She shook her head slowly. "How can we be sure? This was made to warn off those of Yiktor. Will it also work against off-worlders of whom perhaps those who set it never guessed might try their success against the barriers?"

"So what defense have we left against them?" he proceeded.

Her hands arose and sketched a gesture which might have expressed helplessness. "We can only wait and see."

But Farree was not ready to accept that answer—the first he had ever had from her which carried no certainty, only confusion in it.

"How would one unlock this"—it was his turn to gesture—"if it was known?"

"It is a code of sorts," she explained. "One must move from pattern to pattern in a certain sequence and then it will open."

"And that invisible door will be gone?"

She nodded. "But the code was devised by those long gone, and there could be a hundred, even a thousand different sequences—the trying might go on for years, many seasons—and those who searched could come no nearer to success. There is nothing even in the far legends of the Thassa—those which are known to every Singer—which mentions such a find as this."

It was Farree's turn to study the strip of pictures. Those he sought were at the very end. "These four are patterns on the roof—are they any closer to the ones you know?"

She leaned forward. The gray of early morning light since the fading of the rings had deepened, and she squinted and then shook her head. "I cannot tell as yet. There is not enough light."

Lord-One Krip had arisen. "Let us get under cover," he said. "They could not have brought a flitter through the mountain way but they may have a course-setting device with them, and that would give them air support once they set it within this valley."

Withdraw they did under the fringe of trees beyond that ribbon of beach. There they huddled, not too far from each other, easing their tired bodies from the night's labor and travel. They drew lots for first sentry go and Farree had the shortest. He found his wings most difficult to manage, even when furled to the smallest and tightest extent it was possible to set upon them, and he had to push clear to the edge of their cover in order to have room.

The sun arose, almost reluctantly, and the glitter of the water as it had lain under the third ring was now a glare against which he had to shade his eyes. He chewed on one of the strips of journey food, finding it dry and tasteless, and listened intently for any sound of approach by air.

Even though he tried to keep his attention for what lay about and above him, he could not help now and then looking to the tower on the island, wondering if, under the sun, those complex patterns set in the stone were any clearer. Certainly they dared not attempt to solve the code now—the Lady Maelen had pointed out—as that might be a task which would take them long to solve, if ever. He found himself wondering what traps awaited those who did not know the secret at all. He was about to learn.

There were a continued rustling from the layer of jungle as if the plants therein were restless and were changing their positions. But there were no bird calls, no cry of beast, nor chirp of insect. The sullen green growth might have been bare of any life except that of its own. At times that continued rustling took on the sound of a muttered conversation, one which he could almost follow. Then he shook his head vigorously and moved about a little, thinking that it was lulling him into sleep.

The interruption came from a distance and he had plenty of time to reach out and touch Lord-One Krip's shoulder, the Thassa coming into instant awareness at that warning as if he had been only lying conscious with his eyes closed.

"Flitter!" Farree mind sent as if he could be overheard by the enemy even at this great distance. He jerked a thrust toward the south—that narrow rift through which they had come into this valley. In turn Lord-One Krip aroused the Lady Maelen, and the three of them drew a little more together, listening. There seemed to be no search pattern on the part of the air craft. By a continued and ever louder sound it was headed straight for the lake, no pattern of circling to pick up a trail.

"Back!" Lord-One Krip urged. The Lady Maelen was already burrowing into the bushes, and under the sound of the flitter Farree thought he could still hear the hum of her voice as if she once more used a Singer skill to help penetrate the jungle growth. That seemed useless—perhaps it would only work under the radiance of the ring—for he saw a branch spring back at her face, and, only because she threw up an arm, were those thorn marks on her forearm instead of across her very eyes.

At least they were under the edging of the wood and the gravel behind showed no discernible track. Though the off-worlders had their own ways of trailing, rumored machines and devices that picked up fugitives by their body heat when they were close enough.

The flitter was out cruising above the lake. Now it circled in a tight orbit around the tower. If they did know where the three lay in scant cover, they seemed to wish to learn more of the building they had chanced upon, for the craft made a third circle. Then it held steady about the tower and a ladder, such as Farree himself had once used to escape, tumbled out of a hatch in its belly.

Down that swung a man while another crouched at the exit, a laser across his arm at the ready, waiting to cover the journey of his comrade. The invader must have made some suggestions, for the flitter swung forward a fraction, and now he was descending past the roof of the tower into the patterned courtyard. He disappeared behind the wall, and a second explorer took his place on the ladder.

Sound—sudden, both sharp and deafening—cloaked even the clatter of the off-world engine. Then a rainbow of light fanned upward. All that glory of the third ring might have been condensed in that.

"No! Do not look!" The Lady Maelen's thought reached Farree and only half-consciously he obeyed, bending his arm across his eyes. He felt a warmth which was not that of sunlight but rather arose to near the torment of a fire as if he had set his hand to pick up a coal from a brazier, and his wings quivered under that fiery assault. The heat which reached them in such a flash must have been a hundredfold worse within that walled courtyard. Farree heard a scream that lasted only for a second and then was blasted away by the deafening sound rising to a crescendo. What luck had attended him last night when he might have encountered that same trap!

The heat seemed to hold for a long time, but he heard the sound die away and with it the noise of the flitter, in full retreat after losing two of its crew to whatever disaster was the guardian of the tower. A scent reached the three under the edge of the wood—not of the moon flowers which had perfumed the night, but a horrible stench of meat burnt to a crisp.

"They are gone," Lord-One Krip said. Farree wondered why he had not tried to track them himself by mind touch, catching that emptiness which was a shrouded mind. "They will be back," the Lord-One Krip added a moment later. "They will not let this puzzle be."

"Have they anything which can unlock the code?" asked the Lady Maelen. "Have you ever heard of such?"

"No. But that does not mean that they do not possess

one. The Guild have knowledge beyond that of any Free Trader such as I was. There are stories enough of what they have achieved."

"Then we must do our best. If this thing which is guarded here is by the will of ancient Thassa, they must not have it!" She crept on her hands and knees out of the shadow of the bush which had left the scarlet wounds down her arm and reached again for the pictures that had issued from the mirror. Now she turned her attention from those of the courtyard to the patterns Farree had found on the roof of the tower. With her forefinger she traced one design after another.

"They would put their most formidable weapon in the courtyard," she said slowly. "I do not think that they would much expect any to enter from the air. Thus these are the important ones for us." And her finger went once more over the designs, and she was humming again but not the lazy half-sleepy sound which she had uttered in defense against the jungle belt.

"We cannot dare to try until the moon rises—"

"By then," Farree interrupted, "those may be back with something to open that tower as one opens a bra-crab shell."

She nodded. "That is so. Time lies on their side of the balance. But I cannot believe that the Scales of Molester are so weighed against us who would save patterns of time and space and not blast them into nonexistence. We must wait through the day, save our strength—"

"I cannot carry you to the tower and there is the lake to cross," Farree pointed out. He wondered if they would dare to swim—could they swim? The arid country which seemed home to the Thassa might not have given them any reason for the sport. And though Lord-One Krip had been first a Free Trader spacer, certainly he would have had little enough reason to perfect such a skill either.

"I know," she returned and there was a troubled note in her voice.

"A rope"—Lord-One Krip was looking back into the gloom of the jungle—"one of those lianas, were it tough enough, or a weaving of vines—"

"They live," Lady Maelen told him quickly, "with more of a real life than any rooted thing I have seen before."

"But they also die." He pointed in two places where the full roundness of life had shrunken away and there were brownish loops which were plainly dead or near that state. "Can the dead protest?"

"I do not know," she answered frankly. "It is of importance, this rope of yours?"

"It is the only way, I think, of reaching the island," he returned firmly. Though Farree could not see any reason for such confidence.

"Ah, well—" She arose and went to where one of those dead coils spanned a tree from branch to branch. Slowly she raised her hand and set it on the brown surface, tugging at it a fraction. Nothing around her moved or strove to make her pay for her audacity. She pulled harder and began her humming song. Within a few moments the arc of the dead vine was free of the branches, looping to the ground and beyond out on the gravel of the beach. Lord-One Krip was on it instantly. So she wrought with two other vines, and they were in time laid along the surface of the beach in lengths beyond the height of the tower itself, or so Farree believed.

"Leaves." Lord-One Krip stood up from stretching the last of those vines in place. "Such a leaf as that." Again he pointed to a bush standing taller than his own head. The bottom leaves of that plant—the ones reaching out over the beach—were also spotted with brown and plainly dying. Their hard, thick sides were rolled up so that they formed a half tube and were large enough for the Thassa to lie upon. "Can these be detached also?"

The Lady Maelen went to the plant and knelt as it towered over her. Her singing became another series of notes, and Farree thought he could almost read a petition into that. Then she leaned forward and set a hand to either side of the leaf and strove to draw it to her. There was no movement save the constant tensing of her body. At least, as it had been with the dead vines, the growth itself made no attack. Then the rotted core of the leaf gave away suddenly so that she sprawled backward, the broken stem dripping with a black liquid which gave off the foul odor of decay.

When a second leaf had been so released from a similar plant Lord-One Krip set them all to work, braiding the tough vine lengths into one knobby rope. When he had done, he took one of the long leaves down to the water and floated it, throwing himself facedown upon it and pushing out a little from the shore. Though it bobbed downward under his weight, yet it supported his head and shoulders above water.

"This"—he indicated the rope—"well fastened to a rock over there"—his wide gesture indicated the island—"can be used to draw us through the water." He would be trusting a great deal to dead vegetation, Farree thought, but there was a small chance that such might work. His own part of the task was simple compared to theirs. What if they reached the water and the flitter returned?

He had great respect for the Lady Maelen's third ring powers, but this they must do now and the sun gave them nothing but light. However, the trial must be made.

With the end of the coil fastened to his belt he soared up and out across the lake, heading directly for a fringe of rocks before the wall of the courtyard. Once there he hastened to make fast the rope's end to the most slender of those rocks. Lord-One Krip had to wade into the water a little, holding the other end, but it did reach, and he was tugging hard on it, testing its stability.

The Lady Maelen came first, lying in her curled leaf with both hands overhead on the rope, pulling herself along. Against a troubled and current-riven water she would not have succeeded, but the pull across the calm surface, though it seemed to take endless time, was at last accomplished, and Farree flew back with the rope's end to the waiting Krip.

For the second time a leaf made that hardly believable voyage and then, the rope coiled about Farree's arm, the three of them stood before the wall surrounding the courtyard.

··•)18(•··

Farree crouched on the top of the wall and determinedly did not look to the two twisted burnt things that lay before the invisible door. A laser had fallen from the charred claws of one to skid across the courtyard against the wall not too far away. Could he manage to reach the small strip of pavement there which was free of pattern and retrieve it? The thought of such a weapon for their defense was irresistible. He laid aside the rope which he had carried up and gestured toward the two below, off before they might object.

Down he fluttered, not sure yet of his wing power but impatient to get his hands on the weapon. He made a swoop, gasped suddenly as he lengthened out with his body parallel to the ground, and managed to claw up the butt end of the laser, climbing up into the air and then bouncing over the wall top to the two Thassa below. He offered the weapon to Lord-One Krip, who reached for it quickly.

Now, whether his weight on the end of the rope would

be anchorage enough he did not know. In the end he picked that up and did not try to fasten it on the wall but spiraled over to the tower where he could anchor it on one of the jutting bits of the parapet. Then he returned to the wall top where they speedily joined him.

The Lady Maelen lay down and edged along that length of barrier top until she could see the pattern which had been the fatal trap for the Guild men. Farree could sense her aversion to what she saw there, but he also knew that she was driven by duty to consider what manner of trap that was—if she could equate it with something her people still had knowledge of.

"Force released," she said slowly. "After all these tens of tens of tens of seasons that which was set answered."

"But I landed there earlier and nothing happened," Farree commented.

"By luck you must have touched a pattern which was not one set for defense."

He studied the designs carefully. Yes, he had stood at the edge of a crimson circle a foot or so away from the square of wavy blue lines which had been the downfall of the dead men below.

"Dare we cross?" Lord-One Krip wanted to know.

With a pointing finger the Lady Maelen was tracing in the air the patterns between them and the narrow edging of plain stone about the foundation of the tower.

"I do not know. There is a maze there, a curve here, a suggestion of a code. But without full knowledge . . ." She shifted her sight toward the two bodies and shivered. "They will be back," she said then as if speaking thoughts aloud.

"With enough power to blast the place open," Lord-One Krip returned. "Perhaps they will so trigger that as to destroy all of this wholly."

She shook her head. "They want this too much. Or what they think it holds. Remember Sehkmet. They have traced us—some of them—believing we can uncover such another cache for their taking. Now on Thassa world they have found this. Their first defeat was a small one in their eyes. They will be ready to follow through."

"Look you"—Farree gave a tug to the rope against which he had been pitting his full strength—"can you use this to swing across and land by the tower, then climb?"

Lord-One Krip stood up and eyed the rope and its tower anchor with narrowed eyes. "One can try."

His hand twitched the rope out of Farree's hold and bent its own strength in a grip which kept it taut, then jerked at it. The rope held. He clasped it tightly and swung down and out across the treacherous pavement, descending so far that Farree was afraid his feet would scrape across the inlaid stones. Then he was at the foot of the tower and was climbing. His feet set to the wall itself, his arms extending one above the other, he used the rope to raise him. They watched him, tense and frozen, until he was at the parapet and over. Then Farree leapt into the air and spanned the distance between them with the aid of his wings, caught the end of the rope, and bore it back to the Lady Maelen.

For the second time, he witnessed the dangerous swing past the dead and saw her being drawn up by the man on the tower. He whirred across and was there to meet her. For a long moment she leaned against the parapet until her breath steadied, but she was staring down at the patterns now revealed below her.

"The third ring," she said slowly. "These are markings very old—if I had time I could perhaps trace a key to this locking. But we must have Sotrath above us when we try."

Lord-One Krip looked to the sky. "There are hours before we shall have that. They may well be back long before the third ring shines."

She shrugged. "In that we must take our chance. If they come—"

"He will come." Farree knew that as well as if it had been announced out of the air above his head. "Their leader will make this his own venture."

Lord-One Krip nodded. "That it seems we must chance. If he is the regular Guild Veep he will make sure of his armament, of no more losses such as he has suffered here. And—"

Toggor suddenly turned from the place he had climbed to on the parapet, his eyestalks out to their full limit, his gaze on the shore from whence they had come. If Farree had caught that message, so had the Thassa. Beyond the maze ring of vegetation the enemy moved. Those who had followed them through the mountain were now prepared to batter a way through the tangled growth.

"Yes." The Lady Maelen nodded. "However—" She, too, had wheeled about to face the growing barrier and now she planted both hands palm down on a curling line of vivid green set with yellow stars of gems which crawled toward them as part of the tower pattern. She knelt so, unable to see now above the parapet, though she faced in the same direction as Toggor.

"Feed me!" she commanded fiercely. "Feed!"

The Lord-One Krip went down on one knee, his hand cupping the point of her shoulder, his other hand reaching out toward Farree. Not knowing just what was to be done, the winged man settled down, awkwardly now because of his wings, but placing one hand within those groping fingers which caught on his with a painful grasp.

Farree gasped. Something was being drawn from his body, flowing on to Lord-One Krip, then presumably to the Lady Maelen. Her face was so tense and set the flesh seemed but a shallow covering to her bones. She began to sing, first in the low hum he had heard her use to force a path from the growth—then the notes scaled up, grew louder, some ringing out as if she had beaten a gong rather than used her voice to shape them. In the day she sang—would the power without the moon answer?

Though Farree had knelt to take Lord-One Krip's hand, he could see above the parapet against which his shoulder rubbed. Suddenly it was as if a storm cloud had released a wave of wind instead of water. The growth tossed. He could see branches move, vines writhe, some even appearing to unknot themselves and toss loose ends in the air, darting about like the heads of scaled things. This wild rippling ran in both directions. He believed he could even sight bits of leaf and vine which broke loose and wafted along on the surface of that wind out of nowhere.

Farree felt the energy drain from him. Something he had never known existed was being tapped and going through his hold upon the Thassa to sustain that desperate song. He put his other hand to the parapet where Toggor crouched. Now he saw that the smux was rocking back and forth, clacking his larger claws together in part rhythm with the song.

For a while it held loud and steady, and then it began to slow. He could see the drops of sweat running down the Lady Maelen's cheeks, felt her fight to keep on. However, there came an end at last. She swayed and would have fallen had not Lord-One Krip seized her, snatching his hand from Farree and pulling her back against him for her support. A last bit of song, hardly above a whisper, came from her lips and then, eyes closed, mouth gaping, she lay limp in his hold.

The wind or stirring out of nowhere died. Farree tried hard to pick up that nothingness which was the mark of the shielded enemy. There! He had touched one—quickly he searched but there seemed to be no others. Toggor had sunk down, drawn in his eyestalks as he did when he must rest.

Rest! Farree leaned sidewise against the stone, his wings together and folded, an ache in his head and a feeling of emptiness inside him. He was as hollow now as if he had been squeezed by some great hand and flung aside to lie without substance.

For how long that lasted he could not tell. There was a feeble stirring in his mind that they must be again on guard ready for death coming from the skies. Yet he must have slept, for he awoke from that place of nothingness with a hand shaking him, and then Lord-One Krip forced into his hold some of the rations which they had relied upon so long—dry and tasteless, yet he choked mouthfuls down.

The sun no longer burned down upon them but sped

across the sky into red sunset clouds, and the Lady Maelen was sitting up, turning her head slowly from one side to the other as if she had awakened out of a dream and could not recognize where she was. Then recognition came back to her eyes and she smiled wearily.

"Let Sotrath rise," she said slowly, "then we shall see whether, though I am wandless, I am still too lacking in the Gift to do what must be done. At least this day past I have wrought more than I would have believed possible. This is truly a place of power."

"Lacking!" Lord-One Krip burst out. "When you awoke the woods rang . . ."

Her smile grew a little stronger. "Yes, that I did. I am still a Singer."

"One of the mighty ones!" Lord-One Krip said forcibly. "Let them try to deny you your due now!"

"Hush." She put her hand to his lips. "I do what I can, but to claim full mastery is false." She reached out to touch that line set in the stones, to fit fingertip to each of the stones in it. "That this answered the three of us after all the lost time—that is not *my* mastery but that of those great ones who set it here."

"And those who hunt us?" Farree sputtered through dry crumbs.

"Ask that of them." She pointed toward the wood. "They are a greater barrier than even I could guess. Look!" She pointed now to the eastern sky where the dusk crept down like a curtain. Showing just a tip about it was a thing of glitter which he had come to cherish. The third ring was beginning to rise—the time of the Thassa power at its height was coming!

It seemed to Farree that the dusk came more swiftly than usual. As if the very longing of the Lady Maelen had the power to summon up Sotrath and the moon rings. Yet she did not look to the sky but ran her hands up the curving side of one pattern and down the arabesque of another as if her touch could find what she sought quicker than her sight. Perhaps that was so far; just as she had chosen certain stones to rub when she sang their partnership to the woods, now did she settle at last at the farther side of the roof, waving the other two to the blank border beside the parapet while she settled herself on her knees, leaning well forward so that the palms of her hand each cupped a series of three greenish stones which gleamed the brighter as the third ring crept up the sky behind her head.

Once more she began to sing—this time no hum without words, but rather a chant that accented some syllables with the beat of a drum. That sound gripped Farree and perhaps also the Lord-One Krip, for Farree noted that the spaceman's hands were opening and closing, where they hung by his sides, in time to that beat in words.

Farree had begun to believe that indeed she could accomplish great things by her words alone. He had seen sound shatter crystals once or twice in the Limits, when some sleight-of-hand dealer was showing off skills. Why then could such not pick up the resonance of a voice at proper pitch and be moved by it as was a lock with a key laid into its proper slot?

By the time Sotrath itself was showing on the horizon and the arc of the third ring well advanced, bringing rainbows of light from the pavement, she did indeed achieve what she had set to do. There was another sound across the beat of her voice and before her a dark outline framed a good section of the roof.

Her voice arose in a triumphant crescendo and the block so outlined was sucked downward out of their sight.

Farree gave a cry, clapping his hands to his head. Into his mind there burst such a flash or lash of sights and sounds, of places and people, he felt that his very head would split open, not being able to hold or control this wave of otherness. Lord-One Krip likewise doubled near over as if some mighty blow had sent him reeling, and his hands also clawed over his ears; while the Lady Maelen crouched low, her face drawn and contorted into grimaces, her whole body tensed and resisting.

It was, Farree decided, as if a whole world of different thought had been launched at them. He fought, trying to set in his mind a wall behind which that that was he himself could crouch protected.

Half expecting a company of Thassa or their like to come boiling up through the door, a company the Lady Maelen had sung into their defenses, Farree could see only the dark oblong at their feet, and in that nothing moved nor climbed to meet them. Wall! Think a wall! Farree's wings moved without conscious thought and he was up—into the night, soaring above the top of the tower. Yet those hundreds, thousands of thoughts (though they were a little muffled) beat at him. He thought a wall, barrier so tight set that nothing could breach it. As he circled on wings about the tower, unwilling to desert those two who did not have his advantage for a quick escape, he was aware that the thought stream was thinning, that now only a trickle of such came through.

The Lady Maelen was on her feet, though Lord-One Krip still crouched low, his head swinging from side to side as if the very weight of that storm of thought was launched against him in one wave after another. The Lady Maelen held forth the light globe which had guided them through the mountain passage, and that gathered to it the ring's glory until she had cupped a great ball of fire. With that hand stretched before her, she approached the opening, looking down into the depths beneath.

What she saw there Farree could not imagine. When he watched her prepare to descend through that opening he swooped, determined to catch her before she was swallowed up by that maelstrom of mind speech. But he was too late, and, in spite of all his efforts, the clamor caught him again, driving him in self-protection to the edge of the parapet where he strove to shake the Lord-One Krip into action.

Only, it would appear that the man was also still caught in the invisible storm they had loosed. He moaned a little, and his eyes had turned upward in his head so that the whites were visible. Had he been able to manage the other's weight Farree would have hoisted him up, gotten him away from that perilous open door. Now he could only stay beside him, strive to move in his own mental picture of a wall set against the flood.

The light beamed upward from the opening. He did not think he could have entered, even with his mind at rest. It was not big enough to take his spread of wings no matter how much he could try to compress those. But for the Lady Maelen to go alone into that place! Urgently he shook Lord-One Krip until the other's head flopped forward and backward on his shoulders. Then he felt the other begin to gain control, and a moment later the man's eyes were turned up to meet his.

"The . . . m-minds," he stammered, "they are—"

"Can such a place hold an army?" demanded Farree. "Whence comes all this?"

"Memories, all the thoughts—of a race!" Lord-One Krip straightened in his hold, and Farree released him.

"She's gone—down there! I cannot reach her. Can you?" Farree demanded.

"Not now. If I loose—I am lost."

Yet they both crept on hands and knees, one on either side of the trapdoor, striving to see what did lie below. Whether that wave of mind touch that had been building for generations could be loosed suddenly without disaster Farree did not know, but he felt that the pressure against his mental wall was less than it had been. And now he could see.

The Lady Maelen stood below a short ladder, and around her body there was an aura of the light from the globe—perhaps that served as her defense. About her also were racks towering side to side, leaving only the small space where the ladder had given her entrance. And the racks were filled with a series of blocks which pulsated with rainbow colors in a mixture that hurt the eyes almost as much as the wave of mind touch had near toppled their other senses. Scarlet, vivid orange, green in five or six violent shades, blue the same—violet to purple. It was unbelievable. She was just standing there, her head slowly swinging from side to side, her face a mask in which not even her eyes moved—like one asleep who yet walked.

Before either of them could move, she shifted the ball into her left hand and with the right she reached out toward one of the racks.

"No!" Lord-One Krip cried out, and Farree could have echoed him. But if she heard, that protest had no meaning for her. Her fingers closed about a cube which was gem-bright in green, and she plucked it out of the serried ranks of its like and held it to the level of her eyes. It was as if she both saw and heard something in its heart which kept her mazed. Then swiftly she stored it back with its fellows and turned to the ladder, coming up to them in haste.

Under the light of the third ring her own gleaming hair, her ivory-pale skin, took on ripples of the lights, but she still walked as one in a trance. Lord-One Krip reached for her as she came within grasping distance, pulled her up toward him as if he needs must draw her out of some great trap. She did not try to throw off his hold, but she turned with it, holding her globe up to the glory of the third ring and then lowering it to focus its beams on the very stones she had used to open the door. And her chant sounded clear in the night air, the drumbeat of the unknown words harsher and faster as if now she worked against time itself. Even as that aperture had opened so now it closed. Only when that was done did she look to the two of them as if she knew them again.

"Down. We must get down. To the courtyard!" She pushed away from Lord-One Krip and indicated that treacherous pavement below.

"It is"—Farree swinging upward dared to look again at the two huddled bodies below—"a trap."

"Yes," she agreed. "And it must be reset—reset for greater prey! I must do that, by the third ring!"

With the aid of the vine rope they made it. She waved Lord-One Krip away and pointed to certain lines of the patterns.

"Walk so and so." She motioned. "Get to the other wall and up! We may have very little time. Those others will come." It was as if she had knowledge they did not share.

Lord-One Krip stared at her for a long moment and then did as she had told him. Farree flew to give them an escape route, knotting the vine this time to a hard rock near the shore and feeding the free end into the courtyard. But Lord-One Krip would retreat no farther than the wall itself.

The Lady Maelen was singing again. She did not approach the part of the designs where lay the dead off-worlders, but she paced other sections, showing great care where she trod, and sang the same harsh song she had used to close the door above. Three times she rounded the tower and each time the uneasiness in Farree rose. He felt Toggor crowd tightly against him, and the fear in the smux fed his own.

Then, having trod on the pattern before all the four walls, the Lady Maelen ran toward them. Lord-One Krip caught her and tossed her body a little upward so that she clutched the vine rope at a higher level. Then he was hard behind her as she climbed and slid down to the other side.

"It is done." She was panting, her body sleekly wet with sweat, her face drawn and haggard. "And none too soon— The rocks—those—take shelter—" She did not have to utter any warning. They had already heard the beat of the flitter in the sky, saw riding lights like the eyes of a vast insect coming down the valley even as it had earlier flown.

They lay belly down behind the screen of rocks, Farree crimping his wings into the smallest possible space. On the flitter came, and he heard the Lady Maelen: "They know something. Surely they would not come under the ring. But no Thassa would deal with them. What secret has been betrayed that they hunt so?" It was as if she asked that question of the world at large.

Over swung the air craft. It hung at hover, and this time dropped two from its belly onto the top of the tower. At least they had learned that much from their abortive earlier attempt.

"Yes." The Lady Maelen's voice was only a breath of whisper, and then she added, "Now, let it be now!"

As to what followed Farree could never afterwards settle in his own mind. It was as if the rays of the third ring awoke to life every gemlike stone so that beams of raw and eye-burning color flashed out. Not only at the men who had landed on the roof but upwards far enough to transfix the flitter in turn. Farree thought he heard screams—he was never sure because it all happened so suddenly.

But the beams of gem light became flamelike and they licked about the flitter, drawing it down into their heart fire. Then the tower itself quivered and blazed until he dared not look at it any longer. It—it melted! There was no other way he could describe what happened, for its sides grew soft as thray wax under the sun and spun oddly outward in droplets—though none of those sped beyond

the courtyard wall. But the tower sank and was gone, and
the lights failed so only that of the third ring held. There
came sobbing from where the Lady Maelen lay and Lord-
One Krip edged closer to take her into his arms.

"They are . . . dead," she stammered, "they are dead
and with them all their knowledge. It is a second death
and one—one which I delivered to them!"

Farree answered, "But they were Guild and—"

"Not the Guild, those are dead of their own greed. It
was—the ancient memories—those stored lest Thassa
need the weight of them again. But they had their own
defense, and that I set. You do not understand. We were
once so great a people that the Guild, all off-world could
not have troubled us. Then it was chosen that we should
take another path. But there were those who argued that
all knowledge should not be wiped from the face of Yiktor.
So they set the memory tower and each memory was
stored there—all the knowledge of untold time which we
cannot count in seasons or Sotrath rings anymore. All of it
gone—and by my doing!" She was weeping now, and her
head fell forward onto Lord-One Krip's shoulder.

They stood again in the great hall that Farree had first
seen after the landing on Yiktor. The Lady Maelen was a
little before them, facing those leaders of her people, her
head proudly high. There had been a reading of minds,
and she it was who insisted upon judgment. Now it was
the elder of the women who spoke.

"Always you have gone your own way, Maelen. And
always trouble and sorrow comes from it. So the great
memories are gone. Well, none can bring them back.

Nor"—she spoke more slowly now—"since there are those who would take them for a bitter use, can we wish them so. But we say to you a second time, Kinswoman, there is no place for you, by three rings or two. You are no longer Thassa but something else—we know not what. Nor can you slip within the shell of the people. Come to us when you desire but do not hope to stay—for there is that within you which cannot be fitted into our life again any more than a flower can be fitted back into the tight curl of a bud. We do not exile you—"

"No," the Lady Maelen said slowly. "That I have done for myself. I am grateful that you do not turn from me."

"There is this—" The woman held forth a wand which one of the men had handed to her.

"No, that I leave also. I am no longer a Moon Singer, Elder. I sang death to the past—"

"You did as it seemed fit. But, yes, the wand is not a part of the future for you. And you are wise in your own way. Where do you go now?"

"Out to the stars!"

"And the enemy who would trace you?"

"Perhaps dead, perhaps alive. But that is a matter for the future—"

"And you, Krip Vorlund?"

He took a step forward until he stood equal with Maelen to confront them all. "Where she goes thus do I also."

The Elder nodded and then looked to Farree, whose wings moved wide to show the gleaming patches on them. "And you, little brother?"

He drew a deep breath and voiced it now, just as it had

come to him from the moment that those spans of glory had broken from his ugliness. "I would find my world—"

"So be it. And we wish you three well. You have done what was to be done—hold it not in your memories as any evil. Time turns awry and straight in many ways. We grant you time as a companion, and may it serve you well."

Farree opened and closed his wings, his head held high now. Time—there was time always ahead, even though a man could hold nothing but now in his two hands. He would have *his* chosen now—he vowed that. Suddenly he felt his hand taken by the Lady Maelen and he realized that his time would be their time also. For the first time in his life he was warmly content.

Dare to Go
A-Hunting

For Ingrid who wanted a story of the People—

Up the airy mountain,
Down the rushy glen,
We dare not go a-hunting,
For fear of little men.
—William Allingham

··●) 1 (●··

It was warm, too warm for one of the room's inhabitants. However, it was probably discourteous to remark upon the heat though a round drop of sweat gathered just below one of his slightly slanted eyes to trickle down his cheek. There was a small rustle when he shifted position on the uncushioned stool which supported him an uncomfortable height from a floor of tiles matched in brilliant color to form patterns which he could only glance at or it made his eyes ache. That his host not only accepted all this as natural, but took comfort in it was one of those irritating situations which had filled Farree's life for some time.

He had seen aliens a-plenty during his bad time in that sleazy portside district, the Limits, which formed his earliest memories. However, such strangers in their own homes were something he was now only being introduced to by the full swing of fate's finger crystal.

"Hot." Togger's thought, always pitched so high that his own sense could hardly understand, came testily. Farree's jerkin heaved and wrinkled as the smux crawled out into the open to gaze up into his face with stalked eyes.

"Soooo—it is hot, little one?" Not a thought this time but words uttered with a hissing intonation. At a goodly distance down the room a third inhabitant arose, the extended talons on his webbed and scaled feet scraping across the stone pattern on the floor. "Courtesy is all very well, my little friends, but allow me also the privilege of displaying it." A yellow scaled arm, banded at both wrist and above the elbow with well-worn cuffs of an iron-hard wood, reached out to the wall and flipped a switch.

There was no sound of any winds, yet there blew across the room now a swift breeze, tepidly warm to be sure, but at least better than the slow baking heat it disturbed. He who had summoned that now came threading a path between small tables and large—all piled with learning tapes and scan plates in boxes. Farree gave a, he hoped, concealed sigh of relief. Those folds draped across his shoulders, extending down his back so that their edges swept the floor, rose in turn. He did not flourish the wings in full display—he needed more room for that—but at least he could give them a stretch.

The tall old alien watched Farree almost eagerly. He had swept a whole cascade of scan plate boxes to the floor and seated himself with a little grunt and some rubbing of one scaled and plated knee.

Then he leaned forward, setting the palms of his hands on both knees. Farree did not know how long Zacanthans continued to inherit this plane of existence (which was how they referred to life and death) but he was sure that Grand Hist-Technneer Zoror was indeed a long-time master of that skill which, as with all his species, centered upon the collection of information about oddities in a well-spread galaxy—especially the history of such new races as were introduced from time to time into the records of exploration. They were indeed long-lived, these lizardlike people, but even the oldest of them often asserted that he was only beginning his labors.

"Soooo—" Once more Zoror made a hissing of the word. "You wish now that this old man of scales would come directly to the point and tell you what you are and from whence you have come." The Zacanthan nodded so that the pleated frill of skin which lay about the back of his head and shoulders unfolded into a fan like some large ornamental collar.

"It is not easy, you know," Zoror continued. "We cannot walk to the records and say 'Tell me who is this winged one? From what earth and people did he spring?' These," he again flung out an arm to gesture at the unwieldy piles of tapes and spools fencing them both in, "these are records of voyages, many, many voyages, also contributed by men who tell strange tales, sometimes merely out of their own imagination, but other times bearing a truth which—if the Ever Mighty is helpful—can be traced about this far!" He held up a hand to display a thumb and forefinger with a space between them maybe as big as one of Togger's second claws.

"There—there was nothing then?" Farree had curbed his patience all morning, ever since all he could remember had been fed into the read-all of the big computer. His scant store of information had been recorded to match mixtures of still dubious details.

"No, I do not say that. There are stories of such as you. Those come from the bards of Loel, the Rememberers of Garth, the Dance-think of Udolf. Stories, mind you, garnered on more than a hundred planets. But—it remains that they are stories without concrete proof. Those who retell them gather details on this world or that. But the strongest of all—those come from Terra—"

"Terra? But that is but a tale, too." Farree did not try to hide his disappointment.

"Not so—" Zoror's neck frill fluttered as he shook his head. "However, there is something common to all the worlds from which the clearest and most detailed of these stories come. Those were the planets first colonized by people from Terra. Yes, most certainly there was a Terra. It bred several races, in all of which there was one abiding gift, that of curiosity. Terrans were not the first explorers of the space dark, yet they spread farther in less time than many of those who came before. And with them they brought, as we all do, tales which were old and yet part of their lives."

Farree's face creased in a frown. Zoror, for all his learning, was apt to tell stories, too. Ordinarily Farree would have listened with interest. However, what he wanted now was truths, even if they afforded only a very thin thread to trace. "These from Terra—they were certainly not like me." He put up a hand to touch the edge of one wing.

"No. They were not Farrees—" Zoror assured him. "Only stories of such they did carry. In their tales—much of this was researched and put together by Zahaj in a mist of years ago—in their tales they spoke of 'Little People,' which lived sometimes underground—"

Farree unfolded his wings another fraction. "With these they could not!" he countered.

"True, true. But there were different species or races of them. Some were wingless according to the tales. They all had a strange relationship with the men of Terra. Sometimes they were good friends, again they were blood enemies. It is said that they often stole the children of men and raised them, to renew and enrich their own blood. For they were very old so at times their race dwindled until only a handful of them remained. They were supposed to have great treasures—perhaps even records!" Zoror's voice soared high. "Only there always came a time when the men drove them from their homes—perhaps not wantonly (though there are legends about such deeds as that also) but because they held land men wanted. And all know the stories of the ever-living greed of Terra which spread like a mist-dark cloud wherever their ships touched, until there came the Great Reckoning.

"Before that these winged and unwinged ones fled along the star roads not knowing where they might land. They found worlds to settle for a space. But always the same such worlds drew the Terrans. They would come so that the Little People must once more take to space. This has happened many times over, judging by legends we have recorded. However, at last there were no more reports of them, only what remained in songs and stories."

"Did they war with the Terrans then?" Farree's mouth was dry. He must have squeezed Togger too hard for the smux twisted about and gave a warning nip to a finger.

"There was a war, yes, though we hear little of that— mainly a ballad over some Terran killed by the evil magic of the Little People. From Udolf, for example, there comes a whole set of dance songs lamenting some leaders who died from weapons known to the Little People alone. They must have practiced also some form of mind control, for they would keep men within their hold for what seemed a day or a year and then let their captives go, for them to discover that they had really been gone from their homes for a matter of years. There is also the Mingra report. Come and see for yourself."

Farree followed the Zacanthan to the larger table where there were even more piles of tapes balanced perilously. Zoror began to clear these away, piling them on the floor. Farree stooped quickly to help him, folding his wings tight again lest he cause some disaster.

"This is old, too, by the reckoning of most." The Hist-Technneer was fussing with a reader, making sure the machine was in proper position.

"Mingra?" That was a word Farree had never heard before.

"The darkened world—the world of the dead-alive—" Zoror was more intent on the disc he was fitting into the reader than he was to any question. "Now this"—he gave the roll a last turn, slipping it into place—"was the Shame of Mingra, the Shame of all who are space travelers— though perhaps it has so faded during the years that it is only alive as a poisonous whisper by now. Watch with care—for into it has gone the hate of one species for another and yet there is nothing to explain—"

His voice died away in a final hiss. Farree obediently looked at the small screen. Togger moved impatiently in his grasp until he placed the smux down carefully on the table before the screen. Togger drew himself into a ball and perhaps went to sleep. For Farree there was no sleep.

He had seen plenty, since his arrival at Zoror's home which was also headquarters for a whole quadrant of researchers, of such records. Some had been so wildly fantastic that he had been sure they were indeed travelers' tall tales and not any true garnering of knowledge.

A picture formed on the screen. Farree jerked, half arose from his seat. For there was not only an ominous picture of a sphere, half lit at one edge by a red beam. But in his head—

He could not say it was a song, he could not even distinguish what must be wholly alien words. Yet deep into him had struck the thought-feeling that this held a truth which was evil and powerful. Gripping the edge of the table he made himself sit again but he did not loose his sustaining hold.

"Hurt—dark—hurt—" The smux had unrolled from his sleep ball and crouched before the screen, waving his great claws back and forth as if he were facing some dire danger.

That thread of sound swelled and, as if it called for sight, the red light on the screen blazed higher to display a barren stretch of riven rocks which were eroded, or perhaps storm-clawed, into ridges and plateaus. Shadows still clung to the feet of those outcrops and these dark wisps moved as if thrown by some source other than the rocks against which they sulked.

There was fear—a fear which arose and strengthened—which began to twist within Farree. A pile of reading rolls crashed to the floor as his wings answered to the unconscious stimulus.

With the speed of a laser shot a head flashed into the

bloody light. It was the epitome of all evil Farree had ever known. It clashed broken-toothed jaws together, and eyes like pits with a fire deep held stared straight at him. It knew, it hated, it was coming from him! And it was—

"Boogy—" The hissing of Zoror broke that fearful hold which the screened creature had half woven about Farree—either to draw him into its place or to burst forth from the screen—how could it? This was unlike any reading roll he had seen. From whose mind had this horror been shifted for future study—and where— when—?

"This was a collective nightmare," Zoror said. Farree heard him but more than half of his own attention was still centered on that thing. It had emerged from the shadow now. The mist lay shrunken behind as if its substance had been stolen to give the creeper more reality. Creep the creature did. Stunted limbs supported it—no, not limbs but rather thick tentacles; and Farree believed that he could actually hear the sound of suckers being pulled loose from the rock to be set again as it advanced.

Nightmare? This was more alive than any nightmare. Enough to bring death if it struck through sleep.

"Which it did," the Zacanthan said. "Look to the rocks at the right, my little friend."

Farree felt that if he withdrew his attention from the crawler he would leave an opening for attack, even if this was a read-roll. However, he gave a quick glance in the direction the Zacanthan suggested.

There was no shadow at the foot of this standing stone; rather it was crowned with such. The form was humanoid and—Farree sucked in a breath and swallowed a cry.

For it was a winged one standing there, and he knew without being told that this one controlled the creeper, was sending it at some prey, not to slay—at least not at first—but to torment with fear. A winged one. He gave it full attention now. Its flesh, shown in limb and arm and face, was a dirty grey. The eyes, like those of the thing it commanded, were red and burning. About its body was tight clothing, also of a red to match the ever-lightening sky. Those wings which lazily fanned the air were not like Farree's, broad and colored, with one hue melting into another, so that full-spread the pinions were things of soft beauty. No, this leader of merciless shadows had wings which lacked the feathery down which covered Farree's. Instead they were the same foul greyish shade as the skin. Spread out they displayed perilous-appearing hooks at the top.

"Winged—" Farree half whispered. To the fear which still coiled within him was added now true horror. Was this what could claim him as kin—in spite of Zoror's talk about true tales and false? Somehow he knew that this *was* a true tale—

"Only to two." Zoror picked up his thought, and, for the first time since he had discovered his gift because he could communicate with smux, Farree resented that this was so.

"Two," Zoror leaned over and one of his well-smoothed finger claws touched a control which sent the screen dead again. Yet when Farree looked at it, he could still see that abomination winged and aloft on the rock waving forward the horror born of shadows.

"The two," the Zacanthan was proceeding, "being he

who dreamed and he, or perhaps it, who sent such a dream! This was taken from the dream sleep of a small child, one of the many who were brought for treatment from Mingra to Yorum well over a hundred planet years ago. Five only of those little ones survived. The rest—nightmares such as you have just seen pursued them, until some died of fear alone and some then retreated so far from the outer world in their terror that none could reach within where they cowered. Thus they became the lost which we could not help."

"But you speak of shame—" countered Farree. He had seen what could be unending fear perhaps, but there was no shame that he could understand. Any child, yes, and fully grown adult, too, would have no shame for such fear.

"There was on Mingra a colony of dream-sleepers and they were learning how to control their dreams," Zoror explained. "When they were called upon to help, when children howled and screamed in their sleep—they fled and refused any aid. Those who dream-sleep hover always on the thin line of what most men call madness. They have been known to strike out in their sleep, even take up weapons in their hands, to the hurt of any who may be with them. Thus they are sent into wilderness until they learn to control their powers. If this dream recording you have seen worked upon you, think what it might have done to one who was drilled to be sensitive to such encounters? It was not only themselves that the dream-sleepers sought to protect. However, men and women who had seen their children rave in their sleep, a sleep from which there seemed to be no waking, no matter how the medical officers of that colony tried to rouse them—such are not always answerable for red terror which they wreak on their own. There was a wild descent upon the colony of the sleepers. They were taken and given to pain of many kinds when they said they could not awaken nor help the children. They died, not quickly or easily. It was a ship of the Patrol on a regular duty that landed on a planet where hands were bloody and more than one mind could no longer bear the burden of remembering what had happened. The children who had survived that long, and that were very few of those, were brought to Yorum and there healers of the mind wrought ceaselessly to banish the boogyman—"

"The boogyman," repeated Farree.

"That is the name they screamed out of their sleep. However, it was a name which was already very old— another bit of Old Terra come to the stars. For the boogyman was an old creation designed to frighten children into good behavior. And we discovered that some tales of such had been told on Mingra where they were deemed harmless and amusing."

"Harmless? Amusing?" Farree sputtered. "But that was a scene of evil! What child could build such a dream? Unless his race was one of swift punishment and violent tempers?"

"Which they were not—until the plague drove them into such action," the Zacanthan replied. "Nor were any of the dream-sleepers so unstable that they played thus with their own gift. As you must have heard, those who dream-sleep are under vows which are set in their very innermost spirits so that their work can draw no ill upon anyone. However, all the children we were able to draw dream pictures from were caught in the same general horror. And you did not see the worst of this, my small friend. There are some dream pictures locked in stasis since only the very steady and exceptionally well stabilized dare look at them. To dream alike is possible—the dream-sleepers have brought that to a high art. Those who are trained almost from birth can serve for communication even between worlds."

"Therefore if the children were all haunted by the same dream then that dream had a pattern. The Patrol, my own staff, others with one power and another, strove to find the source of this common dream but to no avail. What we did discover was that through that section of the galaxy, comprising some five solar systems, there was uneasiness, there had been riots, even small wars fought. Also there was a rumor which will have meaning to you— the enemy sought was a winged race. Yet no man had actually seen any such, though our net of inquiry was far spread and touched some sources which were usually closed to authority—the Thieves' Guild for example."

"But the outbreak on Mingra appeared to be the end. There were no more nightmares, even though volunteers of trained tenth class dreamers offered their services to the search. Then the Patrol and the authorities said that the whole thing was doubtless started by either some mischief (those who said that had to lie away the very evidence before their eyes) or by a tendency to sensitiveness which was awakened by the old tales. It was then that authority set upon the settlers the brand of Shame for the massacre of the dream-sleepers, and all was to be left alone, with no more time or trouble about the outbreak which, after all, was a very small happening compared to the violence which is ever snapping at the heels of sanity in all inhabited worlds."

"Then the dream—they never believed it was true?" Farree asked.

Zoror rubbed two talons across his chin just above his first throat wattle. "Oh, they believed. And for a while they had their eyes and ears wide. Many of these," he gestured again to the read-rolls, "are their reports. That is why we have easy access to the material now and it is not buried in some storehouse. We add a fact or suspicion now and then—always stories, many of which match one another. The Little Men—the People of the Hills—"

Farree stiffened. People—of—of—the Hills!

"You have heard that before, have you?" questioned the Zacanthan.

Farree rubbed his hand across his forehead as if he could pluck out some very deeply buried memory. Back—back—He was in the sleazy, tent-board place curled up on the pile of mouldering reeds which was his only bed. And the man who owned him sat at a flimsy table, a-twirling between his filthy hands a broken-handled mug which still contained a mouthful or two of the ill-smelling drink he had been gulping. Lanti raised his head to look at Farree and there was promise in his scowl which the boy knew well. It would please the hulking outcast in a few breaths of time to summon Farree forward and beat him well; most of that storm of blows would fall on his hunched back. He could remember that right enough—but what lay before that tent-hut and his miserable captivity was gone.

"Yes." Zoror nodded. "Somehow, sometime, you were

brain-erased. Yet when I mention one name given to the People in the past, you seem to know—"

Farree shook his head. "I can't remember. But—I have heard that name—surely I have heard it! Only in the Limits where all manner of spacers come and go, one hears scraps of many tales, or boastings of ventures."

"Still"—Zoror looked at him kindly—"that is one of the lesser-known names of these people who, it is true, might never have been. Well, it remains, Farree, that I must give you a warning. Maelen and Krip brought you here at night, traveling by air car. Very few must have seen you and it is true you can fold these"—he pointed to the wings—"amazingly small. At a distance in a subdued light they might be taken for a hunched-up cloak. However, by day there would be plenty sharp-eyed enough to note a difference. And—boy, you are not safe!"

"The Guild?" It was true that he had done enough to break up one plot of those masters of menace. But was he high enough among their lists of enemies to draw their attention? If so—

He frowned. Maelen and Krip Vorlund were his friends. It was by their efforts he had won out of the misery of the Limits. It was with them and working in their service that the wonder had happened to him—his wings had displayed themselves for the first time. If he were so noticeable, then staying with the two who meant so much to him might bring them into danger in turn.

"No." It was plain Zoror had followed his thoughts. Farree had made no attempt to shield them, he was so absorbed in what might be an unhappy discovery. "It is true that the Guild have no reason to cheer any of you."

There was a rattle of a chuckle from the throat of the Zacanthan. "Much trouble you caused them, you three, as well as putting them to a form of shame should the story get around. But I believe you are all discreet enough not to talk about what was done. Rather you look forward to what lies next. However, among the many other noisome activities of the Guild is a form of slavery which they indulge in whenever chance offers. They have a list of clients (many of whom could buy this whole planet for their pleasure) who desire to own novelties. You are certainly one such and would bring a very high price on certain pleasure worlds. Then the Guild have their source of information which may not equal ours but is clearer than, say, the information tapes studied by the Patrol. It is quite possible that they have news about the Little People—especially since the Shame of Mingra. One of the often-mentioned tasks of that winged race, according to legend, was the amassing and guarding of treasure. Just suppose the Guild would take it to mind that you were of that mystery race and that you could lead them to a treasure—Ah, I see you understand me. So it is largely for your own sake that I ask you to take precautions against being seen."

Farree's head jerked on his shoulders. He almost stumbled over the stool from which he had just arisen. Zoror's words might be the humming of insects, for Farree's head was now held high, his nostrils were distended to their limit as he drew in a great breath of air. It had smelled musty, of dust and time in this chamber. Now there came another scent in a wave. Just as fear had caught him when he had watched that horror on the read-roll, so now did he welcome this—fragrance. It filled his lungs, sent him stumbling towards the door. All the flowers he had ever known—the spice of bushes—the keenness of water in a dry land. He dodged about a table and his wings raised and opened. Air—he must fly—

..●)2(●..

The barrier winked out and there stood Maelen and Krip. But where was the other? Not hidden behind the two, for Farree would have still seen the edge or tips of wings. He knew—

Where was she!

"For whom do you search, little brother?" asked Krip. There was a shade of concern in his voice as he studied Farree.

"The one—the gracious one—she who flies in beauty! Where is she, my brother, my sister! Have you hidden her?" He suddenly recalled the warning Zoror had given him only moments earlier. "On the ship? Surely she is not of Gragal! For they have not seen our like before—he"— Farree signaled with a finger—"has told me so."

He wanted to shout—to sing—to fly triumphantly up and up—to meet her above in the clouds where their own road ran. Yet there were no smiles on the faces of his friends. Rather Maelen's thought reached into him, dampening the excitement that filled him.

"There is no one with us—nor at the ship, little brother. Why do you think—?"

Farree reached her, his hands outstretched, then a chill extinguished all the sudden joy he had known for the first time in his hard and barren life. The scent—no, he could not mistake that! And it came from—His hand shot out and he grabbed from Maelen's hold something wrapped in a sheet of luxwool such as was used to protect some fragile ware after purchase. The sheet flipped apart, letting him see something which shimmered in a melting burst of color: rose, pearl-white, and the warm grey of first twilight. Farree continued to stare as the fragrance arose about him in a cloud of scent filling every breath he drew. She—she—

He uttered a harsh cry and dropped upon the nearest pile of dead tapes that wondrous thing—wondrous, yes. But the feel of raw cruelty was a part of it: such torment as to sweep away all he had first felt, giving instead a sense of harsh pain. Then out of that pain grew an anger, fierce, filling him to the point where he threw out an arm and swept to the floor two piles of tapes, his lips drawn back so tightly against his teeth that his face was now that of a snarling animal unable to give vent to anger save through claw and fang. His other hand flew to his belt and freed the short defense knife which was his legacy from their meeting with the Guild. Who could be made to pay for this—this hurt, sorrow—DEATH!

"Where—" The demand came as a slurred snarl. "Where was this?" He dared not touch that thing of many colors again; it racked him now even to look at it.

Maelen moved deliberately, coming up beside him.

Farree's whole body quivered as he longed to turn on her, large as she was, to shake from her the knowledge he must have. She picked up the scrap of beauty, shook it out so that he saw, having to watch in spite of his rage and horror, she held a length which might form a scarf. The strip had been cut at an angle which led the colors to play in and out.

"What is this?" Maelen did not try to pierce the turmoil in Farree's mind, rather spoke aloud in a quiet voice such as she would use with her beloved little ones—those beasts, strange or familiar, which shared her life.

"What is it—brother?" she asked for the second time. Farree had given room to too many strong emotions in too short a time. Now he felt dizzy and sick, having to hold onto the edge of the table. Three times he swallowed before he could bring forth a word.

"It is—from a wing!" His own quivered as he answered.

"So!" That was Krip Vorlund who answered. "Perhaps a wing such as yours?" he asked.

Farree turned his head so he did not have to watch that flutter of color which Maelen had taken up again. Memory—did he have any memory of this? He wrestled with his rage and got its explosive force under control. "A wing—maybe like mine." Save that it was far more beautiful in its warm colors than his own shaded green pinions.

"Can you tell us more, little brother?" Maelen, who was the friend of all winged, pawed, other live forms, was watching him very intently.

Farree did not even raise his hand. His mouth twisted and there was a burning in his throat—anger was still there but here now was something else, a sense of loss so great that it bore down on him as had the burden of his wings before time and dire effort had freed them. "She is dead—" He spoke the words, and in his mind he wept.

"How did death come?" Vorlund's firm voice steadied Farree enough so he could answer.

"I—I don't know. If I try to learn"—he waved his thin lingers inches above the length of the scarf—"I will only feel what she felt, not the way of death, nor where it came for her."

Zoror's neck frill was fully raised. He leaned forward a little as if he could force from the length of wing silk more.

"Smuggled—contraband?" His hiss was nearly lost in the sharpness of his demand. But he did not try to handle the length which continued to flutter even though there were no breezes here to set it in motion.

Vorlund asked the question for them all. "This then is a forbidden import? Why would anyone risk exile from space to peddle such a thing? What virtue does it have besides beauty?"

It was true that smuggling was a major crime on all planets, one which brought a full force of all law enforcement officers, on planet or off, to find and punish the miscreants.

"I do not know," the Zacanthan returned. "Because I officially deal in off-world curios, things which might add even a word or two to our records, I have a full membership in the Importers' Guild, not only here but on five other worlds. This is on the forbidden list—"

"And how is it listed?" Maelen laid the strip carefully back on the table.

"As spider silk—a new type—to be reported to the nearest Patrol post at once."

"I do not know this spider silk." Farree looked at nothing but that shimmering mass. "But this cannot be that—"

"No." Krip Vorlund shook his head. "It appears to be far more. Taken from wings—"

At his words Farree shuddered and had again to grab at the table's edge to steady himself. He must wall off that beginning of thought. In the scum of the Limits, where these two had found him, had saved him from rotting with the rest of the drifters bogged there in the mud of evil which the straggling settlement near the landing space really was, he had had the first beginnings of thought to thought—sharing with the smux, also a prisoner. Then these two had come and swept up Togger, and him. He had seen sights a-plenty which were a mingling of fear and horror, but somehow none of those had touched within him as this did—as if it strove to unlock a door which, if he opened it, would sweep him up into another time and place which he must not enter, not yet—

"If it is on the forbidden list," Maelen said, "then its nature and source must be known to someone—it's likely been seen before."

It was Zoror who answered the question. "Wings—brother." He looked now to Farree and there was concern in his eyes, hidden partly by wrinkles of scales. "Could you tell us who or where?"

There was a wave of sickness rising in Farree. "I—"

"No!" Maelen interrupted him. "That is one place he dares not venture—into the past from which this came."

She put forth her hand and pushed back a sweat-damp lock of hair from Farree's forehead.

"Where did *you* find this, Daughter of Moon Power," Zoror asked in a formal tone, as if she were to give evidence.

"For open sale at the market. To search bodily, that we can do!" she returned. "There Farree may find a clue that he dares draw into his mind."

"Watch for a spacer, down on his luck, far down," commented Vorlund.

"A spacer who has been to many worlds, perhaps, known and unknown," Zoror added as if he were attacking some problem with the full strength of his own knowledge. "It follows that we must see this spacer again—and perhaps best in his own setting. There may be more—!" He did not touch the scarf which his talons indicated. "But our little brother here—he must have some protection. Let us see—"

"Protection?" Vorlund asked.

"Yes. When we have more time I will explain. But twilight is here and I would say that we had best be about what we would do before the coming of full night." There was a hooded cloak which Maelen proved adept at putting about him, fixing the hood above the upper jet of his wing tips, leaving him a seeing space in front. Farree's height now was akin to that of his companions. Before he left Togger leaped from the table where he had been squatting, seeming no more than a fistful of outward pointing scarlet quills, dodged within the eye space they had left Farree and settled down, holding on with all eight of his claws.

As they came out upon the small court where the Zoror's team had their quarters, the Zacanthan spoke into a wrist dial, summoning a scooter. Vorlund shook his head.

"With all respect, High Tech, within that we shall be as bare to sight as a half token on a swept pavement—"

"That is so," Zoror returned as the small flyer set down, waiting orders. "But it will take us to the port entrance. There will be many coming and going—and we shall make us a path through such a gathering to the Faxc entrance— from there it is but a step to the Street of Traders."

Maelen looked at him keenly. "Elder brother, you speak as one who leaves a stricken field and expects the victor on your trail. You say that Farree walks into danger. What pot is boiling here?"

"Of you I could ask the same, little sister," the Zacanthan returned. "But there is a watch which has been placed on this small brother—of that I am sure. Yes, he goes into what may be the very heart of danger. Thus we take what precautions are possible to us."

They climbed into the scooter and Vorlund leaned forward to tap out a destination.

Farree took up more than his share of room because his cloak-covered wings returned to him the hump which had once weighed him down so much. At least they had left that length of wing stuff behind and he was free of the influence which it exerted over him—though he was not free of a nagging ache—the now firm belief that some- where there had been such trouble as, in spite of all his own sufferings in the Limit, he had not known. He looked from one to another of his three companions. The Zacanthan by what expression his scaled face could show was the same. Maelen's head was up and there was a spark in her eyes which Farree knew of old, just as he recognized the tightened lips of Vorlund, and the fact that the spacer's hand slipped back and forth along his belt as if he sought the hilt of a long knife or the grip of a stunner, both of which had been lawfully put into a locker by the port officers when they had landed here.

"Where is this trader?" Zoror wanted to know.

"Close to the edge of the stalls," Maelen answered, "near those places which rent at night space to those low in credit." Her hand covered her own wrist dial, which stated what lay behind her in buying credit.

"Then we shall land by the Gate of Unregistered Aliens." Zoror's talons clicked against the scales which guarded his lips. "And—"

"We are followed," Vorlund interrupted. "There is a private scooter which flies this line and does not take another course. Merchants have house colors here, do they not, sir?"

Zoror did not turn to look and satisfy himself that the spacer was right, paying Vorlund the compliment of trust.

"They do so, yes."

"Then who among them puts up three red stripes with a sun yellow in the middle?"

Zoror blinked twice. Farree longed to turn and see what Vorlund had reported but was too tightly wrapped in his cloak to try.

"It makes no sense," the Zacanthan said.

"What and why?" the spacer countered.

"You name the colors of a house which trades by sea and would not show such a sign this deep into the continent. The sea-based houses are of a different breed;

there are few of them who take to the land for anything but a Call Out from the Council—and then they do it protestingly. None of them even has a secondary quarter here."

"No!" Maelen's voice was an order; enough to bring all their eyes towards her. There was a grim set to her jaw and on her knees her hands moved in patterns which Farree believed were those of a Moonsinger.

"Do not think," her voice dropped until it was hardly more than a murmur, "there is none who seeks!"

Farree followed the old path of his own. There was a tower, he speedily constructed in his thoughts. One like that on Yiktor where he had come into his proper inheritance and Maelen had discovered the buried history of her own kin, long forgotten. But this tower was not of stone, nor of any of the building materials which he had seen; and it was fast deepening before the eyes of his imagination to a deep rose. Now it lightened slowly from one story to the next, then darkened again into a grey which became the velvety shade of the early night sky—

So intently did he fasten his attention that it was with something of the shock suffered by one who was shaken hurriedly awake from a deep sleep, that he swayed under Maelen's touch.

The scooter had landed. Just behind them was the gate Zoror had mentioned though there was no one passing through now. Before them, not too far away, was the beginning of a sprawling port within a port which was as dirty and unrulable a place as the Limits had been. There were plenty to call it home after a fashion: spacers who had committed such errors as forced them to surrender their active tickets, those who dealt in smuggled wares. Here one doubtless could re-equip oneself with a stunner such as Vorlund and Maelen had surrendered upon landing here.

It seemed to Farree that the very air above the jungle of decaying and half ruined buildings showed against the sky of growing night as might smoke from a noisome fire. He drew the cloak closer about him and touched Togger gently. It might have been that gesture which brought the in and out pattern of the creature's mind to meld with his for a moment or two.

"In—in—!" There was such urgency in that beaming that Farree found himself trotting until Vorlund caught him by the shoulder.

"Not so fast, brother," the spacer said quietly. "They still watch—let them not take such an interest in what we do that might bring them down upon us, if that is what they are prepared to do."

However, Farree's head was up, and the cloak twisted back and forth as he turned from side to side. That scent! Once more he had caught the touch of the same fragrance which had filled Zoror's room. This was far fainter, having to fight against all the stenches of the place. But he could not lose it once he had picked it up.

"Right, brother." That was Vorlund. "Lead us—but with care."

Farree paid little attention to that. He moved to the front of their party, leaving the rest a step or two behind.

"Bad—hurt—bad—" That was Togger again. But Farree did not need the smux's warning. For the scent which was his guide began to change in quality. Fear—yes, certainly fear! Farree paid no attention to his companions as they reached the first stinking pathway which served this new version of the Limit as a street. He gathered up the skirts of his cloak and held them closely about him as he met with two staggering drunks and used all the craft he had learned in the past years to dodge them, though one aimed a blow at where his head might have been had the cloak really covered the tall man he seemed.

There were more and more people on the street. Some slipped quickly and furtively along, taking all advantage they could of every shadow. There were more drunks and some who were heading to become so. The potions and drugs one could get within this maze might be watered down and cut to a lesser strength, but those who must have them headed toward their places of supply.

Two taverns leered crookedly at each other across the filthy street. Farther in there were lights beginning to show and one could hear from there the crash of ear-tormenting music.

"In—" Togger might have shouted, so loud did it seem. Farree put a hand inside of his loose over-tunic to touch the smux's back bristles. He did not need Togger's urging now—the beacon he followed was growing stronger and stronger.

Pain and fear but now he was almost certain that both those were of the past—that he was not on his way to rescue some captive. However, where fragments of wings were to be found, there also one could certainly learn from whence they had come. Naturally the trader would lie. Farree's pointed teeth showed for an instant as he grinned in promise. However—there were he, and

Maelen, and Vorlund, and the Zacanthan, and, of course, Togger. All of them had the reading gift. His own had been honed and polished during the past months when he had traveled with the two spacers—he knew that he was far better now at this ploy than he had ever been.

There was a crowd ahead. Farree halted for a moment and looked to what lay between him and that which he sought. To push into that crowd—it would take only one drunken jostling to have him uncloaked and betrayed to a trader who dealt in wings.

Most of those he surveyed were crowded about a platform set the height of a man's shoulder above the surface of the street. On this a tall and very thin man, who wore such a skin-tight article of clothing that he might be thought to be bones alone, was waving a narrowed hand with six long fingers back and forth. From the tip of each finger spouted a flame. He took up from an upturned box which served as a table a pannikin half full of liquid, turning it as far as he might without spilling its contents so that the crowd, or at least those immediately before his perch, could see that the pannikin did have contents. Having made a portion of his audience believe that, he held the small bowl with a pair of tongs directly above his own flaming fingers, chanting aloud words which apparently none of his listeners could understand. Now he had won their full attention. As they crowded closer Farree was left with a small space to push by. What he sought was very near; the anguish of the message had become stronger and he traced it to a booth right on the other side of the magician. There seemed to be no one in charge there, though a man in a stained and worn spacer's uniform from one of the large company ships stood directly before its entrance, eyes on the magician.

Farree reached the end of the booth, searching with his eyes the wares laid out there. Some of that was trader trash—such as the companies used with natives on planets newly opened, where the inhabitants did not know the true value of off-world things. But this was not what he sought. He felt Togger move and knew that the smux wanted out; but it was better, he counciled with a swift thought, to wait yet a while.

He himself held his hand over the counter, clutching the cloak as tightly around him as possible. Slowly he swung it palm down, fingers straight and together. No, not on the board at all. But close, very close. Farree would have to risk Togger after all. With a quarter of his attention on the back of the man he believed was the trader, Farree dropped the smux on the piles of stuff. Togger could hurry if there was a good reason and he did so now, speeding over the trade goods, though he had to stop once and shake a gaudy necklace of fake Ru crystal off one of his claws. Reaching the other end of that narrow shelf he swung part way out, only two of his hind feet anchoring him to the surface. There was a sudden surge of the fear-torment. Farree braced himself as if he stood in the path of a tempest.

The smux came into view again, dragging a flat package which pushed some of the trade trash before it. Farree was shaking now. The fear-terror was fast changing into anger. He looked down at the stuff but there was no weapon there. No, the unlicensed trader would not want the State Pacifers to find him with such. Instead Farree grabbed up the packet. His trembling had become worse, and his hold had fallen from his cloak so that the garment was ready to slip from him. Togger sprang, landing on Farree's chest. His claws went out, caught at the cloak and dragged it shut toward him. In Farree's hands the packet shook and nearly fell.

"Hey, you! Trying to get that without a credit, eh? Well, you don't play that game with Ryss Onvet, no, you don't. I can call me a street warden good and clear. We may be trash to your up-nosed crowd from the town but we still got our rights, always being that we ain't on any list."

"But of course that is so," Farree felt the Zacanthan move in on one side of him and Maelen and the spacer on the other. "My friend here wishes to make a purchase. He was waiting to attract your attention. The magician, I must admit, is quite good, very good indeed. Now, if you are willing to conduct business, how much does my friend owe?"

The man had a heavy scar across his forehead which twisted his eyebrows unnaturally, but Farree, in spite of the overwhelming discharge from the package, could sense that the merchant was squinting at them narrowly as if he looked for something or someone who was not there. He must have made up his mind quickly for he said in a rush of words, in trader tongue for emphasis, that he had no business to do with strangers—

"Do you then," Maelen wanted to know, "deal only with your neighbors here? Certainly that makes your market a very limited one and I should think your sales were few."

"Gentle Fem,"—he got out the polite address as if it strangled him to say it—"I deal with all comers, yet I also take specialty consignments. One of those your friend there has taken up. I can also add theft to my complaint against him since that which he holds is *not* for sale at all."

"No? Look at me, merchant, and at my friend here." She indicated Krip Vorlund with a small gesture. "Did you not sell to us a short time since a curiosity which was indeed better ware than any you show here?"

The man opened his mouth as if to refute her at once and then seemed to look beyond them as if he sought for some help.

"Was this not true?" she pressed.

He coughed and stroked his throat as if he had swallowed something he could neither control internally nor heave out again. "Yes," his voice was hardly above a mutter.

"Sooooooo," the word was such a hiss from the Zacanthan that, for a moment, Farree could believe that he companioned some great reptile. "What isss sissss sing?"

He reached across to Farree and effortlessly freed the packet from his hand.

"Treasure? Sssso you mussst declare it sssso—" Even as the hiss grew more pronounced the Zacanthan effortlessly put a talon under the top fold of the wrapped package and gave one short pull to display its contents.

Farree already knew what he would see. There were two more lengths of the shining wing stuff. One was a red-brown shading through warm yellows and oranges. And the other—green, several shades of green: not the darker shades which made up the glory of his own wings; lighter. Not green—red! The whole world had turned red about him. He mouthed a strange cry which he had never voiced before and his hands shot forth—not to seize again upon what the Zacanthan held—but to grasp that throat rising above the grimy collar of the disgraced uniform, to dig into the trader's dirty red flesh and squeeze, squeeze and squeeze!

··●)3(●··

"Get off—you—!" The trader's hand rose. From some-where he had procured a band fitting securely about his knuckles, the metal plates of it starred with sharp pointed spikes facing outward. He crouched a little behind the warped board on which lay his wares, his armored hand moving outward and to the side.

The red mist which had filled the world for Farree did not lighten, but of a sudden not only was there the weight of hands upon his shoulders but in his mind there was a binding as secure as if he were entangled in a hunter's net. He could think, could see that which he wanted, but he was being dragged back by those hands on his shoulders, held helpless by that swift barrier in his mind—but not so helpless that he could not catch up the length of green wing.

The grasp which held him then swung him bodily around and pushed him towards the port end of the crooked street. Then the hold relaxed enough to let him stumble on as long as it was forward and not toward the trader's booth. Yet inside him there was a chaos, first nurtured by anger, and then by scraps and bits of what were certainly no memories of his!

Heights rising from a green plain into a silver mist: there was no visible sun and yet there shone a radiance as complete as the full light of such. What he saw was only snatches, gone before he could center any in his mind. In his nostrils there was a medley of scents completely covering the foulness of the path down which he was being urged.

There was a sudden darkness in this place of green and silver. No true storm, that much he could guess. If he did somehow look through another's eyes—memories—then there had come a swirling of strong evil to tear away all he witnessed. Nor was he able to see source of the evil. He only felt—first curiosity, which caught him as surely as if a sharp blade did cut into his flesh. Fear for himself, yes, but what was worse, fear for another whom he could not see but who was as much a part of him as if she were an arm, a heart—

He was gone into that dream place, unaware now if any walked with him, knowing only that death stalked and he must stand between prey and hunter. Then—there was a last thrust of heart pain. He thought he cried out, while still he sought to face that which had crept behind him. Only now it was dark, full and complete dark. When that closed upon him, Farree knew he had been too weak, too small, too untrained. The blackness was death and into it she had disappeared. He blinked and there before him was the Gate of Unregistered Aliens at the port. He looked behind. Hands were still lying on his shoulders— Maelen. She was watching him very carefully.

"What chances, small brother?" she asked—and her voice seemed to come from a vast distance.

"Death—" His answer was hardly above a whisper and he wiped one hand across his eyes. There were no tears to be so shaken off, only still the abiding rage. His other hand, the bit of wing silk about his wrist, strayed to the front of his tunic under the rumpled cloak. Togger! Where was Togger?

Taking advantage of the loosened grip upon him Farree turned so quickly that the robe flew out. Only in a few seconds of time did something which was colder, more exacting than his anger warn him. But he was already several strides away from them all.

"Togger!" he thought, as he might shout aloud for another companion who had only speech in common with him.

"Here—we—" Whatever the smux might have added was gone. All that was left was an emptiness Farree recognized. There were devices known both to the Patrol and to the Thieves' Guild which could clamp down against any thought sending. But in order to use those someone must have suspected Togger—and Farree himself.

He longed to throw aside the muffling cloak, to be in the air and so able to follow his friend, for Togger had been on the thin outside edge of response when he had sent that broken call for aid for that was what it was. Farree was no longer aware of their company. The contacts he had made mentally within the past turn of the hour sweep seemed to have in some way severed his close contact with the spacers and the Zacanthan. Only they had not lost him. He was aware of someone moving up close beside him and swerved, having no desire to be once more bound by superior strength of either mind or body. It was Maelen—but she was making no attempt to lay hands on him again. Nor had he picked up that clear sending which was hers.

"Togger," he thought swiftly, hoping to make good use of his present freedom. "Togger goes with one—"

"They have found your small one?" That was Zoror and the thought came from behind.

"I think not," Farree returned. He was already off the smooth surface of the gate road into the dust which would become the muck of the shunned street. He looked ahead. The trader—the magician—somehow he thought of them both together, as if, like Maelen and Vorlund, they were so closely knit that their thought might blend into a single mind voice.

None of his companions tried to stop him. They might have taken council together and decided that Farree's loss was theirs also.

The ever-present glow-light of the port was behind them, but the road took a crooked turn and the evil-smelling splotch of buildings was closing in behind. There was light of a sort—here and there one of the door lights demanded by law was a small spark. But it was plain that none of these were allowed to emit the full glow of the same lamps which hung in the city beyond the irregular wall cutting the port settlement from the place where law walked and there could be questions asked with impunity.

As he went Farree fought to pick up touch with the smux, but the silence was complete. However, he remained certain that sooner or later he would be steered aright.

Around their party clung that scent which had brought Farree into the maze of stinking lanes. Only now he strove not to heed it, since he wanted a clear mind, with no thrusts of rage, to follow any trail Togger had set.

They were all with him, Maelen, Vorlund, and Zoror, but this time they appeared to be content to surrender the lead to Farree. Here was the magician's shaky platform. Some of the boards of which it had been fashioned now lay on the ground but no one had attempted to clear them away.

Farree wheeled to look at the booth where the trader had spread out his sorry supply of wares. They lay muddled, tossed in small heaps, some of them fallen into the muck of the roadway. He who had displayed them was gone, and strangest of all, as Farree knew with particular vividness from his own life within a port refuse settlement, this seller had left his stock in trade behind. There must have been raids already on the tawdry stuff. Even as Farree came up he saw hands which were more like clawed paws than his own working with lightning speed to sweep off the largest pile; it disappeared on the other side of the improvised table. There was a scurry as something small and dark as a blot of night pressed all together scuttled away.

Farree stretched out his own right hand, passing it slowly back and forth across what was left. There was nothing to answer until he came to the extreme edge behind the table. Then his skin pricked and he spread his fingers wider. Here was a trace of Togger at last. But nothing remained of that length of a second plundered wing.

With infinite care, Farree held his hand above what looked like a broken bone—dull and brown and shaped with a cutting edge into a knife. Yes, Togger! Now he raised the hand and turned around slowly so that the hand swept across and took in both the magician's platform and this deserted booth. There! Farree's hand steadied, pointing inward toward the deeper reaches of this dangerous district.

"They have not found him." He was convinced of that. Were the smux captive Farree certainly could have read that also. "But he must have gone with the trader."

"To search such a maze and its many lurking places," Zacanthan observed, "may be impossible. Do you receive any more from him?"

"No," Farree returned impatiently, "but—Ah!" He interrupted his own answer, corrected it. "He is there! He does not send except with emotion."

"Yes, that I have, too," Maelen agreed. "Will he leave a trail or guide you—"

"If he can. It is this way!"

"Wait." For the first-time Vorlund spoke. "There are baits for traps—if they would take you, little brother, how better could they call you so? It may be that they know Togger is with them, but they will let him do as he wishes and summon you—"

"Well thought," Zoror hissed. "We cannot turn for any help to the guards, for they do not venture here themselves by night, nor even far in by day. If there are deaths here they turn their heads and do not look. As long as these prey upon their own kind, so will they be left alone. It is only the very foolhardy who would venture out of the stew to kill or rob. I do not think that even the Guild have more than a token representative here."

"I go for Togger," Farree answered simply.

"He will not be turned from that!" Maelen said. "But if they lay a trap for one and four arrive—four with somewhat better weapons than expected, may not the plan benefit us?"

Zoror chuckled. "Daughter, that is a thought to lighten the heart. Only I would suggest that we do not go openly, marching like a landing party with a talk flag above us. We do not know what we seek—"

It was Farree's turn to interrupt. "The wings!"

"What do you mean?" Maelen asked.

"The wings—such brought me here. I think there is still a link between those we seek and their plunder—and I wear this!"

"Let us not argue this in the middle of the street," Vorlund warned again. "Slip around to the back of the booth. It is only right to believe that we are under constant monitoring and perhaps have been ever since we left the Place of Long Knowledge. However, what precautions are possible let us follow."

Now Farree heard a small sound from Maelen which might be smothered laughter. "Wise, oh, wise. Just let us hope that we do not tumble into some hole of refuse and smother ourselves with nose lifting stenches."

Farree was around the counter in the booth before she had finished talking. And he was barely out of the way when the others joined him.

"Now what have you to say about the wings—you are sure these are parts of wings?" Maelen wanted to know.

"I am sure," Farree replied shortly. "And those who once wore them—" He swallowed twice as if he would bite and hold fast the emotion which the thought awoke in him. "Those are dead."

None of them answered that. Perhaps the very tone of his voice made it impossible to quarrel with his statement. They were behind the booth, going single file down a narrow way between the rear of two lines of booths which backed upon one another. Farree forced from his mind all but the seeking.

At the end of that narrow cut with its soft foul footing rising nearly ankle high he stood for a moment, his head turned a little as if he were listening to something which should be audible to all of them. Then he slipped into the wider alley which ran towards the center of the maze. Not Togger, not yet. But he again caught the faintest trace of the other odor in spite of the stenches about—the scent of the torn wings. Abruptly he turned to Maelen and held out one hand while with the other he drew his concealing cloak even closer about him.

"Give me—yes, give me that other piece! The one you bought before."

She asked no question, but unsealed the long pocket which was part of her suit at the thigh. There came a rustle and then he felt the length of silky stuff she passed to him—felt and SAW. For, though here were not even booth lanterns with their dull smoky light—his eyes could detect a faint glow from the stuff he had wound about his wrist. And with both strips so tightly in his hold he felt a drawing again—not from Togger. The green length seemed to wrap of itself about his flesh. There was a bitter chill which crept from it up his arm, down into his fingers. Dead—worn by the dead once—but alive in a way he did not understand—save that he was sure it was acting with him, perhaps for him.

Farree darted across the opening of the wider alley and once more sought a very narrow way. He had to be careful to twist and turn to accommodate his wings. The faint radiance from his wrist band was growing stronger— or was it that he was trusting its guidance the more?

"Here." He backed a little away and nursed the banded wrist against his body. The shadow against shadow which was Vorlund moved closer.

"There is a door here," the spacer reported. "It is set in as part of a wall—I see no latch or way of opening it."

"Let me, brother." It was Zoror's turn before the wall. Farree caught a glimpse of a larger shadow moving in behind Vorlund. There were always noises in these streets—more so now that night had come and most of the inhabitants who sheltered or swaggered here were rousing for another night's pleasure or darksome business. Yet Farree caught a faint clicking and knew that Zoror must be trying his own way of gaining entrance through the wall door.

"It is ssooo,"—the Zacanthan sank his speech to that hiss which served his species as a whisper. "This is most easy—Thus!"

He was gone and Farree caught only a quick sight by the fading color of the scarf he carried to show that the Zacanthan had gone apparently through the door or wall as if that had been an illusion and not a solid barrier. He himself was quick to follow. There was a narrow hall running before him, but what was most important there was also a flight of narrow and splintery steps to his left. Light came from a globe fastened over their heads wherein luminous insects crawled and spun threads which shone brightly.

The steps were narrow and very steep. Farree wondered if he could take them with the cloak still bundled about him. He had lowered and folded his wings to the smallest possible size but still they were a bigger obstacle than the case which had once held them and made him a hunchback.

There was a sudden thrust with his head. Togger! Perhaps the smux had been casting out for him all the time but the beamed message had not been able to reach him before.

"Here—bad—bad—" A recognition and a warning. At the same moment Maelen caught at the fold of Farree's cloak and held him back.

"Not yet—" As the Zacanthan had used his voice in whisper so did she use her mind speech in a similarly low key. "There is a cover here!"

Farree stopped. He could beam in on Togger right enough and now he sharpened his contact. The Zacanthan, with the usual silent steps of his kind, was already on the stairs, Vorlund only a little behind. Farree tried a trace of touch. There was nothing—none from his companions and curiously deadened for those beyond. This was not the first time he had faced a mind shield in action, though such would certainly be of great value to any of the dwellers in this filthy tangle of rotting buildings and swampy streets.

Instantly he clamped down on his own thought. Did they have some warning—and he suspected that they might well have—so any who would follow them must be thought proof? Had they picked up the smux's broadcast and were the four of them indeed now entering a trap?

The stairway led the four to an upper hall where there seemed more substantial walls and some pretense of cleanliness. Two doors opened on one side and one on the opposite—all closed. However, the murmur of voices reached them. Zoror noiselessly passed to the farthest room and there stretched out his hand, planting it palm down against the surface, but not before Farree caught a quick glance of what was a small disc. Having pushed that against the door, he reached back his other hand and took firm grasp of Vorlund's; the spacer in turn caught Maelen's in a similar grip with Farree ending the chain.

He could hear! By now he should not be surprised by anything which could happen. Instead he strained hard so as to not miss a single word uttered within the room.

"It is so." The voice so brought to them lacked any expression of feeling—it might have been a tape left to run. "He was in the Painted Street tonight. I tell you, the information Varis gave was right."

There was still only a murmur from a second voice, a deep-sounding one which seemed easier to hear yet could not as well be understood: it uttered words which were disguised against Zoror's spy disc.

"Three of them with him—"

Murmur.

"A Zacanthan! You would not say go up against that one? He was carefully watched I tell you—it was the scarf which brought him—near pushed into an act where we could have taken him easily. But not with a Zacanthan there. Also those others—there has been a lot said about them—powers they have."

Murmur.

"Yes, he seemed to know—there was a killing anger in him then. They have said these would never go off-world— well, whoever swore that would take oath to Zambut and then go and spit in his god's fat face!"

Murmur.

"Certain—yes, I am certain. He might still be shaking the dust-smoke from the Red Dunes off his shoulders. He wore a cloak—and underneath were wings! Wings, I tell you! You heard the report, saw the spin record. He is one of a kind and he is of his own world—he can play no tricks here. Take him and you'll find your backwards-running River and Old Saptal's treasure all laid right to your hand. They all have the secret—if that is the secret you wish to uncover." A murmur which interrupted.

"We have tried that before—you have seen the reports. They will die rather than talk—and they will their own minds to crack rather than answer with the truth. Get him and—"

Maelen turned her head a fraction toward the stairs and then she alerted Vorlund with a small pull which he, in turn, passed as a warning on to Zoror. The Zacanthan moved away from the door, but he did not loose his hand tie with Vorlund. He retreated back down the hall and, holding the disc between two fingers, he gave a push to a second door. It swung open upon a small room. Another of the luminous insect globes showed a bed, narrow and stripped of all bedding, a small table and two stools. There was nothing else and the air within seemed stale. Zoror let go Vorlund's hand long enough to shut the door behind them and make a sweeping gesture which took in most of that side of the room. Then he crossed to the wall which separated this chamber from the one which now held the speakers. When Maelen briefly dropped her hand, Farree used the free moment to knot the second wing strip over the first around his wrist.

Their hands linked once more, again they could hear. "Speak it, then! If such action is correct, can you do it?"

Murmur.

"Try then!"

There was the sound of footsteps outside. Someone who had no reason to fear those in the far room had just walked past the hall door towards that same room.

"Guide here." A third voice. And then it came again, undoubtedly from inside the room itself.

Murmur.

"I have promises, High Ones. Three pieces for covering your capture—" Once more the murmur interrupted.

"It is not my failure, High One. What I was to do, I did. That others could not carry through the plan was no fault of mine. You, High One—what is THAT!"

"Bad—bad—" The smux was broadcasting in a calling frenzy which Farree had not heard him use since he had been freed from the cage and the torture of Russtif on that day when a better life had come for both him and Farree.

"Catch it, fool with a head of feathers! Why did you bring that here?" The murmur had become speech, unscrambled by any device.

"I bring it?" That must be the trader. "I never saw it—this rotten wall hive may have many stranger things hiding out. Who can swear the Great Oath that ships landing here do not sometimes carry more than is on their cargo listing? It is nothing but a—a thing. Crush it—"

"It is a key," the growling voice began and then sank once again into the murmur. "The thing thinks." That much arose from out of the low notes.

"High One, it is then a way to spy upon us. Let me crush it—" The magician sounded shaky.

Murmur.

"Bait, High One? But is it possible that this is of *their* company—rather than a creature from a ship?"

Murmur. Then from Togger a mind cry as terrible and hideous as the ones the smux used to make when Russtif used the prod to send it into battle.

Togger! Farree pulled loose from their chain of communication and started for the door. Just as rage had taken him over earlier that day so did it rise again to drive him past all thoughts of safety, leaving only the need to rescue the smux.

There was a second cry from Togger. Vorlund had stepped between Farree and the door. He reached out and caught both of Farree's hands in what could be a merciless grip. There was no chance of evading that. But—Togger!

While Farree struggled fruitlessly against the hold the spacer used, he jerked, his body bending backwards, the cape falling to the floor. His face was a mask of pain.

Through the door, or the walls, or the whole of this warren of a house there sounded a shrill, ear-shattering call. Farree was frozen into the position in which he was held, filled with a torturing pain which spread from his head down the length of his spare body. His wings, now that he could no longer hold command of his body—or his mind—swelled up, to open.

He could hear and he could see, but all else was sealed in some fearsome case even as his wings had been. He rocked on his feet as Vorlund changed grip upon him. Maelen had taken a step toward him, he could see her only from the corner of one eye. The Zacanthan swung closer to the wall. He had broken all contact with the others and stood pressed against the stained surface, only the palm of his hand between his head and the disc. He fanned his other hand—a gesture which could only mean for them to remain in silence where they now were. Farree's panic was drying his mouth and throat. Even if the Zacanthan had not signaled silence he could not have broken through that which encased him now. Vorlund drew him closer, supporting Farree against a fall.

Togger! Though he was cold with fear, with the fear that they might indeed have fallen into a trap, Farree thought first of the smux. He was fearful enough to try mind touch. Instantly there was more movement beside him and Maelen's hands came out to clap upon his head just over his ears.

Now he could not see! Streaks of brilliant light played back and forth before his eyes as did lightning over the heights of Yiktor. She was a wisewoman of her kind and she had knowledge. But to use that against him—No, Togger was his own friend more than any other in this world. For a moment there was fire—fire to cut through the chill of that which imprisoned him. He could see the scarves he had looped around his wrist. Along the edges of the wing-strips there flashed sparks of white, of green— and last of all a sun-brilliant yellow. The force of their coming to life shot through his body.

••◗)4(◖••

During all his life Farree had chosen to do the prudent thing and withdraw from danger. The uncasing of his wings but a short span ago had given him self-confidence to be sure, but to face up to an enemy infinitely larger and more muscular than himself, an enemy fighting on his home territory who might perhaps call on any manner of forces—Only this time all the common sense had been shaken out of his trapped body. He could summon no strength to lunge against Vorlund, somehow to shoulder the tall, battle-trained spacer out of the way, and win to Togger's aid. He was still dumbly in the toils of that mysterious force which the whistle had laid upon him. Dumbly, then, he allowed himself to be shifted between Vorlund and Maelen till the three of them were again handfast with the listening Zacanthan.

"We are under a silence?" That was the magician who asked. Some sibilance of his trade speech betrayed him.

"Do we look to be brainless muck worms? Yes, we are under silence, only one begins to wonder—"

The murmur broke for a second time and they could catch intelligible speech. "Yes—wonder—there is nothing can come upon us here—or is that also false? What traveller can ever weigh the marvelous strengths and defenses of a new world? Be silent!"

Straightway there came something new to plague Farree. The force which held him was sloughing away as if it were a covering which he could rend from his body. That which had struck him at the whistling broke—was partly gone. On his wrist the yellow light of the scarf bands was shading down the scale of color, green-brown-red, and then a red as true as would come with new shed blood. In his mind there was a queer beat as if some drum or rattle was pounding out a code, while the now scarlet band flickered.

Vorlund shifted his grip again, and still Farree was without the necessary energy to pull free. He saw by the mingled light furnished by the band on his wrist and the single dim lamp a pulsating to match the beats. At first he thought that he was swinging from side to side in the same pattern and then he saw that Maelen, Zoror, and Vorlund himself were all one with him and that pounding. Vorlund's lips moved; he might have been speaking, but the drum beat in Farree's head had deadened his ears to outer sound—only the pattern of the drum remained.

It was the Zacanthan who made the first move. Catching at the purse and sheath at his belt he brought forth not one of the knives forbidden to off-worlders but rather what looked to be a curved and shining talon twice the size of any of those which sprouted from his fingers.

The silver length of it was patterned by bits of blue

which sparkled like jewels. Stepping away from the wall Zoror used that talon as if it were indeed knife, slicing it back and forth through the air as he might engage some invisible enemy. The talon weapon began to change color, those bits of blue inlay shading into darker and more violent shades just as the scarves had done. It was difficult for any but his own species to read any expression on the Zacanthan's scaled face; however, one could not mistake his eyes—not dark with anger but bright with interest, as if some new bit of learning had been drawn to his attention and he was about to pluck all or any secrets out of this encounter.

Maelen held her own hands out, palms down, her fingers quirking up one by one until they stretched to their farthest reach in fan shape. She was staring at each finger in turn, as if assuring herself that she still possessed them all.

There was moisture on Farree's wrist. He glanced down. Drops were bubbling out of the double band. He might have just taken it out of a stream or pool. Save what fell was not the clearness of true water, rather it was first a pinkish froth and then took on more substance, becoming the same shade of red as the band now was. Blood! Surely that was blood such as might ooze through the dressing on a wound. It fell, but not to the floor, for it diffused again into small balls of mist before it reached even the level of Farree's knees.

It was as if that moisture filled the air it had disappeared into, for it seemed now as if he could actually taste blood, smell it.

Now the color was draining out of the band. It became

wrinkled as ashy spots grew on it. Then both layers of it thinned, flaked away as might ashes from a burning. Only on his flesh there remained a brand, red as a burn. That which had held him prisoner was gone and Farree's medley of thoughts could be sorted out into messages again.

Togger! He quested outward.

"Bad—" He managed to pick up that, but it came very faint and low.

What followed then they all heard clearly, having no need this time for any disc or connected line of search: A cry which was not of the mind but rather had broken from a throat of flesh.

"Ahhhhh!" Togger! Not that cry from him. Rather another mind send: a sensation of being held tightly, of being flung through the air—

"Fool!" They could hear the snap of that voice without any aid. "Spaquet!" There was a blurred mind image of a pale animal bulk plodding into a thick soup of mud.

"The little one"—Zoror's hiss of whisper came as he moved to restore the silver talon into his belt pouch—"he has struck one—I believe he who was the spider of this net weaving. What weapon has Togger, little brother?"

"Poison—on his foreclaws." There must be more than a lethal dose available now, for Farree had never tried to milk away thin yellow beads of moisture which Russtif had always forced from the claws when he had kept Togger captive.

"Soooo." The Zacanthan crossed the floor with noiseless tread and Vorlund slipped aside to let Zoror reach the outer door. "This one so assaulted will die?" He had put out a hand and drew Farree away from the spacer and closer to him.

The youth was rubbing his hands together, wriggling his shoulders, reversing as best he could the spreading of his wings, back into a burden the cloak would cover once more.

"Will this one die?" repeated the Zacanthan.

Farree shook his head. He felt as tired as if he had marched all day through a Nexus swamp. It took much of the will left in him even to stand and then turn his mind to what might be happening in the other room. "I do not know," he answered. "There is a poison—but to some life forms it might not be deadly. There is so much difference—" He let that explanation die away while he rubbed his hand across the brand left upon his other wrist. "What may promise death to one kind, may be no more than the bites of a Lugk fly to another. Togger!" He went from words to mind call.

There was an answer, but it was very hazy and he could not understand. At least that meant that the smux was still alive.

"Let him lie," again the voice speaking clearly instead of in a deep rumble. Whatever had cloaked those within these walls must have gone. "He was without a useful thought, a helpful bit of action. Now—get you down to that hole where he burrowed and bring me back—" Not words but rather a series of clicks followed.

"They may be searching, High One." That voice verged on a whine and was certainly from the magician.

"If so it is better that you not be caught, is *that* not the truth? Remember, we have our own methods for resisting capture—the body can fall into the hands of those who would stand against us—but the mind, ah, now, that is a very different thing. You have seen what you have seen of that, is that not so? A certain ship owner from the Circle—"

"High One, no—I will go. But what of that thing which has done this to Guide? Should we not seek it out and—"

"And die? You seem doubly eager to bring down upon you evils this night, Ioque. Almost one could believe that you yourself had hints of how one might safely use that crawler."

"Not so!"

"You speak that like an Oath of Heart Blood, Ioque. Look out when below where that went out the window if you still tremble with fears. Bring your heel down on its head—"

"But, High One, was it not your saying that this creature might bring to us what we want? Did not the scout swear that the thing belonged to him we have been tracing?"

"At least your memory works, Ioque. But deal with it as you will. We no longer need it."

"How—?"

"With ease." Once more the voice went even higher as if to address a party. "Thus!"

Farree fell to his knees as if his bones had suddenly turned too soft to supply any support. As before he was helpless in the clutch of something invisible which enfolded him both without and within.

It was Maelen who caught and steadied him, once more with her hands on his shoulders. While from the fingers of those hands there poured into him new energy. With a gasp he stiffened and clung in spirit to what she gave him.

There was a new battle in him. He must seek the source of this weakness—if he crawled on his hands and knees to do so—which was a dark urging, and meet it with what remnants of power he still possessed, awakened and armed by Maelen as she fed into his mind belief in his ability.

The room was gone, as if wiped away by a giant hand. He was caught up in a swirl of color, and somehow that in itself made him able to think—or feel—or—what was it—a dream?

There were winged ones in the air. As they dipped and soared or alighted near him he felt a vast peace— or perhaps only the shadow of it—that he was a part of an enduring something which had no failure—which had been, was, and ever would be!

He could not see the faces of those who danced with and on the wind; there seemed ever to be a glittering mist which enshrouded them when he looked too closely. Yet he did not doubt that he was one of them and that this was his own place. He strove to use his own wings, to mount and become a true part of their game, or dance, or the ceremony which he knew was of great meaning and needed only concentration to give up a truth greater than anything he had known before.

How long was he in that place of color, life, and peace? If it were only a moment or two then it possessed a kind of energy which itself vanquished time—the time which ruled the world he knew. There came a sudden flurry and the winged ones gathered together to face him as if they had but that moment become aware that he was there.

From them came wind-carried bands of color. These swirled around him yet did not touch his body. Instead they wove a pattern as among them spun in turn bits of glitter. This glitter did not float purposelessly but rather came to hang unsupported in the air until he looked upon something which was a distinct pattern and about which there glowed light of another kind, green and white. Each of the bits were stilled in turn and hung quietly before him while he knew, though he did not know why, that this was a thing he must use—

The color, the place, the dancers—gone! What had he seen—with his eyes, or with his mind? He could not have said. But he knew that what he had seen did exist; and there was growing now a new ache within him, an ache like the hunger his body had once known which had come to be a part of him, in the dark days of his previous life.

"Come—" Who said that? One of the winged ones whom he could not see? Or was it an actual voice in his ears? Come—to that place—Yes, with all his heart he would reach for it now.

He was suddenly as aware of a force restraining his body as he had been of the place beyond the darkness. But this was not a holding within him as that other had been, but rather the pressure of hands upon him. He blinked and then blinked again and saw that he was back in the room where Maelen stood behind him, Zoror before, looking down at him with what could only be concern in his large green-gold eyes. The terrible fatigue which had struck Farree was gone. Rather he was filled with an eagerness to be gone—where he was not yet sure, only that he must answer that new hunger which had come.

Without his willing it his right hand twitched. His hand rose and the index finger pointed to the door while the brand the scarf had left on his flesh warmed and there seemed to be even a faint glow from it.

"What—" Vorlund spoke first.

"No!" Zoror shook his head, his neck frill extended to its full extent. "There will be time later for questions and answers. For now we shall find us a way back, one that no eyes shall light upon when we take it. You can go?" He addressed that last to Farree.

Shaking a little the other stirred in Maelen's hold. Her hands moved to help to draw him back to his feet. He shook his head a fraction and fought for steadiness, for the world about him had a tendency to heave and to flicker. "I can go—but there is Togger."

"Call now," the Zacanthan returned. Farree sent forth that mental signal which had so long made a bridge between his mind and that of the smux. He hardly dared believe that he would be answered. Yet there came to him a clearer signal than any he had used to locate his companion before this evening.

"Out—wait—out. Big one—throw through hole— out—" A longer message than he had ever received and yet one he was certain was true meant, not sent to entice him into the hands of those others.

Vorlund had gone to the door. Now he opened it a crack and stood listening, perhaps for both any sound and with his mind for a hint that they were facing trouble once more. Looking over his shoulder he nodded and slipped quickly into the hall beyond.

There was no one to be heard or sensed. However, Vorlund did not withdraw to the stairs, as Farree saw as they followed the spacer. Rather he slipped along the wall towards the closed door of that other chamber. Maelen reached out and tapped Zoror on the wrist but the Zacanthan was already on his way. As they all wore soft-soled foot coverings and not the heavy metal-soled boots of the space borne, they did not raise a whisper of sound.

Once more Zoror planted his spy disc against the other door and stood statue still, the others as frozen behind him. Then with a quick nod he fingered the door itself and that portal opened, letting them look into a larger room. There was a slit of a window and through that came not only the seething smells of this muck heap, but also the sound of the settlement which was more alive at night than by day.

At first Farree thought the room was empty and he wondered how the inhabitants had gotten past their own hiding place without revealing their passage. Then he came two steps in on Maelen's heels and saw the crumpled body by the far wall. The man's face was swollen and flushed purple on one cheek, his eyes fastened in their direction. Dead eyes! It would seem that Togger's defense against this particular enemy had struck nearly twice as potently as Farree had ever seen it before.

The dead man held no interest for Vorlund. He was across the room in a hurry, edging by the body and coming to the wall against which it huddled. His hands were out and he traced with arm sweeps and the tops of his fingers that barrier itself.

"A hidden door, yes," Zoror nodded. "Though I would say he is long gone."

"Do we go hence also?" Maelen wanted to know. The Zacanthan reached above and beyond Vorlund's shoulder to rasp his talons along that stained and crumbling surface.

"I think not."

"Togger—" Farree had no intention of withdrawal until he was sure of the smux's safety. He certainly could have been flung through that slit of a window but that did not mean that he would otherwise be hidden from harm where he to fall to the way below.

Thought might have been a shout in summons. There was a hump which appeared at the sill of that window and the smux clambered through, taking off in one of the leaps his kind could make when they were forced to it. He reached Farree and a moment later was clinging to his chest, all but two of the spike-mounted eyes retreating into cover.

Farree was quick to put the smux into a safer perch in an inner pocket of the cape. Only those stalked eyes protruded enough to follow what he did.

They slipped along the outer hall. The light supplied by the bowls pulsated but was strong enough to let them edge safely down the staircase. Again Vorlund took the lead, peering out the door first while holding it partly closed. He beckoned at last to the others, but there was a look of concentration on both his face and that of Maelen, as if they prepared to face a struggle or some wily attack. It was now Zoror who kept a hand on

Farree's shoulder under the bunch of the cape, drawing him forward.

They were out again in the muck of the lane and Vorlund had his back against the wall. He had no weapon, but his hands were out in a position Farree had seen before. There were tricks of attack and defense which could be wrought by muscle alone which were as effective as any delivered by steel. Spacers were adept in such as well as in an array of weapons. Those who were prudent never questioned that they could return in full any attack upon them which did not begin with them at once rendered unconscious in some manner.

Just as Farree had been led here earlier by a silent compulsion which no longer existed, so was he now being moved away. He strove to throw off that feeling that he must obey some strange order as delivered by an unknown voice. From that pocket at the level of his chest he felt Togger changing position and there nibbled at his mind a thought which certainly might have been from or relayed by the smux.

"Go—far—"

"We go—at least from here," he returned by mind touch, setting his own pace to match the Zacanthan's. Maelen was now in the advance of their party and Vorlund was behind. They might have been guards escorting some VIP whose life was under threat.

Farree himself could hardly believe that they were withdrawing without facing an attack, and he was about to question this when the Zacanthan drew him close as Maelen had held him earlier. He saw the lips of the wide mouth shape a word, for they were hurrying past a smoking torch.

"We are followed. Take care."

Farree held out his hand and felt Togger's claws close gently upon his finger not with the poisoned claws but lesser ones. Moving more awkwardly than usual the smux allowed himself to be hoisted out of the pocket and settled on the front of Farree's jerkin. If they were attacked now the smux would have a better chance for defense.

However, the need for that did not come. They were past the trader's wrecked booth. Then the magician's tipsy platform was also behind them. They quickened pace until once more the smooth surface of the port gate was underfoot. Here lights blazed and they must pass in that full glare. If they were still followed their tracker would have no difficulty keeping them in sight. For the first time Farree dared to try mind seek. Instantly his sending or searching was cut off by the heavy power of the Zacanthan. He did not need any further instructions to keep silence.

They were in the main room of the port now and there were enough travelers, staff, and guards, to form a crowd so that the four from the port slum could weave back and forth among them. Farree knew what they would do. In any place such as this where there were minds in a number—then-owners intent on affairs only of consequence to themselves—this should provide shield for their own passage, as long as they could blend their own identities into that of travelers interested only upon reaching some important destination. Swiftly he withdrew behind a simulacrum of his own constructive thought, a servant eager to finish a task for a departing master, then to be on his own for the night. He had not had much practice in such action but he had been introduced to part-playing roles by Maelen and knew a little. His companions were adept at this and he was certain that they could draw about them cloaks of hallucination as strong in their way as the fabric one he clung to. But he longed to turn and look behind, to test his own power of unmasking any pursuers.

The Guild—of a certainty those they watched for would be of Guild employment. On Yiktor the game of that mighty force had been spent by what Maelen and Krip could summon—with some help from him, and the smux, and the two other animals who had become Maelen's people in fur, rejoicing to be numbered so. Only even there the Guild had had their defense—a man-made thing which could deflect any mental probe and protect the wearer from such interference.

His memories of that—No! That could provide a counter to what they needed now. Farree expelled memory. He made himself once more into the persona which he had seized upon earlier—a servant, hurrying to deliver a message. Yes, that was surely who and what he was.

They came down the length of that very long room and passed through the gate where those only visiting the port would exit—avoiding the passengers' section. Zoror's talons on his right hand tapped out a call on the credit dial about his wrist. A carrier swung out of the line of vehicles moving slowly towards their take off. Fighting the desire to rush for the escape that promised, Farree controlled his anxious need to be away, in order to follow Maelen and the Zacanthan at a reasonable pace. They had all boarded the craft and Zoror had tapped out their destination before Krip said: "Human and yet not—Terran to the eighth degree in body. Something else in mind."

Maelen nodded. "Off-world—and with a different mind pattern from any we have crossed." She looked to the Zacanthan as if she expected he would know the proper answer to the identity of the follower they had detected in their careful search.

"A Plantgon—" Zoror said.

Krip's lips shaped a whistle and Maelen looked as if she would deny Zoror's identification.

"How—"

The Zacanthan shook his head. "His shield is very complete. I might have pried a little and learned more, but then he, too, would be aware that we are not altogether without the same defenses and weapons. Yes, he is one— No, in that I am wrong—*it* is one such as we seldom have here. That it passed the port detectors makes it formidable enough for us. It is plus ten to be able to reach a place where it will have all the defenses known to a great many more races than live or have lived. We may be grateful to some explorer whose wind-blown ashes have fallen into the smallest of tracing and whose race and time can only be guessed at. There is one place where even a Plantgon, and I know all which had been said and guessed about them, cannot pierce with either mind or dream body."

They were winging, at the speed allowed in the fast lanes, straight for the headquarters of the Zacanthan study team. Farree relaxed. He had heard one or two whispers concerning Plantgons but he was not quite sure what they might be. However, if the name meant so much to those about him they truly must be formidable opponents.

..●)5(●..

"What have we then?" Zoror was settled in an easyseat which accommodated itself to his body. He held in one hand a blackish-skinned fruit into the skin of which had been inserted a tube from which he sucked now and then. His companions of the late adventure were all occupied with restoratives, each matched to taste of the drinker.

Farree rolled his tongue about his own drink tube. The tart liquid was refreshing, seeming to wash out of him some remnants of the ordeal through which he had gone.

"Qun Glude 'p itho." Vorlund looked to the small screen of the reader on the table. "No identification with the Guild. Was second officer on Halfway in last employment—legal one, that is. He disappeared after his flight right was cancelled. That was on Wayland's World near five planet years ago. Activities unknown but was seen in company with Xexepan, commander of a Free Trader under suspicion by the Patrol. Entered into the records because Xexepan has twice been accused of smuggling—mainly in the Wormost slave trade. Apparently"—he raised his eyes from the screen from which he had been reading aloud in trade code the few lines on a val slip—"Xexepan must have been a shrewd voyager. But what was a slaver doing so far into the civilized lanes? He could not have been—"

Maelen leaned a little forward. "There is always kidnapping," she pointed out. "No tie for Xexepan with the Guild?"

Vorlund flicked a switch with his finger and the lines of code flashed on again. "No straight tie, no. Wayland's World?" He looked now to Zoror.

The Zacanthan made reference to his own call screen. "Fourth quadrant—Ast showing. However, this Xexepan sounds of interest. What was his cover on Wayland?"

"Straight trading. He had some skins, a full cargo of yale sap containers. That was all on the landing permit."

It was Farree who interrupted, for a dark picture had touched him, but not from any screen. "What kind of skins—are they listed?"

They all three glanced at him. In the Zacanthan's eyes there was a sudden gleam. "Little brother—yes, perhaps you have put thought to something there. Indeed skins may be a key—" Vorlund turned back to the reader. "No other definition—only skins. We might use a chart, High One," he addressed Zoror.

Zoror swung his seat a little to the right. There was a second screen there, its picture surface now occupied with a viewing of a broken stone slab across which ran a wavy line of nearly time-erased scratches. With a click of a button this was gone. Zoror inserted another plate. This time the screen flared to life with a star map which grew larger and larger, hurtling towards them. "Wayland—to the left." He prodded a button and one of the dots flared green for a moment.

Farree felt giddy, as if he had been wafted into that screen without any safe anchorage or propulsion. His gaze flickered, almost as if he had been ordered, not to view the planet Zoror had pointed out but to look for another. His wings spread, not from any conscious order of his mind.

"Farree!" Maelen's voice broke the beginning of the spell. "What is it?"

"The chart—there and there!" He had reached the table, edged past Zoror, as his fingers jabbed at the sector far distant from the flashing representative of Wayland to the northeast, nearly at the end of the frame itself where there was only a scattering of stars.

"Why?" Zoror asked. "Wayland is near the rim—there is very little beyond save unexplored worlds, mapped by chart swimmers but with no information taped to draw either First in Scouts or Free Traders, as venturesome as those are."

"No!" Farree pounded impatiently at the table. Togger squeaked and tumbled from his hold on Farree's shirt. He fell on his back and lay for a moment waving his claws, wide spread to show all their vicious promise. One of those scraped along Farree's hand as he raised it to point again at the bright dots on the screen, but luckily did not cut flesh. "There—that is what I saw—the sky dancers! That chart—it was what I saw behind them!"

"Sky dancers?" echoed Maelen. "Little brother, we have not been there."

Farree was impatient now. Within him there was a tug, a need to answer something which was neither words nor mind touch from his companions. "I—when we were there—in the shiptown. I saw—because of this." Now he ran his fingers around that brand the vanished scarves had set upon him. "There were the winged ones—the Mist Dancers—and then before them the lights. I tell you—the lights are those!" Again he pointed to the screen. "They are there!"

Vorlund leaned across to see the chart better. "You say this Xexepan is a Free Trader—and a slaver?" His tone was cold and his jaw was set. He spoke not to Farree but to the Zacanthan.

"My son, there are rogue traders. And if a Guild man wishes perhaps to find himself a cover—can he not use such a listing?"

"No!" Now it was Vorlund's turn to explode. "We are not dirty handed, no matter what others may say of us. As for this Xexepan—if he wears such a registry mark and is not one of us—then he is an outlaw and no one can stand between him and any trader who calls him to account. We can take his ship, him—" Vorlund drew a deep breath. "There was the affair of the Angol—Surely it is remembered! Those who used her so—they did not space again—unless walking on the emptiness outside an air lock can be considered spacing. The Free Traders take care of their own name—those who would push it into darkness will have every ship against them. I say that your Xexepan was either a liar—or the worst of fools—to name himself so!"

"Well enough," Maelen's calm voice, measured against the heat of Vorlund's, was very cool. "Wayland—let us see now." It was her turn to survey the chart closer. Zacanthan drew aside for her. "I have been a spacer for a short time but—" Now she tapped the screen with a forefinger. "Look you—a ship riding outward from this"—it was the cluster of stars Farree had indicated—"what is the first planetfall suitable for trade or perhaps for contacting some emissary of the Guild? If one stumbles upon a treasure which is too large for one to handle there are but two solutions—one, to bring forth a part of it and seek a partner, or—to leave it, to be ever more regretted. I do not think that Xexepan is the type to nourish regrets. Therefore with a token cargo he would search for the nearest planet to serve his purpose. It may even be that he was already one of the eyes and hands of the Guild—to search out what will be of meaning to them."

"Somehow I do not think he is a slaver. The Patrol rides the space along the rim. There would be too much risk in slaving. Perhaps he did go to Wayland to hunt what he did not have—a Guild contact."

"He came from there!" Farree held to his own interest. "This Glude"—the name twisted in his mouth—"had—the wings—the parts of them! You say he had skins—what if those 'skins' were wings?"

Vorlund drew a breath which sounded almost like a whistle. But it was Maelen who asked in that calm voice of hers, "What *did* you see, little brother? Tell us."

He frowned, trying to remember every small detail. "There was an open land, very fair—" For a moment he was caught by the memory of that place so totally unlike any world he had seen. "There were mountains—and those who danced upon the air. I could not see their faces in the mist. But they possessed wings"—he put up a hand to touch the outer ribbing of his own—"like mine. They—danced and then came the lights through the mist and those formed that!" Once more he indicated the corner of the chart.

"A far reader." Maelen looked to him. "It could be possible. Try—" She reached out to the top of the table where sat the screen and caught up what must be a lump of earth, or so it looked to Farree. This she pushed at him until, without knowing why, he took it up. Again without the volition of any thought his fingers enclosed it tightly. He looked to Maelen for an explanation. "What comes to your mind, little brother?" she asked.

Why did she do this when there were other things to be thought of? But under her compelling gaze he looked down at the clod he held. In that part of his mind which could and did speak to Togger and the others something stirred.

He closed his eyes, again not knowing just why. Before him was darkness, then into that night came—

A creature moved. It was slender of body, and was raised on stiltlike limbs—four of them. Two more jutted out from the body and those gripped a black wand or stick. The slim body was round in comparison to those legs, as was its much smaller head. And it emitted purpose—and that purpose was killing. Behind that no rage nor fear, rather the neutral state of a thing which grew because the instinct of growth lay within it, as might a seed within the earth. It raised its weapon, if weapon that was, to bring it down with what appeared to be the full strength it possessed.

Yet that defense did not save it. Rather it stumbled

back as a sharp lance of what might be flame centered on the creature's body. It twisted its limbs as it fell, twitching and kicking. Still Farree knew that it was dead. He opened his eyes then and looked to Zoror. Choosing words as best he could he was about to speak when the Zacanthan said it for him.

"Death—yes—and a being who knew enough to arm itself and strive for defense." He spoke to Maelen and Vorlund. "You saw—?"

They both nodded. Zoror took the lump from Farree. He tapped it carefully against the table then brought forth that talon instrument which he had used to such good effect in the shiptown. The nearly iron hard covering flaked away, to show a contorted mass of fine yellow bones—hardly larger than a finger.

"This is from my own world," the Zacanthan explained. "Zatan made an expedition when I was but a fingerling. He went into the Canyon of Double Dark and what he found there was this—" Again he slipped a tape holder into the screen rim and the scene vanished to display something else—a bulky cylinder lying on a table, a hand and part of an arm of a Zacanthan resting next to it to show that it was indeed small.

"The remains of a ship," Zoror continued. "Old beyond even our counting, but truly a star ship. The crew must have been both small and limited as to numbers. We sent inner beams to explore and classify. It's like had never been seen before. That"—he indicated the bones still entombed in the stone hard lump—"was found not far from the exit lock. What our little brother here has shown us may be a crew member of that ship. This lump was caught against the ship which our expedition brought back. I have kept it as a reminder that there may be strange things even in one's old world—puzzles which have no solving—as yet. We have talked, Farree and I, about legends and tales, both encased in 'history' as these bones are in this petrified soil, but perhaps still alive in the speech of some races even today. The Terrans have such stories, which they carried with them out among the stars. A winged race, a race which once inhabited the same planet as they sprang from, a race which was feared both for their strange knowledge and its enmity with the dominant species of that home world."

"The legend sprang up again on many worlds as those of Terran descent spread among the stars: Little People sometimes friendly, but mostly to be feared for the powers they possessed, which could not be equaled or understood by those of other blood."

"It is perhaps not mere coincidence that such a story could be known on Wayland. In fact that world was named by a scout who was known to be a collector of legends. He served my people also with what he brought back in strange tales and artifacts. When age caught him he retired to Zorp where he was received with honors and his lectures were deservedly popular. I, myself, attended the one which dealt with 'Wayland,' which world he named after a legendary 'god' or storied hero. There was part of a memory song which he told us then—and it has lingered always in my mind, for to my race it carries a hint of interesting speculation. To his kind it was meant as a warning, to my race a challenge in our quest for knowledge. The bit of old lore went like this:

"*Up the airy mountain, Down the rushy glen, We dare not go a-hunting, For fear of little men.*"

Vorlund's lips had moved in company with the Zacanthan's as he repeated the rhyme. The Zacanthan nodded. "So you know this also, far traveler?"

"I heard a part of it once—from a tales teller on Dawn. But it was then part of another story which ended—'because of the grind'—which was a local story monster—one who was an eater of children."

"Little men," repeated Maelen. "And the knowledge of them spread—yet none have been seen?"

Zoror nodded toward Farree. "Perhaps they are seen now. As for gifts which would seem strange and even dangerous to those who did not have them—here is our younger brother able to mind speak, and also to read the past in part." He tapped the broken lump.

Only Farree was thinking of something else. "The wings," his hand went up to touch an edge of one of his own. "The wings—'skins'?"

That rage which had possessed him earlier was returning. Again his hands met before him so he could rub fingers about that brand which had been set on him, as he looked over Zoror's shoulder to the screen where he saw not the miniature space craft still pictured there but rather the star chart. It would seem that the Zacanthan's thought moved with him though Farree was not aware of the invasion of that other mind this time.

"It would seem that there is trouble there."

"The Patrol?" questioned Vorlund.

Slowly the Zacanthan shook his head. "What evidence have we? You have read the data existing on the man with whom we have had contact. Xexepan is under suspicion, but unless more evidence comes to light they would not move. The Guild? One can believe anything of them. What we overheard makes plain that there have been seeing eyes following Farree and doubtless you also. But it is our younger brother here who I think is their main objective. Yet he does not have any knowledge which would benefit them. Thus they want him because he is how he is."

"And who am I?" flared Farree. Sometimes he felt as if he were entangled in words when he wished only the freedom to do—to do what? He could not answer that.

"That is what you have come here to learn," Zoror returned. "A race new to us, save in old legends—"

"A race," Farree repeated, "which was once feared, which has a feud perhaps with the Guild—" His mind sped from what he believed to what might be believed. There were odds and ends which might well be woven to form the truth of that!

"West quadrant." Vorlund might be still staring at the chart but it was plain that his thoughts were speeding elsewhere. "There are journey tapes for Wayland, that must be so. But do those exist which will lift a ship still farther out?"

"Officially?" Zoror picked up his drink again. "That would be only the brief one of the scanner. There may be another—perhaps Xexepan has it."

"A scanner tape," Krip said musingly. "We have operated on such before. It is a chancy way to travel, to be sure. But my people proved that it can be done—over and over again."

"So they have," the Zacanthan agreed.

"You cannot go there." Farree spoke against the surge of feeling which was filling him. "You have done much for me—" He held out his hands, one toward Maelen and one to the Free Trader. "Twice you have freed me. From the stench that was the Limits, from the hiding place I carried with me." His wings waved as he remembered how he had walked under the burden of his tight-furled pinions, thinking that he was one deformed, a bit of refuse. They had called him, those of the Limits, "Dung," and he had accepted that he was not one who had any future save the days and nights of a scavenger. Not until when venturing with these two into danger had his wings at last broken free, and he had done for his friends what they had done for him—a service beyond their power of body. They did not look at him. Krip might have been turning over in his mind some problem, viewing it first from one side and then the other, as he often did. Maelen again flexed her fingers—she could have been painting on the air some picture which only she and those of her people might translate.

Zoror leaned back in his chair, putting aside the drained fruit. "Yes." He was not answering Farree but appeared to speak his own thoughts aloud. "There have been expeditions outfitted from just such a thin thread. But two things will be needed—authorization from the Patrol and credits enough to outfit for what may be years of search."

Krip's mouth quirked. "And neither do we have." Farree stared again at the star pattern. He was without any influence, without any credit save what had been his part of the reward for their smashing of the Guild conspiracy on Yiktor. He wore wings to be sure, but they were not such as would bear him across the star lanes. Yet there was a hunger growing in him, the feeling there would never be any peace for him unless he could find out—

"No, you do not," Zoror conceded.

"But—" Maelen interrupted. "An expedition for the purpose of studying a new race, or ruins remaining: what else do you have but the best reason of all! Your own life has been spent thus, and if you should add something to that great storehouse of knowledge your people maintain—"

There was a throaty chuckle from the Zacanthan. "Sister, you need not tempt me. As all my race would be, I am already won to this quest. You are right, we do not value any reward save that of knowledge gained. We heard those space vermin speak of a treasure. That must be the lever used to move the Guild. However, we can adapt that rumor to our own use. Treasure has many times been found in the remains of a dead and gone race, or even species. Wait—"

He pulled out of the embrace of the easyseat and crossed to a second screen. Before he dropped his hand to the call button there he waved at the others. They caught his unvoiced warning—to scramble out of the range of that screen so that whoever might answer would not learn that Zoror was not alone.

The face which flashed on the screen at Zoror's summoning was that of a Tryistian, her sleek feather crest lying flat, her large eyes half lidded. By the badge on her jacket she was one of the records keepers and also Patrol, but of the Scouts.

Zoror spoke first: "Serve-Wing, is it possible to locate for my seeing the spotter tape covering—?" And he recited a jumble of figures which meant nothing to Farree.

"Your purpose, High One?" she asked.

"Recent information. There may well be a find of note to be made there. Before I make my report I must check this."

"A spotter tape, High One, has little information. However, if anything so reported would be of interest to you, it is freed. Switch to inner files—"

"My thanks-giving, Serve-Wing—" Her picture had already disappeared from the screen. What flashed on in her place was a diagram composed of figures and symbols making no sense to Farree, restraining his growing impatience. However, both Krip and Maelen now went to look over the Zacanthan's shoulder to watch the procession of data.

Impatience continued to eat at Farree, for it seemed that the streams of formulae would never cease. Twice those lines were halted for a moment or two by a sharp motion from Krip. He had taken from an inner pocket a small hand recorder and was holding that up to face the other broadcasting unit, apparently taking notes on some portions which he must believe to be important. Then the date was gone leaving the screen bare except for the flickering light. Zoror typed out an answer which would carry his thanks for the information and list it as Zacanthan research.

"Two solar systems," Krip said. "A sum of twelve planets.

I think even Zacanthans might think several times before an expedition was fitted out for such a prolonged hunt."

"Some of those worlds," Maelen pointed out, "are such as would not sustain any life with the same requirements as ours."

Krip nodded but did not answer otherwise. He was busy with his own small record. "There are three Arth-A, six which are borderline, the rest—" He shrugged.

"So you have three now, not twelve," Maelen pointed out.

"Two in one system, one in the other," the Zacanthan agreed. "If you were a far trader—as you once were, brother—to which would you first chart your way?"

"To a doubtful gamble—that one." His finger indicated a choice. "But there was no reading of life on that report. Should it not have checked for that?"

"Some do, some don't," Zoror answered. "The probe making this report was a long way from its home base, or the ship which launched it. Its data banks were nearly full. They are sensitive enough to anticipate a shut down and allow for one as they clear their complete fill up, and it is time for them to return. This was launched on 7546G and it returned on 7869G."

"The time of the Pan-wen War!" Krip cut in.

"Just so. And during that time the Patrol was fully occupied. The report may have just been added to others, lain unnoted for a hundred planet years or more. I wonder." He tapped his display of fangs with a talon on a forefinger. "We may not have been the first to be so interested."

"Who could reach that information without authority?" asked Maelen.

Again Zoror gave that throaty chuckle. "A good many, sister. There are many secrets which the Guild hug to themselves. It is said, and with truth, that new weapons and informational devices are often obtained by bribery, murder, thievery. No matter what arms they may run and sell for planet wars, the most effective ones are kept for their own raids and secret attacks. That they have access to sealed information is well understood. So that if they tap into such storehouses of exploration tapes as that we just witnessed they will have their own method of making it profitable. Who knows, they may hold rights auctions to their own newly discovered worlds with outlaws bidding, and a large cut for the Guild at regular intervals. Just as your people, younger brother"—he nodded toward Krip—"buy 'traders' rights from Survey."

"So," Krip returned, "then we have a secret which may not be one?"

"Our Farree here says so with his very presence," Maelen answered. "How did he come into the Limits? He is mind blocked, and with such an unknown power that even the Ancient Ones of the Thassa could not search far into his memory. Perhaps one of your stolen Guild devices did that. He is here and we—what do we know?"

"Only the bits of legends which are deemed more tale than fact," the Zacanthan said.

"The wings!" Farree burst out. What if the Guild had as many devices as the stars sprinkled in the night heavens? There were those lengths of beauty which he had held. That dream, or vision, also—the dancers with the wind who were like himself.

"The wings," Zoror repeated. "And a measure of what

we overheard this night. So—" His words carried more of a hissing as he spoke faster and with emphasis. "We have a chart, we have the edge of a mystery wherein the Guild may be at odds with all comers. We have a ship." Now he pointed with his taloned forefinger to Krip. "We have a Moonsinger whose talents perhaps even the burrowing, spying Guild do not understand. We have one from an unknown world and his valiant companion." Now he indicated first Farree, and then Togger. "We have an old one who wishes to learn a little for himself and no longer, for a space, pore over the reports of others—" Now the finger pointed to his own chest. "Do we mix the lot of these and what do we do with the sum of it?"

Maelen laughed. "I look to you, High One, and I look to my comrade in adventure, as to our younger brother here. To your questions there is only one answer. Let us go and see!"

··•)6(•··

Farree hung suspended in the webbing which protected him during take-off and transition into shift. With his wings he could not lie on one of the bunks. As usual he was giddy, with a sickish taste in his mouth, and was for the moment content to remain within the restraints. Around him the walls of the ship vibrated with the force which was its life. It was Krip's ship, Maelen's ship, the one which they had thought to travel the star lanes with those in fur and feathers who would go, to prove to the other worlds they might visit that there was a brotherhood between life forms which must be recognized. They had begun on the world of the Limits with a bartle and Yazz, both of whom had played a part when the Guild threatened them on Yiktor. Nor had those two chosen to remain behind now although Maelen, mind touching, had explained what must be done.

This time, they need not depend upon an unknown pilot, one who might even be a traitor to them as had been so before, for Zoror was himself a pilot and had carefully studied the tape he and Krip had patched together from the data of the searcher. They had lifted off-world recording a goal which was far enough from what they sought that their actual destination might remain their own secret.

Zoror was sure that no spy set by the Guild could penetrate his own library-cum-laboratory. That building was manned largely by robots carefully constructed to obey his voice alone. Though the Zacanthans spoke trade talk, their own language demanded a voice range no other species could project.

However, Maelen had detected a mind search seeking vainly to enter their stronghold several times during the counts of twenty days while they were making their preparations. There had been no difficulty with the authorities. The sector Patrol Commander had stamped his own private seal on their permission papers. A Zancanthan was never questioned when he or she voyaged.

With Zoror's own equipment tuned to a new use, they had inspected—and Farree had been able to join in handling that—every shipment of supplies before it was sealed into the ship. There would be no stowaway surprises to attack them.

Farree himself had lapsed now and then into meditation. To his continued disappointment there were no more visions. He might have been concentrating upon Zoror's own home. On their last night a-planet he at last ventured to speak of this—for if there was no truth in his vision they might even now be acting at a long range motivation induced by the Guild.

He had stood among them, his own wings folded as tightly as possible, and voiced his fears.

Maelen shook her head. "Not so, little brother! Had your vision been a trick its falseness could be speedily read. We who did not see with you might well have seen instead a lashing of the web in which that was bait."

Zoror agreed with her. "There is this too: an object which carries a message may be set to carry such only once. Having made contact with you the charge was exhausted. That one did indeed leave its mark." He gently touched the brand on Farree's wrist. "But only we know of this."

Though he had a great deal of awe and respect for both the Moonsinger and the Zacanthan, and their similar though different ranges of mind send and thought examination, Farree was not convinced. However, he did not mention his fears again. At least on his wrist he did carry proof that there had been power a-plenty in those remnants they had found.

To his shock and disappointment his memory of the dancers and the sky chart did fade even though he strove to hold it in detail. Zoror's story of unknown devices which the Guild could control was part of a private distress. He had been helpless prisoner for a time to one such when they had made their foray into the Field edge town. Could he then have also been marked, even by the scar on his wrist, so that he could prove a guide for others without his knowledge?

They made the change into warp drive easily enough. Farree had to move carefully through the ship, with his wings tight folded, as the passages were narrow. His sleep periods were uncomfortable as he must also accommodate those pinions within another cramped space. Some of the time he spent down on the lower deck with Bojor and Yazz. The huge shaggy bartle that had come from the world of the Limits passed easily into slumber, content to spend most of the voyage in a kind of hibernation. However, Yazz sought mind contact and asked questions Farree could not adequately answer.

Yes, there was a world awaiting them which had open spaces where a fisual could run to her pleasure. Though he himself could not remember too much of the world of his vision, the bright green of the land below the mist clad mountains remained with him. He was sure such a world existed elsewhere—he could only hope that the tape Krip had spliced together would lead them there.

Since the ship was running on a locked voyage tape, with all the alarms for any emergency set, Zoror did not occupy the pilot's seat any longer than it took for him to check at certain intervals that all was well. When hunched back again into the long seat at the end of the bridge, he triggered a small scanner and set a procession of pictures, interspersed with more lines of the intricate script of his own species. Maelen shared his seat and his interest in the records of finds which had been made—Forerunners' long lost works. Rightly she might search such, for the body she now wore was that of a Forerunner—some queen, goddess or ruler of a people totally forgotten until their hiding place of treasure and long sleepers was uncovered in a secret mountain hold where the Guild had come to meddle with that which they might not have been any longer able to command had they gone some steps farther in their investigations.

Dying, Maelen had taken on the body of another long

sealed into a chamber to await a waking which had not come in the millenniums between the time when the last barrier had closed and that hour when spoilers had broken through. There she had fought a battle with the remnants of an evil will which still clung to the body, banishing that other after a hard fought engagement. Now she asked Zoror if her present like existed in Zacanthan records, only to be told that she who was gone might have been one of half a hundred races who had sought the stars in years now so far in the past that the numbering of them could not even be tallied.

"It is, you see," Zoror said once when they were all together, Vorlund swung about in the co-pilot's seat to face the other three, "for us a matter of putting together many bits of discoveries, like striving to set in position the shards of a Trysua glass picture which has been broken past redemption. There is perhaps the find of a derelict ship, preserved in space where it has hung past our accounting, or one of the wind-beaten ruins of the Uavan Desert on Tav where one can only guess what the original form once was.

"And there is also the shifting of old tales, of stories told by far travelers. There was that of the Numerod—"

"Captain Famble's find!" Vorlund cut in.

"Just so. Famble might well have been one of my own race, so diligently did he search for that which was only known because of a few sentences gasped by a dying spacer taken from a life boat. The richness of his find on Scar nearly matched that which your own ship discovered on Sehkmet. Only of the people who fashioned those works of art, those things of great beauty, we know nothing

more. In none of that treasure was there any hint even of
their race or species. They used many motifs of flowers,
strange birds—or at least winged creatures—and others
which ran six-legged, inlaid with gems to remain for all
time. But of the representation of any creature which
might be deemed one of the makers—of that we had no
hint at all. And Scar, as you know, was a burn-off, half of
its surface congealed slag, so imbued with radiation that
any close search was impossible, even for one well suited
up; while over the rest of the world there was a tangle of
vegetation gone totally wild. We have deduced by what
we saw and found there that those who had left their
belongings in the caverns had done so in haste, yet thought
they might come again. However, they did not—"

"There was also," Maelen said, "the skull of Orsuis. Not
even your people, High One, had seen such as that
before."

"That has proved to be a puzzle which many of us
seek to penetrate when we are in youth studies." Zoror
nodded. "The skull might be that of a modern spacer of
the old Terran breed—but it is wrought from a single
lump of Cris-crystal which the experts tell us today cannot
be worked by any known method. Yet it exists, and plainly
it was in some way a manner of communication. There are
many puzzles for the finding here and there."

Farree nodded, rubbing the brand on his wrist. During
his time in the Zacanthan's headquarters, he had seen
many strange things. There were also the legends Zoror
had stressed about winged people, the Little Folk who
were supposedly known to Terrans, not only on their own
world but out among the stars.

Flight time was wearying at best—especially when the ship was on destination tape. However, the Zacanthan used this period to keep their minds alert, holding their interest to more than just winning through to the end of the voyage. During the arbitrarily set ship's hours Farree and the others listened to Zoror's fund of stories of finds and mysterious worlds dead from some war or catastrophe, where ancient weapons yet fought on and anyone trying to land was attacked. Farree paid eager interest at first. The world of his childhood—the malodorous Limits—had had nothing to feed his imagination or instruct his mind—and this was heady stuff.

Only when he was back in his own cabin, Togger occupying the bunk Farree could no longer use because of his wings, he would rub his wrist until the skin was chafed—wishing he had the other silky scraps the booth owner had had, trying, until his very mind seemed to ache, trying to evoke an answer alone, but possessing nothing to read it from. He shivered now and again when he seemed to be answered by a thrust of pain as sharp and fleeting as if he had faced a laser beam. Each time that occurred he was left sick and hurting.

Farree was squatting on the edge of the bunk, his back to compartment door, when one such a session had been so sharp and debilitating that he swayed back and forth. Togger gave a claw rattle that made plain he had picked up a strong broadcast of Farree's pain. Nor was he the only one for a voice reached him from the compartment door: "Farree! That—is death!"

His arms were wrapped over his chest as if he must cling to some part of himself against a fear that was near unbearable. Almost, almost he had been able to pierce that fear, to reach who or what was behind it. His cheeks were wet with drops which gathered on his forehead and ran downward. Fear—yes, fear, but with it anger—Both emotions seemed to lie as a brand upon his thoughts even as that length around his wrist had put its burden on his flesh.

"Farree." Maelen had moved along the wall until she could look directly into his face. "You must not do this—"

He shook his head. Then he half whispered, "I must know!"

"And what will be good for you to know, younger brother, if it puts its mark so deeply on you that you cannot function? See?" She reached out to draw her fingers down his wet cheek. "You labor and that which you would draw near you is—death. We also have the inner sight, we can follow so far—to go farther means the upsetting of the Scales. Molester gave us the gift of such sight; we are vowed not to use it wrongly."

For the first time he looked at her. "I must know," he repeated; but his voice was dull, that painful awareness gone.

"Perhaps—but not that way—never that way, Farree. None can see beyond when they take the White Path, just as none may return." Again her hand stretched forth as she held it palm down and a little above his wrist. "This— even I can feel what this holds, little brother. That which is implanted with sorrow and death cannot be used lightly. For your own sake do not seek to do that."

There spread into his mind something more than the words she spoke—it was a soothing, gentling feeling, like hands bandaging a gaping wound. Dimly he realized that what Maelen was mind casting was that same assurance that she had many times used with those she called her little ones, whom others might term beasts. Sighing, he nursed his wrist, for, under the soothing thought, he realized that there was truth in what she said. He dare not waste he strength on this search—not when there lay more arduous trails ahead. That there was danger coming he had no doubt.

"Good," she spoke aloud rather than thought. "I promise you, younger brother, that there will be a time for you, and when that comes you shall have a great part in what will follow."

He glanced at her, surprised. There were always hints that those with mind speech could also do more—even as he had proven he might read from touch. Only to foresee was not widely known and all he had ever heard of it was rumors.

"Not foreseeing." She picked that up quickly. "It is rather by reasoning, Farree. This is no easy voyage which we make now. If we raise the planet of your people it is well we be prepared for trouble there—"

He nodded. Yes, it did not take any mind skill beyond thought to understand that. Also she was right, he should not waste what gifts he had trying to compel answers, for that was useless. Any mind skill came and went spasmodically and you could not force it.

So he did not try to summon up again what he had seen so briefly in his one vision. That must have fulfilled its purpose when he had remembered and read the chart which had sent them on this voyage. Instead he set himself to another way of preparing for that which might wait ahead. Not only did he coax more and more reminiscences from Zoror, but he visited Bojor in the cabin which had been specially fashioned to fit the huge furred body of the one-time wild hunter, an animal on its own world so greatly feared that even the stories of its bloody meeting with settlers roused terror.

Farree was learning now from a source which lived and breathed, far from the tapes and scrolls the Zacanthan guarded so dearly. His own short life—or as much of it as he could remember—had been spent in the filthy dregs of the Limits—infinitely worse than even the portside on the planet from which they had risen. He had never seen open country until they had finned down on Yiktor. There events had sped by so fast that he had not had time to think of what they saw but only of what must be done, and as speedily as possible. He had acted mainly from instinct and not from knowledge.

Now he matched thoughts with the bartle and so lived the life of the great furred hunter. He padded down mountain trails, his head up to savor the wind and any message that it brought. Claws were sharpened on a favorite rock which also marked the boundary of Bojor's own hunting ground. And so did he slip from one outcrop of rock to another, eyeing a small herd of grush feeding the shoulder-high grass. Thus he squatted on the banks of the stream, one paw ready to dip in with a gesture seemingly too delicate to be used by a bartle, and bring out a swift-swimming creature which had the sinuous body of a reptile.

It was not a one-way meeting for thought which tied

Farree to Bojor during those sessions. For the bartle roused from his hibernation enough to display a curiosity of his own, and demanded that Farree return adventure to balance adventure. The life of the Limits was something which Farree recalled very briefly and from which Bojor turned away in disgust. Those hours he had spent on Yiktor were all he had to offer.

He could still recall the wonder of that time when the hideous hump which had made him a matter of disgust all through his days split and peeled away and his wings were born. The first moments of his beginning flight, when, unsure and clumsy, he had made the attempt to raise himself above the ground, he remembered well—and all the rest of what the wings had brought him—the chance to serve Maelen and her people as no one except he who was so endowed could do. That memory appeared to interest Bojor above all others.

His own experience with flyers had been only with birds, one species of which had followed him boldly from place to place, feasting on the scraps of any kill. For creatures such as himself and the others aboard this ship (Farree discovered from the first that Bojor looked upon them all as fellow beasts, clearly apart from the hunters who had first entrapped him, even though they had worn the same kind of bodies as his present companions had), flight was very strange indeed. He plied Farree with thought questions as to how one felt speeding above and not across the earth.

There were not only Bojor's memories to be tapped, but also Yazz's. The slender-legged, beautifully coated animal had other information to add to that which Farree was eagerly assimulating. So and so did it feel to come upon a strange track in the muddy bank of a drink-pool. A nose at such times was greater than an eye to tell whether this was an enemy or a stranger who need not be feared.

Farree rubbed his own nose ruefully at that. Though he had been able to trail the wing patches into the ship, he certainly lacked such sensitive and selective nostrils. Thus Yazz added to his store of knowledge about what one might search for in a new territory.

Zoror, Bojor and Yazz all had something to add to his lessoning in preparation for the future. But it was from Maelen, and from Vorlund, that he learned that which would be of most importance if they descended from the stars to discover their chosen world had other menaces— perhaps from those whose interest they had already brushed against.

"They had that wing portion." Vorlund gestured to the mark on Farree's wrist. "It is true that trade after trade may swing from planet to planet, nearly across the space lanes—but those wing portions, while they are rare enough, might have little value in themselves. They might have been brought to back up some story, to entice backing, even as a form of introduction from one Veep to another. Perhaps they thought to use them not only as bait for you—but for all of us, little brother, who must now be well known to the Guild—did we not spoil their game on Yiktor? And they do not easily forget losses and failures. It would not be well for them to either lose or fail without exacting punishment—they have enemies enough who might be so encouraged to fight back. Yes, if this is bait—then we are perhaps heading straight into a trap. So for that we must be prepared."

Thus Vorlund became his instructor in other ways. There was the use of the slender knife which the spacer carried concealed in the top of his space boot. Though their room for practice was greatly curtailed, Farree learned how to throw. In addition he listened as carefully as he did to all his other instructors for useful information which could only come from a Free Trader who had known a number of different worlds. Not the least was Vorlund's collection of Guild information gathered from years of listening in ports and to shipmates.

Farree had thought that life was of little worth in the Limits where not even the peacekeepers walked except in pairs and then with tanglers at alert. However, the more he heard, the more he came to believe that there were dangers he had never dreamed of when he had slunk through the shadows of that pest hole. He had once thought that life in the upper town would be ideal and now he was certain that peril was even more complex and ever-present there also.

Dream—It was one night when he had settled in his cabin hammock that he began to dream. He was hovering above a rich green spread of vegetation where bright touches of color rose up to the sun as the worlds appeared to spark a star chart. A stream of water bubbled along, so clear that one could well view the stones scattered over its sandy flooring and spy upon the fleeting shapes of water dwellers.

There were taller growing plants along the stream edge and among those fluttered gauzy winged insects, their armored bodies jewel bright. For there was warmth and light—not only from a sun, but also shooting from the mountains which stood high to protect this peaceful cup of valley. Here, too, there was the drifting silvery mist which floated, now and then veiling off one of those heights and then another. Only this time no flyers winged through it—there was only an empty land. Farree was struck of a sudden with a sensation of vast loneliness containing not fear but despair. He was unaware of his own body—only that he could see—and feel: settling upon him was a need to go elsewhere. There was a flashing of light and he faced an opening of what might be a mountain cave. From the throat of that spiraled the glittering mist.

If this was a natural fault in the rock there had been those eager to re-fashion it, for there were workings to smooth the rock and then overlay it with crystals such as he had never seen. Pure white, like water frozen into clusters, shading downward to the threshold and upward to a squared-off space. Those jutting points near the foot were dusky, yellowish, as if soil had worked into them before they had been frozen into immobility and, far above, the water-clear stones were tinged with a faint shade of violet which deepened into a rich purple.

The doorway drew him and he floated (for he was not aware of flying in this dream) towards the entrance—only to be so sharply and suddenly repelled that he was driven out of dream and sleep in the same instant. He lay, gasping, his heart beating so fast that he felt it must be shaking his whole body. For a space of time which could be measured only by his hurried breaths he adjusted to the fact that he was in the cabin and not before that burnished, gem-studded and open doorway.

Far in his mind something stirred as if a door long and securely locked was shaken. He lay inert and strove to reach that door, only to have a sickening whirling possess him utterly. While he pressed his hands to his mouth to help control the rising sickness in him, there came a signal from the wall of the cabin. They were coming out of overdrive—if Krip's efforts had been successful, the system they sought lay waiting for them.

Farree moved cautiously, levering himself up in the hammock. The sickness was still with him, but so was that vivid and complete dream—as much of a reality as if he had specifically sought out the crystal door.

••●) 7 (●••

"There it is!" Krip pushed forward in the co-pilot seat to view what lay on the vision screen.

Green, blue—a round ball rapidly approaching them was before their eyes. For it seemed to Farree that that world was approaching them rather than they were seeking for a landing place on it.

"Ah—" Zoror's hands were busy on the controls. A feeling of tension spread from the Zacanthan to the rest of them. Just as in the dream the crystal door—or something—had warded Farree off—now the feeling arose in him that danger waited—

Zoror's attention was all for the bank of buttons and levers before him, but now he spoke to Vorlund: "Station for entrance—do you use the controls also—" The Zacanthan's shoulders were braced as if he were exerting force against more than buttons. Vorlund's own hands flew down on the co-pilot's controls and his face drew grim.

Did a flicker on the screen actually waver for a

moment? Farree was almost led to believe that it did. In that breath or two out of time it might have been that their ship was warded off, held from entering the inner skies of this unknown world. Then, if there had indeed been a barrier, it was gone. They finned in with the same ease as if the Zacanthan had held the ship in his hand to place it neatly on a solid surface. Vorlund leaned forward to touch the level of the vision screen which would turn slowly to give them a full view of the space where they had landed.

There were wisps of smoke rising which veiled much; the landing rockets must have found something to set alight. Maelen was reading symbols which flashed on a smaller screen near her right hand. Those blazed up in small green flashes, each one of which Farree knew stood to reassure that beings such as themselves dared explore without wearing ponderous equipment meant to battle hostile atmosphere.

The air, the light, all seemed well; there might not be a second warn off. Farree wondered if any but him had felt the first. However, when they prepared to down ramp and go to view this world he saw Vorlund buckling on a stunner belt. Maelen flexed her fingers as if her bare flesh was also a weapon.

That the Zacanthan was also reaching for a stunner was a surprise. So respected were the Zacanthans across the star lanes that even a Guild Veep might consider carefully any idea which included interfering with one. In fact rumor had it that Hist-Techs' continued studies of the past had included experimentation with outre weapons of the Forerunners and that they were better left strictly alone. Farree had his knife in his boottop but he doubted his own efficiency with that in spite of Vorlund's careful schooling.

They came out on the ramp which was slung out over the strip of burnt vegetation. Maelen paused, fingers lightly clasped and held out as she slowly made a half arc turn, sweeping from one side of the country before them to the other, Vorlund and Zoror pushing back a little to give her full room.

Farree used his mind without any link to an instrument. Of a sudden he took to the air, soaring up above the ship, winging out and away from the circle of destruction its tail flames had caused as it rode those in for their landing.

He headed for a point in the cup of valley in which they had landed—a green-covered hump to the north of the ship. It was the first, he noted, of a series of such which sprouted upward in a straight line. They varied in size, however, some being taller even than Zoror afoot and others so small their presence could be overlooked unless one was searching for any rise in the vegetation.

The careful placement of the hummocks made Farree believe that they were not the work of nature. Burial mounds? Ruins well concealed by years of abandonment? He loosed his mind touch, but there was nothing, not even a fraction of a hint as he earthed on the first one of the line.

This vegetation was thick, curling upward about his feet near to knee height. Hidden by the many three-pointed leaves were small flowers of a dim grey-white, as if the sun, so warm on his wings, never touched them. The weight of his feet loosed scent, sweet-spicy, while from near the patch where he had alighted there burst into the air pellets, some of which struck against him and clung. Those, too, were the grey-white of the flowerets. He pried one loose from his jerkin, finding it sticky, holding now to his fingers. But the moment he took that into his hands he had again a pain-edged flash from that inner part of his mind which had been always sealed until he began this venture. He—he knew this!

Salenge! Ill-bane! It banished ills and made the heart light—only how had he known that? "Salenge," he repeated aloud. His fingers closed of their own accord on the tiny clove he held. It burst under pressure, releasing another scent, sharper, making his nose tingle, the saliva flow in his mouth. Again, without conscious thought, he raised his now juice-coated hand to his mouth and licked the remnants of the burst berry from his flesh. It was cool in his mouth and hot as he swallowed.

Farree flung back his head to look at the sky above the arch of his wings. Salenge—that he knew—and also its use. Only he had never seen this before—or had he? Impatiently he thrust at that barrier in his memory and then swayed at a second bite of pain. No, do not push— Maelen had told him this and she was right. There was nothing but emptiness when he sought. Yet when he let his thoughts settle elsewhere there came hints such as this. He stooped and shook the plants gently. On his other hand and arm he caught as many of the expelled balls as he could. Then he winged up, to circle the ship in an outward swing, studying the ground below.

They had not landed in what could be thought a valley, rather in an odd formation of ground. It was indeed cup-shaped, a perfectly round stretch which was walled by cliffs and rises, with no sign of any break through which one might depart without a climb. Through the lower of those cliffs were partly masked in curtains of vegetation, as thick-matted as the ground, with many entangled vines, the reaches higher up were of a stone which was of a grey close to silver. Through that ran a pattern of veins of a clear white which in places caught the sun and flashed as if they were embedded with gems.

There were no trees or large shrubs—only the rippling of the salenge which was thickest about that line of undulating mounds, then grew less and less until on the other side of the finned-down ship, beyond the black marks of its landing fires, there was a sprawling of what seemed to be leafless vines across a grey-brown soil, hardly distinguishable from what they rooted upon.

Farree climbed with strong beats of wing until he reached the level of the sparkling stone. The air was clear and the scent of it was the scent of growing things which he gulped, after the recycled atmosphere of the ship, in mouthfuls, fairly drinking it down. The exultation which came with free flight was like a heady draught. Almost he forgot all else when he swung around over that space where the vines made odd ridges, leafless against the ground.

For the first time he centered his attention completely on that. Its contrast to the verdant growth at the other side of the space ship became more and more apparent. He dropped to fly closer. There was something about—

Again a sword of memory cut at him deeply.

Hagger—a hagger run. He could see in his mind a

bloated brown body, a thing which ran stomach down on six legs. Yet the shape of its head—! Hagger!

That which controlled his flight did not wait for memory to grow any clearer—it sent him climbing, heading for the gem rocks with wildly beating wings. Then he fought free of that fear, turned back, coming once more to his first perch on the mound. Again around him arose the scent of trampled salenge, soothing—relaxing—

Hagger and salenge—where under the moons of Three did such ever come together? The moons of Three! He dropped his harvest of burst berries and held his head in both hands. Again a memory flash—why did such torture him so?

"Farree!" Maelen's mind call brought him out of that haze of pain. "What is it?"

He did not answer. Instead he took wing, flying back to the ramp outsprung from the ship and there stood before the other three. Plucking a salenge berry from the edge of his sleeve he held it into their full sight. "This is salenge— what they call also ill-bane for it heals all ills and wounds if it can be used in time. And"—he gestured to the ship— "behind that are the hunting lines of the hagger. Do not ask me how I know this—I cannot tell." He shook his head slowly. The pain had eased, yet he knew that it was lying just beyond—waiting—

"Where have we landed?" To Farree's surprise Zoror asked him nothing concerning what he did know.

"Thus—" Quickly Farree replied with a picture of the cup in which they had planeted.

It was Vorlund who broke the silence first when he had ended.

"No way out then?"

"Not unless you climb. But I have not had time to search thoroughly."

Maelen let her hands hang free. "No life registers—save our own party."

"Those mounds." The Zacanthan nodded to the humps Farree had first sighted. "Grave barrows, ruins—" He spoke as if to himself. Then he asked Farree the question for which the other had been waiting. "Salenge—hagger—?" Repeating the words he made them an inquiry.

Farree shrugged. "I cannot tell you why," he repeated, "but that much I know."

Vorlund sealed the lock with a word code they all repeated after him and then they moved off, Zoror heading straight for the nearest one of those hillocks. Vorlund stood eyeing the nearest wall, now hidden under that thick coating of vegetation and Maelen held her head up, staring straight northward, as if from a breeze now rising she had gathered a message.

Farree's gaze followed hers. He actually staggered as the strongest hurt from that hiding place of his memory struck home. "Caer Vul-li-Wan—"

Not part of the barriers which closed them in now, no—rather a peak upstanding like a narrow tower surmounting a keep. White against the sky which was a rich green-blue—Down its sides he thought he could see flickers of glitter even as far away as it must be—perhaps the same gem light as on the upper reaches of the cliffs about.

Almost as if his small flash of recognition had sent out some unknown message to alert sentries, there was a gathering of haze about that spire, a cover which might have been drawn from clouds too high to be seen, and it was gone from view.

Zoror's thought struck with almost the same force as the memory touch had given Farree. "Caer of the Seven Lords? So—it would appear that we have indeed been caught up by legend, younger brother. But whose legend? Have you come in summons by the 'Little People'?"

Farree paid him no attention; he thought only of the sight of that slim uprise against the sky. No, he had never seen that before—Then where had he gotten that name, and known that it was truly the right one? The haze which hid it now—the Breath of Merl-Math wafted in, to confuse any not of the true blood. But not raised to confuse him.

No, there was other cause to wear the wind veil! Other causes—! He was airborne once more, hardly aware that he had beat upwards with what was near a leap. It did not matter that the Caer—that which called him—lay elsewhere. Farree wheeled in the air, looking not to the north where the peak was now hidden but to the west. At that moment the ship, those from it, everything which made up the mystery of this new world was wiped away. In him was a compelling call which only he might answer.

Already he had passed above the lip of the cliff which walled in the cup. There was no stretch of green beneath him as he dropped a little lower, skimming across a space filled with many pillars and wedges of rock, where there blazed forth with force enough to make him squint and strive to see only through a narrow slit, flames of light, red, green, blue, yellow, and also rainbows of many colors.

"Farree!"

He blocked that call out of his mind. Beside the compulsion which sent him on it was but a fading whisper. He was needed—he, alone—not those of other blood—those who plundered and took, killed and enslaved—"I come!" He thought that with all his might, all the power he had learned from Maelen and Zoror. It was as if his own thoughts broke and tore as had that rough skin which had covered his wings, freeing him in another way.

Even as that tatter of some other's wing skin had led him through the crooked lanes of the portside town, so did that appeal, growing ever louder, draw his mind. The stretch of country where the jewel fires blazed fell away. He saw before him now a sloping into another valley but one much wider and more uneven of shapes. There was the glint of water there, and clumps of what might be trees. No bare soil showed the crisscross of hagger ways. Yet there was life here. Across the valley a number of dark animals were apparently grazing the short turf. One flung up its head and pointed that in Farree's direction. On so low a thought band that he almost missed it, he sensed part of what might be a question. He had no desire to linger and answer. The creature reared, flashing forelegs in the air, perhaps in challenge, while those others about it bunched swiftly, before taking off first in a trot and then at a rocking gallop.

Up from the copse of trees not too far from the river whirled a flock of birds taking to wing with the speed of warriors summoned by a chief's horn. They drew near to Farree and he saw that, though they appeared at a distance to resemble birds, this close he could see no feathers. Their brilliantly hued wings were more like his own and their bodies were covered with scales which were as jeweled in this light as the cliff rock he had crossed moments earlier. Their heads were long and narrow, split near the beginning of their sinuous necks with gaping jaws which showed teeth.

He eyed them warily and soared higher. There was a wind now which was chill and had what could be a snow bite to it. Perhaps it had come from the taller mountains to the north. For some reason the bird things did not try to join him. Instead they wheeled as if on some shouted order and headed north, leaving the sky clear.

The sight of this alien life had, in a strange way, dimmed the message which drew him on. Now that was strong again. Suddenly he was looking down at a disturbance of the turf and soil below. There was broken earth, gouges and ruts. Surely those were of such a size as to make certain they were no beast spoor left to be tracked by a hunter. Oddly enough they had sprung from a point in the middle of a bare space of ground as if whatever had left those marks had issued from beneath the surface itself.

Farree flew on. Now he discovered that the call which drew him lay in the same direction as that trail. He winged ahead to where a fringe of small hills were a screen between any ground traveler and the land beyond. But the ruts found a way among these barriers, weaving in and out. Here the valley, which had appeared narrow in the beginning, widened out, though even from the air he could not see what lay far beyond. The same haze which had veiled Caer Vul-li-Wan cloaked it as fully as if a curtain, hung high in the heavens, lowered folds to hide the earth.

For the first time Farree faltered. That plea which had brought him so far had been cut off—as suddenly as if death itself had been the portion of the one who uttered it. Also there was something about that haze curtain which struck him with a greater chill than even the snow breeze had raised.

He turned track and flew south—only to find there again the curtain in place, while the call was not even a whisper of a whisper. The haze did not hang to the north or across the eastern sky through which he had flown. As he coasted along still a good way from its edge he tried to search with mind call for the cry he must answer, only to shrink backward—for it was as if his own thought, badly distorted, had been thrown back at him. Nor was there anything in his treacherous memory to match this.

To fly above was no answer for, as if it were indeed some weapon aimed at him, the haze spiraled upward also, matching him. From it that deadness reached outward. He was sickened, drained, having all he could do to keep a-wing. The ebbing of energy brought him at last to ground level where, once he felt the firmness of the sod under his feet, he struggled to keep on those feet, unable to do more at first than to gasp for breath.

The haze might have defeated him at this first encounter but that certain stubbornness of spirit which had kept him going as a homeless misshaped creature of the Limits held him now. His wings folded down about his shoulders like a cloak as he crossed to a big rock which showed a deep scoring, as if that thing which had made the road had grated along it. There he sat on the stone, his hands on either side of him, bracing his body as he strove to master the weakness assaulting him in deep waves. His move raised the scent of salenge. There must have been some of the seed globes still clinging to his clothing. He inclined his head to draw that reviving odor into his lungs. A flicker of more recent memory came uneasily—He raised one juice-stained hand to the front of his jerkin. There was no familiar bulge there.

Togger! It was the first time since he had first known the smux that he had actually forgotten him entirely. Now, finding him gone was like losing part of a wing—or a hand. The discovery shattered the spell of compulsion that had kept him seeking westward. He viewed the haze squarely. It appeared to be drifting in his direction. There was a curl of it reaching out to where he perched. Without knowing why he put out his hand and—felt actual pressure against his palm!

Instantly he jerked away. The Wall of the Carrion Wind! There was a faint odor of corruption which flowed from his hand, where it had rested against the unseen, up into him. Farree closed his eyes, and saw darkness shot through with hard brilliant beams of light—light which was as straight as a laser ray. Between those beams there were shadows, some leaping forward as if to drag down a hunted creature for the kill, others falling away because some flash of light touched them and slew. In the midst of the whirl of light and dark someone stood. At first he thought it might be Maelen or even Zoror.

Then he knew that it was neither but one who ruled the

Carrion Wind and set it as a barrier against which the living might beat in vain. Only he could not see the one who labored so.

The brand about his wrist awoke to pain, almost as great as that which had first struck him when it had been set upon his body. Farree opened his eyes. He might even have whimpered aloud as the torment grew. He looked down at the hand which he had raised against the force of the haze. There was a blaze of color above the brand mark, hiding that with a brilliance of gem radiance.

He raised his other hand to nurse his hurt, wavering to his feet, feeling as if he burned in a fire from which there was no escape. Farree cried out.

"Utsor vit—S'Lang." His voice seemed to slant outward—almost as if he could see the words take shape and strike at the haze.

There was a curdling of the mist; it might have been stirred by some great ladle. The barrier began to thin before him, first forming a window of sorts through which he might look upon what had been hidden. Then that slit lengthened into an open portal. Farree blinked, shut his eyes. The vision of the darting lights was gone—

Carrion Wind: once more his lips shaped the naming. The stench from the drifting filaments was strong enough to overcome the last trace of the salenge which had revived him.

He did not take to wing again. Instead, with his pinion-cape furled about him, he went forward on foot, picking a way with care because of the deep ruts and holes in the surface of the strange road. The inner call which had summoned him was alive again but very faint and faltering, as if the one who formed it was near to the edge of strength.

Farree stumbled and kept his balance with difficulty. That which tripped him was only half buried in the broken earth. He stooped and dragged it free and stood staring at his find almost stupidly. He knew it—it was out of the past which he well remembered—the hell hole of the Limits. A pulse whip! His finger slid along the indentations in the butt. No weaving of force answered him. Burnt out. Only to find this favorite weapon of slavers here! He made to cast the evil thing from him and then reconsidered. Zoror—the Zacanthan knew such disciplines; it might even be that he could pull out of the torture weapon some idea of who had wielded it last, advance an idea of what enemy they might be about to face.

The haze was near dissipated. Farree had wondered what lay beyond the portal his shouted words had opened. But there was only the churned-up earth, which vanished when it reached a curve of height beyond.

That which had called him faded again and died. He still felt the renewed pain in his wrist but he was no longer imbued with the drive to fly ahead. Instead, with the whip thrust safely in his belt, Farree took wing again, heading back towards the ship.

He half expected to see the haze rise again, to the east, shutting him away from his shipmates. But there was no more clouding of the sky. The sun was farther away—and the chill winds buffeted him. He looked to the north, half expecting to be able to sight the spire of Caer Vu-li-Wan; only it was as if that had been erased from the sky.

There were similar heights to be sighted—the one most important was gone.

Farree scowled. Now he could no longer trust his eyes—That calling, was it responsible for this blindness? There were too many questions and no answers he could pick up for himself. What words had he shouted? Now he could not remember. Maelen, Vorlund—to them things like this were known. The Zacanthans closed no doors upon the hope of knowledge, even though it was yet only a hope. What had he? Fragments of a tormenting memory, but so little more.

He shook off his sudden self-pity to look around, seeking some landmark. There were the cliff tops ahead, not so alive with flashing colors now that the sun was nearing setting. To him now all looked alike and he had not even the sighting of Caer Vu-li-Wan to set him aright. He was startled by a harsh call—one he heard with his ears and not his mind.

He was not alone in the sky. Above and beyond him a second pair of wings beat, wings as large and wide-spread as his own. But they were not mounted on anything which could in the least be thought his kin.

It was black, that elongated body, which twisted as easily through the air as a snake would cover ground. The head was turned in his direction and he saw a half open mouth, not unlike the ones he had seen on the smaller thing which had flown ahead of him earlier.

It screamed again. Farree needed no other warning, and he flew with all the speed he could summon. That thing also had great clawed feet. Those talons now flexed as if ready to close on prey and as it was fast overtaking him, a third cry sounded almost in his ears.

..●) 8 (●..

He was over the cliff top now, streaking at the highest speed he could muster to elude that flying thing. Its body twisted and turned as lithely as that of a snake, matching speed with him, but keeping a little above on a parallel course, while from its open jaws flashed what could have been a tongue of flame. Still, though it hovered above him, giving every indication that if it wished it could attack, it remained two lengths of its own long body behind. Why it hesitated to pull him down was a growing puzzle.

Farree's head jerked up and a lock of his hair flopped across his forehead in answer to what did reach him.

He was meeting a stream of thought which wriggled back and forth as did the body from which it sprung, its message now clear, now snapped just short of fading out with the speed of a breath.

"Darthor, Darthor!" The words burst from him. The stab of memory did not come so sharply this time.

He no longer strove to flee and at the same time

somehow keep eye on what had been a menace. Had been—? Of a surety it was so.

"Darthor, varge!" Surging in beat, his own wings carried him higher, brought him around in a glide to face the monster. The creature cut speed. It veered to the north, though it still kept its large orange eyes fastened upon Farree.

"Darthor, varge!" He shouted as one who has mastered a captive horror from some unknown world and impressed his will upon it. It squawked, lashing the tail which was a good third of its body length. A shaft of what certainly looked like real fire shot again from between its jaws. It did not spiral away from him, only altered its line of flight so that it flew tandem with him, matching its speed to his.

Farree switched from voice to mind send. "Darthor, servant one, hunting lies not in my shadow." The words came to him in curious formal fashion as he thought them slowly and with the emphasis of one who would be obeyed. A dim picture hung behind that voiceless speech, Darthor a-wing after something which fled in frenzy, while behind him was one who was also winged, who carried a glittering rod in one hand. Himself! No, that could not be—Not him, but one who was his like, before whom Darthor flew as a hunter. Yet Farree's first fear was not quite appeased. He was no master of this creature. Still why did he know it and fear its coming?

For the moment he could do nothing. Darthor was flying in odd spurts even as a land-running thing might give sudden leaps, and always it kept its eyes on Farree. There was a sly sullenness in that gaze, as if the hold he had on it, keeping it from the leap which would tear him from the sky, was only tenuous, that at one moment or the next he might lose that unsteady control.

They were in sight of the edge of the cup valley now. Shadows had crept from the heights to reach out toward the ship. Farree headed toward that mound where he had first trod the earth of this world.

An air-splitting shriek which seemed able to rend the rocks themselves startled him. Even as his feet met the mound he looked up. That creature who had accompanied him was lashing its tail, its whole slender body, back and forth through the air. It would attempt to fly in Farree's wake only to be hurled, actually hurled, back in the air, wings beating frenziedly, other shrieks following the first.

There was rage in every assault it made from the edge of the cliff top. Its clawed forefeet reached out as if to tear the air itself into shreds. Farree was aware of movement beside him. Vorlund came to a stop, his stunner unleashed and ready for firing.

"No!" Farree cried out, striking at the other's stiffened arm as he took aim.

"Darthor—guard—" He fitted together the small scraps of knowledge which he had. "It fears—you!" Saying that he knew he spoke the truth. The air creature was centering that yellow-eyed stare on Vorlund while lashes of the seeming flame burst from between its jaws. There was rage in it which was as strong a weapon as the one the spacer now held.

"It cannot come here." That also was true Farree knew. There was no billowing haze to present a wall and yet there existed a barrier, unseen, unfelt by Farree in his flight—only set against other things. At that moment there was released from the squirming, flapping thing another kind of attack.

Vorlund cried out. Though the stunner wavered in his hold, he did not drop it even as he fell to his knees. Farree had been on the edge of that blow delivered mind to mind. But not from Darthor—that creature had only released what was being fed to it.

"Fragon, Shadow commander, I name names." The pain in Farree's locked mind nearly sent him sprawling beside Vorlund. "Name names," he thought again. There was a mad whirl of color in his head, but he still held to what was blanking out, or attempting to black out his mind, as a blindfold might have cut off his sight.

"Fragon, Fragon—" He chanted that sing-song aloud as well as holding firmly to what he directed toward the flyer.

"Fragon," he repeated. Then he was chanting: "By the sky hold, by the throne, by the green, and by silver worn, I do call the name—thy name!"

The thing on the cliff top writhed, spinning as if some great fingers had closed upon it to wring it like a rag. It was screaming again. But pain had arisen to blot out what it had been transmitting. Vorlund was shaking, his face strained unnaturally, but he was rising, though the stunner now lay in the thick green growth about their feet.

A new power possessed Farree. He felt a surge of such strength as he had never known. His wings spread wide and he held clenched fists above his head.

"Take your Shadow one, Fragon!" His thought had somehow grown louder, more demanding also. "Take

the Darthor, Fragon. There is no meat for its rending
here!"

Abruptly the fading turmoil the creature broadcast
ceased. It still hung aloft there, its head lower than its coils
of body. Farree knew, even without being able to see at
this distance, that it was closely observing them, still a tool
for another, but one who was wary, angered, yet not ready
as yet to take the lead into battle. Then the creature
whirled in the air and the steady beat of its wings carried
it northward where a thickening haze cloaked height after
height, hiding well what might await them there.

Farree caught at Vorlund's shoulder, steadied the taller
spacer who leaned forward to catch up the stunner, only
to slap it deep into its holster. Then he looked straight at
Farree.

"What was it? It would have killed—"

Farree shook his head slowly, rubbing one hand across
his forehead where the cessation of that confrontation had
ended for him in a dull headache and a mistiness of
thought. He knew—knew what and why? He was unable
to sort it out now. There had been contact and now there
was emptiness, total withdrawal. "I—don't know—" he
quavered. Within both his mind and his body there was a
sickening churning. Pain, which might have been there
during the attack but which he had not noticed there, bit
deep.

"You named it," Vorlund countered. "There was a
second name also—Fragon—"

Farree shivered and then heard another voice, speaking,
not intruding into the place of growing torment in his
mind.

"A mighty mental power is this Fragon." Zoror came up behind them. Now he looked directly at Farree. "So, little brother, your mind barrier still holds?" He reached out one hand and gently pulled Farree's fingers away from his pain-wrinkled forehead, pressing his own to Farree's head in their place.

It was like a draught of water to soothe a dry mouth and throat: from that lightest of touches spread a cooling.

"I have never been here before," Farree answered in words, "yet I know!"

He felt Vorlund stir beside him, but it was Zoror who spoke: "Know what, little brother?"

"This country—or part of it!" Farree swung out his arms to indicate not only the valley but what lay beyond. Then he looked around to see Zoror still studying him. It was difficult to read expression on that scaled face so different from a humanoid's, but he thought that the Zacanthan's usual one of wide interest was now narrowed into a beam like the Darthor's fiery tongue, reaching out to him with the same force that flying creatures had used.

He closed his own eyes momentarily, in a hope to shut doors against the other's unspoken probe. Farree could not rid himself of the feeling that Zoror was willing an answer out of him.

"Where did you go, brother?" He had been too closely observant of the Zacanthan to note that Maelen was now also here. Her fingers pointed to Farree himself.

"Up," he answered dully, gesturing towards the gem-banded cliffs. Too much had happened to him. He wanted a time of quiet, or the ability to shut out the lingering tumult in his mind. "There is a large, very large valley over there." Now he gestured westward. "Animals—I think they are animals. Something like a road worn by heavy wagons—then"—he lifted both hands in a hopeless gesture—"there was the fog—the wall—" He strove to make plain the nature of that barrier but he had hardly finished when it was Zoror's time to question.

"Why did you so leave us, little brother?"

Farree answered with the truth. "There was a—call. I had to answer."

"And—" prompted Zoror.

"With the wall it was ended—that call."

"Ended so that this Darthor might take its place? Perhaps," suggested Vorlund, "you did riot answer quick enough. The impulse to incite you was not strong—"

"No!" Farree interrupted sharply. He moved a little so he was facing to the north, to that sky finger of a peak now completely hidden. "They are not the same!"

"What are *they*?" Maelen's voice was soft and low, and she did not strive to touch mind to mind. For that Farree was deeply thankful.

"There is—" He looked down at his hands and then was aware of a sharp tug at his boot. The ill-bane grew in a thick mat but it was trampled here and Togger was easily seen. He stooped and caught up the smux, holding him tightly. In all this maze of wounded memories Togger remained real, alive, and an anchor Farree could cling to. He cradled the smux, taking pleasure in feeling the creature's body pressed close to his own. "It comes only in bits. It hurts to think," he said slowly. "But I believe that there are . . . two forces here which do not work together. Fragon—and do not ask me to tell who or what that name is given to—controls the haze—and has spies along the land. The Darthor projects visions of what happens on the ground by cruising along the haze. I think"—he was frowning and the smux wriggled a little as if he were now grasped too tightly for even his tough skin to take—"I think that there is something beyond the haze—that which or who summoned me. And that other is in great peril and needful of aid."

"Which this Fragon would not allow to be given?" Vorlund wanted to know.

Farree nodded. "Only I could not go through the haze—it was a wall. And perhaps another exists here—for the Darthor could not come to us. Two—two forces—" His voice trailed away. Farree recognized the listening look Maelen wore. This was the Lady as she appeared when in contact with one of the animals or birds which were her lifelong other-being.

Zoror and Vorlund were quiet now, also watching the Moonsinger. Shadows were swinging closer as the sun descended, reaching easily the cliffs they could not climb. Her hands showed the beginning of a flush. Farree guessed that she was taxing to the utmost one of the few defenses her people had kept when they had destroyed a dangerous and contorted past to become wanderers on the earth of the planet they once had ruled.

She began to hum, and that faint sound throbbed also in him as her flush traveled over her skin and grew deeper.

Maelen opened her eyes. "There *is* something there. It does not yield to any search my people know. But it is aware—of us. It—" She did not complete what she would have said then but her hands no longer held straight. Rather they tilted towards the mound on which they stood.

Farree caught his breath even as he heard a whisper of hiss from Zoror. Then from beneath them as they stood— It was as if something climbed with ponderous movement up towards them, its passage setting the earth to rock with warning. Farree's hand swept out, knocked up Maelen's fingers. He knew that what might now be awake and stirring was no friend to such as disturbed its slumber. He dared to shake Maelen hard, as if he could force her to throw off bonds of a compulsion. Then she spoke directly to Farree.

"What comes to my call?"

A source outside his consciousness supplied an answer and as he gave it, he was also entirely convinced of its truth.

"The Sixth Champion of Har-le-don. He who shall rise in the last days of the Far hosting, no longer oath bound to any lord, but shadowed by the binding—" He cried out then, and threw back his head to look up into the evening sky. There was no flutter of wings there, no heart-rousing song of battle to face.

"Come not the dark for our day is not yet dawning!" He knew the meaning of the words he cried aloud, but he did not speak in the common language of the trader tongue.

It was Zoror who moved first. A scaled arm wrapped about Maelen's shoulder and she was swept from the mound top while Vorlund leaped outward, putting a side distance between him and the hillock.

"Farree!" His voice and Zoror's rang together. However, it seemed to the one they had left behind that the herb growing so profusely there entangled his feet and would not free him. Still he sensed what stirred beneath the ground. With that came something else, a thrust—though weak—into his mind. Not painful this time, rather cold, diffused. What or who might have aimed that might be only a little aroused—not yet returned to—

Using all his strength Farree repelled, defended. His wings opened to bear him aloft, but not toward the ship where he had thought to go: rather as if he had received an order he could not disobey. Farree landed on the next of the mounds, then after only a breath or two of resting, he was aloft again. Once more gripped by compulsion he crossed the open space, flying from one mound to the next, some large and some small, until he came to the northern cliff wall. The hold on him was broken there. He turned and flew back to the ramp of the ship. When he touched down there he felt free, as he had not been since they had made landing. What had forced him to make that flight he could not have told. He clamped his wings down into folds and walked, for the first time suspicious of the pinions he wore, back into the ship, trailing after those who had already gone in that direction. Nor did he wish to look over his shoulder, to see if the Great Mound showed any of the disturbance which was troubling it from below. He found the others in the pilot's cabin, Zoror holding a reader, his large eyes fastened upon a screen smaller than the palm of his narrow hand.

"People of the Hills." His voice was half hiss as it was always when he was excited. "That is the ancient name—People of the Hills. And their kingdoms, their places of refuge, were often said to lie under mounds!"

"That was glamorie." The three of them raised their heads to stare at Farree. Maelen and Vorlund wore expressions of no comprehension but Zoror's eyes glowed.

"Ah, glamorie," he repeated.

"Do not ask me questions!" Farree threw at him. His hands again bracketed his aching head. "I do not know where I find these words, or why—"

"It is no question," Zoror continued. "Rather this is a part of the old legend of the 'Little Men.' In many tales and fragments of tales, which have been gathered from the planets where the old Terran breed settled, there are such small scraps to be harvested. One of the stories which is told over and over again consists of two main elements. First, that the People of the Hills (and you were very right, younger brother, in giving them that name) had a different reckoning of time. To be in their presence for perhaps a night took a mortal man or woman away for a year from the life they knew, to stay under the hills for a year meant several centuries passing for the captive or guest from the outer world.

"The other strange gift they had was that of glamorie, of allowing those of the upper and outer world to be deceived easily, thinking they saw something very different from what was real. One of the People might pay for service in coins of gold, the one paid only to discover in his pocket not long after dried leaves or a twist of grass. The People could produce a great dwelling worthy of a high noble and he who feasted there with them would wake in the morning to find himself in a ruined and deserted pen for the safe keeping of animals. Also it is said that if a human was by some chance able to see through these webs they spread he or she might be blasted sightless when this knowledge was betrayed."

"Then they were always avowed enemies of other races?" Vorlund wanted to know.

Zoror's horny fingers rasped along his lower jaw. He shifted his stand a little so he was facing directly north.

"They were, according to the old tales, ever changeable. Some that were not of their race they would aid freely, making common cause with them against danger. Others were for their sport and suffered from their careless cruelty—"

"In other words," Vorlund said as the Zacanthan's voice trailed away, "they were much like us after all—save they perhaps used weapons which we could not wield."

"True," admitted Zoror. "What they would do with us now—for that we must wait and see."

"See!" Maelen was not repeating Zoror's word, but rather summoning their attention.

It was well into early evening. The sun had been cut off so that only the fading of a deeply rose-blue swath across the sky marked it. However, there was other light in the cup valley. Points of glimmer touched the top of each of the mounds as a flame might spring from a candle. They differed in shade or color from one another—here there was a rose shading nearly into crimson, there was one which flared first blue and then green; beyond was yellow, scarlet, even a deep rich purple. Only that largest mound was different yet.

There the blossoming light was not a candle flame;

rather it flowered into a circle, from the rim of which shot spears of gemlike brilliance. In color it was different also, being a frosty silver such as might appear on a winter snow bank when a full moon stretched across ice crystals. The points of each of those spears flashed also blue and green.

"A crown," Maelen said softly.

Farree bit hard upon his lower lip and fought for control. Just as that summons had taken him into the air and out over the unknown land, so now was another compulsion gathering within him. Without knowing what he did his hand stretched out—although the mound was far away from him in reach—his fingers crooked as if setting grip upon the crown. Then he shook his head as one who strove to drive away some inner fog, and his hand folded into a fist.

"Staver's Bane—" His voice was hardly above a whisper. "Take up that and the world is one's for the having!" Then he raised his voice in a shout which carried out over that display of jeweled flame. "I do not trouble you, Old One! I want no power from you! Sleep again, Havermut—your time has not come!" He was shivering, one hand clinging to Togger who somehow provided an anchorage in a place of whirling strengths rising to battle one another. He leaned over the rail of the ramp, and then there came from his twisted mouth those ugly obscenities which had studded the language of the Limits. Farree cursed the crown of light, those night candles about it, and fear fought anger in that cursing.

As if his words, expanding outward, possessed some visible power in themselves, the flames flickered. But that which he had hailed as Staver's Bane swelled larger and larger, embracing more and more of the hillock on which it was the crest, the silvery radiance of it slipping farther and farther down the rounded sides of the rise. No longer did it resemble a crown—rather it was a wheel which began to spin, so that the lights of its spear points became circles undistinguishable one from the other.

Farree, hoarse from shouting, caught at the rail of the ramp. He had only to—No! another part of him shouted in his brain, drowning out the first—it was truly a bane to him who would lay hand upon it. For this was no crown of the blue moon, it was rather a trick, a trap, bait to catch the foolish! Of that much he was sure.

The circle now had reached the ground level, forming a wall about the mound. There was a haze arising from it—Farree shuddered. With one hand still upon Togger to anchor him safely to the here and now, he fumbled with the other in the air, jerking fingers back and forth as if he were able to so erase what he saw.

High above the wall of the cup from where night had gathered with racing speed, there came a shaft of light like the force of a laser beam. It sped across the still gleaming candles and struck, full upon those who stood at the top of the ramp. Zoror cried out and slumped down. A rainbow of sparks shot from Maelen's fingers. Vorlund caught her as she stumbled back, and held her against his own body. In that moment the spacer appeared the strongest of them all. But Farree was held motionless, as if pinned within the space he occupied by that needle of light.

It came from the north, and, though he looked into the full glare of it, unable to turn either head or eyes away, he saw not the blasting of the light but behind and beyond.

There was a balcony, set into a wall and on that stood others—he could see no faces, no bodies clearly, yet he knew them for what they were—these were the masters of this world and to them, all who came in ships were dreaded enemies.

••●)9(●••

A moan sounded. Farree rubbed smarting eyes and turned his head. Vorlund leaned against the wall of the door port to Farree's left, Maelen was limp and motionless in the spacer's arms. Her eyes were closed and yet she moaned again feebly and tried to raise one hand.

Zoror had reached that point of what might be temporary safety before them. He was sitting up, his head clasped between his two hands, his fanged mouth open as he panted, drawing in breaths as if he had been on the point of being strangled. Still, as Farree glanced outward once again, the light was there, yet stopped at the port through which they had come as if some tangible force had cut it off. Zoror pulled himself up on his knees. He was still breathing heavily, yet it would appear that his condition did not keep him from the quest for knowledge which was the ever-present employment laid on his species.

From his belt he drew the talon knife which was both an honor badge of his people and, most times, his only weapon. He caught the tip between the two fingers and tossed it out to clatter down the ramp towards the ground.

What followed was like being caught near the tail of a ship taking off. There was an explosion of searing light which again left Farree blinded. Then—something which he had sensed—a compulsion, a stern will—vanished. He pawed at his eyes with one hand—they were still watering. However, that spear of light from the north was gone. The weapon of fire might have failed; he was sure it had not willingly been withdrawn. There remained—like a whisper in his head—unease—counter-fear—astonishment—all. Then that, too, vanished and there was nothing but dark and silence.

Those candles on the mounds had snapped out of existence as quickly as had the weapon of light. There was only thick dark outside now, dark and a rising wind which beat with an icy lash against Farree as he staggered a step or two forward to look out into the valley. At first he had a fraction of terror, the belief that he had been blinded by that last shattering of flame. Then, as he turned his head frantically from side to side, he saw that each of the mounds was still sending into the cold of the night thin trails of faint luminescence—it might be the breath of unseen monsters turned visible by the icy air.

There was no crown, no candle flame. Farree leaned against the side of the door opening and he looked beyond—toward the north from whence that spear had come. His teeth caught hard upon his lower lip—there—and there—and there—!

Not as bright as the mound candles, in fact tenuous enough to be only ghosts of those flames, there were pale lights. As his eyes adjusted he could count them—nine—They were too faint in color to be camp fires, and from

each streamed a thread of grey unnatural mist. Outward
to the south they were reaching over the valley, waving as
might banners. The first of these now dipped down, as if
to lap them out of their refuge, but it came no farther than
the foot of the ramp. There it wavered and clung, sweeping
back and forth, joined and fed by those other traces of
vapor, which made it more visible.

It was trying hard to get to them but it was walled away.
Farree heard an exclamation from behind him. A stunner
clicked, aimed at that wavering tongue of mist. It did not
vanish, no, instead it appeared to draw energy from the
power sent against it, so that the tongue of mist spread
wider, its movements becoming more energetic and
threatening, though it still did not reach beyond the foot
of the ramp.

"No—!" He heard Zoror's voice. "Cold iron—your boot
knife—let that feel iron!"

His cry might have been for Vorlund but it was Farree
who heeded the order first. He grabbed at his own boot
top, caught the hilt of the weapon which Vorlund had
taught him to use, though he had never done so except
in practice. The hilt was warm in his hand, the warmth
growing into real heat as he raised it. Then, as the
Zacanthan had done before him, Farree threw, aiming at
the tongue of mist. He saw the black spot that was the
speeding knife, and then the whip back of the mist. It
broke into tatters which waved wildly in the air. A
moment later he was aware that Vorlund had joined him
loosing the infighting weapon of the spacers.

That mist fluttered, a thing now of ragged, dissolving
wisps. It drew back to the mound which had been

crowned, but no farther than that, changing the direction of its advance, pointing rather to the ground than to the ship beyond. Once more it was rebuilding in shape and strength.

"Cold iron! That is truth then!" Zoror's hand fell upon Farree's right shoulder. The Zacanthan may have yielded to the strike of the original beam but now his voice was full and deep again. He was, to all appearances, his old self as he leaned past Farree to blink out into the night.

"Cold iron?" Vorlund demanded. "What do you mean?"

"Mean?" Zoror's voice carried all the force of one who has chanced upon a long-hunted treasure. "That once more there is a kernel of truth lying snug within legend, brother. It was said many times of the Little People that the one weapon they could not circumvent nor withstand was iron itself—iron which made man the master of the worlds where, one after another, they disputed his lordship."

There was a moan which was closer to a sigh. Farree swung around. Vorlund was down on his knees now, supporting Maelen. By the ship's lights her face was pale and drawn. She might have lain for long in the hold of some illness. Then her eyes opened and she looked up at the Zacanthan.

"They have power—such as even a Singer cannot summon—"

Zoror nodded. "It was always said of them that they were not to be easily overcome. There is something here, though, which we do not know—why should they attack without warning when we mean no harm?"

"Because of me!" Farree said bitterly. "And I do not have the knowledge to be able to discover the why of that either." Once more that ache in his head strengthened. There was something—something to be done—and the need for doing it gnawed within him; only he knew not what it was or why he must do that unknown act.

"We are safe within here," Zoror glanced around at them, his gaze lingering a moment on each as if he measured their strength and abilities. "Let us rest the night in iron-governed safety and see what the morning will bring."

Farree, half blind again from the pain in his head, lurched obediently into the corridor beyond the port. Somehow he got down to the level of his own cabin and there collapsed into his hammock, aware of nothing more than that his body rested and perhaps his head might follow. One hand moved restlessly. His palm felt sticky and not knowing nor caring what he was doing he brought up his hand and licked at it, so gathering into his mouth what was left of the bruised leaves and berries of ill-bane. He chewed and swallowed that harvest. The pain which had been a tight band about his head eased. He slid, as he might have on the ramp had he lost his footing, down into darkness.

There was a great hall, and panels in its walls were a-glitter with light, cold light, in spite of the fact that some of the colors were the red and yellow of flames. The pavement underfoot was silver, perhaps even true blocks of that metal. He did not tread there so much as waft above it, yet he did not feel any expansion of his wings.

Between the glittering panels were others of the same silver as was underfoot. Those were wrought with patterns in high relief. Some depicted strange creatures such as the fire-breathing snake which had hunted him back to the valley. Others were humanoid in form, yet differed one from the other. There were bodies like his own, winged and plainly traveling aloft. But there were also other things, grotesque, some monstrously so, and more merely strange, exuding no menace, as did a few.

There were no torches or lamps within the room—the radiance seemed to flow from the flooring beneath. Then he became aware of swirls of a milky mist which was coiling and recoiling, reaching every time farther out into the middle of the chamber. From somewhere there sounded a single trilling note. Two of the pictured wall blocks vanished sidewise into the flanking wall and there entered two whose wings were furled about them like colorful capes, even as he himself went where he trod the earth.

One was slightly taller than the other; since the wings sprang from the shoulders, they concealed most of the body, and were of a deep crimson shading into a silver as glinting as the pavement. His head (for the features on that calm and nearly expressionless face were ruggedly masculine, with a seam of scar across one cheek) was held high and there seemed to be flickers of fire in his large eyes.

His companion was just as plainly female. Her enclosing wings were the delicate ivory of the ill-bane flower, but they were also touched with silver which glinted gem-bright as she moved. Her long hair was braided about her head and woven in among the pale yellow of those coils were gem-set threads. Once in the room she loosed the tight covering of her wings to show that she wore a short, form-clinging robe of pure silver, girded by a wide belt of gold and brown gems. To the first glance she might look like a girl only on the verge of womanhood, but when one saw more closely, especially her eyes, there were signs of years of knowledge.

The man moved on into the center of that hall, his wings, too, now rising. While his body, even to arms and legs, was hidden in a glossy red mesh, he wore about his narrow waist a wide belt of silver scales which supported a weapon. Farree recognized it from pictures in Zoror's collection: it was known as a sword. The man's hands played with the buckle of the belt and he was frowning, his eyebrows near drawn together by a scowl. Now he stood staring down at the pavement as if he might find on the surface some answer to a problem which troubled him.

His companion did not come so far into the room. She held up her head as might one who was searching the sky and it was plain that her attention was caught by something which she sought aloft. Before either of them moved farther or spoke, if they did speak aloud, there sounded another note of summons, this time a double one which might come from within the earth. Two more of the panels opened, but those who entered thus were very different from the first comers.

They were small and they were wingless. Their shoulders were hunched a little forward, almost as if they were used to walking ways where the roofs pressed closer to the footing. Both arms and legs to the knees were bare, showing rough brown skin, wrinkled and pocked with small dark splotches. Their bodies were covered with clothing almost the same shade as their flesh. And, far from being beardless, the faces of both were covered from the cheek bones down with mats of crinkled yellow-white hair, thatches of the same apparently covering their heads, as tufts appeared under the edges of dingy, rust-red caps. Their features—large hooked noses and deep-set eyes— were nearly masked, and as they drew nearer together and came forward a few steps, there was the air of suspicion about them, as if they were far from easy in this place or with such company.

The winged man looked about and jerked his head in a nod which both the gnarled creatures echoed. However, the woman continued to look aloft, now turning her head as if so to view the whole of the large chamber. She took no note of the newcomers.

A third sound followed speedily on those which had brought the bearded ones. A last panel opened and there came through a masked figure who, because of its muffling, could not be clearly named man or woman. The mask has been made to cover the whole head, fastened at the shoulders on either side of the throat with dull brown brooches. It had been fashioned to resemble the head of a beast, even to a covering of bristles, like needle spikes, planted along the large pointed ears and across the back, as well as along the drooping jowls, which helped to form the face (if one might term it that). There was no true nose, only a snout above a half open mouth. Small eyes were dark pits on either side of that snout, and there had been set in place within the jaw a full showing of greenish-yellow teeth with a rounded fore-fang sprouting out both to the right and the left.

The robe about the body of the newcomer was masklike also, falling in many folds. In color it was red, and over its surface were black lines which appeared to move with each step the creature took, sometimes forming patterns, only to dissolve at the next forward movement.

As the masked one advanced, ponderously, as if the robe covered a large bulk, the two capped men drew back hurriedly and shifted to one side so that the winged man was between them and Beast Head. Again the woman paid no attention to latest addition to their company, her head remaining up, her eyes searching. It was Beast Mask who broke the silence. He spoke gutturally, almost as if he found speech difficult for his tongue and lips to shape. The words he spoke were slurred into a monotone.

"Why the summons?"

It was the man who answered him, though somehow Farree was surprised that he did so in audible speech: "They have come in greater force. Also they have more bait—one who has been turned to their service—"

"Where?" the Beast wanted to know.

"They have landed their hunting cage in the Valley of Vore," the woman replied, never looking away from whatever she must be seeking.

One of the small men laughed and the sound was like a rusty bolt grating in a long disused lock. "Ah, and them what sleep—they have stirred!"

There was a moment of silence. Farree believed that perhaps of them all he could read the greatest surprise in the attitude of Beast Mask.

"There cannot be an answer." That voice came even more harshly. "The dead have long since returned their substance to the earth. That which was the real part of them fled upon the coming of the strokes which separated them from life—"

"Ho." Again the dwarf laughed. "Good teaching that. So we can lie snug and not think of old ill acts and the payment thereof. The earth hides much—but its doors he opens to us!" He held his head back and as far above his bowed shoulders as he might. "Bind the dead down with wand—even with iron"—Farree noted the small start of the winged man at that word—"and there comes a day when ties will break, for even iron is eaten by rust. Do not think that you are rid of the Hunters and the Shield men because they were planted with the best of your spelling. Time may also wear that thin—"

He was interrupted by the woman. Her head had moved down and now it seemed to Farree that she was looking directly at him: her eyes widened with surprise and she held out one hand towards him, her fingers crooked in what he guessed was a warning sign.

"There is one here!" Her words came as sharp as a knife thrust.

All the others stared in his direction now. The man had drawn the sword, the blade of which looked like a flame stiffened into a slightly curving length. Had Farree been able he would have fled. However, that which had brought him here did not release its hold on him.

"Who?" the man demanded of the woman. Beast Mask had moved up beside her, snout seeming to expand, as if its wearer could indeed pick up an alien scent.

"Atra—" The gross voice within the mask pronounced that word as if it were a loathsome oath.

The woman answered with a decided shake of her head. "Not her, no. They may have made her their tool, but she would carry then the stench of them with her. This one comes not in body—"

Beast Mask brought out of body wrappings a hand which was long and thin in contrast to the rest. This was turned palm upward. Farree caught a suggestion of glitter from a round disk which appeared fixed to the hollow frame of flesh and bone.

A finger of color, or colors, for it was rainbow hued, corkscrewed about, aiming in Farree's direction. The woman uttered a single word and that hand shook, while Beast Mask gave a short cry as from pain. The man was beside the woman with one stride, his wings fanning out so the tip of one came near to buffeting Beast Mask. "Fool!"

"Fool, thrice fool yourself!" spat back the masked one. "How do we know what weapons the Hunters have made for themselves through the centuries of time? Can it not be that they have projected a defense to cover the incoming of a spy? What have we done? Gone behind our cloud walls, sealed ourselves in as a way of escape. I tell you that this will never rid us of these vermin who have trailed us on through space for more than five lifetimes of the Star!"

The upward gesture of that muffled head drew Farree's sight even though he felt as if he must be fastened there, easy food for the killing. The ceiling of this great hall was again silver—but it was a setting for something else.

There depended a huge crystal on a single chain, as Farree had seen in miniature made into amulets favored by those who believed in the power of luck. This one was divided into three points—the two on the sides jutting out from the middle one as branches might grow from the trunk of a great tree.

Rainbows of light not unlike those imprisoned in Maelen's fingers played along its surface, and there were flashes from the pointed tips of the three branches. Inside Farree there was a sudden mighty surge of feeling. What had filled him on the hillocks of the valley—that sensation that he was a part of something he did not understand, that ignorantly he might lose that which none could control, was back a hundredfold.

"Atra!" He had certainly never spoken that. It was only a reaching thought which made him try to raise hands pleadingly to that triune of crystal.

"Here!" The woman's voice arose in what was close to a shout. "One of the blood here!" She ran forward before Farree could attempt to move and swung her hand as if she would seize him. He saw the flash of fingers close to his eyes but he felt nothing. So real had this all seemed that he could not believe for a moment that he was *NOT* there.

"Not Atra—" The man joined her again. He had reversed the sword which he held and was now prodding with the hilt, passing through the very space Farree seemed to occupy.

"No." The woman's hand had fallen by her side. "If it is not Atra—then who would be so spying? None else has been captured alive by the death dwellers. And none of those has the inner power to enable them to come here!" the woman added. "Who else or"—now her expression changed from one of astonishment and wonder to a smooth mask in which only her eyes seemed alive. Yellow those were like the ones which Farree faced when confronting a mirror—"has there perhaps been some greater folly—some attempt to bring forth Atra? Someone of the Icarkin may have gone against the oath. A second capture—"

"So oaths do not hold you flutterers—" one of the small men growled. "Are you then foresworn?"

"Aye," his mate echoed. "Is not Atra of the High Blood? Mighty close do you stick together, you flutterers! Did they not set the trap with her as bait as speedily as she fell into their hands? These 'men' are not fools and they are all sick with greed. If they have caught another such as Atra and set him or her to watching—Did not Sorwin here say that they may have new weapons to bring against us? You!" He swung his head toward Farree or towards where Farree would be if he *had* invaded this centermost defense in person. "By rock and rap, by thunderclap, by sword and stone, and voice alone—"

"By heart and eye," intoned his fellow, "earth and sky."

"Show you must!" Beast Mask's voice, more than half snarl, ended the chant.

It was as if he were one of the candles' flames on the crests of the hummocks back in the valley; Farree felt a pull from one side to another. He might be clasped in giant hands and so shaken back and forth—Shaken back and forth. There was no more hall of silver and crystal— no more winged ones, no dwarfish workers of spells, no beast-headed monstrosity. Instead it was as dark as if a cloak had been flung over him. Then Farree opened his eyes. He lay on his hammock in the ship and he was blinking into the eyes of Maelen, who was regarding him with concern. Behind her stood Vorlund, and the taller Zacanthan was in the doorway of the cabin. Under one of Farree's hands there was movement and he felt the well-known contour of Togger's spiky body. Dreaming— he must have been dreaming! Only the memory of all he had seen and heard remained as clear as the ceiling crystals of his vision.

"You have been—elsewhere." It was Maelen who spoke, and she did not ask a question, she stated a fact.

Farree licked dry lips. Part of him was still Farree the outcast of the Limits who had been given new life and hope, but another part was stirring into wakefulness, an awareness which was born in the familiar pain within his skull.

"Under the crystal—" That part of the memory suddenly seemed the most important. "They—they have fear—of us—No," he corrected himself, "of men." For the first time another thought came into his mind and with it a spurt of excitement. "Great One," he spoke directly to the Zacanthan, "are we—men?"

Zoror blinked. "Each of us has a name for our own kind, a measurement against which we rank others. 'Men—women'—to a fellow of my blood I am 'man.' To other Thassa"—now he nodded to Maelen—"she is 'woman.' To Thassa and perhaps Terran also, because he held once Terran identity to come by chance and fate within a Thassa body, Krip here is 'man' to those two species. Yes, to ourselves, our kind are 'man—woman.'

What we may be to others—" He stroked his jaw with a taloned finger. "To those others we may be different. Extees is one word that is used. We have intelligence in common, and perhaps some extra natural gifts of mind or body—but we are not 'man—woman' in one meaning of the word with each other and his or her kin."

He was right, Farree knew. Here was a Zacanthan, two of the Thassa, and he who really did not know what he was. They were working for a common purpose but they were not a common species—"men—women" by some measurements—that used by those who pioneered in space.

"They fear, I think," he said slowly, "some like those of the Limits. But perhaps we can find an understanding—"

"With whom?" asked Maelen. "Little brother, where have you traveled this night?"

··•) 10 (•··

Trying hard to make with words a picture of what he had seen, Farree outlined all which had happened in that dream that was not a dream; but he knew not what else to call it.

"Ah." Zoror was the first to break silence when he had finished. "Here then also are several different races. There are the winged ones, the small ones without those pinions, and this one who wears a beast head. Tell me again, little brother, the manner of the mask that one wore."

Once more Farree repeated his description of that figure. Maelen and Vorlund were looking at him intently as if they hoped in some way to enter his memory and view that scene for themselves. But Zoror was nodding as if some bit of unexpected knowledge had suddenly fallen into his hands.

"Swine—" He said when Farree was finished. "Another of the legends come into life for us. You speak of an animal which was known to the People we seek—one the keeping of such they reckoned part of material wealth. Perhaps this masked one was a—" Then he frowned. "But Zargo said in his twin worlds research that this was a matter of women's religion and that a priestess would play herder—though his authorities were few and very obscure."

Farree thought again of the masked figure. A woman— or anyway female? That one's voice had sounded harsh and low pitched. However, it was also certain that the masked one was not of the same blood as those whom he might call kin—it, or he or she, was wingless.

"We can take it," Vorlund said sharply when Zoror's words trailed into silence, "that there is another ship downed here somewhere. And that the crew or owner has captured one of the winged people and is using her as bait."

"Also," Farree broke in, "her people are not trying to rescue her—Ah—" Now it was his turn to lapse into silence. Then he added in a rush of words—"She—it must have been she who called!" Even as he said that he experienced some of the force of the compulsion which had carried him from their landing place off across the mountains until he was stopped by the haze. The haze! Was that a barrier which the winged ones were using to cut off any of their people who would try to answer the captive's call? To him that instantly seemed possible.

Maelen read his thought. She reached for the far end of his hammock where his head had rested such a short time before. It was faintly alight with green and she clasped it tightly, her eyes once more on Farree's as if she willed him into some action. However, it was Vorlund who asked a question.

"You remember nothing else—nothing of these winged ones? Of how you went from here into the Limits?"

"If he came from here—" Zoror corrected. "There may be more than one world where such dwell. If it is true that they must have a world like to that which those of the old Terran blood required for settlement—Well, are there not numerous planets with such attributes, and not all of them settled, or, if so, only thinly. Our records report that these People have shared many different abiding places with those whom we well know. But there always came a time when the People of the Hills were forced to withdraw, to take flight again for the search for a place of their own, for they never lived in peace long with the human kind. Another planet may be such a home also—"

Farree rubbed one palm across his forehead. The ache was beginning again, becoming a dull torment behind his eyes.

"Guesses." Vorlund shrugged. "That Farree has found those like him may be the only answer. If we could only get behind that mind block which weighs upon you so, little brother!"

Maelen had leaned forward a little and now her fingertips touched Farree's forehead directly between his large eyes. That contact was almost as if he had taken a drink of water when he had been long parched with thirst. He saw that her eyes were closed and now her thought came into him.

"Loose—loose your thoughts, little brother. Do not try to raise any barrier—"

He struggled to do as she asked; the need of his own to find answers made him eager. Farree whirled around and stumbled back until he half fell over the hammock he had just climbed out of. About him streamed colors and those colors were pain which he could not subdue. He clung to the hammock, feeling as if that flood of color strove to carry him away. Then it winked out and he was once more in the dark, shivering and weak.

"It is a lock which I do not understand." He heard Maelen's voice but it sounded very far off.

"My lady, it is a death lock!" That was surely Zoror. "You must not try that again. Such a lock is unknown to us—even to our records—"

"But perhaps not unknown to the Guild," Vorlund cut in crisply. "Is it not well understood that they have secrets in advance of much of ours? Perhaps they held and lost him, and then only found him again when we battled on Yiktor and he came into his power of flight?"

"Possibly—" Zoror was saying, but Farree had his eyes open though there were tears wet on his cheeks. The ache behind his eyes seemed likely to blind him.

"Little brother—" Maelen touched his cheek, then smoothed his tumbled, sweat-slick hair. "There will be no more, this I promise you."

He was still shaky and weak when he joined the others on the bridge of the ship from which by the landing screens they could view the world about them as they ate ship's rations and watched the sweep of the outer mirrors. The ship itself was locked against any invasion and as an added precaution Maelen had alerted Bojor and Yazz, saying that their minds, being different from those who were seeking knowledge, might stand sentry into the bargain.

Those candles of light had disappeared from the mounds attendant on the large one, but every time the mirrors' report flashed on the last they could all see that there was still a pulsing circlet about it—no longer in the form of that wondrous crown, yet visible as a pale ring.

The ramp had been run out again for a short time, long enough for Bojor to shamble down, his thick-furred pelt, having been grown for the season of chill on Yiktor, making him look twice the size that he really was. But the bartles were never to go unmarked by anyone invading their native mountains. Although Bojor had been captured as a yearling, he still retained inherent in him the strength and cunning of a nasty fighter were he to be aroused. As all those Maelen called her "little ones" (which was a misnomer in the case of Bojor, for his breed was notorious for their handling of any would-be trapper and also stood taller than Vorlund when he rose to his full fighting stance on his sturdy hind legs), the mighty beast was able to thought meld with the Moonsinger to an astonishing degree, and had welcomed the chance to be a part of the active forces from the ship.

He melted into the dark as they tried to follow him with the ship's sighting equipment. However, he had been given directions to stay away from the hillocks and to head directly for the cliffs, prowling along the foot of those. Suddenly, as they sought to watch him, there appeared to burst from the ground itself a number of light dots. As if those, too, were under orders, they clustered, outlining the body of Bojor. He squatted back on his haunches, one of his huge paws, meant to deliver crushing blows, waving through the air. Yet he was unable to beat them off. They flashed so quickly that it was apparent he could make no contact with them. As length he went again to four feet and moved on, still revealed by the light dots so that now he could be easily watched by those within the ship as well as by anyone who might have summoned that form of illumination to keep spy sight on the ship and those within it.

Twice Maelen communicated with Bojor, only to report that the bartle had not been attacked, that the sparks of strange fire only hung about him. Yazz, who had come up into the cabin to watch the mission of her furred companion, whined deep in her throat, her attention all for the screen. She raised a forepaw suddenly as if she could scrape the surface of the view plate and so release Bojor from his strange escort. Even Farree, who had only limited rapport with her compared to Maelen's ability, felt her uneasiness, a kind of foreboding. Though the bevy of lights had made no really hostile move, it was plain that Yazz did not trust them.

The bartle's speed was deceptive. Though he appeared to amble along at hardly more than a strolling pace, he had almost finished a quarter of the wall's length. He had passed well beyond the carpet growth of ill-bane and was into the withered land overlaid with the pattern of the hagger web. Yazz once more whined. Farree dropped a piece of leather-tough dried fruit on which he had been chewing.

"Back!" he cried out. The advancing lights gave only a partial sight of Bojor, not clear to ground level. Farree had felt through his body, as clearly as if he stood out there beside the bartle, that beginning of a stir; not what had moved earlier beneath the hillock but something of the here and now. It was like an evil stench projected to his mind instead of assaulting his nostrils.

Yazz threw back her head and gave voice to a growling which was her own battle cry. She turned swiftly and pawed at the door of the control cabin, at the same time looking over her shoulder to Maelen, her whole attitude expressing her need to be loosed to join Bojor. In the days they had spent together these two, so different in species and early training, had thought themselves into a team, a team which had drawn Farree, too, into its being.

Farree had pushed past Vorlund and was busy with the door latch, Yazz crowding in beside him, ready to leap when that portal opened.

It must have been their united fear which reached Bojor. For the bartle had halted and was standing now, back to the cliffs, facing outward to where that webbing lay across bare earth. Maelen accepted the warning of them both. With no questions asked she pointed directly to the screen where Bojor was to be seen.

The light sparks shifted as the bartle settled back, again on his haunches, a favorite stance to await attack. His paws hung down before his barrel of body and, though Farree could not see them clearly in the minute flashes of light, he knew that the bartle was extending to their fullest length those broad punishing claws which could tear apart any attacker who got too close.

"What—" Vorlund moved, planting one booted foot over the fastening of the trap door in a stride so swift that Farree had only an instant to get his fingers out of the way. "What are you doing?"

"The hagger—Underground!" Farree returned impatiently. "They can attack, never coming into sight, from below! Lady, call him back!"

Maelen's fingers blazed, building up, as Farree knew, power for her mind sending. But if she reached Bojor, the bartle gave no sign of having received any such orders. His mouth was a little open and they could see his head more clearly, for the sparks were now clustering tighter there about. Though those within the ship could not pick up the sound, Farree knew that the bartle was roaring a challenge. He grasped a fleeting mind picture of a dark tunnel in the earth and things moving along it. Had he or had he not also glimpsed for just a second just such a figure as those small men he had seen in his "dream"?

He thrust his shoulder against Vorlund's leg, the suddenness of his move pushing the spacer off the door even as he struck a fast blow with the side of his hand against the latch. With his other hand he jerked up the plate which formed that barrier and Yazz, snuffling and whimpering beside him, leaped down, not touching the steps of the ladder. Farree swung, folding his wings as tightly as he could. But it was always difficult to struggle through such passages with what he bore on his back.

Vorlund was following, but he could move no faster than Farree lest he push before him, perhaps disastrously, the smaller, hunched body. He asked no more questions and Farree would have had few answers for him if he had. There was only one thing true—that Bojor was about to face such an attack as none of his kind had ever known and against which all his strength and native knowledge would provide no defense. They were in the lower corridor now and Yazz was on her hind feet against the wall, pawing at the controls of the ramp. Farree reached up also and snatched from the rack mounted there a stunner kept for just such emergencies when trouble awaited outside. He brought the butt of that against the ramp controls just as Vorlund caught him by folded wing edge. Farree glared at the spacer.

"Out!" he said between gritted teeth. "Bojor will be taken else."

The ramp had answered; the hum of its expansion vibrated through the ship and the scent of ill-bane was wafted in to them by a brisk breeze. Yazz had already taken the lead and was riding the ramp out and down, her formidable rows of teeth locked around one of the railings to steady her as she was swung by the motion of her footing.

Vorlund loosed his hold on Farree. "What and from where?" he snapped.

"Hagger and from underground! Their webs already lie out there. But those are old. Now they are being led!" Farree leaped ahead, free of the ship port. His wings expanded and he was airborne in the night, wheeling about to face that part of the cliff where Bojor waited at bay.

The spots of light were larger and brighter here, making a beacon easy to see. Farree shook his head a fraction; having left the interior of the ship, he could feel better and stronger that warning of the coming of the attackers. Beating his wings against a strong flow of air he headed toward the splotch of light. A moment later and he himself gathered up attendants. For the same sparks of fire which had hailed Bojor sprang to life around about him, outlining his body, gathering in a tight cluster over his head.

At the same time his wings faltered in their beat. He was nearly sent earthward as their power failed for the pace of a heartbeat of two, while in his mind the old ache steadied into an ever-growing pain. He forced himself on but it was as if he were trying to beat his way through some viscous invisible flood in which his wings were being tangled and slowed until he was brought down so low he was skimming across the ground, the toes of his space boots caught now and again by some higher tangle of growth.

Yet he refused to answer a compulsion and go a-foot, for there grew in him the strong feeling that as long as he continued to fight so he was free of another entanglement, this one ready to grip his mind. He was able to pick up Bojor's rage now. Not since the bartle had helped to retake their ship, captured by the Guild fighters on Yiktor, rescuing Maelen and Vorlund from imprisonment, had Farree known such anger to fill the brain of the huge furred one. However, threaded through that anger was puzzlement, for Bojor as yet faced no visible foe, only sensed, as did Farree himself, the threat growing ever stronger.

Those sparks of light which clustered over his head and followed the likeness of his suddenly too-heavy wings were glowing brighter. Pressing against him was the power which attempted to bring him to earth, perhaps to render him useless in any confrontation to come.

As Farree fought on, throwing all his strength into the struggle with the pressure, he was suddenly shocked by such a spear of thought as he had not felt even from Maelen, the acknowledged leader in their own communication.

"Come—die! Traitor, losstreek, demni—"

Loud and firm as that rang in his mind, he could not pick up, save as a wavering and faceless shadow, who thought that. But that opponent had erred for, by the very storm he so loosed, he gave Farree himself a goal for a counterattack.

At the very edge of that part of the valley floor which was crisscrossed by the web lines, Farree settled, though he kept his wings spread, and kept so little of his weight on the ground that he hardly crushed the last straggle of ill-bane.

Instead of concentrating on keeping aloft, he now bent all of his strength on a mind thrust—dragging out of the depths of himself anger engrossed by fear—a fear he projected on that other. Because he had no other clue and very much needed a target, he pictured his opponent firmly—one such small man as he had seen in the hall of the crystal—giving that vision all the details he could summon.

Above and around him the points of light blazed—no longer white, but green as if the ill-bane itself had become a fire and he had wound the flames about him as he might a cloak. The green motes swirled now, all gathering above his head and moving so fast that they appeared to form a ring. But Farree was more aware that his mind touch had vanquished a shield. It was not a shield like any he had met before—either the science-produced ones the Guildsmen had worn on Yiktor, or those he had encountered with

Maelen, Vorlund and the Zacanthan when they had tested him in hope of finding some answer to the barrier which he found so crippling.

Having damaged it, Farree now threw strength against it. At his second raging attempt the barrier went completely down. He was caught up in a chaos of thoughts but the greatest and clearest was intelligible enough. The one who broadcast was afraid, yes, but under the spur of that fear was determination to act. It was true that the broadcast came from underground and the general direction showed that he who was coming into attack was heading toward Bojor. Only the mind Farree was now reading in part did not see the attacker to be physically engaged in any battle.

There ran before this other mind and under his control, others, perhaps for their size the most dangerous entities Farree had ever known—and since he only had a half knowledge of them sifted through another mind it could well be that they were even more dangerous than he believed. Hagger! The picture was clear in his mind, sharply clear so that he saw in only an instant or two of holding it a horror which made him shiver. Oddly enough in shape it was not unlike Togger, save the pulpy, fattish body was covered with mud-streaked hair. Like the smux, the foremost pair of feet were equipped with great claws, the inner side of which were saw-toothed, a visible threat to any likely to be caught by those. The heads were round, bearing to the fore flexible antennae on the tips of which were balls which he knew, from the thoughts of the enemy who had herded them ahead, served as eyes and had an astounding range of sight in the dark of the tunnel through which they traveled at a speed which was seemingly foreign to the fact that they crawled on three pair of legs, the armed ones held aloft as if ready for battle at any moment.

Farree quested ahead, seeing in a strange way through the eyes of the herder. The underground traveler was aware of him now, but unable to push him out and away, though his increasingly frantic attempts made him strive to read Farree as Farree had already reached him.

Farree struck. The command which he thrust deep into that other mind was already aimed at the grotesque army scuttling under the surface of the ground. But with the necessity of keeping hold on the herder, and, through him, trying to reach the other creatures, Farree had to sacrifice sight of the burrowers. Whether his push reached them, or whether they surrendered to his unvoiced command he could not tell. Something hit the ground before him with a thud. For an instant that broke his concentration. Togger had lurched out of Farree's jerkin to leap to the ground between two of the crossing web lines. The smux flung himself, with a powerful thrust of his strong hind feet, at the nearest of those lines. His foreclaws whipped out, cutting into the earth, and when he brought them together with an audible click there was a crinkling in the dry soil as if, freed from a very taut hold, the web lines had snapped away from that break, carrying part of the earth with them.

"Bad—" Farree caught that but he did not catch the smux whom he tried to snatch up again. Togger was running over the webbed earth in the general direction of that glow which marked Bojor's choice of battleground.

Time and again the smux stopped for only an instant or two to snap the lines just under the surface of the soil, though for what purpose Farree could not understand. However, that thickening of the air, or what had seemed that, which had kept him from speedy flight, was gone. He soared up and out across the web Togger was so effectively destroying, heading toward Bojor at the foot of the cliff.

Over his head the circle of lights had broken apart and now fell behind him like a headscarf blown by the wind. Twice he bent all the strength he could muster into trying once again to take command of the underground party, only now he encountered the blankness of a new shield, one strong enough to stand firm against his probing. Thus he concentrated on reaching the cliff, the ship stunner in his hand.

"Bad—come—" Not Togger this time. He had already flown past the smux, could no longer see him. That was Bojor. And if the bartle had assessed the enemy enough to add come, then indeed the attack would be a formidable one.

Farree reached the edge of the webbed country. Bojor squatted almost directly before him, the crest of longer and stiffer hair between his ears standing up. The light which had marked Bojor when they had watched him from the ship was now plastered against the cliff side some distance away from the stout body. Bojor's eyes were red and opened to then-farthest extent. He looked up to Farree but did not hold that glance very long; his attention dropped quickly to the ground immediately before him. Farree winged a fraction closer and lit, not folding his wings, but feeling the security of the ground beneath his feet. He had the stunner in a tight grip and now dared once more to mind search.

Almost he leaped into the air as he met a surge of what was not thought as he knew such, but rather a great hunger, a need which came from many minds. He tried to separate one of those threads from another, to trace it back to the mind which gave it birth, but they were so entangled there was no hope of that; and they were very close.

"Togger—come—now—" There was that sending and he saw in the dim light sent off by the motes a blotch of shadow which sped in closer to one of the bartle's legs. Once there, crowded in against the bartle, the smux turned around, claws up and ready in something of the same stance that Bojor had taken in defense. Outdistancing the smux was Yazz; she was not running, but weaving a pattern with short jumps from one clear patch of ground to another. It was manifest Yazz sensed some danger which was inherent there.

..•) 11 (•..

Their only source of light were the motes hovering in the air, a patch over the head of each. When Farree, in one wing-aided bound, joined the other three by the wall of the cliff, only to whirl around and stand ready, waiting for the charge he was sure was coming, his attention was all for the ground. There was a swirl of light which whipped about him as the lash of a whip might have cut at his body. He gasped and choked. The lights were lower, circling about him at throat level, drawing in closer. He flung up an arm to beat them off and small pains stung his skin as if they were in truth sparks from a fire. Nor could he so win free of them. The circle was at chest level now. Unconsciously he had furled his wings as the fire sparks flicked along their surfaces.

His left arm was pinned to his body by the sparks, but the right one still held the stunner. There was no way he could spray those strange attackers. Nor had he any belief that they were even insects ready to sting him into submission, for his mind did not pick up the slightest hint of life as he knew it in those minute flashes.

Farree tried to expand his wings again, to perhaps rise above the attackers. At that moment, as his struggles grew stronger, the ground itself burst outward, spraying earth and stones into the air as there boiled out of a crumbling hole the first of those things he had mind seen in the tunnel. He had already set the stunner to full strength and part of its beam, though his arm was unable to hold steady as he was being jerked back and forth, chopped across the first two of the ground runners. Yazz showed her teeth and made a rush at the third to climb out of the runway below.

Above her head the sparks which had accompanied her formed a ball aimed at her. However, like all of her species, her movements in attack were delivered so swiftly that her body became slightly blurred to the sight. Though the ball swooped, Yazz was gone, only her hind legs and thrashing tail visible, the whole forepart of her body now within the hole.

Farree kicked and twisted his body. At last there was an instant when he could bring the stunner to bear on part of the star ring about him. There was a winking and he felt a relaxation of the pressure which had been squeezing him. Bojor roared, that vast surge of sound echoed from the cliffs about. Farree stumbled back, one of his furled wings striking against the bartle's bulk. A vast paw fell heavy on his shoulder drawing him farther on toward the cliff. The lights, which had surrounded the bartle and brought him to bay here, divided into two clusters, one of which struck at each paw.

Yazz drew back from the entrance to the burrow. Her jaws were fast set upon a thick round body, just behind the head of the creature. It was beating its forefeet against the ground in a vain effort to win free. Its efforts merely broke loose clods which the claws showered through the hole from which it had been so unceremoniously ripped. Yazz gave a quick snap and threw her captive to the other side of the hole. It landed on its back, kicked feebly, then was still, while its killer was already heading back into the hole after more prey.

As Farree was swept against the cliff, those sparks of light which had snared him before formed a new ball, drawing back several paces. He gasped air into lungs which had been compressed, took aim at that ball. He never fired. Instead he gave a cry as the balled lights sped at his head. A solid mass, it struck an instant later with a force which snapped his head back. The sparks wheeled endlessly before his eyes. Then, on the tail of that strike there followed pain so intense he could neither hear, nor see, nor understand anything, save that the world was a place of torture. The brilliant, eye-searing white which had followed on the stroke of the sparks darkened and then even the pain, at last, also was gone.

As he had been in his dream he was somewhere else, not in his body, though he searched frantically for awareness of flesh and bone and could not find it. Yet he was able to sense that he was not alone. Bojor—Yazz— he tried to hail them—Nothing of the warm sense of friendship, which should follow on his thinking those names, came to him. He tried to advance the mind search. As it had been when he met the haze he could not pierce the unseen envelope which appeared to hold him.

No, he could not reach out—but he could be aware—aware that he was not alone in this nothingness.

Farree drew back into himself with a rush. For a moment he wanted to cower in hiding as he had in the Limits when some drunken and sadistic inhabitant of that hell was seeking him to afford amusement, for that which was without him projected a feeling of strength and ruthless purpose. Only he was no longer Dung, the outcast of the Limits; he was Farree, winged and—free? No, not free; he was caught in a trap, held to await the pleasure of those who had set it.

"—Langrone? But none of the guards survived!"

Thoughts, not voices. Only he could not send any reply. He was mind-dumb but not deaf.

"They were found—" Farree was granted an instant or two of a picture of a green hillside and on it lay forms sprawled. The nearest lay face down and dribbling down a bare back, from twin pools of raw flesh, was blood. Wing! The wings had been cut from the dead!

"—dead—" He had been so intent upon that picture which one mind broadcast that he had missed part of the sentence.

"Langrone," repeated the first mind voice emphatically. "Doubtless poisoned like Atra—bait!" There was contempt in that. Through the darkness there came a thrust of pain but it seemed far away—accompanying the body which he could no longer feel for himself.

"Blind!" The mind voice was very sharp, cutting into him as a knife could have cut his flesh—it was undoubtedly an order delivered to him. "Prisoner with ho hope!" a second contemptuously delivered.

If he had for some reason accepted the fate the first comment had laid upon him there was still resistance in him against the second. Prisoner he might be—somehow dead-alive—but that core of him which had awakened with his wings, had been nurtured by Maelen and Vorlund, remained strong enough to refuse to surrender.

"—Selrena." Again he had missed part of the thought speech.

"We cannot carry—Ha—what is that thing?"

"What? Where?"

"It moved over there!"

There came a time of quiet and then the first of his captors spoke again: "It is one with the beasts that these death givers have brought to serve them. A rock finished it off. Now—we cannot carry him. Let Selrena lift him if she wishes. Or let him lie; he will be true dead soon enough. The winged people do not take well to the dark ways. If he is Langrone he is really of no matter to us."

"Say you that to Vaspret's face?"

"Langrone!" The other repeated the word as if he were spitting it out in a gob. "Air Dancers! What does it matter that they are being hunted?"

"Remember that which the death dealer from the other ship found? Do you think that they will let go of any of this world now that they have laid hands on that? Roxcit's lying place they are going to search for. With what they have in their ways of strange knowledge they are going to find the second cache soon. That they hunt the winged people—yes, there is no real harm for us in that. But that they break the guard we are set to—"

"Well enough, well enough! Remember, if this Langrone is one with Atra he has been blinded by those others. He will be able to draw them—"

"Not so. For them perhaps he shall be bait now." There was satisfaction in that.

The darkness in which Farree was closed drew tighter about him as if to force the air from his lungs, even as the lights had earlier done. He was aware of that frightening increase of pressure even if he was no longer aware of his body. Then—there was nothing. Farree opened his eyes. There were no longer folds of black choking him—rather what he saw was grey—like the light of very early morning or the haze which had turned him back from his first scouting on this world. He rested on his side but a small attempt at movement told him that he was still the prisoner the mind voice had claimed him to be.

However, the haze of grey seemed to sway sluggishly in an odd way which made him feel ill. He was entirely aware of his body again but the ills of that were of less importance than what the swaying of haze revealed or obscured.

There was a chair which towered above him as he lay not too far away from it on a floor covered with a pavement of alternate green and brown blocks of stone, the brown blocks veined with threads of green. The chair was white and the legs, arms, and the frame of the back were heavily and intricately carved, the arms ending in balls as clear as if they had been solidified from fresh stream water. The chair had a padded back and seat of heavily patterned stuff, green leaves, flowers of every shade and here and there a band of what appeared to be such runes as Zoror had once shown him, saying that it was believed that the People he sought once preserved knowledge by such markings.

Before the chair was a footstool and on this sat a small

creature which he could not immediately determine as a sentient being or a lower animal. The small body was covered with spotted scales, golden in shade, but its contours were humanoid. A head which was round in the back and narrowed to a point in front crowned a long and sinuous neck. It had four limbs, stick thin, the upper pair of which ended in webbed six-fingered paws; the back ones ended in broad pads. Between the forepaws it rolled back and forth a tube of white which was patterned by a series of holes. Putting one end of that to the sharp snout mouth and lingering along the length, it now produced a series of notes which sounded like trickling water. The eyes were very large and were glowing like green flames, if such could exist.

Those eyes were regarding Farree and he knew that the creature was perfectly aware of him. Cautiously he tried mind touch—but was astounded to find that he had apparently been deprived of that sense—it was like the haze he had faced before. He met a wall.

The tinkling notes of the pipe grew louder and the room haze was thinning, disappearing. He could see more of the room now—the sturdy legs and lower surface of a long table, the color of walls where ran the runic patterns of the chair cushions; but these were clear, unhidden by any other designs.

Farree licked dry lips, preparing to use his voice as he was unable to mind touch. But he never got a chance to see if the creature with the flute would be able to understand vocal communication. There was movement beyond the table and he then saw fully the figure who came around the end of it.

To his first glance the newcomer looked like many of the spacers he had seen—tall, humanoid—perhaps taller even than Zoror. He wore tight covering on his legs and feet as if foot gear and clothing were one—above that a laced jerkin clasped in to a narrow waist with a broad belt which glimmered and flashed with a silvery radiance. His head was covered with hair which was mingled red and gold. The skin of his face and his uncovered hands was pale—there was no space tan to darken it.

There was something set and remote in his expression. Heavy-lidded eyes were half shut in a face which was as perfect as if it had been carefully carven out of a substance as white as the chair he now sought and settled in. Remote that expression might be, but he was regarding Farree closely, and there was that about him which suggested that he was in complete command here.

"So—" Though Farree had not been able to pierce the interference resisting his own thought, the barrier did not exist for this stranger. "Who may you be?" The feeling that question suggested was a cold curiosity. Again Farree strove to answer but for him the barrier held.

On the footstool the flute player leaned forward. It no longer played that instrument, but flopped down to its pad feet and advanced a step or so. As if it controlled Farree's body it leaned forward and tapped the captive's lips with the tip of its flute, clearly an invitation or perhaps an order to use vocal speech. Having done so it padded back to the footstool and once more resumed its seat.

The man in the chair had watched that action and now he nodded. "So—" He once more turned his gaze on Farree. "Who?" He made of that single word a sharp order.

"Farree—" To his own ears that hoarse sound was extremely loud as if he might be shouting—there was even a murmur of echo to follow.

"There is no mistake that you are that." The questioner's speech sped smoothly into his mind. "What name have you or *had* you in Langrone ranks? Or have they taken that away from you, cripple, along with all the rest?"

"I am called Farree." He did not understand what the other meant.

There was a faint frown on the man's face. Then Farree shook as a spear of mind send invaded him. He was no longer aware of the room, the man, the flutist—only of the same torture which engulfed him when Maelen and the rest had attempted to break the barrier which existed between him and much of his own past. He could not defend himself against the power this other projected, but neither could that one penetrate the shield which someone or something had used upon his captive. The pain became darkness and he was only aware of weak relief that the force was gone.

Breathing fast as might one who had nearly gone beyond the ability to breathe at all, Farree was again aware of the room and those two watching him. That frown had grown the darker on the face of his interrogator and the creature on the footstool had drawn arms and legs back against its body, shivering, as if it also had been the target of sudden assault.

"How did you escape?" The send did not ravage him now, rather it was softer. In the great chair the man was leaning forward, his hands on his knees, his eyes no longer lazy.

"They freed me—" Farree tried to summon up pictures of Maelen and Vorlund as he had seen them first, when they had rescued Togger, and incidentally himself, from the filth of the Limits.

"No—" The man straightened in his chair to eye Farree with open surprise. He pointed a finger at Farree as if flesh and bone were a weapon. "No, you cannot be made to hold a lie such as that! Then there are two parties here!" He was out of the chair in one movement, walking at a swift pace away from Farree, out of the captive's range of sight.

Farree began to test whatever it was which held him so tightly prisoner. He looked along his own body and could see no sign of any bonds. The light particles which had entrapped him were gone, but still he could not move. Move, repeated his aching mind, still weak from the force which had been used to try to pluck his past from him. What had Zoror said about glamorie—that it was a weapon, or a trick, which could be used to entice or deceive those who did not understand it? It was true that he could not transmit to another, but did that barrier also keep him from working on himself? There was certainly no reason not to try.

The flutist on the footstool was playing again. Farree moved his head slowly, trying to shut that music out by concentration, for it seemed to him that the tune filled that very part of his mind that he must use, lulling what was left of its power into uselessness. His hands—in his mind he pictured his two hands as he had seen them last—not stiff and straight against his body but free to move in any direction he willed for them. Fingers—curving so! Yes, he could picture that in spite of the drone of the flute.

Move slow—He had a sudden small rise of triumph. One finger had indeed arched away from tight contact with the rest. Farree fought the euphoria of that triumph and held tightly to his mental picture. He felt the trickle of moisture, summoned by his effort, across his skin. Two fingers now—a hand! He shifted his hand and felt it move against his side. Two hands—A snatch of thought—had the flutist noted this? Was he a guard sent to do sentry duty and summon help if it was needed?

While patches of sweat plastered his clothes to him Farree fought on. The flutist had made no move. But that did not mean that he would allow Farree to win this battle. Feet—Farree rolled over on his stomach and used his hands to lever himself up. He looked over his shoulder as he managed to rise to his knees.

The sentry no longer played, merely slipped the flute back and forth through its webbed hands, its head cocked a little to one side as it watched Farree's floundering fight to get to his feet. He expected any moment to see the man rushing in to put him once more under restraint—still that had not occurred.

He was up at last, though his wings were still folded into the narrowest possible bulk. The flutist continued to watch. Farree moved quickly, putting the table between him and the other. From the size of the table as well as that of the now empty chair Farree believed that the room was intended for the use of the large man's own race or species, since all was clearly too big to be easily accepted by one of his own stature.

The top of the table was crowded with a variety of objects, including a mirror. He hooked his fingers over its edge to study himself in the surface. Near him there were flasks, some of them transparent, so that one could see either liquid or powders inside. These were as rainbow hued as the flashes from crystals, which were present also. Two had been carven into balls and were positioned on stands—one of them white and carven intricately, the other dark and plain; the ball resting on the latter was also murky in shade. Other crystals remained in their natural forms, holding jagged surfaces aloft. There was also a roll of greyish leather (which resembled those records Zoror consulted from time to time). This had been flattened out and was kept so by smaller chunks of crystal of a greenish shade. A little farther away was a second sheet of the stuff, and a pot of dark color with a pen made of a stiff feather lying beside it.

A brazier occupied the middle of the board. From its pierced lid there curled a faint coil of smoke, bearing with it the scent of spice. Plainly this was a work place for someone whose interests lay along the same path as those of the Zacanthan. Thinking of Zoror now brought Farree back to the matter at hand. He tried to expand his wings, centering in his mind his vivid memories of free flight. However, though he might have freed his body, he was not successful with his wings. They remained cramped, as tightly furled as bones and flesh would allow.

Still holding onto the table Farree surveyed the room carefully. The haze which he remembered had now vanished, although all the corners of the chamber were dark and shadowy. Walls were cloaked with stiff panels which bore both dim pictures and lines of runes. There was another chair and a smaller table by the far wall, and, beyond the large table, a piece of furniture which he also had seen in Zoror's rooms: This was a tall standing rack, each shelf divided into a number of small cubbies, many holding rolls which matched that one outspread upon the table. Zoror had very ancient rolls fashioned from the skins of beasts (from many worlds and scores of years) which he stored so. Farree had seen some of them—those the Zacanthan had consulted in his search for the People.

To his left there was one wall bare of any drapery and broken by a large window, now curtained, though that curtain stirred as if wind plucked at it. Here was a bench fitted into place. Farree drew away from the table, testing his ability to walk alone. He staggered, grasped again at the table, and then, taking steps with care, he made for that promise of an opening beyond. If there was a door to the room it was hidden somewhere behind those lengths of stiff folds.

He reached the bench, ever listening for any cry of alarm from the flutist. However, when he edged partly around to see, the creature had not stirred, though it was watching him. The sill of the window was high, again not suited to one of Farree's small stature. He pulled himself up on the bench and then got to his feet, one hand to the wall to steady himself while with the other he tugged at the curtain, dragging it a little aside.

There was darkness beyond, the gloom of night, perhaps even a storm-summoning one. In spite of the fact he could not see much or clearly, Farree believed that this room was well above the ground and that there was no way out.

For upon the moving of the curtains he sighted a barrier which was a web of silvery metal patterned in the form of entwined vines, the leaves of which glimmered as if drawing some light from beyond.

He shook the web, or tried to, but none of the metal shifted, being too well rooted in the stone about it. Then he flinched back, nearly falling from his perch. For driving straight at the window was one of the flying lizards such as had escorted him back to the valley where his ship had finned in. It uttered a grating cry and swerved just as it appeared that it was going to hurl itself against the bars of the vine. At its full-lunged screech Farree hurriedly loosed his hold on the curtain and dropped back to the bench.

The fluttering notes of the flute sounded. But the creature had left its perch upon the footstool and was moving in a queer way which was not a walk but a skittering kind of dance.

It was not coming towards him but rather was headed toward the wall behind the chair. And before it quite reached that goal it shimmered, its outlines becoming unclear. Then it was gone. Farree rubbed his hand across his eyes and drew a deep breath.

Of course this might all be a dream, as his other venture among these people had been. Perhaps they had indeed taken over his mind and he saw only what they desired to show him. Had he fought that battle which had freed him from what he believed was a trance—or had they only allowed him to do so in order to test him in some way? Was he waking or asleep?

He hunkered down on the bench, leaning well forward

to accommodate his furled wings. Could one dream such reality? He clipped a good pinch of skin on one wrist between his fingers and applied full pressure. Pain—

Still Farree huddled where he was and fear such as he had never known, even in the worst days in the Limits, stirred within him. Who was he? Was he here at all or had some other mind taken over, putting all this into his mind? Perhaps he was even back at the ship bodily—and here in another form, no matter how real this seemed!

Sliding down from the bench he once more approached that crowded table. Deliberately he leaned forward and cupped his hands about the clouded globe, which was nearest. He had to draw closer to the edge in order to hold it.

There was an answer to his touch. Within the globe there burst a fiery circle. Then the flames died. He was looking straight at Zoror, but companied with the Zacanthan was the Lady Maelen. Her eyes widened and Zoror blinked. Farree was sure that even as he viewed them they could also see him. Then the Zacanthan edged aside, and only Maelen stood there. She raised a hand and from each fingertip there flashed a light which darted straight toward Farree. The globe trembled in his hold and such a heat seared him that he had to jerk back. But the flames continued to coil about in the crystal globe, slipping along the inner surface as if that fire fought for a way to reach him.

··•) 12 (•··

There was a burst of the flame within the globe, and all sight of Maelen was seared away. From somewhere sounded a piercing note, sharp and jarring, bearing no resemblance to the tinkling music of the flute; this was an alarm. The globe moved in Farree's hold, seeming almost to twist itself into freedom. It forced itself between his fingers and fell, not to the top of the table but to the floor beneath.

A thunderous sound followed. The ball had splintered at impact, shards flying. The light it had held vanished and the pieces on the floor turned a dull black as if a real fire had burned within it. Only for a moment or two they lay so, then crumbled, becoming a pile of dust. There puffed from those last remains a strong odor of burnt meat. Then that, too, was gone. Farree stood, his smarting hands to his mouth as he blew upon them, trying to abate the pain, though there was no sign of any burns on his flesh.

Suddenly there was more light, this time snapping into life in the clear crystal which had accompanied the murky one. This pulsed irregularly as once more sounded that

446

piercing note. Farree dared not try to take the other one into his hands, but he leaned forward, staring into its flutter of light, striving with all his might somehow to summon again Maelen or the Zacanthan—to no avail.

However, the light began to take on form. He was again looking into eyes, but, though they were in a woman's face, they were not Maelen's. There was no age to her; she might have been young or old, for her skin was as fair as it was unmarked. What he could see of her hair was part of a dull brown braid which formed a crown above her wide brow. Her eyes were dark, so dark Farree could not have named their true color, while her lips were a brown-red, thin and tight at the corners. There was no brightness of welcome in her, only something of a faint expression which spoke of cold curiosity. Inwardly, Farree shivered. Even if he could not read her thoughts, there was a strangeness there. She was so alien he could not even think of a meeting mind to mind.

Still that was what followed, shaking him as if each word was a blow aimed at rocking him. Once more he saw only through a haze which clouded sight, and even cloaked his mind.

"You are not Langrone—" It was not a question but a statement. "Throstle?" That was a question but he had no time to answer it if indeed he could. Instead he felt as if he had been gathered up bodily and hurled through time and space in an instant.

Again he crouched in all his filth and rags against the wall in an alley of the Limits, suffering the hurt of Togger as the smux was disciplined by the master of that unsavory show of pitiful wild things beaten into submission. Once more Maelen and Vorlund came to him. Memory spun on—he was reliving in a series of flashes his life with those to whom compassion of the heart was abiding. He was in Yiktor seeking out some needful thing. There was Maelen about to fall from the mountain trail. His hand went forth once more, just as it had on that real moment in the past. He felt the split of that thick growth on his shoulders which had pressed him forward through all the time he could remember as one who went hump backed. He had a flashing moment of wonder once again, as that tightened, itching skin broke, releasing the wings he had never known he carried.

Once more he crouched in the stinking alley and now he was shot backwards from his meeting with the space people into the days before. He endured blows, starvation, all the evils one who was small and handicapped might know in the Limits. Now he arrived with a rush at the earliest memory of all—of looking out from his hiding place in Lanti's tent to watch the renegade spacer killed, which freed him from the first of his bonds.

Perhaps he screamed then—if so he did not hear his own cries. It was as if a great force was pushing him back against a wall which would not give, that he was about to be crushed, flattened against that hard surface. The force which inexorably thrust him so hard was crushing—He screamed again as pain burst in his head. Then, mercifully, he was in the dark—he was nothing within nothing and there was nothing—

"—Throstle?" Far away that sounded. "Selrena—"

"Tricks again. Do you doubt he should be dragon meat? Where is the globe of storms?"

Memory stirred, willing him back once again. There was an urgency to the attack upon him.

"He is empty—gone. It is of these others we must think now. In him there is no thought of harm—"

"You grow simple, Vestrum. Thoughts can be erased; they might also be inspired to confuse. We have learned much; through the same generations they have also. He is of the blood, yes. That could not be faked. But of what clan—Langrone? We can account for all of that kin."

"Atra has been brought to serve them. Why could this one not be shaped anew as she was?"

"His memories say that is not so. But you are right. Many things have been learned by those, our ancient enemies. We cannot count this one as any but a danger."

"He can be taken by the Hoads—" There came a sense of outrage or strong denial.

"We do not waste the blood. What has come to you, Vestrum, that you would suggest that? Is it that the old blood *has* run so thin that we can think even as those do— to slay for safety? Do we not know of old that that would be a deed to break us forever apart? Are we then so great again that we can move mountains and roll up seas to confuse our enemies? If they have learned through the centuries, have we been in exchange dull of mind? Should he be their proposed key to our gate, then since he is in our hands let us study how they would use him. But he is not part of those in Dakar's Valley."

"True. So what do you make of this other ship?"

"Have you not read the answer to that, wrung out of this one?"

"They trouble the inner sight. There is among them

such power as we have not found in the enemy for ages. They seek him now, their thoughts running here and there until they are a torment to all Listeners. It is true that they are not openly akin to the dark ones, and so far they remain a puzzle. It may be they who placed this one among us—"

"And he broke the Globe of Ummar."

There was a pause. In vain Farree tried to trace the thought pattern back to the last speaker, only to face a wall once more. There was a coldness in these words which shifted through to him—mind words. If they realized he could hear them, they did not care.

"You think then that that is what he was ordered to do?"

The asking came to him again, growing easier and easier to understand with every mind touch.

"There is no shadow of the Restless One on him. It might have been chance only—"

"If there is only a small doubt that it was not—Yes, you are right. Let him be prisoned—near the Hoad Ways. If he receives enough of their probing he will be weakened, the better for our purpose. Let it be done!"

That last was a sharp command. Farree expected some action on it, only he was aware of nothing at all. The darkness held him as tightly as if he were the meat within an uncracked nut shell. He was, however, gaining some strength of mind and that he hoarded. He could not understand the nature of the bonds which they had laid upon him. Yet it was plain he was again a helpless captive. He was once more able to see by physical means, but dark first met his eyes. About him was a sourish smell, combined with that of fresh turned earth. For one moment of heart-thumping fear he thought he had been buried. Then, putting his body to the test, he strove to sit up and was able to do so. His upper wing curves scraped painfully along a rough surface and soil shifted down on his face from the hands he had put out to judge the size of his cell—if cell this was.

When the fingers of his left hand rubbed an uneven surface, he used that point as an anchorage, drawing near to it. It marked a wall right enough. Sweeps along that surface told him it was of stone, but sometimes he felt the ridges of what could be bunches of roots depending from above. The smell became foul once as his nails scraped across something slimy. From that spread a faint glimmer of light, enough for him to see a tuber clinging with hairlike roots to the stone—now oozing viscid stuff from a hole his fingertip had punched in it. He wriggled the tuber back and forth until the hair-thick supports were torn free, so he could carry it with him as he went on—though the light was very dim, showing him no more than the patch of wall immediately around his improvised candle.

It was twenty strides from the place where he had awakened to a corner where wall met wall. Halfway up the new barrier was a dark hole and from that trickled some liquid, which coursed down the stones to collect in a runnel at the wall's foot.

Seeing this suddenly awoke in him a raging thirst. How long it had been since he had eaten or drunk he had no way of knowing. Did he dare to touch this oily-appearing streamlet? He was not sure. Debating the safety of that he turned and edged along the side of the stream, using that now for a better guide.

In the end that disappeared in a round hole in the floor.

His torch was failing him and he tried to find another such. Only here the growth from above looked more like ends of stout vines. There came a sudden sound. The stream had flowed silently, and the silence itself had pressed in upon him. He had not realized the full depth of that quiet until it was broken.

There was a kind of flutter, as if the roots from above swayed. He looked up. Overhead was nothing but the thick dark. Cautiously Farree tried to open his wings. Once more the edges scraped over his head. The passage was low of roof. He pulled his wings into as tight folds as he could manage.

The thirst which he had tried to put out of his mind was joined now by hunger. He longed for the pack of emergency supplies still back in the ship.

The ship! The Lady Maelen—what had happened to her when the murky globe had broken in his hands? What had those who had put him here done? Had they in some manner moved into that bowl valley and tried to fetter those on board as they had him? He had great respect and awe for Maelen's powers—even more for those of the Zacanthan. Through unreckoned time Zoror's people had collected knowledge, had developed latent talents. Not all of them had followed the same paths—he knew that Zoror had experimented with mind speech and mind control. But Farree did not know the scope of the historian's talent. He paused for a moment to put his own mind send to the test once more—only to strike that barrier.

Well, they might have bound his mind, but they had not fettered his body this time. During his brief halt those roots above seemed longer. For some reason that awoke a dread in him. Being under the earth was difficult enough; he had to fight an ever-present fear of being shut in—encased in this evil-smelling pocket of soil. The light from the tuber continued to ebb. Farree faced around to look back, although all there was blind dark.

Not quite. He sighted a small spark of light—fiery orange-red, like a minute, awakening flame. Two—close together—another pair slightly behind the first. At the same time an effluvium, a stench strong enough to churn his empty stomach, puffed in his face. He gagged and fought to control the nausea that awoke in him.

At the same moment his mind was touched. He was in contact with one of the things which had run the dark ways underground back in the valley. What he could read was ravening hunger, and a picture of this foul thing hurrying to seize upon his flesh. The odor grew stronger, and the lights which marked their eyes brighter and larger. Hunger drove them and he was the food.

Moving backward, Farree edged as close as his folded wings would allow him to the wall at his right. His hand groped for the knife and then he remembered his sheath was empty. He had no defense except his two hands. Still he backed and the creatures followed. Now and again he gave a hurried glance over his shoulder to make sure that there were no other eye lights showing ahead, that he was not being driven into a trap.

He expected them to charge, but it seemed that something kept them from making that last run which would bear him down. They were coming up on him to be sure, but not as swiftly as he expected. The tuber in his hand lost its light. But he could still see the eyes.

As Farree went he was careful to test each step with his heel, making sure that he was not about to lose his balance. Then he kicked something and there was the sound of metal striking stone. He dared to stoop and seek to feel what he had stumbled upon. His hand closed about a chain.

Part of it was loose and yielded easily to his jerk but the other end appeared to be fixed. He pulled again and was answered by a glow of light. Again where his fingers pulled he saw a glimmer. The hunters had paused—Raw hatred and purpose still filled them but there was now caution, he believed, in their halt, as if he had chanced upon something in which they foresaw trouble. At the same time the links gathered into his hand began to warm, to burn as had the globe; but he refused to drop his find. The fact that the very picking up of the thing had slowed the others' advance made him cling to it the tighter.

Light sped from the links in his hand out along the rest of its length. This was a far better light than the tuber had given. He gathered the metal linkage up in both hands now to give a strong pull. There was no give. Only more of the chain was alight, so that his eyes, already accustomed to the dark, could follow it to a wall. There it had been fastened to a loop apparently deep set in one of the stone blocks. Farree followed it up to that anchorage. He had to divide his attention between what he was doing and those menacing eyes. But the latter had stopped their advance.

Farree's fingers found a loop set in the stone. From his touch there came a stab of agony as great as if he had put his hand into real flames. He drew back but he did not drop hold of the chain. Unlike the links he held the loop did not shine. Pull having achieved nothing, he tried twist, winding the chain as swiftly as he could to the left, its links clinging together and its length becoming less as he wound it into two strands together. Once more he jerked.

There was a clang and the link locking the chain to the loop gave way so quickly he stumbled back, his wings brushing painfully against the other wall. Now he held several arm's lengths of glowing chain free from its anchorage. Though it remained fully in his hand it did not sear his flesh as had the single stone-set loop. Winding a fair portion about his right hand he swung the rest back and forth as one would swing a lash. With a clank of metal against rock it met the pavement behind him. Only then did its light reveal something else—a skull, teeth a-grin, as it rested in the midst of a pile of bones. What manner of creature had been left to die here Farree could not tell, but to his eyes the skull looked as if it were humanoid in shape.

He took a stride across that mass of bones, striking the skull without intention with the toe of his boot. It rolled back along his trail, toward the waiting eyes. Farree shivered and began once more to edge along the right hand wall of this place, which changed quickly into a narrowed passage. The glow from the chain remained constant and he swung it back and forth now—not only as a warning to those who followed him, but as a method of seeing a little ahead on his own path.

The dim light picked up a heap of something and for the second time he viewed a pile of bones. But the method of securing this unfortunate prisoner to the wall had been different. The upward swing of the chain showed a small cage of metal secured to the stone about as high as a man such as Vorlund would stand. In that cage a second skull rested, with the bones piled below. Farree hurried on.

He passed two more chains looped to the wall but neither of these contained a prisoner held to his or her death. Then he came to the end of the way he followed to be faced by a flight of steps and a matching rise overhead to give that flight room.

It was at that moment that the hunters attacked. Farree must have been about to pass out of their territory and they would not allow that. He got up four of the worn steps and stood ready to face them, the chain dangling ready. They came and he lashed out. He struck solidly the one in advance of the other, then hit at the second with less chance to aim. For the first time the things gave voice—a shrilling so high and piercing that it hurt his ears. Twice more one leaped at him only to be caught by the lash. The first one he had struck lay struggling where the first blow had thrown it. Now its fellow joined it. One pair of eyes lost their light, and Farree thought that perhaps the creature was dead. Now it seemed that if not at that last state yet the second was badly injured, for it did not attack again, only lay near its fellow eyeing Farree with a hate near great enough to cancel out pain.

He watched it narrowly before at last turning away and beginning to climb. Farree still glanced back every step or two to see if he were again being followed. The heightened color of the chain dimmed to a light glow. He wound it about his forearm and held it out before him to light as much of the way ahead as it could. Once started on that climb the upward path seemed endless. Twice he made his way through an opening overhead to come out upon another dark passageway. He was not tempted to explore, keeping rather to the stairs still reaching upward.

Used to the subdued radiance of the chain he was not aware at first of a faint light up ahead. At length the shape of a grey square drew his attention and he found by means of this some remnants of his decreasing strength to hurry on to the head of the stairs. This left him in a room of some size. There was a furnace at one end, and hanging on the walls at intervals were objects he had no desire to examine closer, for in this place there was such a residue of pain and fear as to make him shudder. Farree opened and flexed his wings—there was room here. At the far end of this chamber was another stair, while far above the reach of any one standing here, there was a row of barred windows, square cut along one wall. From them the mist-light of the grim place came.

Underfoot was a layer of dust in which Farree's tracks were very plain. The bitter cold here was that of a place which had been deserted. Farree wove the chain end once more about his hand as he fanned the cramps out of his wings and stood looking about. Here the glow of the chain was subdued, but Farree thought it looked like well-burnished silver. Certainly it did not show any rust, as had the anchorage loop and the cage of the skull, both of which had red flakes falling from them. He wound the length more tightly about his arm and started up the second flight of stairs. As had the one in front of the earth ways, there was a second flight beyond a first landing. A corridor ran off to his right but to his left there was a

window—narrow enough that he had again to fold down
his wings, and high enough that he had to loosen the chain
from around his skin to catch the bars with both hands
and pull himself up to look out.

He was staring into open air as he had done in that
chamber of his first waking. The bars prevented him from
leaning far enough forward to see what lay to either side.
In the center crossing of those bars there was a plate of
metal which was a dull red in color. Rust from the bars
sifted off on his hands and his fingers jerked in pattern
with twinges of pain until he loosed his hold again. The
center plate had a deeply incised pattern, and there was
no mistaking the picture it bore. He had seen in it some
of Zoror's prized records—the ancient hand weapon
known as a sword—longer than a knife and more difficult,
he thought, to handle. The point and half the blade of this
had been driven, point down, through the representation
of a humanoid skull a-grin with teeth as long as fangs. Just
as the room below had brought him the ache of pain and
ancient fear so did this tug at him—but in a different
way—as if there was an important meaning in it which he
could almost guess.

Hunger and thirst drove him on, up the next length of
the stair, and he came out at the far end of a hall which
stretched before him as had the hall of his dream except
there was no crystal brightness here. The walls were hung
with tatters of woven stuff which were now rags, and most
of them had fallen to the floor, lying at the foot of the walls
in mouldering lengths. Down the center of this huge
chamber was a table. Dust had reduced its vivid colors,
but here and there some chance had brushed away the fall

of years to show that the board was of a deep red stone veined with black and glittering. There were benches on both sides of the board, their supports carved of shining black, the seat hidden by the dust. At intervals down the table were set large footed goblets and these had a shadow of sheen. Perhaps if they were burnished they would show the glow as that chain which was his weapon.

There was a backed chair at one end of the table, also of the black glittering stuff. The top of the back was a mask of a skull, bone white and thus vivid against its setting despite the dust, pierced by a black sword. Along the left wall as he started down the length of the chamber, rotten rags had fallen from covering large windows, each barred and centered with the sword and skull device. Through these came air which was so fresh and sweet after the burrows beneath that Farree made his way to the nearest.

These were quite large and he found them closer to the floor than any of the others—as if they had been fashioned to accommodate inhabitants of his own size. Also, when he leaned forward he was able for the first time to see something besides sky.

Judging by the sun it must be after middle day, a clear day. The frightening gloom of the building through which he wandered was forgotten when he looked down. Below there were indeed walls. It was what was still lingered within the wall which made him gasp. For this was like a sea of green, although after a first incredulous glimpse it sorted itself out into a tangled mass of shrub and tree, with an inner core of what could only be a pool. A bird of clearest yellow arose from one of the trees with a burst of song.

Farree could see a terrace farther on, a stairway leading down into that miniature wilderness. He stumbled in the general direction now, trying to find the door which would give upon this freedom. He shuffled through a large mound of rags which became dust at his touch, puffing up to set him coughing and blinking his eyes against the flying particles. Then he found his door—closed. He jerked down on a time-fretted latch and came out on the terrace.

He was staggering, and had to make his way down the stairs crab fashion, holding on with both hands to the banister, the chain now looped around his neck. The water drew him—to find that pool locked within the green and drink from it—that was the only thing important now.

••●) **13** (●••

Yellow birds were screeching over his head, expressing their anger at his plundering fruit from a tree they must consider their own. There was no sign here that any but the birds and a small furred creature who had scrambled out of his way, its teeth firmly fixed in one of the same pale green balls as the one on which he feasted now, had been here for a long time. He had dared to drink from the pool and to cram the fruit into his mouth, taking the chance that neither carried any seeds of death for off-worlders.

Only—he was not an off-worlder, Farree thought, as he reached for another of the fruits. There were those like him here. Also there were those odd small flashes which managed to work past the memory block which cursed him, letting him know that his kind were not strangers here, though this castle might be utterly strange to the Farree within its walls now.

His hunger for the moment satisfied, he climbed back to the terrace where there were no trees or bushes to impede the full spread of his wings. From there he launched himself into the air, the better to see the nature of this lodging which chance had brought him to.

The walled garden became a single bright green square as he spiraled upward, while the dark mass of the building looked all the more sinister from this height. It was not the height of the walls and towers alone which rendered it so for him. The fact that it crowned what might be a high-set plateau, with lower heights crowding about it, made it all more impressive. There were three towers, one large one springing from the bulk of the building through which he had come into the garden, two smaller and of less bulk to one side. The building was unique in that the pile of masonry rose sheer from the very lip of the level on which it had been built—as if it had sprung directly from the native rock.

He wheeled down closer to those two towers and the small open stretch before them. It was now plain that they guarded a gateway—one where a massive portal was firmly closed upon the outer world. However, from an open space there led downward a way which had been cut into the rock—steep enough in places to turn into steps of stone.

That was also closed he saw as he swooped downward, for not too far down that stepped path was abruptly cut off. There was only the rock of the mount on which the castle stood, though some distance below there were signs that broken traces of it still lingered.

Below at ground level there was a trace which might once have been a road, and that pushed between ranks of oddly twisted trees bare of any leaf or sign of life. Farree swooped lower again until he was near skimming the top of a dead forest. Limbs of all these trees were twisted as if they had been deliberately wrung and left contorted. There were splotches here and there of a sickly yellow and a disturbing red-brown, masses which clung to the trunks or to the spindly branches. As he had felt in the unpleasant chamber within the castle, so did the same faint fear touch him here. There had been evil here, strong enough to utterly defeat all that was of life and hope.

The dead forest spread out and away from the foot of the plateau on which the castle was rooted. There was no sign of green no matter how high he flew. And at the end of that stretch of tormented woodland there were again mountains such as stood between the ship and that other mountain hold which went veiled in haze.

He circled back and flew along the wall of the two towers, seeking again the garden with the food he needed. Between the towers on that gate which was so firmly set there appeared in high relief that device he had seen elsewhere in the castle—though this time the skull was red and the black sword had lost its hilt.

Farree's flitting was joined suddenly, as he passed the second tower, by a flight of birds, not the yellow ones of the inner garden but larger and more aggressive looking. If they were birds—Farree wondered as they circled in a wheel formation around him, taking turns to fly closer until he feared one of those curved beaks would strike at one wing or the other.

In color they were almost the same yellow as the growths on the dead trees, and, although their bodies were feathered, their wings appeared with patches of what looked like dirty grey skin exposed. Their eyes were always turned toward him—they might well have been examining a suspected enemy before they ventured an attack.

So wary did the sight of them make Farree that he almost sheered away from the castle, to wing out across the dead forest. Only the need for food and water kept him on his way toward the overgrown garden. He was above the bulk of the castle, the tallest of the towers to his left when the birds, which had flown in silence, suddenly voiced a series of harsh screams. The encircling flight broke apart. Out of the uppermost slit window of the tower there shot a beam of light. It had not been aimed at him, but rather at one of the birds. That one screamed again and veered, flapping its ragged wings with frenzied haste, yet losing altitude.

The others were already on their way back toward the gate tower from which they must have first come, while that one which had fallen afoul of the light shaft landed on the roof below where it lurched along, one wing dragging, as if it could no longer be folded against its body. Farree kept out of what he believed to be the line of fire. Who still defended a place which had seemed deserted for generations by all the signs he had so far seen?

The slit window through which that light had come was deep as well as narrow and he caught no sight of anything— or anyone—within, although he now discovered the sensation of peace within the garden disturbed. Certainly he had no wish to go exploring in the dark pile again. However, he selected a place where he could fit himself under the cover of a tree if he remembered to keep his wings well folded. There Farree busied himself with some tall grass he had wrenched out of a bed at the foot of the

terrace. He began to knot the lengths together into a kind
of net, with a care which seemed to draw into his fingers
skills he did not know he had.

Sunset was already just ahead as he tied the last knot.
He allowed himself a long drink at the pool and established
a rude nest of leaves he had scooped up from under the
largest tree. To sleep here was perhaps rank folly, but his
flight outside had showed him no place better and he was
very wary of ever entering the castle again. Having nearly
gorged himself he settled down, not to sleep as yet,
though the sun was lost behind the heights, but rather to
test once more his ability to search by mind sense.

Surely it reached farther now! He fastened upon the far
end of the tangled garden as his goal and went slowly, ready
at any moment to snap back into hiding within himself if any
danger arose. There were flutters of life, birds, and perhaps
the small creatures that had raided the fallen fruit. Neither
of those showed any trace of another purpose. He thought
of trying to reach the tower and then decided quickly that
there would be little profit in perhaps drawing upon himself
once more the notice of the various owners of those voices
he had not been able to answer.

Once he started up as a cry of one of the ragged birds
sounded near, was even echoed back by the walls. His body
was tired and longed for rest but his mind was like another
creature, alert, prying a little here and a fraction there. He
found another life form, ground dwelling, which was a night
ranter and fastened a thread of search upon that.

As the thread spun out, he grew excited. The barrier
about him must be either gone at last or worn thin. This
creature he so accompanied scuttled along what could

only be one of the inside hallways of the dark deserted bulk behind him. If only Togger were here! It was hard to keep in touch with a small mind which seemed to wander in and out at the lowest range he himself knew.

It was in the castle—and it was hunting, though what other life form could be discovered there he had no idea. The stone-set walls were too bare—there would be none of the possibly edible refuse which might be available if the castle were inhabited. Up—the creature was going up and the runway was a tight one. It managed to squeeze through places where it must flatten its body to half size in order to pass.

There was nothing in its mind but hunger and the anticipation of finding food. Also it was very sure that there was that food only waiting to become prey. As a fisherman might play some sea life larger than himself, allowing it to run fruitlessly, keeping only the thinness of a line upon it, so Farree followed where that night hunter went. There was excitement in the creature now; it was nearing its favored place for finding what it sought. He did not have Maelen's power or Vorlund's; he could not see through the hunter's eyes or even gain a picture of what it pursued.

It was slowing, showing more caution, advancing by short spurts which carried it apparently from one spot of cover to the next. Then—Farree loosed his touch, whipped it back, hoping that he had not been detected. There had been another mind—not that of any of the creature's kind— powerful, overwhelmingly so, though Farree had only brushed lightly against it. Someone was on watch. He pulled himself to his feet, his wings compressed as tightly as he could hold them, and strove to look inward to the east—toward the tower which was only the faintest of shadows in the swiftly fallen darkness. Were there any windows on this side? He could not remember. His mouth was dry, and he felt his hands sticky on the heavy branches he had pulled into place before him. This was fear again, perhaps the stronger because the object from which it spread was unknown. He forced the barrier of mind nothingness on himself and waited—for what he could not tell.

Time passed. The throb he had fully expected to feel did not come. Still he dared not try such a search again. Togger—he longed fiercely for the smux. They had played games before, those which took the two of them for the playing. Still he waited for an assault, although there had been no light in the tower, no sign that anything but the creature was there.

At last Farree settled down once again in his leaf nest. His only defense could be to keep strictly away from any more such experiments. Scent from newly opened night flowers was heavy and there were insects in plenty which gathered around each of the large blooms now giving off a pale glow.

Glamorie—that strange word which Zoror had used. Farree thought he detected a new softness in the night air, a kind of defense against the harshness of the stone which walled in this place. Slowly he studied what lay around him, half expecting to see some change strike this spot. His initial wariness was fading and with a start he recognized what danger might be in that. He might be under the edge of some control which had not alerted him as it came. He loosed the mind send because he had to know—

He could sense the small lives of the garden, and there was no fear, no uneasiness in those. If something was striving to move him now, it was narrow-beamed to touch him alone. He looked up once more, sweeping aside a flower-studded branch to try and see again the tallest tower, for he was sure that all he sensed as intelligence must be located there.

Then he saw a round coin of blue, the same blue as had marked that beam which had swept the bird from the sky. This was not fixed, for, even as he watched, it swung a little to the right. Not an eye in reality, of course, it was too large. But that it performed for someone that function, yes, of that he was sure. Now it had circled so far to the right that he could sight only the edge of it. Again it must have moved on for there was nothing suddenly. Could he, during the time it might be turned away, wing to the west and away? It might be possible but to him at that moment the chance was too thin. Instead he watched as now the eye appeared to his left and moved on until once more he could see the disc in its entirety. Then it did not shift any longer but remained fixed in the blackness of the night sky.

That it could look down to where he hid well below its level was another thing he could only guess at. Any moment he expected to be caught in some unknown trap. His presence here could have been sensed from the first moment that he had climbed out of the depths of the earth into that foul lower chamber. Surely he *had* been at least noted when he had taken wing out over the dead forest—

He had—what he had expected so long came—not with the force of a blow—but rather of a greeting. There was no danger—

Farree slipped out of his nest and reached the terrace before he took to wing—then as he arose above the scent of the night flowers a picture came full envisioned in his mind as to where he had been summoned. It was there—that landing place firm and square on a roof at the tall tower's base. Furling wings again he went to a door which was a little ajar as if to greet him. He was only aware that there was need that he do this and as time passed that need grew more demanding. Once more he mounted stairs that wound around within the tower, the treads just wide enough to give him foot room, his furled wings brushing against each wall. He hurried faster, a kind of breathlessness plaguing him. The need—he was needed! Time was so short—

Time for what? queried a deep-buried part of his mind. He was unconscious of the desire for any answer. Light spilled down the last part of the stair—not the red-yellow of flame nor the glow from ship's walls, nor any other he could call to mind. Blue—as the watching eye. He stepped out into the room which must form the whole of the tower at top level.

She sat there in a chair of brilliant crystal which caught and reflected the light until it seemed that her resting place was formed of gems. Her full sleeves had fallen back from hands which were together so that her forefingers touched her lips, the arms braced with elbows on the arms of the chair.

Farree's wings trembled, half spread. He stared and met her stare eye to eye. She was certainly as tall as Maelen, and she wore no wings. Hair, which in this light was palely blue, must be really silver, fine spun. It lay loose on her shoulders, rippling down until it formed a shoulder cape above her robe.

Jewels as brilliant as the flashing throne on which she sat glittered here and there among the strands as if they had been threaded on her hair itself. And there was a device on the breast of her robe—wide wings of glitter outspread.

Farree stared. One hand went uncertainly to his head where the pain once more built up swiftly. His sight clouded and his other hand went out in protest.

"So—the wheel has indeed turned." The words dripped through the pain into him. "What went down to defeat in darkness struggles to arise again. But not wholly, is that not so, small one? Fragon's seal is not easily broken. Tell me now—who am I?"

Farree's mouth felt as dry as if it had been scrubbed with desert sand. He whispered: "Selrena—"

She moved her hands so that those forefingers no longer stayed at lip level but pointed straight at him as if to impale his body on their pointed nails.

"So—" She nodded and the jewels spun into her hair danced to dazzle him. But the pain was lessening, and he could see her clearly once more. "And what am I, little one?"

For that he had no answer. The wall within his head was as intact as ever. "I—I do not know."

She did not frown but he sensed a momentary impatience in her. "Fragon!" She spat that word and then appeared to school herself into patience. "At least you are Langrone. Look!"

So impetuous was that command, the pointing of her finger, that he immediately stared floorward to see that between them was a circle of the blue shining surface. The eye—but—?

She appeared to catch his thought. "Eye? Yes, it is something of an eye. However, we must make sure—"

He was invaded. There shot before and about him fleeting pictures. Once more he relived what he knew of his life. Then, feeling as if he had been caught up and sucked so that most of the strength in him was stolen, he stood again, swaying, at the edge of the blue disc. Selrena had not moved out of her chair but she had placed her hands on its arms and for the first time there was real expression in her calm face.

"From off-world"—it was as if she mused to herself— "and those with you—What is planned can be changed when there are new strands for the weaving. Now—" There was the same force in her voice as had been in the command which had been given for that brief return to the past. "Look—reach—"

He went down on his knees, mainly because he could no longer stand erect, and he leaned over to stare down into the disc even as he had stared at her upon their meeting.

There was nothing to herald the scene which flashed instantly into sight. He was almost as much a part of what he saw as if he did stand in the control cabin of the ship. Zoror sat in the pilot's place, but Maelen and Vorlund were on their feet and now both their heads swung around and they looked in his direction, but their expressions were puzzled. There was another will uncoiling inside of him. Even as he had used the creature from the garden for a chance to seek out what might be of danger, so now he was being used in the same way.

Vorlund continued to look puzzled, but Maelen held up her hand and the fingers moved. Farree was shaken by a sense of surprise—that which was using him did not expect such a response. Beneath the surprise was now a thread of uncertainty. Farree's mind sense was commandeered, thrust at Maelen, and flattened so against a wall. Then he was hurled against Vorlund and found entrance, but only momentarily. There came a wry twisting and he was once more outside. The Zacanthan then—

Again the defense was too much for him to hold.

"Farree!" Maelen had returned the sense. "Farree—where—" She did not complete that question.

Between his eyes and the disc a white hand passed, fingertips brushing the surface. The scene which had been so sharply clear was erased. Slowly he lifted his head to look again to Selrena. She was one of the Darda and they were always set to keep their own council. To them the winged ones were as children: this was another weight of knowledge from the past. She was standing now, towering above him, no longer looking down but at a narrow opening in the wall to the west. Her lower lip was sucked in between her teeth, and a lesser person might have been thought to be in a state of indecision. He felt as tired as if he had gone for days without any rest, and he had to fight to keep his eyes open.

"New one—with power!" Selrena said slowly. "And not come against us but—for you!" She swept her robe about her and went to a small table which stood a short distance away. Picking up a bowl which she cupped in the palm of one hand she shook into that the contents of two small boxes and added liquid from a tall bottle. In her two hands she tilted the bowl slowly from side to side and then brought it to Farree, stepping around the side of the disc. "Drink!" she ordered sharply.

He found that he could do nothing else then but obey. The contents were thick but fluid, and the taste was tart, nearly fiery, so that he swallowed hurriedly, to get it out of his mouth. Heat sped down his throat and suddenly he realized that the grim walls about had forced a chill not only on the room but into him so that he had been tense against it, whereas now he relaxed.

Selrena had reseated herself in the crystal chair and sat watching him with the expression of one striving to solve some problem. As he put aside the bowl she gestured again to the disc on the floor. He leaned forward a little, wondering if he were again to face his companions. The fatigue which had ridden him ever since he had come upward from the ways beneath had somehow vanished; neither did he feel as if he were under any compulsion. Perhaps this was more of Zoror's glamorie, but he had no desire to fight it.

"Who are these friends of yours?" She was direct and to the point.

Though she must have learned from her mind hold the major parts of his story Farree retold it again, partly by mind picture, partly in speech. Though he used the universal trade talk of the star lanes it would seem that she had no difficulty in understanding him any more than he found her words untranslatable. When he talked of their adventures on Yiktor she stopped him several times, mainly to ask that he repeat something he had said concerning Maelen or those of the Thassa whom he had encountered.

"From whence did they come?" she again asked abruptly. "These who share thoughts not only with each other but also with the animals and other life of their present world?"

Farree shook his head. "I do not know—only that they are an old, old people who once lived in cities but who now travel over their world, having no true homes."

"Yet they have power." The hand resting on her knee clasped itself into a fist. "Now"—she switched to another subject—"tell me more of this Zacanthan—from whence did he come and why does he comb old legends? Does he hunt treasure as seems to be the goal of many races and species?"

"The Zacanthans hunt knowledge. In their own world they store all that they can learn—"

"For what reason?" she pushed him.

"I do not know, except that they find knowledge itself treasure. Sometimes they go off-world as Zoror has done—either to stay, as he does, on another world where many ships planet and where he can gather the news from many far places—or sometimes they explore ancient ruins to hunt there some clues as to who built them and when and why—"

"And it was this Zoror who told you of the People—who came with you seeking them—merely for the knowledge he could add to his gleanings? Or had he some other reason—perhaps to hunt for the Doomland? Only death comes to those seeking there for any treasure. There are many stories of what can be discovered, but those are rightly distrusted. Death guards its own. However, that the People are still remembered and that someone seeks them"—again she was looking over Farree's head toward the wall of the round chamber—"that is something to think on."

"He does not hunt treasure—" Farree began and she laughed, though there was nothing but chill in that sound.

"No, he comes to return you to your kin. Is that his boast then?"

"He does not boast. Yes, he wished to follow the need which brought me here. And the Lady Maelen and her lord—they were of a like mind."

"A pretty tale." She laughed again. "So here you now sit in the hold which was once Fragon's and give me puzzles to be solved. I am always one needing answers, wingling. However, there is"—she tilted her head a fraction and eyed him intently—"this is just—Yes!" She brought her hands together with a clap of sound. "How better can you all play our purposes, wingling? Since you are here, be sure I shall make good use of you. Come—" She had arisen from her chair and beckoned. He got to his feet.

She waited for him to draw level with her and then laid one hand firmly on his shoulder, compelling him to walk with her. They were facing the wall when she halted to set her other hand to the stone. What she did there he could not tell, but a large portion of the wall fell outwards, providing a ledge open on three sides to the night. Swiftly Selrena lifted the hand on his shoulder to touch his forehead between his eyes.

Farree lunged outward onto the platform. There had come a question—one only he could answer and that he must—now! His wings expanded and he leaped out and up into the night.

··•) **14** (•··

This was the same call which had drawn him earlier from the ship, and he could not do anything else but answer it. Under him the earth was dark; an evil greenish glimmer from the dead forest provided all the light except the very distant stars. No birds arose to fly with him or harass him during his flight. Farree tried to reach ahead, to pinpoint the source of the call but he could only learn that it lay to the west. While to the east—He thought fleetingly of the ship and those waiting for him there, but there was no way he could escape the urge which kept him flying directly away from what might be safety and help.

The fatigue which had enfolded him in the castle was gone. Perhaps, he thought fleetingly, banished by the drink Selrena had pushed upon him. He was flying with some speed. Now the dead forest was overpassed and he was above another line of cliffs which towered to match the heights on which the castle was perched. There came an end to the glimmer of the fungilike growths, and once more he was over bare stone.

Farree was well out across this, discovering that he had more night sight than he had ever been aware of before, when ahead he caught a beam of a far stronger light than the forest had produced. At the same time the cry which drew him swelled up into what was like a mighty moan before dying away completely. After that was silence, and some of the urgency which drove him on was gone. He slackened speed, once more somewhat in control of his own movements. The beam of light head became just that, a column pointing skyward. Ship's light! That must be it!

A ship in this direction could not be the one he longed to home in upon. With the cry no longer ringing in his head, deafening and deadening his other senses, he could think clearly again. To rush straight for that beacon was to be a fool. He tried to break from the compulsion, to head east once more. But he had not been released to the point that he could do that. The heights over which he had been flying curled away to the north and he discovered that he could vary his advance enough to follow their broken line.

"Limit! Limit!" That might have been shouted in his ear. He swerved a little under the shock of that mind send, the strongest and most punishing he had yet felt. He headed left and there were four strong and frantic beats of wings before he could escape the punishment of that ringing in his head.

Torment or no he was not allowed to go free. He flew in and out, heading always northward against his will, striving again and again to cross some invisible barrier which set off, each time he tried, that burst of ringing in his head, even affecting his sight so that he could not see as clearly as before. He veered once more to the left and gave a leap in the air. "Limit!"

Dazed by the pain in his head accompanied by a feeling of all beneath him whirling madly around, Farree winged on. He must have broken through, but he was only half conscious that he was still aloft, flying again towards the pillar of light in the distance. Slowly Farree recovered from the latest sharp encounter. He was again in the open, leaving the cliffs once more behind, as he headed, whether he willed it or not, towards that distant finger of brilliance.

There was no more of the crying which had pulled him here, yet he was sure that it was associated with the light. Shortly he was circling what was manifestly an off-world camp.

The ship which had finned down in the open was somewhat larger than that which had brought him here. Its ramp was out and there was a cluster of planet shelters set up about its foot, which suggested that this planeting had been established for some time. The beacon which had attracted him was aimed from the nose of the ship, straight up into the night sky. Perhaps it was more of a guide for those traveling on the planet—a warning or a summons.

There were lesser lights at ground level. Farree coasted down, slapped wings hastily together and trod earth again. Was his arrival still unknown as far as those in ship and camp were concerned? He had seen too many ship devices to believe that there were no guards set against strange arrivals.

The principal light at ground level shined at a place

where a flitter—the light exploring craft—rested. Farree could see the forms of those working about that ship; repairs, he guessed. There were five of the planet shelters. Four of the smallest size, hardly large enough to shelter two men at the most, clustered about a single one three times their bulk. His eyes had adjusted quickly to the glare given off by the beacon and the working lights at its foot. Now he could see who labored there—or stood looking on. From this distance they all looked humanoid. However, there were no recognizable uniforms among them, certainly nothing that marked them as perhaps a Patrol scout that had come to some grief and had only the chance of making a landing and setting a beacon to call for help. Certainly the ship was no broad-bellied freighter, even a one of limited tonnage such as a Free Trader crew would bring in.

He counted seven men—three hard at work on the inner parts of the flitter, two watching, and two more stationed by the entrance of one of the small shelters, their attitudes suggesting they were guards—which should mean a prisoner. His memory fed him a quick flash—could this be where that unfortunate Atra he had heard spoken of was kept? As if the thought form of the name released a tight grip, mind send reached him.

"Help, oh, wing-kin, help!" The plea did not strike hard nor very deep; rather it was a whisper which he had to strain to hear. He snapped up mind shield instantly and pushed himself further into a nearby mass of brush for hiding.

"Wing-kin—" The cry was piteous, the reaching out of someone deep in the grip of some peril who called against all hope for succor. It did not have the compulsion which had brought him here; the last of that had been burned away in his battle with that which had cried "Limit" to him. Still it held him uneasily, making him uncertain as to what he did here and why.

A man came at a run down the ramp of the ship, pounding towards the shelter which was under guard. The faint echo of a shout reached Farree. The guards whirled, one facing the door, weapon in hand, the other hastily circling about the bubblelike structure to view its far side. The runner pushed past the guard and jerked up the tent flap. While both of the guards now prowled about the circumference of the shelter, their heads turned outward, weapons at ready.

Farree longed for Togger. If he could have sent the smux in, seen through his eyes as he had before—Only there was no Togger within the front of his jerkin, and no one or nothing to depend upon save himself.

"Wing-kin—Farree—come—come—!"

The wail in his head was strong enough nearly to drag him out of hiding, lead him down to the camp. Bait! That was bait set to entrap. However, in this second call for help there was a difference—something which overrode any anger or fear he felt.

"No! Noooo—!" His hands twisted in the branches about him. Pain, real pain, hot and sharp. Farree felt as if a lash had been laid across his back as had often happened in the old days. The one who summoned was forced to it!

Farree strove to build a barrier against the send. It was meant, he knew, to set him running or flying in to its source, unmindful of anything save the need to help.

Perhaps that would have worked well had he been indeed wing-kin, raised here among those who certainly appeared to be of his own kind. Only he possessed no real ties with any he had seen or heard. The Darda, Selrena? To the Darda winglings were of no value—the Darda lived by different rules. And that animal-masked one who had been in the palace of crystal? He had picked up no suggestion that he, she, or it would be moved by any desire to go to the rescue. The one who cried, that must be the Atra they had spoken of—

"Come—" The mind voice was a frail shadow of itself. He could feel the waver in it, believe that the one who called was failing with the plea.

There came a silence which made Farree shiver in spite of his fight for control. Such a silence could perhaps fall when death came. Was the prisoner dead? His hands curled about branches in a grip which broke twigs, sent their sharp ends digging into his flesh.

The guards who had been on duty below separated and two of those by the flitter joined them. They fanned out—two going west, weapons at hand, and the next two coming toward his hiding place on the east. That mass of brush behind which he had taken refuge was separated from any other chance at cover. And he was without any concrete form of defense. To take to the air should make him fully visible, and Farree was well aware that the off-worlders might well have very sophisticated tracking devices. He could already be within a trap, but he had not fallen into their hands as yet.

One thing to do was to blank out all mind send. Once before he had come up against enemies who were well protected by artificial thought dampeners which protected them, yet also left them well aware that there was some-one near at hand to be reckoned with.

Farree began a slow crawl to the right. The hunters were coming at a very deliberate pace. Now and then both men halted for a moment or two near some thick growth of vegetation. Then both would bring left wrists in at waist level to stare down at something they wore. He wondered if perhaps they were even seeking underground for the source of the alarm. Underground—were those who had seized him also busy hereabouts, either building traps or spying?

He was at the inner edge of the bushes now, crawling on a parallel path which he hoped would eventually slope upward so he might reach the foot of the cliffs. The high stand of the vegetation would, he hoped, provide him with a screen. He was trying, so far vainly, to plan what must be his next move after he did gain the bare earth beneath the cliff. Then, without warning, darkness snapped about him. That beacon of sky-pointing light was abruptly cut. There was a long moment or two and Farree desperately took advantage of that.

He leaped into the air with a wild beat of wings, climbing up and up. Not a moment too soon, for a smaller shaft of light now shot from the nose of the downed ship, not vertically this time but rather horizontally, flicking through a rapid circling of the camp site. He rose above it until the camp below was small enough to be covered with the palm of one hand. This was his chance—to get back to the cliffs, out of a trap which apparently had its limits after all. Yet even as he turned west, there came the knowledge that the force which had brought him here might have relaxed, but it was not totally gone. Below him the light was now not only making a circle but reached skyward in fast jumps. He was barely able to avoid one. It was plain that even as the guards had appeared to fear something under the earth's surface, they also watched for what might come from above, out of the air.

Farree threw himself toward the cliff crest, but it was as if he tried to fly with wings beating through a viscous flood; it was difficult to keep airborne at all. He fought both for altitude and then more speed. So far he had been very lucky that he had not been caught by the wandering beam, though it seemed to be focused lower than he sought to fly. Farree was nearly to the cliff edge when there were other movements in the air. Birds—? The dragonlike creature which had once herded him back to the ship? The light stopped suddenly, then flashed, and caught in its glare the edge of what could only be a wing as large as those he wore—only it was black, and it was gone in an instant.

Farree tried to soar higher, sure that the light would be back. Yes, the sweep was already returning! Now it was one of his own wings that was revealed, and by more than just its tip. As he climbed out of that edge of beam, the light flashed up to transfix him. A downward drag seized him, which he could not break. He was coming down too fast, having no control any longer.

Farree could only hope that he would not smash against the wall of rock which the cliff offered. A last beat of wings, a mighty effort on his part, and he reached the cliff, managing to make a forceful landing on a spur of the rock, scraping his body painfully against that ungiving substance as he struck. But he had a hold, in spite of the pain in his hands, and he scrambled up a little, coming onto a fraction of ledge where he just managed to turn, pushing his wings back and apart to give him the most room possible.

He had freedom only until those men he could hear now shouting one to another, reached him. The light was centered on him, to keep him where he was, while the brilliance of it made him blind. There was a sudden flicker of the light: something had swung between him and its source. Wings again—dark wings—invisible in the night—then something else flew through the air. At first he thought something had been cast at him, but it was jammed into a crack beyond his reach. He saw a rod which quivered from the force of its strike.

Farree crept along the ledge. The beacon no longer pinned him so tightly, for it was swinging back and forth again, striving, he was sure, to pick up that other winged one. As far as those below could see it might be that they thought him safely at their mercy, and they were now endeavoring to bring down a second captive. Farree reached out, swinging his arm and hand as far as he dared extend his body. Those groping fingers closed to meet around the rod, which still moved a little. Exerting what strength he could, Farree deliberately added to that quiver, fighting to pull the shaft free from the crevice. At first he thought he had no chance, then it yielded so suddenly that he was nearly tumbled off his perch.

What he held was a hollow rod almost the length of his body. For all its size it was light of weight. The beacon had not caught his move to free it—instead it had risen yet higher, sweeping along the edge of the cliff, once more catching part of a wing which was as quickly gone.

Farree ran the rod through his hands. It was smooth for most of its length, but at one end there were protrusions like buttons—four of them. He had a strong guess that this might be a weapon of sorts but it was totally strange to him. Huddling as far back on his foothold as he could, Farree shifted the rod from one hand to another. There was no cutting blade which he could discover, nor was it either a stunner or a tangler. A simple staff of defense, he believed, one which would be less than nothing when used against such weapons as those the hunters below carried.

The light was swinging back and forth at a high rate of speed. Then a flash of brilliant red cut the air. Though he had not seen any trace of wings again, some one of the men must have fired a laser. However, that single burst of lethal flame, for Farree was sure by the depth of color it had been on kill strength, was not followed by another.

All at once he uttered a small yelp. The light had not turned but, out of nowhere, there had sprung a force which beat upon him, shoving him hard against the rock, making him entirely unable to move. That held for only a few breaths—breaths which his lungs labored to draw in and exhale. Then it was gone. Farree guessed that whatever it might have been must be being used methodically against the cliff, striving to catch and hold the unseen flyer.

He fought to see. There were small lights below now. These spread out along the cliff side. Like the beacon they swept back and forth, also up and down. Twice they flicked over him but did not linger. He was judged, he thought, a core of anger starting to glow within him, to be safely pinned—they were intent now on locating possible other quarry.

With those beams, the great and the small, playing back and forth so close, he dared not try to climb. If he took again to wings he could well be burnt down by the lasers. In his hold the rod moved, turned of itself. He gripped it the tighter, not letting surprise rob him of what he had thought was a weapon if a very weak one. His finger caught upon one of the buttons, and his tightened grip pressed a second one.

From the opposite end of the rod sped a small projectile, or so he believed because he saw a chip appear on the wall. From where it had struck a small bead of glitter grew rapidly into a tiny hollow of fire. Farree loosed his touch on both buttons hurriedly. Whatever chance or the concern of that other winged one had brought him was far more potent than he had expected.

For the first time his anger grew to equal his sense of caution. Let them try plucking him down and he would now have some kind of an answer for them.

"Come—come!" Out of the silence that had fallen the plea came again. "Come—" The mind touch trailed away. Then it was back, sharp, urgent—"Go, no, go! They come with nets—"

For the second time that communication was silenced as if the one who sent it had been out down. He dared not try to search for it.

Suddenly into the very center of the great beam there

winged a flyer and another behind, two, three—Behind them shot something even stranger—charging ahead, unheeding of either light or those below. It appeared to be flat platform unfitted with wings, far different in shape than any air sled. On it stood a single figure.

Searchlights caught and awoke glitter from the tight clothing the rider wore—she might have been encased in metal. Farree did not mistake the face of the one who dared test the strength of the enemy with such a disregard of their power to attack. This was Selrena.

The speed of the platform on which she rode brushed back the long streamers of her silver hair until it seemed to be a cloak stretched behind her. She held close in both hands what looked to be a twin of the strange weapon Farree grasped.

Her attendant winged ones were of his kind, save that their pinions were black and their hair was the color of a starless night sky. Each of them grasped a silvery chain such as that which Farree had taken from the dead in the underground ways. These chains stretched downward, but hung very stiff and straight, as if their other ends might be anchored. And there was something there—a mass which piled up against each chain in near invisible folds, but able to be glimpsed against the gleam of the silver.

As they came, so did the beacon swing around to keep centered on the airborne party. Laser beams cut high—but the ends of those beams veered outward, as if the firing had been aimed against the surface of a wall. Yet no wall or any construction of which Farree had ever heard could have held off a laser attack of that intensity.

It was certain, however, that the newcomers had the full attention of the attackers. Farree teetered on the edge of his ledge. If he could even reach the top of the cliff he would be better able to take care of himself. He leaped from the ledge. For a moment he thought his wings were not going to support him. The heaviness which had weighed him down before was again a burden. He could not make it to the cliff top. Nor had he any intention of following behind that strange entourage which had already passed his ledge, skimming serenely along, as if they had nothing to fear from laser flashes which cut below, above, before and behind them, but never touched them.

There was one way he might go while those others took the attention from him—and that was out over the camp, heading still farther west. He began to believe that such a maneuver might well be a good choice. To go west and then circle north and east—Thus he chose a path which carried him over the heads of the ship men, fighting for altitude. Their full attention was still centered on the group in the light.

Selrena broke her calm, tempest-riding stance to point to the ground with the rod she held. Farree had just time to see that her escorts were aiming their weapons downward in obedience when a strong blast against him brought him to the ground. He was angry at his own folly in trying such a reckless ploy. On wing he stood out to be picked off by any who sighted him. He expected to be either burned or jumped when his feet touched earth. It was darker here. All the light was gathered near where the other air invaders were traveling.

Out of the dark span a loop snaked about his body at waist level and then set off tendrils to bind his arms tightly to his body. A tangler! He was indeed trapped, forced to yield to the will of the trapper as he was snapped back, losing his feet, and then dragged face down across the ground where the vegetation had been worn away. Those portions of his hands and knees which had been skinned by his cliff landing were rasped raw for the second time.

He blinked. That drag had brought him up beside one of the bubble shelters and the flap curtain closing that had been pulled aside. Out of the shadows came his captor. He was a tall man, matching one of the Darda in size, but there was nothing about him which suggested those cool and distant ones. He wore the clothing of a spacer and that was stained, grimy. From him as he moved there came an animallike smell which was like that of one of the drifters in the Limits. His skin was nearly black from space tan and he had a wide mouth which now gaped as he grinned, showing spaces of missing teeth.

Now he reached down and caught Farree by his hair and dragged him up and into the shelter with one strong pull. "How'ya, lady? Got you a friend for now."

Farree, helpless in that hold, looked to one who was not only more helpless than he but who had suffered from her fate. She huddled on the ground, her thin body seemingly drained of substance, curiously flat, showing bones beneath the skin, for her clothing consisted only of a few rags, and those left enough openings to display old lash marks and new. Her hair was a matted tangle and her small hands and feet nearer to claws than normal appendages. She did not lift her head nor look at the man and Farree.

The spacer took from one of the loops of his belt a thin tube. Crowding past Farree he held that over her head. She stirred and lifted a face so twisted in torment that Farree struggled vainly in sympathy and fear.

"Come on, you. Give us an invite now," her captor ordered.

She stared past Farree as if she did not sight him or understand his presence, if she did. If his mind broke full voice, filled with pain, the cry he had heard before.

"Come—come!" Around him he sensed a strange eddy, as if there were more than words in the mind plea. She moaned a little, her hands going to her head. The tall man laughed.

"You got your wish, lady. Here's a friend come to you. Not that it's going to do either of you any good."

··●) 15 (●··

The jailer stood aside from the girl, but she did not show any more awareness of him nor of Farree then she had before. Her wings were fastened together and over them was a near transparent film packaging them so. They were the same color as those Farree wore—shades of green—but the sheen of the furlike covering was masked by that which imprisoned them. The guard stepped closer to Farree now and tapped one finger against the wings tangled in the cord which kept him prisoner.

"Prime!" The man licked his lips. "Prime stock. Vass will like this. You've brought him luck, flying boy. At auction these will fetch a good round of credits and Vass, he don't forget them as has done a good job. Yessss—a prime pair."

Now he ran his fingers along the edge of the near wing and Farree shivered. There was something in that touch which promised worse than he had expected. There came a clacking noise and the guard hurriedly unhooked a disc from his belt, listening to staccato speech Farree could not identify. The off-worlder barked an assent into the

disc and stowed it away again. For a moment he stood
looking at the two of them, a leering grin on his face. Then
he spoke to the girl.

"You, little lady, don't you think as how you can get out
of here with him." He stabbed a thumb in Farree's
direction. "You want th' silencer?" Something in that
question pierced through the daze which held her. She
gave a little moan and shook her head. The guard laughed.

"No, I thought as how you wouldn't want that! As for
you"—now he looked to Farree—"don't you go threshing
about. Because there ain't anyway you can get yourself out
of that tie up!" With that as a parting shot he left the
shelter and dropped the outside curtain behind him.

Farree already knew that there was no way he was
going to get out of a tangler. Only fire might shrivel those
bonds away—unless the proper signal was thumbed on
the stock which had spun it. He looked to the girl. She
crouched as if she wanted to bury herself in the earth
under their feet, her head bent and her attention all on
her balled hands.

Then she spoke and there was a sharpness in the quality
of her voice—as if she were thoroughly aware and
unmarked by any ill handling, but knew exactly what she
would do. Only the words she voiced in a thin croon, hardly
above a whisper, meant nothing to Farree. It was not
the universal trade tongue with which he was the most
familiar—rather it sounded almost like a song.

"I do not understand." He curbed his own voice until it
was hardly louder than hers. Perhaps there was no hope
that she would understand him in return. He guessed that
to use mind touch here might be the worst of all.

She did not raise her head but glanced up at him through the sweat-wet tangle of hair which fell across her forehead. The dazed stare was gone out of her eyes, replaced by inquiry which was as wary as if he were about to add to the wounds and scars which patterned her body. Now her fingers stretched apart from the tight fists into which she had curled them. She pointed a forefinger at him and her lips shaped a word which again had no meaning for him, but he took a guess at the question.

"Farree," he answered with his name.

The girl looked impatient, started to shake her head, and then winced as if at the bite from one of her hurts. Again she pointed, stabbing the air as if to emphasize the seriousness of what that question was.

He could shake his head only a fraction in the bindings of the web which held him fast. If she did not want his name, but rather his reason for being there, he was unable to satisfy her.

She had settled back a little and was eyeing him intently. Then she held out both hands. Her fingers slowly moved as if they wrote on the air.

Farree sucked in his breath. Just so had he seen Maelen gesture once or twice in the past; yet the prisoner was plainly no Thassa. He could not lift his own arms, which were bound tightly by the tangler. If he could what might he do—only copy her own gesture?

Maelen! He built up a mind picture of her without thinking.

The girl threw herself forward, her one hand out to his head, one emphatic shake warning him.

But that came too late. Skittering in and out of his thought bands was the touch he knew well—Togger! In spite of the continued emphatic warning the girl pantomined, Farree deliberately pictured the smux, down to the last curve of the poison-feeding claws. Once done he held to that—not trying to reach any other of their company. It might be that his call for the smux was on so different a band of mind sense that it would not be detected by any of the sensors, mental or mechanical, which these killers used.

He put into his own call all the force of his frustration. "Friend—friend!" Togger had made contact! Where was the smux—how far away? Farree forced all such speculation from his mind and continued to hold only on the picture of Togger, and to keep in touch with the smux. From the clearness of the touch, and the fact it grew continually sharper, he believed that by some freak of chance fortune was with him—Togger!

The girl was on her knees before him, staring straight into his eyes as if she could see through those into what stood in his mind—the squat body of his first and closest ally. She brushed aside the locks of hair dangling about her face and then she held out both hands, touching his body between the loops of the cord which held him so motionless. Into him streamed a flow of strength. There was amazement in her expression, a recoil that almost caused an involuntary withdrawal from contact with him. Manifestly she had not expected what her touch was accomplishing.

"Togger—" He strained his mind touch as far out on the scale as he could. And touched now another—! That these two had managed to reach him, and yet he had not felt any call from the Zacanthan, Maelen, or Vorlund, was surprising to him. Perhaps some device activated by his captors prevented this. But the party from his own ship must not be allowed to come within range of these who had established camp here. They in turn could be swept into captivity.

The near witless look that the girl had worn while the guard was with them was swept away by her continued attitude and expression of wariness. Her touch on Farree changed. Now she gripped each of his hands, even pinned as they were against his sides by the tangler, in one of hers and a stronger force flowed between them.

"Bad—bad in the air—" Togger broadcast. And repeated even more firmly, "In air, bad."

Still keeping touch with the smux Farree listened. There were more shouts and he could hear the crackle of lasers. Did that mean invaders were still trying to shoot down Selrena and her black-winged escort? Or were the three of his own comrades riding the flitter of their own ship and now taking a part in the battle?

His back was to the door of the shelter but he saw the girl's eyes widen, felt a small added pressure in her hands. Someone was there. Then Farree caught a whiff of the acrid odor given forth by Togger when he was aroused and his claws were ready to deliver poison to an enemy. There was another smell, too.

"Yazz!"

A furred body pressed against his back for an instant and then rounded into his sight. Mounted on the back of the slender hunter rode Togger, holding on to a strip which had been fastened around Yazz's body just behind her forelegs.

"Togger, Yazz!" Farree would have liked to have shouted aloud, but he remembered to keep his voice down. Yazz raised her slender nose, sniffed in direction of the girl, who stared wide-eyed at the pair of newcomers.

"Friends!" Farree, unable to even point because of his bound hands, nodded to the two newcomers.

She dropped her hold on his hands, edging back into the position in which he had first seen her. Still she looked from one to another of the three of them with wonder in her face. Yazz moved in closer and opened a mouth well equipped with teeth, ready to snap at Farree's bonds.

Hurriedly he sent a thrust of danger at Yazz. To touch those might well entangle her in turn. He must have his freedom—but how long they might have before the guard returned Farree had no way of telling. Fire—but there was no fire to shrivel the tangler cords into black strings as he had seen done before. Nor was the whip stock which controlled the spread of the sticky cords here. How then—?

It was Togger who answered that. The smux dropped from Yazz's back and scuttled forward, his large foreclaws slightly raised. There was the shine of poison showing on those, even one or two drops falling as he came to Farree. Was that the answer? Could the caustic defense of the smux work to burn in another way? Farree clutched at that thought. Togger might not be able to nod in agreement as he squatted momentarily before his friend, but Farree was certain that that caustic burning was just what he proposed to try. He clicked his claws and Yazz came to him. Using a dangling end of the strap by which he could ride on the larger animal's back Togger pulled himself up to that place he had occupied before. Yazz turned sidewise and with small, cautious movements she drew as near as she could to Farree without touching one of those white cords. Togger held on with his back legs and his small claws, and reached out to Farree, straining his whole body as far as he could to reach the prisoner.

Despite the growing stench of the poison and the threat of those claws should Togger aim badly, Farree stood as still as he could hold himself. Selecting a length of the bonds which was as far from any bare skin as he could find, Togger clasped it with a light grip.

There came an even stronger whiff of the poison. But the touch of the smux had not tied him into captivity, too. Instead there was a black ring where the claw had clutched as the smux loosed it. That blackness spread, in both ways, from the ring.

The cord loosed suddenly, fell down, while the black spread up the surface of each end of the cutting. Farree started once as part of the blackened stuff which touched his own skin gave him a sharp thrust of pain, as if he had held his arm in an open flame. His hands were free and the darkened portions were falling away. In moments he could shake himself and the last of the smoking tangler loops dropped from him.

He kicked those away and stood steady as Togger now leaped from his perch on Yazz to his favorite riding place in the front of Farree's jerkin. The girl's hand was at her mouth as if she were chewing on her knuckles.

Farree held out his hand to urge her to her feet. He

might have very little hope of winning free from this camp but that was no reason not to try. Then she shook her head vehemently and pointed to what lay along the floor, which he had not noticed before. She was tethered to the large support in the middle of the shelter by a chain and a ring about one slender ankle; her ankle was much darkened by bruises, as if she had tried for freedom on her own.

The anklet was of the same silvery metal he had found in the deeps below Selrena's castle. But the chain itself was darker in hue and looked as if it might be steel. The end which was clasped around the support was even darker in color.

He reached for the nearest of the chain links to test the hold. She caught at his hand and shook her head sharply. He drew as gently as he could of her clutches and knelt, taking the chain up between his hands. The links were warm, even hot to the touch, but it seemed to him that when he jerked the loop around the support, it gave a little. Togger's acid poison had bitten through the tangler cord; could it also act on this?

Farree threaded the chain through his hands, until his fingers were near that other ring about her ankle. The longer he held onto the length of metal the hotter it became, until he had to push himself to touch it. But he straightened it out against the trodden earth and mind sent to the smux.

"Cut!"

Togger slid down from Yazz once more and scuttled in his half sidewise advance to study the chain. His eyes shot out on their stalks to the greatest length, nearly touching the chain, and for a long moment he did not move.

"Back—" The order reached Farree. Obediently he hunkered back on his knees. His smarting hands had gone to his belt pouch to bring out some wilted ill-bane, near crushed into a wet mess. Catching this up between his palms he turned it around and around. The first hurt of moving the reddened skin across his fingers was swallowed up with the healing coolness of the herb. Togger meanwhile squatted down and closed claw about the chain. How much venom remained in the claw pockets? Could it corrode metal as easily as it had disposed of the tangler cords?

Togger closed both claws on the same link and held it tightly. The smart of his hands reduced, Farree leaned forward to set fingers to the chain on either side of the link the smux held. He pulled at that with all the strength that he had. There was no change; the chain held. The effects of the ill-bane were wearing off, and Farree's hands felt the scorch of the strange heat rising again. Togger sat back, supported by his hind legs. It was plain that he, too, was bringing all his strength to bear. The smux dropped the chain out of his claws.

"Hurt—" his complaint reached Farree. There were no more bubbles arising along the edges of the claws. It was plain that the venom pockets were empty. Perhaps half a day—or night—might lapse before they would be filled once again. Farree himself gave a last defiant jerk, in spite of the pain in his hands, to the chain.

The link snapped. Farree looked at the two ends for a moment and then he caught the girl by the shoulder and dragged her to the entrance of the shelter. Unfortunately, it was also apparent that she was in a very weakened condition, and had to hold to Farree or fall face downward. Yazz crowded in upon his right side, Togger once more in place on her back. The girl caught hold of a roll of the loose skin immediately around Yazz's neck and used that hold to balance herself, while Farree, making sure she could stand erect for a few moments, carefully pushed back the shelter curtain a slit to look out. They could hear the crackle of lasers and the night sky was lit by constant flashes—but the main part of the disturbance was some distance away. He wondered if Selrena or any of her winged crew had been caught in the vicious and deadly darting of the beams.

How had Togger and Yazz gotten there? Had they tracked him somehow clear across this country of which he himself was not sure? How had he gotten into the depths of Selrena's castle, by the way?

"Not here! Them Darda will claim anything, 'tis truth enough. But Fragon never built nothing for no one but his own self—"

The words in Farree's mind gave the impression of guttural sneering. Involuntarily his gaze fell from above to below. Beyond the next shelter bubble there was what seemed to be a well-like opening of dull black lying flat, only to be noted for a second or two when the firing above came near. A figure hunched on the lip of that and Farree was aware that the send came from there.

"Go!" Togger's urging was sharp enough nearly to touch another level of mind send.

Though he might be journeying from one trap into another Farree did not hesitate, but turned to pull the girl through the curtain. She was plucking at the transparent substance which covered her wings, without achieving any freedom. Grabbing her hand Farree propelled her toward that disc of darkness. The hunched figure arose to full height, proving as tall as Farree if one did not count the arch of wings overhead. From the glimpse Farree caught of him this was like the leader of that pack which had been traveling underground to attack Bojor. He longed for the strange rod he had lost when he had been captured, for any weapon to hand. From the shadow came a grate of what might be laughter but did not sound like honest mirth.

"Gonna get outta here, wingling? You gonna try up through that?" The underground dweller flung a hand high to indicate the sky, though the light was such that Farree could not tell how many of the flyers were still engaged. To rise into the midst of that Farree knew would be the same if not worse than going back into the shelter to wait spiritlessly whatever fate the enemy planned. He tried to see deeper into the hole, distrusting its size when he had to count on the folding of his wings.

Again that cackle of laughter while mind speech accompanied it. "Not winging will you be this time, wingling! Nor she neither, 'less she puts those flappers of hers down."

The girl was pulling once more at the edge of the transparent covering which held her wings pressed as tightly together as hands palm against palm.

There was little of the night left, Farree noted. Instead a distant greying of black sky suggested that dawn was close upon them. They must waste no time.

Though his hands were stiff and painful after his ordeal

with the chain, Farree tried to help her tear off that covering. Then he caught up Togger. There might not be any more venom—nor could the smux have used it here—but his foreclaws still had their sawlike inner surfaces and these Farree put to use, holding Togger while the smux moved to open a hole in that tightly fastened length. Once that was breached it was easy enough to strip off the stuff in lengths, hurling it away from them.

"Make it quick, winglings!" The underground dweller had popped down into the hole but his mind speech still reached them. "We ain't gonna wait around for any of them Big Folk to come-a-lookin'. Get in here with you!"

Farree dropped Togger back with Yazz and steadied the girl beside him. He still dared not try mind send—with her; Yazz and Togger "talked" in another level of communication, at the very edge of what he could pick up. Maelen was better at communication with all those she called "those little people in fur," but his long connection with Togger made Farree able to pick up the smux easily enough. The fact that somehow the people of this ship were able to force the girl to talk to their purposes kept him from attempting other channels—though the send of the earth dwellers appeared much like logger's on a lower level.

He touched the girl's nearest wing even though the pain in his now very stiff fingers made that a difficult gesture, pushing gently at the edge to attempt the suggestion that she fold them back. Perhaps she picked up the earth dweller's order, she was flexing her wings, stiff from their long imprisonment, though she jerked and shook as if every move caused her pain. But at length she got them as furled as Farree had brought down his and, as she was ready to enter the hole, he held her by the wrists to lower her. Yazz and Togger had already gone in.

There was something of a drop; Farree had to lie belly down until he felt her come to a stop and her fingers moved to free themselves. Then he swung over hurriedly, having to let himself fall until he plopped down on earth and smelled the sour and musty odor which seemed to hang in these underground ways. There was a dull light some distance away towards his left and Togger's send reached him again:

"Come—"

The passage was none too large and it must have been recently dug, for his wings, as tightly folded as they were, brushed clods of earth from both overhead and from the walls, until he feared that the whole way might collapse on him. The light was not stationary but ran ahead as he followed and he guessed it to be some kind of a mobile torch in the hands of one of their party.

Then he passed by a hollow in the side of the tunnel and heard a whisper of stir there. He chilled. Though he was not sure how he could be so sure of it, he was certain that in that hollow, well within reach of him as he pushed hurriedly past, were the furred, leggy creatures who had opened the other way in order to attack Bojor in the valley of his ship.

There was a rustling behind and he called on his sense as strongly as he could. Yes, it was the burrow lurkers, but they were not trailing him as he had feared, rather scuttling back toward the hole which led to the camp. Surely they would be a surprise to any who would come after them, but also they might now be engaged in filling the entrance to this escape route. Farree quickened his pace as best he could, his arm up and ahead of him to feel out anything which might catch on his wings. But he did not touch any of the tubers which had hung from the roof in that other way.

Twice the passage took an abrupt turn, and on the second one he caught up with the rest of the party, hardly more than shadows in the very weak light which came from a crooked stick carried by the one who had overseen all this rescue. His head, in that dim light, looked nearly too large for his body, and his forearms and legs, which were incompletely covered by dull grey-brown, skintight clothing, were nearer stick thin. The rest of his body was haired with coarse black and thick clumps of bristles. His nose was nearly a snout, for his mouth was very large and he had no visible chin. In some ways he looked rather like the animal-masked one Farree had seen in his dream. His ears were pointed and placed well up a naked skull, the ends of them curved over a little. Farree, who had seen many strange wayfarers during his days in the Limits and a-travel thereafter, thought that his ugliness well passed the common.

Having once made the escapees free of this secret way he paid no more attention to them, but stamped ahead flatfootedly, leaving them to follow or not as they would.

The girl was behind Yazz, and she kept hold on Yazz's waving tail as if she needed touch with some creature less disagreeable than their guide. There was no room here to push up closer, so Farree continued to bring up the rear. They passed walls now where the soil rained down and there were streaks of moisture showing. The earth dweller hastened by those spots and they had to hurry, Farree very uneasy at those signs of possible disintegration.

One more turn and their path was much brighter. Unconsciously they all speeded up once more toward that and so they came out into a place so different from the cramped ways down which they had come that Farree stopped short, once he was through a break in the wall, just to stare about him.

··●) 16 (●··

The light was as brilliant as the full day's shine but not steady. As the lasers had flashed in the air earlier, here also shot shafts of rainbow glitter. He might have been back in that crystal castle of his first dreaming. Only here the crystals were untamed. They had not been quarried or shaped by any will save their own. Great, sharp-pointed spikes stood taller than Farree, sprouting from the rock as if they had grown like trees. Some were as clear as mountain water save that they cut the light into rainbows. Others were footed in color—amethyst, clear yellow, smoke-silver. In the midst of this vast cave or hall there were many of grey but these were murky, not silver, resembling the ball, the Globe of Ummar, which had splintered.

These alone showed that they had been worked upon for a purpose. They were packed together, flat sides uppermost, a wall of high points at the back of a level stretch on which someone was seated.

The earth-dweller who had led them here forged

ahead, but those he had guided remained just within the entrance of this place of colored light, dazzled by its brilliance. Their guide shambled on, to stand at the foot of the piled crystals which had been fitted to serve as a seat—or a throne—

He bowed low and then looked up into a face—Not a face, Farree thought, the chill once more upon him, but rather a countenance close to a skull, even if there was yellowish skin laid across the thrusting bone. The eye holes were not empty; there were tightly drawn lids across their sharp edges. And the skin on the two hands resting on flanking crystals was deeply wrinkled, showing long nails, curved beyond the ends of the fingers as might claws, all emblazoned by a bright scarlet which the play of the crystal light could not disguise.

The rest of the figure was muffled in a grey robe which did not look as if it were of material substance, but rather as if an armful of haze had been pulled about a skeleton body. Between the knees of the enthroned one was the massive hilt of a sword and at the hidden feet lay a skull, this one far larger than that of any man Farree had ever seen. Struck well into the dome of bone was the point of the sword—the device which had been so plainly displayed in the castle where Selrena had had her lurking place. At the same time he noted that, Farree was aware of what might be the first stroke of a very strange battle— the throb of an invading mind send.

"Glasrant." That one word pierced his head as the sword pierced the skull before the seated one. There was a stirring, a pushing—such pain as he could not have imagined before strove to split his head open. Through

the tears gathering in his eyes and running down his
cheeks Farree saw that those tightly drawn eyelids were
no longer flat and closed. Somehow they had vanished
and, as he staggered forward to answer an unvoiced
command his gaze was caught and tight held by what lay
in the dark pits so uncovered: cores of flame, red, yellow,
near white-hot—They reached into his head, hunted, sought,
appraised, dropped aside as without value, summoned what
the mist-robed one wanted and formed that into something
which could think, and thinking, hear again.

"You were dead," observed the robed one.

"I was not dead." Farree felt as if some other had taken
over his body, his mind. "Your earth grubbers were not
thorough, Fragon. Then there was Malor—you were not
well served, Fragon." He kept his feet by sheer will; there
was a burning hell of released thought and memory,
which strove to carve more room that it might fill its
proper place again.

"Ah, yes, Malor. One must often be reduced to using
tools which are flawed." Now the skeleton's red-nailed
hands met and bore down on the sword hilt. If that gesture
measured some emotion it was not echoed on the skin-and-
bone face in which only the fire of the eyes was alive.

"So Malor did not gain by his treachery?" There was a
face in Farree's mind—sculptured to resemble his own, so
much so he might have been the other's son—or brother?

"For a season he profited," Fragon said indifferently.
"As a quas fruit he had that much. Then there was a
naming and challenge; he thought himself invincible. The
learning otherwise took but a short space. Quaffer had the
better of a yield flight."

"And what then happened to Quaffer?" Farree asked as in his mind a second face formed, one for which he held no liking.

"Quaffer was a fool!" That answer had not come from the dead-alive Darda on his smoky crystal throne, but from one Farree had forgotten, the girl.

She must have followed him, for now she drew level with him, her eyes also on the Dark Darda.

"Quaffer was a fool." Agreement rang in Farree's mind.

"Fools and knaves, they rise like scum on a meat pot when it is set boiling. Quaffer made a pact with those of the Cursed Ones who had discovered this world. It was he who bought their aid with an offering—you, Glasrant. They sought you the world around. After that star ship rose from the earth, Quaffer swore you dead of the Cursed Ones' malice when the Bright Lady and the Sword Lord threatened him with a coat of iron.

"Yes, youngling, there was a blooding of many shields and a tramping of feet after that. For that the Cursed Ones would return, as was their fashion, all knew; and this time it had been sworn by Light and Dark, Night and Day, Sun and Moon, that we of the Folk, Darda, Winglings, Hodlins, Wisser, Thorm, and Wend, would swear a pact to hold, though there be bad blood 'twixt clan and clan, folk and folk. Still that would be forgot until our time of the last trial would come. Thus we have wrought what we could since the Cursed Ones did come again. Now you appear, Glasrant, and from a star ship with Cursed Ones—" There was a pause.

Farree found himself thinking of Maelen and Vorlund, of Zoror, and of what they had meant to him since his escape from the Limits. His other memories, those that almost vicious unlocking had doomed him to, he pushed away.

Fragon leaned forward a little, his hands on the sword hilt supporting him. "They know—" He shaped those two words as if he chewed upon something which he found as bitter as the poison of Togger's claws. "These know!"

It was the girl who swung half around to stare at Farree. Her fine greenish skin did not disguise a flush, even as her anger burned him along the send between them. "You—" she began when Fragon's heavier and clearer send cut over to drown hers out.

"No, Atra, Glasrant has not played your role. You who have been the Cursed Ones' bait can lay no such guilt on him."

Her flush grew deeper and then faded, leaving her cheeks so pallid that Farree guessed she was deep stricken. Then her head drooped and all touch with her was gone. However, Fragon was not yet done with her. "So, sky dancer, you wish to deal a blow with what you believe to be truth but cannot face such yourself? It seems that Glasrant has found something anew—that there are those of the Cursed Kind which court our trust. The one who is scaled, even as the wisser, the two might be Darda, they have brought you here. But the treasure they have come seeking is not to be ripped from our earth, strained from our rivers, lakes, and seas; instead it is found within skulls!" The hilt of the sword moved in his hands and appeared to dig even farther into the skull.

"There is a very old saying which has come out of the far mists of even our time, which is very long as the

Cursed Ones reckon it. And that is—we who share an enemy may stand together without hindrance, even though not all of us are of one race, one species. These who have come with you, Glasrant, perhaps are part of some such a pact."

The girl's head rose again. "Those from the stars all carry the curse."

"Say you so? Now let us see." On the rack of bones which under the mist robe marked his shoulders Fragon's head swung a fraction; he was looking beyond her to the opposite side of the carven hall.

Selrena strode between the up-pointing crystals. There was a reddened line along her arm, and on the tight silvery garment, which covered near all her body except for her arms, were blotches of dull black. Behind her came two others, a little taller than she, one the man Vestrum, who had faced Farree in the room of the crystals, and the other that cloaked one who wore a bristle-rooted mask—the face hiding the one of Farree's dream.

Behind these three there was a gathering of others, each keeping with those of a like kind. Here was a winged lord who had wings of red, and those whose pinions were as dusky as twilight on a starless night. Behind the masked one shambled creatures such as the earth dweller who had brought them here, and others varying in size; four at least were tall enough that they had continually to duck to escape from striking down-pointing crystals. Vestrum had two of the small flutists capering behind him, piping as if to set all dancing, and three ladies, tall as Selrena, their flowing hair red-gold, and their robes girdled and looped with wreaths of flowers no wider than ribbons.

"You called." It was the Beast Mask's harsh voice which rang out, as he was the first by a few steps to find a place before the crystal throne. And he made no obeisance to Fragon, though those of his hideous and motley following all bowed to the Dark One.

"And you have chosen to come." Fragon did not speak— he thought that. However, it would seem that Beast Mask did not choose to follow that form of communication, for he spoke again. Farree did not feel it queer that he could understand. He was assured by Fragon's very presence, by his own, that here he had once a place, and tatters of memory which might never reweave gave him power he had not yet tried to understand.

"You are free—" Selrena spoke, not to Farree but directly to the girl. "There is"—she held the fingers on her right hand wide and came up to Atra, setting her hand so on the crown of the winged girl's head—"is, however, something of *Them* about you." Her fingers burrowed into the girl's matted hair and Atra gave a small cry of pain, wavering where she stood. Farree turned, caught and held her. Out of her hair Selrena had drawn what looked like a very loosely woven cap of thin wire. It was held tight knotted and she had to tear it free, each tug of her fingers bringing a gasp from Atra. Selrena threw it from her with the gesture of one who had held foulness. It struck the pavement and Fragon studied it for a long moment. He nodded to the earth dweller who had been their guide. The creature aimed a kick with one of his outsize feet, setting the circlet spinning until it brought up against one of the smoky crystals which helped to support Fragon's throne. There was a flash of light bright enough to be seen even in this place of many highs. Nothing was left of the cap but a wad of smoking metal.

"Ahhhhh—" Atra's hands threaded through her hair back and forth. She might have been seeking some other bond which held her. Her wings expanded, brushing Farree back and away. They swelled and small silvery designs were visible along them as they moved. Head held high she looked to Selrena.

"Thanks to you, Lady. What debt does Langrone now owe you—or is there still any Langrone kin to offer such? I saw many fall to the mutilating knife and their blood guilt rests on me—for some I called to their torment, being captive to *Them!*"

"True enough." Beast Mask faced her, and there was nothing but coldness in his or her harsh voice. "There is more than one debt, Daughter of Langrone, since it was Noper here who had you go forth—"

The creature who had led them showed a row of yellow fangs in what might be a smile.

"Not so!" That was the lord of the red wings. "Come the inner ways perhaps she did, but it was this one of her own kind who had her go forth." He nodded to Farree who noted that the winged people were edging away from any contact with the strange beings who followed Beast Mask.

"Have done!" It was not a roar of a voice but one which cut through the mind like a blow, and Farree was sure he was not the only one to receive the force of that order. "This is no time to remember old troubles between our people. Glasrant brought her forth from the first bondage. Sharp Nose sent to him those who served him well. It was a thing done together. It is of more importance that Glasrant tell us what may come from this other ship which brought him—Who are these slave dealers, Son of Langrone? And what new injuries do they think to deliver here?"

Farree shook his head violently. "No injuries—they brought me—"

"For bait!" hissed someone among Beast Mask's company.

"No." It was Farree's turn to sweep his hands across his aching head. That wall within his mind may have been shaken, shattered in places, but still all he could remember came in faded bits and patches as if he looked upon some chronicle in Zoror's collection which had been half destroyed by damp and the nibbling of insects. He knew that it was true he was of the winged people who stood in companies here, and that he had been handed over to smugglers by one of his own people who wished the power Farree, once an adult, might claim. He had an instinctive dislike for Fragon, as if he sniffed now and then some foul odor which puffed from the mist robe. Also he was wary of Selrena and the black-winged ones which made up her escort. But even now he could remember so little—

Selrena must have been following his thoughts. "What you remember—do!"

That was an order Farree discovered he must obey. He began with the misty half-life he had led in the Limits, coming into clarity only with the death of the spacer who had kept him in bondage and his own escape. The dangerous days which followed were so much alike in the constant peril which they offered that they were a single blur of misery, in which only his tie with Togger

made one small patch of light. Then there was the coming
of Maelen and Vorlund and the seeming miracle that they
cared enough to lift him out of the foul mud of the Limits
and admit him into the tight circle of their friendship.

There came the voyage to Yiktor and the meeting with
the Thassa after the Guild had made its move to take them
over. When he thought of the Thassa and of Maelen's
people there was, for the first time, a stir among those
who listened, who read from the pictures in his memory.
It was Vestrum who broke through what was nearly a
trance in which Farree spilled out the past.

"These Thassa—of what world are they? From whence
do they come? And what powers have they?"

"Why not ask that of they themselves?" Selrena
countered. Those who followed her broke apart to form a
pathway and down that came Maelen, the flickering lights
of the crystals seeming to center about her slender body
in the sober-colored space covering, making it resemble
the robe of one who was equal to Selrena or perhaps more
than the Darda. At her shoulder walked Vorlund and he,
too, appeared kin to the Darda, as powerful in his way as
Vestrum. While behind the two was Zoror looking eagerly
from right to left as if to crowd into memory every small
detail of the scene.

Maelen and the two with her made a small gesture to
Fragon, no more than they would have used in greeting
one of their own kind with whom they had little to share.
But Maelen smiled at Selrena and raised her two hands
before her, her fingers moving in intricate patterns as if
she wrote some message on the air.

For the first time Farree saw an odd expression on the

Darda's face—a trace of confusion. Vestrum stepped to her side and his eyes were intent on the off-worlder. One of his small flute-playing creatures made a sudden quick movement, squatting down before his feet between him and Maelen.

From its pipe there arose a thread, thin, sweet-noted air. Maelen listened for a breath or two. Then from her own lips there came a song without words, note matching the note of the player. Wonderment was on Vestrum's face. Selrena's hands moved of themselves, her fingers lifting and falling to the measure of that wordless song.

Among those who were winged there was a stirring, a fanning of pinions as if they would take off to the spaces above Fragon's seat, though none of them did. In Farree there was also an answer—a lightness of heart such as he had not felt since they had started this venture. He found a hand slipping into his and he knew that Atra also was making her own answer to the weaving of this spell. Only Fragon, the beast-masked one, and his crooked company did not move. The faces of some of them were screwed up into masks as ugly as that their leader wore.

"You are—of the Blood!" Vestrum spoke first when the piper was finished and Maelen's own song died away. "Of the lost ones, the far travelers who are apart!"

"I am Thassa," she answered him. "My people are so old that we have forgotten our far past. Long ago we put aside what we had held to—settled homes, land, save for riding over it, possessions, all which had weighed down our spirits. We cut ties with the past—seeking only that which would give us life with the Little Ones—knowledge which brought good, not harm—"

"You are of the Blood!" Vestrum repeated. "And of the Lost Ones! We are few here. There only half a hundred of us left. And of those many have withdrawn into worlds they have created where they choose to be gods, or heroes, or"—he looked to Fragon and then away again—"devils. We age with weariness and the knowledge that wherever we go *They* will follow to bring their deaths and their ills, and, at last, all destruction of what we know. Do you now take to the stars and seek distant kin? If so, you have succeeded—I will say that you are of the Blood!"

"Of the Blood," Selrena echoed him, "but, I think of a different path. You have power but never have you used it to the full—" Her head was up and her dark eyes seemed to grow ever the larger. "You have chosen another way. And"—she hesitated—"perhaps your choice has brought greater content than we have known. What do you with *Them* when they come?"

"We live apart, and because we have no treasure and because we walk another road, we have lived without darkness for long and long. Now there are others who have set up laws that none may be troubled if they live in peace." Maelen looked to Fragon. "What is your peace, my lord? Rule by your order alone? And you"—she turned her head slowly that her gaze could go around the half circle—"until those from off-world came was there peace here?"

Farree remembered the skeletons of the dark ways and that room of shadowy horror through which he had gone.

"We have had our disputes." Fragon made answer first. "Of such ploys there always comes an end. One tires even of power. This I shall say first, I of whom much ill has been said and perhaps with truth. There comes a time when one has fulfilled every wish, answered every desire. Then"—his grasp of the skull-piercing sword must have shaken a fraction for there was a clatter from it—"one is as nothing." Now he deliberately rattled the skull by twisting the hilt of the sword back and forth. "*They* have found us and with us they have played games—setting one against another as they have done countless times before. There are old hatreds which they aroused on their coming. Why not"—it was plain that he spoke to the others behind Maelen—"give them what they want—we are done—"

"That is not the truth." Zoror's slightly lower mind band came alive. "Never yet has one door been closed that another does not wait the unlocking—"

"So?" Fragon asked. "You are not of them, nor of the Blood, or else our records are not complete. What part of this do your people play?"

"We gather knowledge, hunt for the beginnings—"

"On the belief that the ends may be better marked?" Vestrum locked eyes with the Zacanthan and stood still as if they were now bound together. Then he added: "What are you that you can see so far into others? You are—"

"A Zacanthan."

Farree knew that these were claiming him, and that perhaps those he had been comrades with were acknowledging that claim. However, at this moment, he felt no comradeship with those others with wings, though he had sought such ever since his own had broken out of their casing.

"We search for knowledge."

"Knowledge can cut two ways—" began Selrena when,

for the first time, Fragon loosed hold on the sword hilt. His talon-fingered hand arose to make a small gesture which ended Selrena's speech almost in mid-word. "Knowledge is never to be neglected. Tell us, hunter of the lost, what do we face now? For out of past roots grow present troubles."

"What you and your kin have faced before." Zoror nodded. "You have said here that, though you have not been friends in the past, you have now drawn together—"

"Drawn together?" Atra said, her voice high, almost shrill, as she interrupted. "Ask those who winged out of Burdenholm at a sending for an ingathering how that drawing followed! Well did the Earlier Ones name you in-cursed, Fragon!"

"You see"—the ancient Darda did not reply to her challenge, rather he continued to speak to the Zacanthan—"there is little upon which we may build anything which approaches true comradeship. The Langrone are near wiped from our history as we make it now. It is true that there was treachery and ill dealing which began that. This one"—now that free hand pointed to Farree himself—"can be witness to that, even though the memory was near burned from his mind. He is in truth Glasrant and right lord to those same Langrone who are near gone. All happened to him because there was a settling of blood between two who held false honor above the good of all. And Atra who speaks so plainly now, she also has been used as a weapon against her own kind—but not by any will of ours, wingling, earthling, or Darda.

"These Cursed Sky-Riding Ones who have made near a quarter of our world a place of blood and killing—always have they followed after us from world to world. They turn against us the metal which burns and various powers of their own, born in turn of artifacts they make of that same iron. Our wits they can rift from us—Atra can witness that. They fight with fire and all we can do is to call on skills such as we have long known and make what defenses we can. At this hour we do stand together, power with power, that we may not be mown down apart and have no defense at all."

"Now you come also from the star ways and you are not as *They*, for you have that in you which is far nearer kin to us. You brought hither Glasrant and him we have read— to know that in you is found none of the poison that *They* use to besoil all they touch. There are three of you and you are of different races—You, Lady"—he spoke now to Maelen—"are of a people we can call kin after a fashion. And he"—now Vorlund was indicated—"is also of a mind with you, though he is not born of your blood, and within might be one of *Them*. And you, Zacanthan, have no malice in you toward us, only wonder and pleasure at finding our kind. So we are not enemies, though we may not be friends—"

Vestrum shifted a little. "Words upon words, Fragon! You summoned us hither for deeds. We had Selrena and her winglings go up against these enemies by mind will alone, impressing upon *These* who slay without mercy the phantoms which can be summoned by mind—"

"True," Selrena cut in. "Have we not spent too long a time on words? While Atra was with them we had no chance to attack, for she would have known and by their trickery must have given us away. So when that one"—she nodded at Farree—"was near within our hands we had no trouble closing fingers upon him, and using him as a key to open Atra's prison—as he did very well. Now what do we next? Once more summon up ghosts of ourselves to ride the sky? There is little ghosts can do and already we know that *They* have doubts about us. So, I say again, Fragon, Vestrum, and also"—she indicated the Beast Mask—"what do we do?"

Fragon spoke directly now to Maelen. "What do we do?" He repeated the question.

..●)17(●..

"What do we do?" Fragon had asked of Maelen. Perhaps he had not expected her to produce an answer, but she did.

Farree—he could not yet think of himself under that other name they had called him, nor even wholly accept that he was a part of their race—lay belly down on a rock ledge. His outspread wings were the same color as the lichen which grew in patches among the stones here, and now served him as disguise. Togger squatted just under the edge of the right wing. The smux's sight could not reach as far as his own, but Farree was aware that Togger was using all his own senses to the highest alertness.

Behind the two were others of the winglings whose natural pinions were of a color to blend in with the rocks—there grey patched with silver, and the darker ones who had accompanied Selrena. What they spied upon was the off-world ship and the small temporary settlement by its fins.

It was well into afternoon and there had been a great

deal of activity down there to be observed. Three days ago several of the spacers had tried to take the path underground in search of their freed captives, only to discover that most of it had fallen in; after a few feet not even its course could be traced.

They had taken to the air also. The repairs on their flitter had been speeded up so that it could continue to carry laser-armed patrols out over the surrounding country in a gradually widening circle. Twice those Farree had met in the crystal cavern had summoned up the haze which was their most constant defense, only to have the flitter bore directly through it, seemingly unaware that there had been any blinding fog projected. They had not attempted another mass hallucination such as they had used to cover Atra's rescue.

It was plain from the probing Fragon and Maelen, two unlikely partners-in-arms, had used, that those in the camp were well guarded by devices which protected against either mind search or lasting illusions—the two ancient and tolerably efficient weapons of the People.

Nor could they compete physically. Swords and force-charged wands, the other arms which were theirs and had been for untold generations, could not stand against lasers, tanglers, even discordant sound. When the latter had blasted out of the camp earlier that day most of the winglings, the Darda, and several others of the old stock had been rendered helpless for awhile. Only those born of the earth who had immediately retreated underground kept their full senses. Then Zoror had loosed a small shape like a winged tube. That, arching up above the waiting ship and its camp, had blasted back, as a mirror might return a reflection, the same ear-piercing sound, drawing it up the scale as if each note were threaded on a cord and jerked out of reach.

In answer they had seen the men spill out into the opening, staggering here and there, hands pressed over their ears, some stumbling to their knees and then falling forward to roll across the ground, plainly in agony. At length some one of the enemy regained sense long enough to shut off their own broadcast and the ensuing silence was like that of death, so complete was it.

The spying party, in hiding along the upper reaches of the great valley in which the ship had set down, revived sooner than the opposition. While Farree and his companions stirred and came back to themselves, at least three limp bodies had been toted into the largest of the ground shelters and several others had made a difficult business of getting back to the ship itself.

It was not much later that the flitter had taken off and began to fly its spy circles around and around, each one farther than the one before. That the invader might be equipped with detectors was a point Farree considered when he had witnessed the first flight. They had had Atra long enough to run a sensor on her, set her pattern as part of the "memory" of such a machine. Thus any of her own species could be instantly detected when caught on the flitter screen. That the enemy did not coast down the wind and spray them all with laser fire as they lay in hiding was something which Farree himself could not understand. He cringed flatter to the ground—his fingers digging deep into the soil as if he were an earthling used to disappearing quickly from sight into that sanctuary.

Atra herself was up in the heights with Maelen and Fragon, submitting to their examination of her mind sense as they sought any traces of future attack which might have been placed within her, as a buried and unpleasant form of weapon, providing she did execute an impossible escape. Farree did not envy her that; he had too many times in the past undergone such delving into what was a sealed portion of his own mind.

If the invaders had taken a reading of Atra, it must have been too closely turned to her own personality to serve now to locate any of her own species. The flitter was already on a much farther circling out and had not slackened flight speed when it had crossed the place of concealment where his own party lay in wait.

Those three giants who had come into the crystal cave in the company of Beast Mask had left hours ago to tramp back with Vorlund to his ship, their supply of strength meant to transport certain equipment which both Krip and Zoror had selected for this voyage. Nothing had been chosen which would not be permitted for use on a primitive world—if this, which the first comers had named Elothian, might be termed primitive. The People had long ago set up their own defenses, recalled lessons from their history, to make as secure as possible this new world. Their inability to handle heavy metals, especially iron (Farree need only look at the bandages on his own hands covering burns the chain of Atra's captivity had left to understand what damage even that could cause) had handicapped them always when facing off-worlders.

The crystals of the caverns they had uncovered here had provided an array of weapons as deadly as lasers. Only lasers could kill at a distance far beyond that which any of the people could send elfshot, small needle-shaped and sharp fragments of the dusky spikes, which buried themselves within flesh, eventually causing clouded and diseased minds. There were other weapons, mostly mind linked. Those again required a careful assessing of the mental strength of the enemy; but Atra had been under such control while in the off-worlders' hands that now she brought her people a clear picture of their powers.

Zoror was prowling the upper heights—a good distance away. Equipped with a beamer suited to a Zacanthan's greater strength, he was busy sealing up any way through which the People's own holdings could be invaded, except from the air.

The Zacanthan might be so engaged physically but Farree was sure that mentally Zoror was busy in a different direction, that of searching his vast memory for anything of the past which could be turned into good use in this present. As for Farree himself—

He stared at the scene below, now so familiar with it from hours of observation that he was sure he would never forget so much as the curve of each and every one of the shelters. There had been lookouts before him and what they had learned from this intent study of the territory was little enough.

That the beacon which had lighted the scene at his first coming was a recent addition to the scene he understood quickly. This ship was, in the opinion of Vorlund and Zoror, but a scout for a larger force. The nose beam from the ship was set each night as a guide to lead that force in.

To have the invaders thus reinforced would be the end

of any successful defense—that was already understood. Thus—the beacon would have to be taken care of, and that was Farree's part. His answer to that pillar of light in the night rested now just under the curve of his wing—a flat box slightly larger than one of his bandaged hands.

Vorlund had spent nearly the whole of a day fashioning what was inside, helped by a pair of misshapen earth dwellers who worked metal in fire with the ease of those who were master smiths. They had looked at the pictures the spacer had drawn, listened intently to a jabber of firm instruction from Beast Mask, leader of those dark dwellers—who were of a devious and often treacherous turn of mind. Metal had gone into it, but that was silver poured from clay ladles, and thin streams of gold fed into narrow tubes of clay, to be later hammered and twisted into wire near as thin and supple as thread.

Months ago, the winged race among the People had discovered, at a bitter price, that to approach the camp by air was folly. There were various disturbances invisibly cutting the air about the ship able to paralyze wings, dashing the flyers to their deaths; or else, if those wings were to be harvested, bringing them immobile and helpless to the ground where another form of death waited. However, all such flights—and there had been very few of them after their end was witnessed—had occurred only when the winglings had recklessly soared out over the shelters or that part of the ship which was open at a high altitude.

Farree's body now was fitted with two wide belts. On each were seamed pockets into which Vorlund had fitted more small devices he had urged the smiths to make in haste. In the seven days since their meeting in the hall of crystals, they had all been driven by that need for haste. For how long would it be before that beacon would lead in larger forces?

Their one bid for victory depended on so many ifs—*if* Farree could indeed penetrate the air above the enemy encampment successfully undiscovered, *if* he could affix the device he carried to the proper place on the ship, *if* it would really work. All was founded on hope and the best that memory could supply from the observations and lore of the People, the encyclopedic recall of Zoror, the ship knowledge of Vorlund, born to be a star rover, and of Maelen and the Dardas, who had drawn together as they never had in the history of their colony on Elothian. So many *ifs*, Farree thought, but perhaps their only chance now. He watched the slow coming of sunset and his body ached with the strain of waiting.

The flitter swung back at the coming of the dark, landed in the twilight not far from the ramp of the ship. Those who manned the smaller ship, four of them, clambered out—three heading for the shelters and a single one trotting up the ramp into the ship. Farree rose to his knees and Togger gave a short leap, to burrow in beneath his jerkin. Farree sensed the tension of those who remained in hiding about him. There had been neither the time nor the proper material to equip the rest of them with the hereto untried method of defense he wore. However, they had their own dudes and were already taking wing, to establish the trap which would be the next defense.

Between two of the night-winged leaders hung a netted bag and what weighed it down was bait. Piled in it were vessels and ornaments of gold and silver wrought by smiths who delighted in setting crystals where they made the bravest show. They had already learned from Atra, as well as from reports of some of the groundlings who had gone spying on their own, that the invaders equated the People not only as raw material for their trade (when they could rip free the wings of the dying) but also with a strong tradition that all the People were guardians of treasure. To this Zoror gave credence, saying that such stories were an integral part of many tales he had ferreted out.

There was a place where a bank overcurbed a stream, the flood waters of which had cut away a large bite of soil. There the "treasure" was to be half hidden, a piece or two dropped into the shallows of the water itself, waiting for the invaders to spot. Selrena had overseen this part of their preparations and would be moving now into place at the foot of the rise where Farree was poised for takeoff. She had reports from the groundlings as to the invaders who slept outside the ship. Two such she had selected her own prey. They would have dreams this night, for she had been testing her ability to sow hallucinations by subtle mental touch. As she had led the supposed entry of the airborne attack wholly by projected images, so she could reach any of these below by a dream. The "reality" of the dream would enforce itself most strongly on certain temperaments, and both Vorlund and Maelen believed that such temperaments were to be found here. Two down there would dream vividly tonight, so vividly that they would be swept into action with the coming of the morning. Also, they might strive to conceal that action, being who and what they were.

Farree was airborne now, the device he was to plant on the ship clasped tightly against his breast with both hands (Togger crept up to cling just beneath Farree's chin) as he climbed steadily into the cold of the upper night air and moved out towards that beam of light which had already burst from the nose of the ship, spear-straight up through gathering clouds. He winged forward in desperation, not knowing if he would be beaten from the air by some silent defense. Even though that attack did not come in the first few moments when he was out in the open over the edge of the camp, still he could not be sure that his flight was not being recorded by some intricate device below.

He must come up against the outer shell of the ship well below where that beacon sprang. Now he held firm in mind the information Vorlund had drilled into him. The spacer who had voyaged in star ships almost since birth knew well the danger spots and where a ship could best be assaulted.

Farree's fingers caught in the rim of a small port used for the workmen during an overhaul. There was no hope of his gaining entrance here. All such places must be under spy screen since the night of the escape. But this was the guide for him and he had reached it with no sign that he had been sighted by any of the sentries the invaders must have on duty here. If he could have dared mind send he would have been better content—touching any foreign thought patterns would have been warning. Only he must go blind.

He pulled himself up with one hand and now his toes found a small resting place on the nearly invisible seam which marked the door. One of those discs on his belt gave a sudden jerk forward and planted itself tightly to the surface of the closed port.

There were small surges of heat about his bare feet. The fabric of the ship was indeed not cold iron, that deadly metal, but there was enough of it in the alloy forming the surface to make itself felt. He forced the pain to the back of his mind and brought out the case he carried, slipping the cord about its top between his teeth so he could use both hands.

At the same instant the warning came that he was indeed being picked up by some alarm. A trickle of jumbled thought whipped across his mind. Farree clung to the almost invisible seam of the hatch and frantically edged upward as that questing picked and prodded the natural thought defense he had developed.

He slapped the narrow box against the surface of the ship, perhaps the length of his body below its nose. It instantly became so closely a part of the surface that nothing could free it—or not without a lengthy period of careful work with tools, which time those here did not have. Even as the box welded itself to the wall, a touch of Farree's forefinger activated what lay within. Farree pushed back and away, his wings beating almost frantically as he tried to put distance between him and that which he had brought.

He was away from the ship, even past the circle of shelters, when the device Vorlund had labored on blew. Flame torched through the sky, rising to join with the beam of the beacon. That went out abruptly, and Farree heard a roar. There followed a second outburst which might have singed one wing had he not, in his dread, flipped sidewise, no longer in a direct pattern of flight outward from the camp.

Below there arose a clamor. Two laser spears cut the air, which made his body quiver so he near lost the firm beat of the wings which bore him. However, the lasers lanced the air far enough off that Farree believed that he had not been detected, that they had been unaimed, fired only as the result of fear. He was away, flying with desperate wing beats in the direction of the place where he had hidden during the day. He passed over that, to flash on into a place of broken rock pillars which guarded one cave entrance to the lower ways in which there lay the hall of crystal, their agreed-upon meeting place when this piece of action lay behind. Farree alighted at the mouth of that cave and smelt the mouldy stench which told him at least one of the underground people was present. He did not go forward, but wheeled about to look out toward the ship.

The beacon might be gone but there was still light about the nose, hazy as if there were clouds of fire roiling about. Still he could catch now and then clear sight of a splotch of true incandescence which must be cutting itself into the ship's skin immediately below the level of the control cabin. Such vagabond and wandering spacers as this company carried with them means for some repairs, but Farree believed that the hurt this ship had taken could not be mended by any improvised work as the crew was trained to do. Vorlund himself had learned by default—helping to keep other lone ships flightworthy—just what would do the most harm, which also could be delivered by the materials as were at his disposal.

There was a far-off sound which could have been caused by the hungry flame, or perhaps by the voices of a number of men raised in wild shouts. As if in answer, the dark clouds overhead, which bore a reflection of the fire, massed the tighter and then released such a pelting of rain and earth-tearing force of wind that Farree pushed back into the cave, knowing that with wings wet through he could not hope to fly, however much he wanted to join with those winglings who had gone to set the trap, or else beat an air path to where Maelen and the ancient Darda had gone, to an almost forgotten lookout within the body of a mountain.

There came a snarl out of the dark behind him and the stench grew stronger.

"Wingling"—the word was spat like a curse—"get you out of the path—we are not afraid of wind and wet even though you may be."

Farree folded his wings as tightly as he could and edged against the wall to his left. His eyes, still somewhat dazzled, took time to adjust and twice he was prodded by a sharp elbow as a groundling crowded by. He did not count them but he was sure that there were quite a number, and he wondered what was taking them out into the storm. That some of the Darda were supposed to be weatherworkers, that much he did know. But there was purpose in this gathering he did not understand—not that more than the bare skeleton of what was to be done this night *had* been told him. What had been important for him to know was his own part and that seemed now to be over.

In the dark there was no sighting where the groudlings

went, nor did he, he decided, have any particular desire to learn. He hated invading their odorous hole any further but he was bound for the appointed place of assembly so he went slowly along a way which sloped inward. Here and there one of the tubers gave light which revealed hardly more than the area immediately around it. As long as he could see those pallid spots ahead he was more willing to walk away his whole nature detested.

Togger's head wriggled from the front of his jerkin and the stalked eyes of the smux were advanced to their greatest length, revolving slowly as if to make very sure of their surroundings.

Farree rubbed his hands together. The pain of the iron burns lingered on though ill-bane salve had been lavishly applied under the adhesive leaf bandages Selrena used. He thought of the Darda—three only of that race had he seen, unless whoever hid behind the beast mask was also of that company. Fragon had commented that they were very few.

How many of his own kind—winglings—still existed? Those who were of his clan, or the clan claimed for him, had apparently been near wiped out by the invaders. The other clans had not been so devastated, for the fate of the Langrones had come upon them soon after the enemy had finned down. Since the winged race were widespread over territories they claimed, most of their co-species had managed to escape, save for a few surprised when they returned to their territories by crossing the ravaged land of their sometime kin.

It had been easy enough to understand that the People had been divided among themselves when the off-world danger had struck. He himself had been of some importance, not for himself but because of the state of kinship he could claim. However, he had, at the same time, been practically defenseless, condemned to the ground until his wings were fully grown. While he was so helpless, Farree gathered from the scraps Fragon, Selrena, and Atra gave him, he had been a victim of jealousy among his own people. His father, who had led the Langrone, had been brought down during the clan-species dispute which had flared between his people and the groundlings (due to some incitement on Fragon's part for what reason Farree could not guess). He, Farree, had then been taken into captivity by the Museyons, night dwellers and hunters of the dark, answerable—sometimes—to Beast Mask but mainly going their own crooked ways.

From them he had been freed temporarily by a traitor—brother kin to his father and sour-blooded because the rule had not passed to him. Naively the traitor had attempted to bind the star invaders to his cause and had delivered Farree in turn into their hands, hoping so to remove him in such fashion that his trail could not be traced.

Those of the ship Farree had just attacked had not been the first to fin in here—there had been earlier ships. The first one had had none of the defenses which had rendered this one and its crew so formidable. That earlier crew had been made free of some treasure; in fact a "safe-hole" of groundlings who were considered Langrone enemies had been betrayed. But that treasure had been hardly won. Star-based men had died, and, in turn, burrows of groundlings had been stormed, their owners trapped and slain. So that at last, having in turn suffered a loss of nearly half the crew, the ship rose again, with its hard-won cargo, determined to return better equipped for the tearing of the last scrap of precious metal or new-found gem from one-time owners.

How he, Farree, had come into the Limits with Lanti, reduced by drink and graz chewing to a sodden wreck unable to get another berth, was part of the memory which still eluded him. Not that any of that mattered. This was history as far removed from him as Yiktor from the earth into which he was advancing steadily downward. There had been another visit here of an off-world ship, and that had stayed for some time. Traps had been set— they had gathered captives—even one of the Darda. What they did with those they took none could discover, for their ship was blank to all mind probing. In fact the use of this talent could and had led to more captures—the invaders seemed able to home in on any trace of mind search.

Thus, unable to use what they had come to depend upon as one of their most important weapons—the power to contact mentally and even overcome the wills of others—they had realized that once more they had been overtaken by the old, old enemy and against off-worlders they no longer had much chance to win. They had been on Elothian for centuries, so free from the ancient menace that they had no longer had the knowledge nor the materials to prepare for another flitting. Here they must stay and face a losing fight. Furthermore they were not of one mind, for the groundlings considered that the invasion could not move against them—they had their ability to burrow and hide in places too remote for the invaders to follow, unless they were willing to creep or wriggle on their bellies through the dark, unable to stand against ambush. It was easier to battle winglings and the Darda castles. It had taken the fall of one of their cave cities, its inhabitants overcome by fumes from smoke released from balls of metal which had been brought back by some of the smiths, to bring the under-surface ones out against the enemy which thus became a common one.

That ship, too, had vanished in time. But the Darda had not released watch, nor had the winglings and the others. Their history was too plain—with the coming of such invaders their day of defeat was upon them, and there was nothing to do but wait for that to arrive.

Except this time there were other players. Farree thought of Maelen, of Vorlund, of the Zacanthan, who had the results of centuries of learning behind him. What of himself also? He was Langrone but more beside. Having survived the horrors of the Limits he had proven that there was a good measure of strength in him, while his journeying with Maelen and Vorlund had brought him knowledge his kind might never have gained before. Yes, he might not be Darda but neither was he pure wingling.

Before him burst the great light. He now moved more quickly into the chamber of crystals, eager to learn what he might of what the others had done.

··●) 18 (●··

Fragon again occupied the throne of dusky crystal. He might not have moved since Farree had last seen him. There were others gathered about, some finding perches among the lighter crystal outgrowth. He saw Selrena seated so. Her head was upheld but her eyes were closed. On one side of her Maelen was also seated and she held one of the Darda's slim hands between the two of hers. Her eyes were open but there was a remoteness about her face which suggested that she had fastened thought elsewhere.

At their feet was Atra, so removed from the others of her race; they were clustered in a burst of color apart from the center of the cave chamber, their wings folded, their attention on the three they did not approach.

Well to the other side of Fragon's chosen seat stood the Beast Mask, but for the first time Farree saw that mask thrown back, to lie along the shoulders as a limp hood. The features so disclosed were not entirely unlike those of the Darda, save that the skin was dark—greyish—like unto Fragon's, and this was no skull head. That dark skin was puffed and so distended on the cheeks that the eyes seemed very small and near hidden by the rolls of the unpleasant-looking flesh. There was no hair on the puffy ball of the head. Male or female? Farree could not be sure. He felt an instant disgust and beyond that—fear. This one was as powerful as Fragon in his or her own way.

The other Darda, Vestrum, and his flutist were missing. However, even as Farree stepped into the crystal lighting, so did Zoror enter from another angle. He laid down the power conductor which he had carried up the slopes and, doing so, noticed Farree first, beckoning to him. Of Vorlund there was no sign; perhaps his mission to their own ship was not yet finished.

Atra opened her eyes, meeting Farree's with a strong compelling stare as if she had been waiting for him. Farree paused. She edged away from Maelen and Selrena, to cross the cavern toward Farree and the Zacanthan. Her torn and filthy clothing had long since been changed for a short robe of creamy white, girdled with a mesh belt of silver into which had been set small gems of green-blue. A circlet of the same material held her hair in place at the nape of her slender neck.

Farree noted that in her coming to him she made a short detour which took her away from close contact with the other winglings, those whose wings pulsed, rose or blue or yellow. Nor did he escape picking up a flash of thought—just as he had found himself aloof from their company so, it would seem, she, too, had been placed in exile. That she had been released from any enemy mind bond, he was sure, or she would not have been here. However, the shadow of what had been done to her, and through her unto others, still wrapped her in.

There was a small flare of anger in Farree. He moved out from beside the Zacanthan and held out both his hands in a welcome he had not consciously meant until that moment. Her delicate hands, still dark with bruises and rent by seams of scratches, lay palm downward for a moment, resting on his, and into his mind sang words.

"Welcome. Greater that the Seven Deeds of Malfor has been yours! We thought that the days of the Thrice Named were gone." For the first time she glanced away, her eyes sweeping over those of the company which were the closest. "Tallen can we of the Langrone claim, and Asdir, Tullusa, and Rond. You have joined a high and fair company, kinsman!"

At those names, very faint and broken memories stirred in him. He shook his head.

"You do me too much honor, kinswoman. It was not my own powers that I used." His hands dropped from hers and went to his belt to indicate what the smiths and Vorlund had made for him. "The Langrone—" He hesitated. What would it be to her that that word did not mean kin to him— that it was but a name?

"A name, yes." The words were in his mind. "And perhaps only a name—for the clan is gone. See?" She nodded towards the winglings in their ranks. Then her hand went up and smoothed the edge of one of her own wings and he caught her meaning. That color was not to be seen among the others gathered here, save in his own pinions.

"Lanquar and Lis, Lystal and Loyn." When she beamed him those names he knew them even as he would have known something long set in his mind. "But Langrone have no more to answer, unless those by the Far

Rim scattered in time. And of those how many were there?" She held up one hand between them and extended the very slender fingers, once and then again.

In his mind he saw what she had willed—a threatening mountain, rock bare and radiating from it a gloom which was a leaden weight upon the heart. If any of the kin had been driven or had fled despairingly there—

"They have not answered the call—"

Farree was startled by that other mind voice breaking in almost harshly upon his thoughts. It was a wingling who wore red-white wings, and he had left his own people to come to them. Farree could sense no congratulation, nothing but a forbidding chill in his words.

"If they come not at the Great Summons, then they are either dead or overshadowed by thought far and faint. You have no true kin, Glasrant."

"So do you wish it!" flashed Atra. "Who closed the upper flight to Amassa when she was heavy with child? Who sent forth the Doom Singers in that hour?"

"What had to be done, was done. Sometimes one dies for many—"

"That I have heard before." This roused Farree. "Was it not that very thought which this kin-sister"—his hand touched Atra's shoulder and almost he gasped, for that touch had united him with a source of warmth he had not known could exist: it had nothing of the burn of fire but was rather a caressing, a healing—"Was it not that same thought which held you all," he began again, "when this sister lay in the hands of *Them*?"

"As bait—" the other returned. "Better she had taken up the fire metal and wreathed around—"

Farree moved. He stood between Atra now and the chief of Lystal, another scrap of memory supplying him with a use for that name. "Do you speak now, Qua, for all?" he asked, narrow-eyed. Though he still felt apart from these who appeared so like himself, he was also aroused that they seemed so uneager to welcome him either. That denial angered him even more. Granted that he was mind blind, so he could not remember when he had been gathered close into the circle of kinship, warmed and sustained by this whole world. Yet that was a loss which he pushed aside. Nor could he fit into any other clan!

But that was it, he knew suddenly. There were the Lanquar and Lis, Lystal and Lyon—He saw them standing there. However, save for Qua, none had approached, nor was there any welcome mind send from them. Only Atra—

His hand slid down her arm to the wrist and there his fingers closed as if it were a matter of utmost importance that he keep her here. As it had been on the ship when he had depended on Vorlund's device, here was it now—she only was his anchorage and that which he had sought could be found only with and by her.

"I speak—" Qua hesitated and there was a shadow of a frown on his handsome face; his folded wings stirred a fraction as if he would expand them and so employ all the stature he could command. "Yes, I speak for all. You have both been within the shadow, the very hold of *Them. They* have blinded and bound you—therefore shall we not always wonder whether there can be any trust placed with you henceforth?"

"You speak well, Qua." Atra smiled coldly. "Have you in truth matched words with Slitha of Lis, Usern of Lystal, and Cambar of the Loyn?" All the gathering of winglings was watching them now. Farree knew that those others had been following all which was said by mind touch. There was a stir among them at Atra's naming of names. Again his remnants of memory gave him what he needed. He did not wait for Qua to answer that, but instead took the lead for himself.

"If you speak with one voice for all, Qua," he returned, "then put your fears to rest. This is not the first time Langrone has stood alone. Valfor bore green wings—and went to his brave ending because of that. However, we intend no ending. Langrone lives, under the ancient rule, as long as either of us flies—" He drew Atra a little closer. "If you covet our Two Plains and the river land, then take it, Qua. We shall not dispute you for them. But neither shall we be forgotten when the Great Summons goes forth at Year's Ending. Remember that, Qua!" Farree now looked beyond the Lanquar to the others who were waiting. "And you, Slitha,"—he looked toward a slender wingling with a queen's proud stance and wings of gold—"and Usern,"—blue wings quivered as his thought struck home—"and Cambar." The pinions of that leader were grey shading to white and he was much darker of countenance, thicker of body, than the others.

"Remember!" Atra's reinforcement of his speech was more than a warning, it was an order.

Qua stared at the girl and then he smiled as coldly as she had done earlier. "There is now a common enemy; we fly no direction but that." He, too, might be only giving a reminder, but Farree was certain that there was also a warning to be read there.

"As Glasrant has already done!" she flashed. What more the spokesman for the winglings might have said was never uttered, for Maelen opened her eyes, and the skin tightly covering the eye caverns in Fragon's face quivered and also showed a slit break.

"It is done!" Both voice and thought came from Maelen. "*Their* beacon has been quenched, and even more, many of those traps and defenses set up by *Them* are gone. And the dream holds those two we need to make trouble for each other in thrall!"

Selrena spoke to the unmasked one. "Loose your followers now, Sorwin!"

The robed one raised both hands to mouth and with them shaped a hollow like a horn. The puffed cheeks expanded even more and from that horn there pulsed a cry which echoed through Farree's head. It had savagery in it, a lust and a hunger which was like a call of doom. Groundlings growled and left with a rush and a slapping of huge bare feet, and after them came a following of things whose very bodies, swinging and swaying, seemed to alter as they went—and always the forms they wore, forms which slipped from one to another and then another, were those of the blackest terrors any night might know. Ironically it was true that those who were fashioned as entirely threatening to each other marched now against a single enemy.

They were gone, and it seemed to Farree that the whole of the crystal cavern was the lighter for their going. He wondered what harm they might wreak on the invaders, for many of those who had swept on seemed hardly more solid than a cloud of that haze which could spring into being at command of the Darda.

The Zacanthan moved for the first time, turning his sharp-jawed head to watch their going. Farree knew that Zoror was filing in his head all which chanced here. What names would he give to those who had just gone? How many more were there that had long ago been listed in the records he thought he knew so well?

However, if there was an exit of a force there was also an entrance. Farree heard the now-familiar tinkle of flute notes. So heralded came Vestrum. Gone was the clothing he had worn before. In its place he wore silver fashioned in small supple rings so that it moved even at his breathing. He carried a length of crystal rod which was headed by a hilt much like that of the sword which was never far from Fragon's hands. The flutist scampered back and forth as might an eager hound only waiting to be dispatched against some quarry, while the two women who walked a pace of so behind had laid aside their filmy robes and flower ribbons. They, too, wore chain mail and on the out-held right wrist of each there sat a flying lizard, smaller than that which had accompanied Farree on his first trip across this land, but manifestly of the same breed.

Neither was this all of the party, for Vorlund followed but a little behind the Darda and, with him, two of the giant folk, bending heads as they strode ponderously, striving to avoid and painful meeting with down-pointing crystals.

Vestrum spoke, but he did not seem to address any particular one of them but rather the whole company,

from Fragon to the smallest of the winglings. "This one"—
he indicated Vorlund, but as if there was nothing in truth
between them but what might be a distant enmity—"has
done as he swore that he would—he has launched forth
his messenger."

"And you, Vestrum, how has it been with you?" Selrena
was the first to break the silence on the tail of that
message.

"I made sure that there was no treachery in what was
wrought!" returned the Darda coldly. Now his eye caught
on Farree for the first time, and with a lightning-swift
gesture the hiked rod swung up, its end aimed for Farree's
head. Along the length of that sped a dot of rainbow
light. More memory moved in Farree. He took two steps
forward and his bandaged hand swung up, his fingers
caught and held the end of the rod. It was chill, seeming
to generate a cold which bit into his flesh, but he did not
loose it for ten long-drawn breaths. Then his hand
dropped and he met the measuring stare of Vestrum with
as level and probing a gaze.

Was there a faint trace of disappointment in the
Darda's tightheld eye-to-eye measurement? Farree could
not be sure, he only held a suspicion.

"Well and now, Vestrum." This time it was Atra who
broke thought silence just as the capering flutist settled
down at the Darda's feet and made the instrument it
carried give forth a trill of notes. "Do you believe? Or is it
your claim next that Glasrant has power to hide the cast of
all his thoughts from you?"

"Have done!" For the first time Farree saw Fragon rise
to his feet. Standing, he was near as tall as he was spare,

almost shoulder to shoulder with the giants who had come with Vorlund. "What may have been in these two—it is gone. This night Glasrant has done what Valfor in his day might have lifted hand to—save that, mighty as our Elders were in their own time, they had not the knowledge of *Them*. We have been given that which we have not held to us since the days of incoming upon this world. We have lived, we have built, we dwindle, we earth dwell or keep jealous council with one race, even one kin, only our kind. We have lost much and now we are too old and few even to defend ourselves against *Them*. How many more times must their star ships come—each adding death to death? *They* are as many as a hundred times the number of sand grains now under our feet. There will always be more to come and less of us at their going. If they go, for their signal was set to guide others this time. Look to your delving in the ancient knowledge, Vestrum. What discoveries have you made? Small things, things of half-life—Can you bring forth that which is no larger than your hand but can rock a star ship?"

The trickle of notes from the flute ascended higher and higher—until they sounded almost like a cry for help. The Darda in his coat of mail stood frowning, his two hands sliding back and forth along his hiked rod.

"And you, Sorwin." Fragon thrust his head a bit forward, his now widely open eyes seeking out the unmasked one. "Well for you—yes, that has been your thought for a long time. Your groundlings and your wraiths—they have little to fear from *Them*. You and yours think to go into such hiding that no off-world mind or body can scoop you forth! We already know that is less true than you would like. And I say to you that *They* have always sought knowledge, more and more of it along paths which we do not or cannot follow. We can summon a storm, set against them the land itself. Only we cannot hold—there are too few of us and we are too wearied with time. What other secrets have *They* uncovered? Do not think you can lie safe hidden."

Sorwin did not reply but Fragon was plainly not through. He gestured with one hand while with the other he still kept his lingers in tight hold on the hilt of the skull-piercing sword. It was a summons and one they had no thought to disobey.

The Zacanthan came, and Maelen, and Vorlund, edged by his giant helpers, and Farree reluctantly dropped his hold on Atra's hand to stand with the other three. Fragon moved again, down from his dusky throne. He came to wait on a level for their coming to him.

They did not approach him too closely for he was now swinging the sword back and forth and the skull was smoothing out a patch of the sand. When that seemed leveled to his liking, the Dark Darda fumbled at the breast of his hazy robe and tossed out upon the patch of readied sand a ball of the same clouded crystal as Farree had taken up in Vestrum's chamber, though this did not break when it landed. Instead light spread from it. Then it was as if they were all a-wing, looking down upon a scene of constant, almost frenzied change. The star ship no longer stood tall but was canted, and its nose was oddly concave at one side. Hail and wind beat at both the ship and the ground about it. The wreck of the shelters flapped forward and back in the wind. Of any men there were no sign.

Then there appeared to burst out of the troubled air itself a flight of such winged snakes as those Farree had seen before. Only these were four, six times the size of those, and they whirled in a mad circle about the canted ship, one after another in turn darting down to skim the wreckage on the ground.

Then night and storm vanished, and with them the disabled ship and what was left of the shelters. What they were looking at now was a stream swollen with storm water, and it was day. A knot of men gathered on the bank of that stream. Several were on their knees digging into the soil with their bare hands. One jerked free from dark clay a swinging length of shining metal. The one nearest him snatched at it. Their mouths were open and they might have been shouting at one another. In moments a frenzy seemed to grip them all, and then there was the flash of a laser which itself banished the scene.

"These will not trouble us again—" Vestrum's thought came, and there was satisfaction in it and triumph.

"There will be others." Selrena broke that thread of satisfaction. "Always there will be others! It is as Fragon has said, they are as many as the grains of sand. Short-lived they are but they breed and breed and among us the young are very few. Long have we fled before them—now we stand with our backs to tall mountains and even the star roads are lost to us. We are already dead though still we struggle—"

"That is not quite the truth." They all turned to look to Vorlund. "You have wrought with your own strengths." He gestured to the ball now lying quietly on the sand, no longer beaming forth pictures. "We have wrought with ours. Not only as we have done these days and nights just passed, but for the future. You have been long apart—do not believe that now you are standing alone. You have your rites and customs, your laws and punishments for the breaking of them. There are also laws and punishments beyond this world. You believe that I have brought from our ship that which will serve you now. Yes, in truth that is so. Only we have more to offer—"

"Look you at us!" The command came with clear force from Maelen. She held out a hand and it was taken by the Zacanthan. In turn his other hand went to close upon one of Vorlund's while the spacer's second hand was with Farree in hold. "As you differ to the eye and yet decide on a single purpose, so it is with us among the stars. There are those darklings whom you know as enemies: not as many as your sand grains are they. And there are powers known to us which can destroy them, can bring you a defense that no ship of theirs can crack."

"That also is the truth." The Zacanthan's mind send was heavier but as clear. "There are other worlds where those who live upon their lands and within their seas can be easy prey to those of evil. Only there is no fear there—"

"Why?" Vestrum crowded a little closer to make his demand, his chin thrust forward, about him the sharpness of hostility.

"Because in the space about those worlds there are protectors. Not ones who live and breathe and are of our form of life. No, these are like small, very small, ships set to travel in patterns. If a star-roving ship comes near, these sweep swiftly to match its path and loose a warning.

If that is not heeded then that ship will speedily become, while still aloft, like this invader that you have just seen. Only those who know and can think the proper words can pass unharmed. Once each four years one of these who know the signal will come here and land where you your-selves shall appoint and there you and the people of that ship may meet. So through the years to come you will learn of us and we of you and when the time comes we can share peace."

"Thinker and Rememberer," Fragon made answer. "We know that what you say is truth, as you see it. But truth wears many faces when it abides with different peoples. Truth also changes as lives change and what may be right at one time is wrong at another. However, we have little choice. If we are not to be meat for any strange ship which lands here we must accept what you promise. Still, how do you bring this forth? You have a ship and can run to other stars. We are earth-bound, and, in the time we must wait for this you promise, we may attract more spoilers."

"Not so." Vorlund shook his head to emphasize his thought. "There has been set up among your mountains a defense—like that of the ship which was trying to beam in their fellow thieves, there goes forth now another beam. All may fear death, a death which cannot be withstood or treated with any ill-bane. There are certain worlds—your people were star travelers once, perhaps you can remember—where death awaits any who dare to land there. On such worlds the law keepers have set up that which will warn off any ship approaching a landing orbit. You need only tend well this warning and you shall be free of those who discover your world by chance. This will serve until we can come again with the more certain defense I have spoken of—"

It was Sorwin's harsh-pitched thought which interrupted him. "So we wait for the coming of those who will set up rule, a rule of those unlike us. They well hold us in a new bondage—"

"No." Zoror answered that. "I hope to come again, for there is much I would learn. Am I one to put the searing iron on you? There may be others like unto me—like these—" He nodded toward Maelen and Vorlund. "Ask of your own." Now he indicated Farree. "Can we be trusted, are we rulers with orders?"

"They are in their way kin," Farree answered. "Me they brought out of the Deep Dark and they call me friend. Even as I am friends with this one." He freed the smux from his jerkin. "It does not matter the form, only that which lies within it. Also"—he put his thoughts into order—"I swear this by my body after the Great Memory—I shall be with you here where you can do with me as you please if you believe I have twisted truth."

Vorlund laid hand on Farree's shoulder. "This one has been much to us, more and more each passing day. We shall give to him all the knowledge needed to keep you free. He is kin-friend and will always be."

Sorwin grunted but Fragon was nodding slowly. "There is no falseness in what you have said. You believe it. If we are minded to accept slowly it is because we have known it to be otherwise many times over. Glasrant has been beyond the stars as one of you. Indeed we can learn from him. Therefore we accept this much, that you will leave with him such knowledge as you are willing to trade. But to you we offer nothing now—save our thanks for what is already done. Let time prove whether you are right."

Farree stood where his wings had borne him at dawn. He was looking down into the cup valley. They were already aboard. All except two—He glanced down for a moment at what he held, felt the familiar pinch of the legs upon his arm and wrist. "Cold—" That plaint was familiar too. Togger did not relish the kind of wind about them here in the heights.

"Lady Maelen?" A thought swift sent, an answer.

"Lord-One Krip?" A second hail and farewell.

"Lord Zoror—?"

"Only until we come again." The Zacanthan's thought was swift to answer.

Farree watched the flame of the jets, the rise of the ship up and up, out of the cup which had held it, back to the stars.

"Do you truly wish yourself there?"

She had alighted on the grassy surface of the cliff top just too far away for him to be aware of her until the thought wove with his.

"I do not know—Here I am one."

"Here you are kin." Her send was clear and strangely soft. She had folded her wings and now she walked towards him. In her hands was a gathering of ill-bane flowers, and the scent of them was also hers.

"Kin, Kin," she chanted aloud now and each word was like the scented and healing breath of the plant.

Farree threw back his head to the dawn-colored sky. He could only see a very distant trail. Then it was gone.

"Kin!" Atra was beside him and the scent of the flowers brought with it a softening of all sadness.

He no longer searched the sky for the past but looked into the face of the future, and his smile was eager.